The Scions of Atlantis

Leaning Rock Press
Box 44
Gales Ferry, CT 06335
www.leaningrockpress.com

978-1-7328519-4-8 The Scions of Atlantis, Hardcover
978-1-7328519-5-5 The Scions of Atlantis, Softcover
978-1-7328519-9-3 The Scions of Atlantis, ebook

Publisher's Cataloging-In-Publication Data
(Prepared by The Donohue Group, Inc.)

Names: Turner, Claudia, author.
Title: The Scions of Atlantis : a novel / Claudia Turner.
Description: Gales Ferry, CT : Leaning Rock Press, [2019] | Series: [Kat
    Hastings series]
Identifiers: ISBN 9781732851948 (hardcover) | ISBN 9781732851955
    (softcover) | ISBN 9781732851962 (ebook)
Subjects: LCSH: Women intelligence officers--United States--Fiction. |
    Rich people--United States--Fiction. | United States--Politics and
    government--Fiction. | LCGFT: Thrillers (Fiction)
Classification: LCC PS3620.U7635 S35 2019 (print) | LCC PS3620.U7635
    (ebook) | DDC 813/.6--dc23

To Luanne, my sunshine on a cloudy day

The Scions of Atlantis

A Kat Hastings Novel

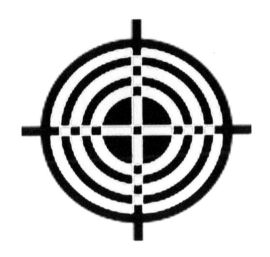

Claudia Turner

Leaning
Rock
Press

Gales Ferry, CT

Chapter 1

Friday, February 26, 1993

*D*espite *the shrill whistle of the teapot, Adheem's eyes were riveted to a small TV atop a marred chest crammed with books and papers. For once, he didn't despair about his pauper's living room with its pockmarked walls and peeling paint. He was too mesmerized by the images of destroyed vehicles, the collapsed roof of the PATH station and the bleeding, panic-stricken, soot-covered office workers fleeing the World Trade Center. His friend, Ramzi Yousef, had done his job. And yet, Adheem's admiration was tempered by the fact that, while more than a thousand were injured, only six people died during the attack. They had hoped for more. Ramzi had predicted that the bomb would topple one of the towers, and the compression would cause the second to fall as well. The cyanide gas would take care of anyone not killed by the building's destruction. Sadly, it didn't happen.*

"You'll need more than a truck for explosives," he had told Ramzi months before at their last clandestine meeting.

"You must have faith, my friend. This is only the beginning. We will bomb the tunnels, the UN and the federal plaza. New York will be in flames before the Americans know what hit them," Ramzi replied.

Adheem limped to the closet-sized kitchen and turned off the teapot, now shrieking for his attention. He poured the steaming

1

water into a plain white mug and dropped the teabag inside. While it was steeping, he pulled out his prayer mat, got on his knees and closed his eyes. "Falillahil hamdu rabbis samawati warabbil ardi rabbil 'alameen," he chanted. "Walahol kibria'o fis samawati walard wahowal azizul hakeem." (Praise be to Allah, Lord of the heavens and Lord of the earth. Lord and Cherisher of all the worlds! To Him be glory throughout the heavens and the earth, and He is exalted in power, full of wisdom.)

Although Adheem praised Allah for the destruction Ramzi had inflicted, there was another, more momentous event for which he gave thanks. His only son, Adam, had been accepted to Harvard and would attend after his graduation from prep school in June.

He had taught his son well. They'd spent their days studying mathematics, literature, science, history and, of course, Al Quran. Adheem was a demanding tutor. Not satisfied with Adam's academic excellence and prowess in soccer and track, he also demanded his son's complete and sincere spiritual devotion, even if it meant employing the harsh techniques he'd perfected while with the Taliban to rob the boy of his will. Money was tight, but the monthly stipend he got from his brethren and the money his wife made at the laundromat provided just enough to allow him to homeschool his son during the crucial early years without having to work himself.

He'd named the boy after a prophet, not just because of the blessing it conferred but because it was a name readily accepted in the west. By the time Adam entered boarding school (on full scholarship), he too had learned the meaning of sacrifice, the nobility of Jihad, and hatred for anything or anyone outside of Islam, the one true religion.

Sacrifice was a way of life. Sharia law, the only law that mattered, commanded it. Had Adheem not weathered the cold of the Afghan hills? Had he not watched brothers die at the hands of the Russians? Had he not shattered his leg in the battle for Kabul? These challenges forged his bond with Ramzi and the others, including the great Osama, but during his convalescence he realized that their efforts would matter only if they occurred on American soil where they could inflict terror in the hearts of the western devils—and not with bee stings like this attack today, but something more horrific, more spectacular, more permanent.

Adheem stroked his coarse beard, pulling it repeatedly as though he were trying to coax thoughts from his balding head. His deep-set brown eyes closed as he remembered his homeland, Pakistan, and the life he'd left behind for this den of iniquity where men were weak, and women strutted like whoring peacocks, baring their faces, arms and legs; where the equivalent of pornography aired on their televisions; where their religion, as blasphemous as it was, was a flagging priority. Money was the only god in America, and the infidels would pay dearly for that. He would see to it.

Adheem remembered the first time that he, Baha and their five-year-old son stepped onto American soil. It was 1980, and they had landed in Boston where the Sharia community welcomed them. In Pakistan he had been a scholar, reciting Al Quran freely and flawlessly, and using his interpretation to belittle, coerce and persuade his peers. By the time he left for America, he had earned the respect and possibly the fear of the Pakistani community he left behind.

But now, his public persona was insipid. He spoke enthusiastically about Boston's teams, pretended to care about the Red Sox and had even bought a Patriots jacket, though he knew nothing about this perversion of football. He smiled to his American neighbors and asked them about their children, especially Ashley, the little blond-haired girl two buildings down who sold him Girl Scout cookies. He occasionally helped Joe, the old man who lived next door, cross the street. Allah would protect the innocents, such as Ashley and Joe; he was certain.

He had also obtained U.S. citizenship and a driver's license, both vital to his cause. Ostensibly, he was now one of them. After Adam left for boarding school, he found a job with one of the local taxi companies. A couple of years later, he had saved enough to buy his own cab, transporting Bostonians to the airport, around the city, to doctor's appointments. He memorized the neighborhoods, got to know a reliable and honest mechanic, and could recommend restaurants. Yet with today's World Trade Center bombing, he knew he would get suspicious looks and inane attempts at conversation. "I don't understand you Muslims. Why do you hate us so much?" one would say. "If Muslims hate Americans, why are you here?" another would ask.

They never bothered to understand the Islamic world. Sunnis, Shias, Sufis, Ahmadis …one Muslim was just like another to them. Little did they know that these sects detested each other. American forces in the Middle East could have used this to their advantage. Instead, the U.S. became the hated enemy that united these otherwise divergent groups. Jihadists knew that if they bided their time, the Americans would lose patience and leave until the next war broke out, a new president was elected, or a new crisis emerged, and the cycle repeated itself.

How many times, when transporting a fare through the Boston streets, had he been tempted to reach for the gun under his car seat, turn, and fire? He couldn't remember a time when he didn't seethe at the mere sight of them and their big houses, their fast cars, their corrupt ways. They knew nothing of sacrifice. To them, wars were an inconvenience, not a commitment. When they lasted too long, the Americans left, unable to stomach body counts and mounting costs.

Adheem rose from his mat and took his tea, spilling a few drops on the pants he now wore instead of his jalabiyyah. The beard would also have to go. He needed to look more like them. Another sacrifice. Sacrifice, patience and faith: the qualities that distinguished him from those among whom he now lived. Soon Baha would be home to prepare his supper and clean their apartment. Once she had been a good wife, obedient and compliant as a woman should be. Now, he detected a percolating resentment, bitterly providing him her body, but only when he forced himself upon her.

"Why can't we go to the movies like our neighbors? The women at work invite me out, but you forbid me to go. I am a prisoner in my own home," she'd complain. "Why must I wear this burka? You shed your robe."

All women should hide themselves, that was fact; but another fact was that the burka also concealed the bruises. The beatings were no longer effective, however. Baha stoically endured them, saying nothing while glaring at him with hatred. It would be good if the burka could hide her spiteful eyes as well.

He sat back and sipped the tea, allowing it to relax him as he reflected upon his situation. Baha had served her purpose by providing him with a son, but now he'd be better off without her. It would make his plan easier to implement.

He had shared his grand plan with the few mullahs and imams he trusted. They promised to convey his ideas to Osama and Ayman al-Zawahiri, the two men who led a disjointed band of militants. Al Qaida, the base, was intent on the destruction of the Great Satan and more enduring than the upstart ISIS. Like Ramzi, they wanted to strike immediately and sow the seeds of fear throughout the west. There was value to that, of course, but Adheem sought a higher, longer-lasting prize. Just as he had once severed the heads of Russian prisoners with one stroke, he would decapitate the United States using his son as the gleaming sharp sword. Only then would he deserve the name his father bestowed upon him; Adheem—the most great.

Chapter 2

Present Day

As I'd done every other morning since we'd arrived a year ago, my day began with a sensory overload: the taste of locally roasted coffee, the sounds of seagulls, the smell of the salty air, the endless views up and down the pristine beach, and the emerging warmth of the sun made early morning my favorite time of day; all enjoyed from the deck of our blissful Nevis hideaway.

The beach house had belonged to my former boss Ben Douglas who had given me the keys right before they found him dead in a suspicious one-car accident. Although I thought of him often, today I merely savored the early-morning tranquility while I waited for Robbie to join me for a run.

He emerged a few minutes later, taking one last sip of coffee before joining me at the railing, giving me a peck on the cheek, squinting his blue eyes toward the horizon. His curly hair was a little grayer now, and he was developing a slight paunch, but every day I fell in love with him all over again. His dedication to truth and exposing those who would destroy it, coupled with his warmth and compassion, made him irresistible to me.

"Another beautiful day in paradise," he said, wistfully. "How about a beach run today?"

At the word "run," Scout, our Lab-Rotty mix, jumped up and began prancing around the deck, anxious to start. The three of us began jogging north on Pinney's Beach, passing swaying palm trees, marine-colored cabanas and the tourists who'd staked an early claim on lounge chairs. Pinney's white sand was gorgeous, but running on it was taxing, especially now that we were in our sixties. Our pace had slowed, and our joints complained more vehemently, but still we ran; our minds, souls and bodies depended on it.

"Hey, Kat," said Robbie, panting a little. "How about going to Chevy's tonight for some reggae? I need to get out."

I nodded. "I know what you mean. The walls are closing in."

Robbie looked down at me. "Yeah? I thought I was the only one who felt that way. I've loved our time together, don't get me wrong, but ... well, I guess you know what I mean."

I thought of all the sights we had seen here during our forced escape: The Botanical Gardens, Montpelier House, Alexander Hamilton's birthplace, the Museum of Nevis History, the fort at Nelson's lookout on Saddle Hill. We were married at the ruins of Cottle Church where families and their slaves once worshipped together. How many times had we climbed Nevis Peak? We had visited every single beach on the island. I enjoyed it all, but in truth, we had exhausted the island's many attractions.

"I know it's not easy for you," I said. "I feel trapped, too. I just don't know what to do. We don't have to stay here, you know. We could go to Europe or somewhere in the States where no one would look for us."

"I was thinking the same thing," he said. "This isn't us. We're not programmed to watch from the sidelines." He stopped abruptly, and I turned back to look at him quizzically. Scout waited patiently for a split second, then took off after a seagull.

"It's killing me, Kat. I can't even get my book published from here. I guess I could self-publish and do it all online, using your secure computer, of course. The mainstream publishers won't touch it. It's too hot. Either that, or ... ."

I started jogging again, motioning for him to catch up. "You're being paranoid. Publishing houses aren't controlled by some clandestine government agency." He didn't say anything, which probably meant he thought they were controlled by some clandestine government agency.

"Come on, Robbie. You have to publish." After a brief hesitation, I added, "If you were to self-publish, could they track you down?"

"They think we're dead, remember? If I did publish, they'd know we tricked them. Maybe I could use a pen name, but they'd figure out it was me. They know I was close to figuring out the Kennedy assassination. I hope your computer really is beyond hacking."

"Greg assured me that it is." Greg Wheeler was my former friend and CIA colleague who developed spy craft for the agency. He had shared many of his gadgets with me, some of which had saved my life and may have cost him his. The sight of him slumped over his desk, his head lying in a pool of blood, would never leave me. Nor would the feeling of guilt that now weighed like an anchor on my soul.

Robbie shook his head. "Just because your computer is safe doesn't mean they haven't hacked people we've sent things to. No telling what they've come up with during the past year."

That possibility had crossed my mind as well and was the major reason I had almost no contact with the friends and family we'd left behind. Still, Robbie didn't need me to stoke his fears. "We have fake IDs. We don't use credit cards. My cell phone is untraceable." I mentally checked off everything we'd done to avoid detection before asking, "If you did publish and they did figure out you're alive, do you think they could find us?"

Robbie didn't respond. His eyes had fixed on something in the distance. Following his gaze, straining to see through the sun glinting off the sand, I realized with a spasm of fear that it was a man with binoculars, standing atop one of the sand dunes about a quarter mile ahead, tracking our movement. "Looks like they already have," Robbie said sharply. Grabbing my arm, he pushed me toward a path to our left and whistled for Scout. "Run!"

This couldn't be happening again. We had been so careful. Stealing one last look back, I saw the man lower his binoculars, leave the dune and turn toward the road.

With sea grass whipping our legs and the shifting sands of the dunes hampering our strides, we raced toward the main road, hoping the presence of tourists and traffic would deter our pursuer from doing anything rash.

Just when I was sure I would drop, Robbie sprinted behind a gas station and pulled me after him. Panting, sweating and spent, with Scout circling anxiously, we flattened ourselves against a propane tank, then peeked around the corner of the building to see if the man followed.

In a hushed voice, Robbie said, "There's something you need to know, Kat. I've stashed some important information in a deserted cabin about two miles north of Tom's house, off a dirt road in the woods. He doesn't know anything about it. You'll see a sign that says, 'Bait.' It's easy to miss, which is why I put the stuff there. It's in the cellar, behind a boarded-up hole in the cinder-block wall. Pry off the boards. You'll see a box. Don't let them get it, Kat."

"And where will you be?" I struggled to keep my voice down. "Robbie, you're not leaving me, not now."

"With luck, I'll be with you, but just in case I'm not, I want you to protect it. You can't give it to anyone, no matter what."

"What kind of information? More Kennedy stuff?"

"No, much more important," he replied, his eyes darting left and right. "I'll explain everything, but now's not the time. It's too complicated."

Seriously? I wanted to throttle him, but I'd grown accustomed to his subterfuges, informing me of his discoveries only when the situation became critical. Perhaps he was protecting me, but now he was asking me to share responsibility for something in which I played no part. If I didn't love him so much, I'd clock him. After a few minutes to reassure ourselves that we'd evaded our pursuer, we emerged from our hiding place, avoiding the suspicious frown of the gas station's owner and scanning the road in both directions.

Ten minutes later, we were back at the beach house. Our neighbor came running toward us, smiling broadly, waving his long black arms and calling me by the name by which I was now known. "Miss Carla, your brother stopped by. He said you were expecting him."

My eyes locked on Robbie's, now dark and hard. I had no brother.

"Really? How long ago?" I asked, attempting nonchalance.

"You just missed him. He said he'd be back." Jackson seemed perplexed that we weren't more enthusiastic.

Mustering as much composure as I could, I replied, "Oh, that's too bad. Thanks for letting me know."

"He seems like a nice guy. So polite," Jackson said. "Good-looking too, though he really doesn't look anything like you. He even saluted when I told him you were out for a run."

"Like this?" Robbie brushed his forehead in a mock salute, the trademark gesture of Beau Foster, a former college friend turned foe who was supposed to be in prison.

Jackson laughed. "That's right."

As Jackson returned to his house, and Robbie turned to me. "You know what this means?"

I nodded grimly. "We've got to get out of here." The scar on my left breast served as a daily reminder of the torment I'd suffered at the hands of Beau and his henchmen, when they'd bound and beaten me repeatedly, trying to force me to reveal Robbie's whereabouts.

Since our self-imposed exile to Nevis, we'd known the day might come when a rapid escape was essential and had planned for it. We ran into the house and checked to see if anything was amiss. I gathered my special phone and the other gadgets that Greg had given me, raced to the bedroom, changed my clothes, and grabbed the pre-packed suitcase prepared for such an emergency.

Robbie emerged from the den, holding his duffle bag and computer case, ready to go. His soft blue eyes were now like steel, reminding me to focus on the present and our survival. Hopefully, there would be opportunity to think and gain answers, but that was a luxury we could not indulge now. After thirty-five years, the fates had allowed Robbie and me to find each other again with our love intact. Yet despite all we had endured, it could disappear with a single gunshot or slash of a knife. I wasn't ready for that and, by god, I would not allow Beau to triumph. I pulled Robbie's face closer, feeling the soft curls of his hair still moist with sweat. "No matter what happens, I love you, Robbie O'Toole."

He returned my kiss with one more urgent. "Just remember what I told you. You must keep the information safe, whatever it takes. The only person I trust with it is Tom. He can tell you what to do with it."

Although we seldom used it, Ben Douglas had left a car in the garage of his beach house. I stole one last glance at the Eden we were forced to abandon. How ironic that we had bemoaned our boring life just hours ago. Our time together had been a gift, even if our thoughts, fears and memories boiled incessantly beneath the surface. We had loved, laughed, and for once enjoyed a blissful respite from the dangerous world we'd left behind. Now that same world demanded our return, on its terms, not ours. We threw our bags in the trunk. Scout leapt into the back seat, and we were on the road within minutes, heading toward Cades Bay. From there we would cross the narrows to St. Kitts, find a hotel and make arrangements to fly out.

Robbie drove while I navigated toward the Sea Bridge ferry that would carry us to St. Kitts. With luck, Beau would assume we'd fly out of the airport in Charlestown. Departing from the neighboring island might buy us time to determine our next move. Our lives depended on it.

As we drove across the narrows I watched the cloud-capped crown of Nevis Peak recede, saw the brightly colored houses fade, felt the ubiquitous flowers cease to bloom. Immediately I began to miss our runs through the Botanical Gardens, along the jungle trails and Nevis' many pristine beaches. I found myself mourning this place and the friendship of some of the gentlest people on earth. Though a stranger when I arrived, the islanders had welcomed us and made us feel at home.

"I don't get it. Why would Beau want us to know he found us?" I asked, my CIA analyst's mind churning.

"He's a terrorist, just like the people who blow up buildings or execute journalists. He wants to make us afraid."

In a barely audible voice, I said, "He's succeeded."

Chapter 3

How had Beau figured it out? My old boss Ben had arranged a new identity for us courtesy of a man who he implicitly trusted. Even more perplexing was how did Beau get out of jail? They had enough on him to hold him for the rest of his life.

Once we were on St. Kitts, the narrow road snaked across the isthmus, passing small hills that sheltered vacant beaches. We turned north around the Great Salt Pond and soon entered Frigate Bay where a pet-friendly room awaited us at the Marriott. Crossing the spacious lobby, we passed black leather sofas and stools, surreptitiously scanning the faces of everyone we saw. At the mahogany registration desk we introduced ourselves as Bridget and Roger Pettigrew, hoping the British-sounding names might throw off potential pursuers. But our efforts to project the calm façade of tourists was foiled by our nerves. I don't know if it was Robbie's drumming his fingers on the desktop or my shifting from one foot to the other, but the check-in clerk finally asked, "Is there a problem?"

The elevator took us to a room with a king-sized bed, a sitting area and a kitchenette. Tall windows revealed tanned, scantily-dressed bathers lounging by the pool or walking the beach that stretched endlessly in both directions. Robbie stared at the scene intently, presumably looking for anything amiss while I pulled out my phone and called Jermaine's number. He answered on the second ring.

"Kat Hastings. Well, I'll be damned. What's it been, a year? Is everything okay?"

It was good to hear his confident baritone. Jermaine had once belonged to Joint Special Operations Command, or JSOC. He knew how the world operated and came through when Robbie and I had needed him the most.

"Beau found us," I blurted. "He's in Nevis."

"Damn."

He fell silent for so long that I finally said, "Are you still there?" His reaction didn't bode well. Jermaine had an uncanny awareness of events, sometimes before they happened, and his ability to manage them was nothing short of superhuman.

"I've been ... away. Just got back." Another pause. "First things first. Are you still on Nevis?"

"No, St. Kitts."

"We've got to get you and O'Toole off the island. I'll call Nate."

"Isn't there someone else you can call?" I didn't want Nate to pick us up. The added stress of flying with both my current and former husbands spelled disaster.

"The fewer folks who know, the better. He flew you down there; he can get you out." He was in command and control mode now and I knew better than to argue. "I'll call you in half an hour. Lay low."

The call ended abruptly, and I turned to Robbie and explained the plan. "Jermaine's calling Nate. He'll fly us off the island."

"The hell he will!" Robbie's eyes blazed.

"You've got a better idea? We've got to get out of here. Now. Nate is just a means to an end. Once we're off the island and somewhere safe, he's gone, out of our lives."

"Why don't we just hire a pilot at the airport? There are plenty of people who could do that. People who weren't married to you."

"And you'd trust they wouldn't sell us out to the highest bidder? Would they take Scout? Come on, Robbie." I tried to take his arm, but he turned away. "Nate does this type of thing all the time. He wouldn't betray us."

"Oh, like he didn't betray you? There's no way I'll ever owe him—for anything."

"My father trusted him. Jermaine trusts him. Ben trusted him... ."

"Your father? Now's there's a resounding endorsement."

My father, known as H2 in the Company, had not approved of Robbie, and his history of covert actions were dubious and often sinister, but he came through in the end, right before he died, leaving me little opportunity to resolve our stormy relationship.

An awkward silence descended. I moved to the sitting area, scratched Scout's head and watched Robbie pace the room, deep in thought. The ring of the phone made both of us jump. Seeing Jermaine's number, I hit the button for speaker phone, so Robbie could listen, too.

"Kat, there's a terminal for private planes at the Bradshaw Airport," Jermaine began. "Follow the road that goes around the main airport and you'll see a small hangar with a Citation Mustang outside. You have Ben's car, right?" I told him yes. "Be there at seven p.m. sharp. Nate will take off as soon as you get there. Don't be late, or early. Just be there on time."

We hung up, and I checked my watch—three p.m. "We should leave by six."

"Four hours. That's a long time, too long. They'll find us. If we split, it will be harder for them to get us both. I'll take the car to throw them off. You can call a cab. It's less traceable."

"No," I yelled. "We're in this together. You can't leave me again. I need you."

"It's the only way, Kat. The information is important, far bigger than you know. Find it and keep it to yourself. Don't give it to anyone but Tom. If it gets into the wrong hands ..."

15

"Nothing is more important than your safety," I pleaded. "You have to leave with me."

"I'll be careful." The door had slammed before I could argue further.

Five o'clock came, and I still hadn't heard from Robbie. I called his cell phone, but there was no answer. Nor was there an answer when I tried again at five-thirty, then six, then six-fifteen. I'd have to call a cab. Maybe Robbie was already at the airport. Reluctantly, I grabbed my things and leashed Scout. Laden with my carry-on over my shoulder, two computer cases in one hand and Scout's leash in the other, I trudged to the lobby and exited toward the cab that was waiting in the drive. Robbie's computer bag fell off my shoulder, and I kicked it the rest of the way. Sweat poured off my forehead, and I was drenched by the time I threw the bags in the trunk, loaded Scout into the back seat, and climbed in beside him. I took one last look back to the entrance and pounded my fists against my leg.

I frantically tried to call Robbie again. This time I left a message. "I'm leaving for the airport. Meet me there. I'm not leaving without you."

The cab pulled away. I looked right and left, hoping no one was following me. Anxiety was now morphing to anger. Not only was I on my own again; Robbie had dumped the responsibility for his important information on me, as usual. He knew how precarious our situation was and the stakes we now faced. Why hadn't he called?

Then anger became worry. This wasn't the Robbie I knew. Yes, he could be obstinate, but he wasn't stupid. Had something happened to him? The drive was torture.

We pulled into Bradshaw Airport, continuing past the main terminal to the private hangar that Jermaine had described. Several planes sat on the tarmac, and I examined each one until I saw Nate checking the tires of a Citation Mustang. No Robbie. As I lifted my bags from the trunk, Nate looked over. His jaw was clenched, his brow creased, his deep brown eyes hidden behind aviator sunglasses. He walked toward me.

"Hi, Nate." His jaw dropped.

"Kat? I knew it. You're Carla Banks." He started to hug me, but I pulled away. The rejection registered momentarily on his face as he took my bags and threw them into the back of the plane. "I thought I was supposed to be taking two people," he said, stiffly.

"I've been trying to reach Robbie. Can we wait for him a bit longer?"

"O'Toole? You're with O'Toole?"

"We're married."

"I see." He stepped back awkwardly. "We don't have time. The sooner we're out of here, the safer you'll be. My orders are to get you off this island by 1900 hours. If O'Toole isn't here, that's his problem. We've got to go. Are you coming or not?" His tone was sharp, perhaps because of the danger, perhaps because of my marriage to Robbie; maybe both.

I stood paralyzed, not knowing what to do. My cell phone rang.

"Kat, it's me. I don't have much time. They found me. Get on the plane now."

"Where are you?"

"Just get on the damn plane. Look in my bag. There's a scrap of paper buried in the bottom. Read it and destroy it."

"Where are you? We'll pick you up."

"Go, just go! I'm so sorry. I didn't mean for this to happen. I love you, Kat."

There was a loud whack followed by Robbie's dull protracted groan. My heart stopped. The line went dead.

I grabbed Robbie's bag before Nate pushed me into the plane. Once seated, I hugged the duffel as though it were Robbie himself, trembling with grief. We taxied to the runway; neither of us spoke. Once airborne, I opened Robbie's bag with palsied fingers, desperately rummaging through clothes and toiletries. There, at the bottom, was a scrap of paper with the words, "Scions of Atlantis."

Chapter 4

June 4, 1998

*N*ot even the Thursday morning chill could dampen Adheem's spirits as he gazed with awe at the pomp and pageantry unfolding before him. After Adam's incessant pleas, Adheem finally broke down and bought a suit for Harvard's Commencement, though it hung loosely over his lanky frame. At 8:30 the faculty, arrayed in brightly colored doctoral robes, gathered in front of Massachusetts Hall. He heard the bagpipe and drum that would lead the seniors along the streets of Cambridge, into Harvard Yard, and to the Memorial Church. He abhorred that his son would have to listen to that sodomite Christian, Peter Gomes, conduct the service.

At last the seniors exited and, tipping their hats as they walked by the flag of the United States and the bronze statue of John Harvard, formed two lines through which the president, faculty and honorary degree recipients paraded into the Tercentenary Theatre. Adheem found it ironic that a country so swayed by the latest whims of Madison Avenue still revered places such as Harvard where tradition still mattered, at least to the twenty-five thousand people now gathered here.

University President Rudenstine conferred honorary degrees upon people whose names Adheem did not recognize, including Mary Robinson, Ireland's president and UN Commissioner for

Human Rights, who stood to speak. Adheem bristled at the thought of a woman honored in this manner. He ignored her remarks until she said, "You have received an exceptional education at an exceptional place when there are many, in both your country and mine, and in many, many other parts of our world, who are just as innately talented and just as ambitious as you are but will never have such an opportunity. ... I do ask that you use your education to pursue only the worthiest of goals; goals that contribute to the betterment of the lives of others."

How laughable that, in this country of privilege and wealth, a woman would speak of such things and expect this audience to embrace them. Theirs was a future of business, medical and law schools, not the slums of the world. True, his son would go to law school, and he would also pursue the 'worthiest of goals,' but they would differ from those advocated by this Mary Robinson. Adheem's lips curved into a grim smile.

But that was in the future. The only thing that that mattered now was that among the thousands of degrees bestowed, one would belong to Adam. When the program concluded, he followed the students who roomed at Eliot House, a dorm known for its elitism. Adheem took solace in the fact that Eliot House was also where a direct descendent of the prophet Muhammad and the Unabomber both lived while at Harvard. He watched with pride as Adam received his diploma. Not only did it signify that his son was a graduate of America's most prestigious university, it meant that a vital step of his plan had been accomplished. He could not erase the smile from his face as he stood, elbow to elbow, with members of America's upper class, surprised to feel a bond with them, forged by a shared pride in their children.

Adheem waded through the crowds until he found Adam talking with his classmates and smiling broadly. Back slaps and fist pumps. It was good to see how well he got along with these young infidels; it boded well. He hung back to allow Adam his well wishes. Once the others had moved away, Adheem approached and hugged him.

"I am proud of you, Adam. You have honored me."

"Thanks. Why isn't Mom here?"

"I forbade her. I was thinking that you and I might celebrate together, man to man."

Adam's face fell. "My friends have invited me to a party. I'd like to go."

"I see." Adheem could not hide his disappointment. He had hoped to celebrate with Adam the way other parents would with their children. True, he had hoped to remind Adam of his commitment to his plan, but it was clear that now was not the time. "Well, you are of age. You must make your own choices." Adheem locked onto his son's eyes. "Just remember Al Quran."

"I know, father. Intoxicants and gambling are an abomination, Satan's handiwork. 'Eschew such that ye may prosper.'" Adam smiled faintly. "I got it, don't worry."

But Adheem did worry. He hugged his son one more time before turning back toward his cab, his thoughts slowing his steps. Everything hinged on Adam's steadfast adherence to the plan which depended on his acceptance by the others. Adam knew this too and was why he chose his friends over his father. That must be it. Adheem climbed into his cab, shut the door and closed his eyes. His monthly appointment with Mustafa was not until late afternoon. Now that he and Adam would not share a meal, he might as well drive his cab and earn some money.

"Taxi, taxi!"

Adheem lowered his window to speak to the immaculately dressed couple rushing toward him, the man sporting a custom-tailored suit, the woman dripping jewels. His own suit seemed suddenly cheap and inappropriate.

"Take us to Logan Airport."

Adheem nodded and popped the trunk. After placing their bags inside, the couple climbed into the back seat. Adheem pulled away from the curb, listening to the man and woman gush about the ceremony.

"Wasn't it grand?" the woman asked.

"I wish they had a better speaker. Someone famous. All this talk about the poor. Too depressing," the man replied. Adheem bit his lip. Hard.

"At least Tyler got through. There were times when I thought he majored in partying, not economics."

"Stuart promised him a job at his firm. He'll do all right," the father said.

They continued their patter while Adheem turned onto the Mass Pike, his jaw clenched and his white knuckles strangling the steering wheel. Traffic was mercifully light, and they arrived within half an hour. He would not have to endure their incessant chatter any longer.

"Twenty-five dollars," Adheem announced. Despite a desire to do so, he would never inflate a fare. He might be plotting something diabolical, but he was honest when it came to his business.

The man handed him two twenties and told him to keep the change.

Adheem couldn't resist. "My son graduated from Harvard today as well."

"Is that so?" The man replied, his eyebrows arching. "Well, uh, congratulations. You must be proud of him. I'm sure he'll do well."

Adheem ignored what he thought to be a patronizing comment. His revenge was meant for clueless fools such as these.

At four o'clock, Adheem turned onto Malcolm X Boulevard in Roxbury, scanning the street for his contact. At length he was flagged down by a tall, bearded man in a robe and whose eyes

seemed to hold the wisdom of the ages. Adheem swerved to the curb and Mustafa climbed in.

"Kayf Haalak, Adheem? (How are you?)"

"Bi-khayr, al-Hamdu lillah, (Fine, praise God)," Adheem replied, using the customary response.

"I trust that you and your family are well."

"Yes, thank you. Adam graduated from Harvard today."

"And what will he do?"

"He's been accepted by BC Law School, so he'll still be close to home."

"Excellent news. You must be pleased."

Adheem checked Mustafa's drawn face in the rear-view mirror. "You have something on your mind?"

"You are perceptive, Adheem, as always." After a short hesitation, Mustafa leaned forward. "There's a plan afoot. Later this year, a plane will fall from the skies. The Iranians will make it look like Libya is responsible. Many will die."

"You know how I feel about such events," said Adheem. "They will stun, but the effect will be short-lived. They only serve to heighten the scrutiny of the intelligence community. This will undermine my efforts."

Mustafa shook his head. "By the time your plan is ready to implement, this event will be virtually forgotten, as will others that occur. We must keep the West in fear. They think we've been weakened by their efforts, but we now have more than a thousand cells, all willing to fight Jihad. Yours is but one of many efforts throughout the world."

"They accomplish nothing. Americans care little about what happens elsewhere. It doesn't matter to them as long as it doesn't occur here." Adheem noticed the Mullah's eyes narrow.

"Your plan is ambitious, maybe too ambitious," the wizened man responded. "We can't sit on our hands, hoping that it succeeds. You have compromised your values and those of your son to

achieve it. Do you know how difficult it has been to convince the others of your loyalty?"

"I've compromised nothing. I'm willing to sacrifice every-thing, including my only son." Adheem fought to keep his voice even.

"Our group does not see it that way. You and your son no lon-ger worship at the mosque. You dress like a westerner. Now I see that you've even shaved your beard. Some say you are becoming just like them."

Adheem turned to look briefly but vehemently at Mustafa. "It's vital to my plan's success. You know that."

"Yes," said Mustafa calmly. "But those unaware of your plan do not. You walk a tight rope, my friend. Do not fall. I won't be able to catch you."

Adheem's anger boiled inside, but he did not dare further in-subordination. It was enough that they permitted him any variance from Sharia law. Through gritted teeth, he muttered, "Amin (let it be so)."

He stopped the cab outside the mosque where many peaceful Muslims knelt side-by-side with the five or six who were commit-ted to the West's destruction. Before Mustafa got out, he leaned forward again. "It is time for evening prayer. Will you join me?"

"You know I can't, and why," Adheem replied, quietly. "I will pray at home."

"You are a cautious one, Adheem. Such caution will serve you well. Just make sure that you and your son don't abandon our be-liefs. There will be consequences. Fi Amanullah (May Allah pro-tect you)."

Adheem said nothing, but the mullah's comment stung like a slap across the face. He knew the necessity of Adheem's and Adam's acceptance by the West. How dare he question his alle-giance? The movement seemed so short-sighted and fragmented. Last month's frivolous attack on the Acropol Hotel in the Sudan was a pin prick that killed only seven; the Americans hardly no-

ticed and didn't care. Something big was needed, something that would rip the souls from their adversaries.

Chapter 5

The Scions of Atlantis—what the hell did that mean, and why, of all the things Robbie could have told me, was that the one thing he scrawled as an emergency farewell? I stuffed the scrap of paper in my pocket. Nate gave me a sidelong glance from the pilot's seat and asked, "Love note from O'Toole?"

I didn't respond immediately, reluctant to reveal anything to him, and galled by his insensitivity.

"It's nothing," I answered.

"After all I've done for you … Kat, I'm on your side, remember?" The heat of his stare made my cheeks warm. I prayed that I wasn't blushing.

"I don't want to put you in any more danger," I said, and resumed rummaging through Robbie's bag. I didn't really expect to find anything else, but at least I didn't have to look back at Nate.

"And I suppose that's why you didn't tell me who you really were when I flew you to Nevis last year." A disgusted snort, then, "I knew who you were. Your build, your mannerisms, you couldn't disguise them, not from me."

"Why didn't you say something?"

"You were in bad shape. I didn't want to make things worse for you." His voice was unexpectedly gentle. "What happened?"

"You probably already know."

"Not really. Jermaine didn't say much, only that I needed to help you escape. I knew about Ben's death and that you worked for him. I put two and two together." I sat silently, unsure of what to reveal. He shrugged impatiently. "Look, I know I wasn't the best husband and there's not a day that I don't regret losing you, but if I'm risking my neck to help you, I have a right to know what we're up against."

"Is that why you stocked the beach house while I was in the hospital? Or were you just doing your job?"

"My orders were just to get you there, but when I realized it was you, well … ."

I finally allowed myself to look at him. He was still disarmingly attractive, but the years had etched a few more lines in his face, and the gray at his temples and in his mustache seemed to smooth his sharp edges the way ocean erodes the jagged edges of sea glass.

"I appreciated it," I said. "I'm not sure how I would have managed otherwise."

"It was nothing. I was happy to help." He squirmed a bit in his seat. "I was recently divorced and had plenty of time on my hands."

"I'm sorry," I said, although I really didn't feel anything.

"Too many hours in the air, I guess. I got a taste of my own medicine. She hooked up with someone else. One day, she was gone. When did you and O'Toole get together?"

"A couple of years ago. We ran into each other at a party thrown by some old college friends. It seems like eons ago. He was, I mean, he is a freelance reporter." I clutched the bag reflexively. I couldn't allow myself to accept that he might be dead. Changing the subject, I asked, "Do you know why Jermaine went away?"

"You want me to tell you what I know, but you won't tell me anything." He tried to say it lightly, but his indignation was obvious.

"I'm sorry, Nate," I said—and this time, really was— "but the less you know, the better. It's enough that you know I'm Carla

Banks." I leaned back in the seat, exhaling deeply before adding, "So many people have died because of me: Ben, Greg, my father … I can't put you in danger, too."

"I'm a big boy," he smiled, patting my knee. "I can fend for myself." Although I didn't think he meant it to be condescending, it was, and I stiffened. He immediately pulled his hand away and stared at the stars before us.

"Ben was a good man," he said. "He wanted to do the right thing before he retired."

"And Jermaine?" I leaned forward imperceptibly.

"Even though O'Toole used an alias to contact publishers, they figured out who it was. Since O'Toole was still alive, that meant Jermaine had lied. He was a marked man after that, so I flew him out."

"But how did Beau get out of jail?"

"Didn't know he had, but you know how the world works."

I chewed on his words. The so-called deep state had evidently struck again. "So, where are you taking me?"

"To a small airport about half an hour outside of Boston. Jermaine will meet us there."

"There are people I need to see."

"I'm guessing that this has something to do with O'Toole's note?" I grunted. "Kat, I know I haven't given you much of a reason to trust me, but I'm trying to help."

"If you really want to help, fly me to Indiana."

"Jermaine wants you to meet this guy first. Said he could keep you safe. After that, I'll take you wherever you want to go. Promise."

"Do you think they killed Robbie?" I asked, my voice quivering, unable to check my emotions.

"What I think is that you have to focus on your own survival."

The black sky masked any rooftops and roads, and it was only when we landed that I could make out "Lawrence Municipal Airport" on the small building beside the airstrip. Jermaine's familiar brown Hummer was waiting outside.

Nate taxied to the terminal and braked next to the car. When Jermaine emerged, my relief was palpable. He greeted Scout first.

"Hey, fella, how ya doin'?" He rubbed Scout's ears vigorously and then looked up at me. "You look a whole lot better than the last time I saw you. Welcome back."

I stood on tiptoes to get my arms around him. "It's good to see you, Jermaine. How are you?"

"No worse for wear. Hop in." Scout beat me to it.

"What about Nate?" I asked, jerking my head in his direction.

Nate called out, "You haven't seen the last of me, but now I've got to get out of here." As he stuck a card in the gas pump and began refueling, we drove off. For some reason, part of me was sorry to see him leave.

"A little awkward?" Jermaine asked.

"More than a little."

"O'Toole didn't make it? Too bad."

I told him about Robbie's phone call. "Someone found him. I think it was Beau or one of his men. I'm worried, Jermaine."

He remained stoic as he pulled onto Route 93 heading south. Normal people were sleeping now, but my life was no longer normal. With virtually no traffic, we'd be in Boston by three am.

"Nate said something about meeting a man who could help me."

"James Treadwell. He was a friend of Ben's."

"Company man?"

"No, but he has close ties with the agency."

"And you want me to trust him? I need more to go on than that."

"Just talk to him."

"Nate also said you had some trouble on my account. I'm sorry."

"Yeah, I had to disappear." Jermaine's eyes were fixed on the road. I could see him working his jaw. He didn't like discussing this.

"Then why are you still driving your Hummer? Won't they recognize it? Isn't it dangerous for you to be back?"

"I've missed your rapid-fire questions. Yessir, you put an Uzi to shame." Still stonewalling.

"So, when are we supposed to meet this James Treadwell? There are others I need to see. They may be able to provide some information ... if you won't."

He ignored my barb. "Not a good idea. Besides, you have to meet Treadwell tomorrow." As he turned onto Storrow Drive, the streetlights revealed his creased brow as well as the concern in his eyes. "Just what kind of information are you after?"

"Before the line went dead, Robbie told me to look in his bag for a note. All it said was 'Scions of Atlantis.' I have to find out what that means."

Jermaine's body went taut. He turned to face me with eyes afire. "Now you listen to me, Kat, for once in your life, listen! The Scions don't mess around. They make people disappear. I can't keep you safe forever, and I'll be damned if I'm going to get myself killed because of your foolishness. Stay away from them. I mean it."

No matter how much his words and his anger terrified me, I knew I wouldn't.

Chapter 6

"You can't possibly expect me to just sit here," I protested as I evaluated my surroundings, a spartan third-floor apartment in a Beacon Hill brownstone; probably another one of Jermaine's safe houses, and certainly decorated like one. "Besides, I need to get some clothes. All I have is the stuff I wore in the islands, and I'll need food for Scout."

"I'll arrange for clothes. You're what, a size four?" Jermaine responded, appraising my frame.

"Close enough," I replied. "How soon can you get them?"

"Why? So you can skip town? I know you better than that."

"At least tell me about this Scions of Atlantis," I said as I pulled the curtain aside and gazed down to the narrow street below. A few early risers, wrapped in winter garb, bustled over the brick sidewalks, their chins tucked under scarfs and hands buried in pockets.

"Get away from the window," Jermaine snapped, grabbing the curtain from me and pulling it closed. "What do you want to know?"

"For starters, who are they? Why should I avoid them? Why would Robbie's last request be for me to find out about them? How did he know about them?"

"Okay, okay." He collapsed into an easy chair and blew out a puff of air. "I suppose you have a right to know." He rubbed his head, and I knew he was already censoring what he would tell me. "First, let me ask you a question. Who do you think runs the country?"

"The easy answer is the president and the Congress, but I know that powerful people pull their strings."

"Right. There's a reason for that. Big business, the wealthy, the power mongers … they continue long after elections end. They are the Scions of Atlantis. They meet secretly, sometimes at an unknown location, sometimes electronically. They are the puppet masters, more mighty than the commander in chief. Hell, they own the president."

"And they don't have to get elected," I added.

"Elected?" A derisive snicker. "They control the elections. Along with the stock market, foreign policy, oil prices, interest rates, you name it."

"For the sake of argument, let's say they control the government, but I can't believe they would do anything to bring down the U.S. They'd have too much to lose."

Jermaine shook his head. "They're global; they don't view the world in terms of countries. Take Cosmoplex Financial. It operates in every major country, America's friends as well as foes, and its revenue last year alone was over a hundred billion U.S. dollars. Cosmoplex could single-handedly ruin the economy of any region just by withdrawing its business, not only because of its own valuation, but because it manages the financial holdings of other industries within that country. All it cares about is money and power."

"So why would Robbie want me to look into them? What can I do?" Despite my sleep deprivation, gears were grinding inside my head.

"He didn't do you any favors by tipping you off. My guess is that he discovered something about them—some activity that threatens the U.S."

"So how do you know so much about this group?"

"Let's just say our paths crossed when I helped you and

O'Toole escape." Hearing that, I shrunk a bit, knowing that Jermaine would never reveal the danger he encountered.

"But all I had was stuff on the Kennedy assassination. They wouldn't care about that, not now."

"O'Toole had a lot more, but it disappeared in the fire ... didn't it?" His eyes bore into mine.

I tensed. Robbie's strict instruction was not to tell anyone. I could not return his glare.

He rose, walked in a very deliberate manner toward me, his face only inches from mine. "What do you know? What aren't you telling me?"

"I don't know anything yet." I stepped back, away from him, and began fiddling with the zipper on my bag.

"You can't hold out on me now." His voice was laced with anger, but something else, maybe fear. Even in the most dire of circumstances, I'd never seen him afraid. That, more than anything, made me afraid too.

Matching his intensity, I responded, "If I told you anything—that is, if I even knew anything, which I don't—they could hurt you. I can't let that happen."

"What I don't know could hurt both of us. Now, tell me." His eyes bulged disconcertingly, and I looked away.

"If I learn anything, I will." I hated keeping the little I knew from him. He had risked so much for me.

He stormed out of the room, slammed the door and locked it behind him, ordering me not to leave. This once, I'd obey.

After a much-needed shower, I pulled out my laptop and searched the CIA database for "Scions of Atlantis." All I found was a reference to the Lara Croft series in which the scion was some sort of device that gave its owner the power to do whatever he wanted. Could the name be a reference to that? When I clicked on another link, a notice popped up saying the page was no longer available. Someone had deleted it. Who could make that happen? Was it that secret—even from the CIA? And how did Jermaine, a covert ops guy in JSOC, know about them?

I looked up James Treadwell next and learned everything I could about the man: CEO of Quantum Bioinformatics. Based in greater Boston. Sixty-five years old. Graduate of Yale and the "B School." The largest individual philanthropist, dollar-wise, in the entire country. Gives to the political campaigns of both parties. Enjoys extreme sports. Other than the trappings of a successful career, nothing jumped out. Why would he want to help me?

I continued to scour various databases for business tycoons and retired members of intelligence or the Joint Chiefs of Staffs. Then, reviving my own CIA expertise, I began tracking their movements to see if any patterns emerged. By the time Jermaine returned, bearing a complete if not entirely fashionable winter wardrobe, I had determined that a certain subset made a yearly trip to Edinburgh in May. Had I just found the Scions of Atlantis? If so, James Treadwell was not one of them, which was somewhat reassuring, but I needed more information. I quickly logged off. Jermaine would erupt if he knew what I had been doing.

If Greg were alive, he could have helped me flesh this out. I had exhausted my computer skills, but Greg's son Cam, a carbon copy of his father and also my godson, might be able to help. As far as I knew, he was still in the D.C. area, working as a contract employee for whomever needed the skills of one of the best IT minds in the country and was willing to pay megabucks for the service. Did he hold me responsible for his father's death? Would he even consider helping me?

Jermaine gruffly announced, "I picked up some Chinese food. It's in the car. I'll be right back."

"Thanks, I'm famished."

"Glad to see you listened for a change and didn't run off." He didn't sound friendly. "What have you been doing?"

"Just getting some background on James Treadwell. He sounds like an amazing guy. Why does he want to help me?"

"In addition to Ben, he's friends with Tom and Rob. They go way back."

"Robbie never mentioned his name."

"Doubt they've had much interaction lately. Treadwell is always on the move. He has to be."

That struck me as worthy of a follow-up question, but I would save it until Jermaine had cooled off. "Do you think I can trust him?"

"As much as you can trust anyone at this point."

"I'm sorry, Jermaine. I appreciate everything you've done for me, both before and now. I don't want this to come between us. It's just that not knowing what's happened to Robbie, hearing about this arcane group, and being on the run again have made me more than a little paranoid. I had to do some digging."

"Maybe if you'd let people help you, you'd be less paranoid." His voice seemed only slightly warmer.

"I can't just sit back. You know me better than that."

"Then you'll be making it harder on all of us," he said as he left abruptly.

I stared at the door with mixed emotions. I wanted to take an active role in my survival, but I also wanted to find out about the Scions. I didn't want Jermaine to be angry, but I didn't want him controlling me either. I didn't want to cause anyone else harm, but I knew there were people I needed to see.

Then my cell phone rang. Very few people had my number and I answered without hesitation. It had to be Robbie. I hit "accept," but before I could say anything, a voice on the other end said, "Thanks to Lover Boy, we've got your number … in more ways than one. You're next."

My heart seized. The voice wasn't Beau's, but Lover Boy was Beau's nickname for Robbie.

Jermaine's knock the next morning came as a relief. My sleep had been tortured by visions of Beau's gleaming teeth, the remembered heat of the branding iron, the smell of my own burning flesh. What atrocities had they inflicted upon Robbie to make him talk?

After washing up, I donned one of the dressier outfits that Jermaine had selected and emerged from my bedroom to find a hearty breakfast of eggs, bacon, toast, orange juice and coffee set on the table.

"How'd you sleep?" he asked. I mumbled something to indicate I hadn't and told him about the phone call.

"Did you recognize the voice?"

"It wasn't Beau, if that's what you mean," I answered after swallowing a gulp of coffee.

"Just because they have your number doesn't mean they can track you, right?"

I nodded, confirming that when Greg gave me the phone, he said it couldn't be traced. After a forkful of eggs, I added, "But that was over a year ago. Maybe they figured out a way to do it."

"We'll play it safe. Keep calls to a minimum. But we have other things to think about now. Are you ready for your meeting with Treadwell?" I nodded. "Finish up. Our meeting is in an hour and I don't want to hit too much traffic."

Leaving Scout behind, we exited the building into an alley. The narrow space between rows of brownstones funneled the frigid wind, and I was grateful for the winter clothes. I turned in the direction of Jermaine's Hummer, but he pulled my arm, guiding me to another car parked at the corner.

"If someone's watching the place, let them think we're still inside."

A short while later, we were on Route 128, heading to Treadwell's bioinformatics firm. Jermaine admonished me to let Treadwell do the talking, but after a while it sounded like white noise as I silently reviewed all that I had read about him. If Treadwell didn't fill in the blanks, there was no way I'd hesitate to push him for answers. I think Jermaine knew it.

We pulled in front of a glass and steel monolith, perfectly landscaped with curving drives and gardens punctuated by statues of Greek and Roman gods. Inside we were greeted by a tall, fortyish, fit-looking man who introduced himself as Josh Harbaugh. Josh rode with us in the elevator to a top floor filled with exotic plants and fountains. If it weren't for the ubiquitous "Quantum Bioinformatics" signs, I'd have sworn we'd entered a giant terrarium, not a Fortune 10 company.

"Please wait here. I'll let Jim know you've arrived." Josh turned abruptly on his heel, like a sentry guarding the Tomb of the Unknown Soldier.

"Remember what I said," Jermaine whispered. I looked at him blankly. He ran his palm across his shaved head, trying to remain composed. "Let Treadwell do the talking."

I nodded as though I intended to comply and moved away to admire the landscaping. After perhaps ten minutes, a thoroughbred of a man emerged and covered the distance between us in very few strides. He wore jeans and a sweater, and only the gray of his hair, pulled back into a ponytail, indicated his age.

"Kat Hastings," he grinned broadly, ignoring Jermaine. "I've heard so much about you. I feel like I know you. I'm glad we're finally able to meet. I'm Jim, Jim Treadwell. Let's go someplace where we can talk." Turning to Jermaine, he said, "You don't mind waiting, do you, Biggs?" Before Jermaine could answer, Treadwell turned and pulled me away. I looked back to Jermaine and shrugged. He placed a finger to his lips, once more signaling me to be quiet.

Treadwell's office looked like a corporate mancave with banks of high-def TV screens tuned to CSPAN, CNN, MSNBC, FOX and Bloomberg. Computers and monitors dwarfed a minimalist desk that sat across from a conference table. A huge window framed a panoramic view of the technology belt that girded Boston's bulging waist. Next to the window was a chessboard with pieces positioned for a new game. I felt instantly insignificant until I noticed the wall behind Treadwell's desk. Pictures of sixties' rock legends, captured in concert posters from years ago, looked down upon us: Janis, the Stones, the Who, Ten Years After, and Robbie's two favorite groups, The Band and Crosby, Stills and Nash. I relaxed just a bit.

"Thanks for coming. I see you've noticed my friends. Those were the days. Can I get you anything? Coffee, water, soda?" I shook my head, and he continued, "This must be a little daunting for you," he said waving his arms around the room, "especially since you've been through so much."

"Uh, yeah, but how do you even know about me?"

"You're important to Rob and Tom, and they are important to me."

"That's it? Aren't you worried that I might be a liability? I'm not exactly popular right now."

"There's also Ben Douglas and your father, both of whom spoke highly of your intelligence and tenacity—or as they called it, your stubborn streak."

I practically jumped out of my chair. "You knew them?" I stared at Treadwell, amazed that this man whom I'd never even heard of until twenty-four hours ago had intersected with such vital parts of my life. "Did you know my father well?" I asked, hoping to hear anything that would bring him back to me, if only for an instant.

"Not as well as I knew Ben, but I knew that even though he

could be gruff, he cared for you very much. He even grew to respect Rob, although he'd never admit it. The day before he died, your father tried to reach me to see if I could help, but I was out of the country. My guys didn't get to his place in time. I'm so sorry that you had to go through that, and I'm worried about Rob too. We need to find him." I might have been mistaken, but I thought I saw his eyes moisten before he looked down at the floor.

That he seemed to care for Robbie was reassuring. "What can I do?" I demanded.

"Help me find him. I know you're a crack analyst, and we've got an incredible system here, maybe as good as the NSA, if not better, if I do say so myself."

His pride was not annoying. If anything, I wanted to hear more, especially if it meant finding Robbie. "Like what?"

He gestured at the devices on his desk. "That's just for starters. We have anonymous routers, sophisticated encryption, and algorithms that are impossible to hack with current technology. With your analytical skills and our IT capabilities, I'll bet anything that you can find him. And maybe," he paused ever so slightly, "help us with something else, something really big." He cocked his head slightly and his eyes sparkled like those of a child who can't wait to share a secret.

"I'm listening."

He leaned in and spoke in hushed tones as though someone was eavesdropping. "It's kind of, well, radical. Can I trust you to keep this confidential?"

"Of course, but it's not illegal or anything, is it?" I smiled but felt suddenly wary.

"No, but it won't be easy." He sat back in his chair. "I don't know about you, but I felt like the last presidential election was a farce; however, it did accomplish one thing. It made us look in the mirror and acknowledge the divide in American society. I can't remember when we've been so polarized, not even during 'Nam. Maybe not since the Civil War. Both parties are controlled by the rich and powerful. Not only is the two-party system obsolete, it jeopardizes our country, threatens our shared prosperity and diminishes everything we stand for."

"I don't mean to be rude, but you seem to be doing pretty well in the prosperity department."

He laughed. "Touché, but even one of the most fiery radicals, Jerry Rubin, became a stockbroker. The difference is, I want to fix the system. What was it Thoreau said? 'Rather than love than money than fame, give me truth.' " He leaned forward and with more intensity said, "We can't let the current oligarchy—and don't fool yourself, that's what we've become—permit so much power residing in the hands of so few with no one accountable. We want—no, we need—to change that."

"Who's we?" I asked, the hairs on my neck standing at attention.

"There are many in our merry little band," he replied wryly, "including some, like me, who believe the time has come for a viable third party, a party that is committed to honesty, saving and improving our way of life; socially inclusive, but fiscally responsible."

"Okay, so what makes your idea so, what did you call it, radical?"

"Democracy is a fragile thing. Aristotle wasn't that keen on it. He preferred a monarchy or an aristocracy, and he ranked a democracy just above oligarchy and tyranny. But since we are already moving toward oligarchy, and our founding fathers arranged things to prevent a monarchy or aristocracy, we need to make what we have work. Despite the challenges."

"Such as the lack of citizen participation and the tyranny of the majority?"

"You know your Aristotle, I see. That's good. And your de Tocqueville. So I imagine you must also know the saying, 'There are many men of principle in both parties in America, but there is no party of principle.' We will change that. The men and women we recruit must be people of integrity. 'I'm not interested in preserving the status quo; I want to overthrow it.' "

"Machiavelli," I stated, uneasy that Treadwell would quote him. "So how can you change a system that's been in place since the country's inception?"

"Think of the electorate as a normal distribution. Whoever captures the middle, where most people fall, not only wins the election, they get things done. Our party will represent the middle. Not only will we meet the needs of the majority, we will force the Democrats and Republicans to be accountable. We will be every bit as powerful as them and work within the system, completely legit."

"Sounds good in theory, but incumbency is too much of an advantage."

"That's another thing. We will advocate for term limits, just as the founding fathers intended. We will eliminate the obscene amounts of money spent on endless campaigns, and legislators will have the same healthcare system they expect our citizens to accept. The people who serve will do so because they want to help, not get rich."

"Sounds like a tall order. If you're to have any impact, you'll have to make large inroads quickly. Otherwise, you'll fail just like the others who have tried."

"Ah, a woman who speaks her mind. I was told you would. I like that." He smiled briefly before standing to pace the room. "A significant number of moderate House members and senators as well as governors are frustrated by the extreme factions in their parties and have already agreed to join us. They are true public servants who want Congress to function as originally intended. We will have the needed critical mass right from the start, not just one fledgling presidential candidate."

I must have looked skeptical because he quickly continued, "When you and I were young, there were three networks. We got our news from Walter Cronkite, Huntley and Brinkley, or Howard

K. Smith. Now, people listen to the news they want to hear. If they are conservative, they listen to Fox; the liberals listen to MSNBC or maybe CNN. What now passes for news is now nothing more than a bully pulpit for an ideology, prompting people to become more entrenched in their individual biases. That doesn't even begin to describe the impact of the Internet. An MIT study of 1,500 people found that a false story reaches them six times quicker, on average, than a true story does, and fake news is 70 percent more likely to get retweeted than accurate news. Our media outlets will provide pure news, no commentary from talking heads, which will enable people to form their own opinions."

"But how will you get people to leave their comfort zones and listen to your network?"

"Do you play chess?"

"Haven't for years. Not since my father died," I answered, ruefully quoting his admonition, "'L'attaque, l'attaque. Toujours l'attaque,'" meaning to always be on the offensive.

"He taught you well. I like to play the Sveshnikov variation of the Sicilian defense. It, too, is an aggressive style of play, but one that gives the second player more flexibility in counterplay. Given that the current government is entrenched, we are definitely second players, but as Bobbie Fischer once said, 'Tactics flow from a superior position.' We have worked hard to establish that."

"How so?" I asked. He had me riveted.

"We already have many baby boomers from our personal contacts. In addition to them, we will target millennials, using the latest social media platforms and creating some of our own. Maybe we can actually get them to vote. We've run numerous focus groups to determine what resonates with this demographic. They are the future, and they despise the way the current president got elected and how he's caved on gun control. Their 'Never Again' movement is impressive. We've also hired many minority and female advisors, to help us address their concerns about the white supremacists, voter suppression, and sexual misconduct. We've landed some big sports contracts and feature presentations that will lure a broader segment of the viewing public to our station. Our launch will be epic. The establishment won't see it coming."

He was an enthusiastic salesman, and he was right that the credibility of the media had been undermined. Nonetheless, it all sounded overly pat. There were other demographics to consider, and cable TV was loaded with competition. Besides, I had a gnawing unease about a party with its own media outlet. It seemed counter to the checks and balances that allow a democracy to thrive.

"I see you still need some more convincing," Treadwell said. "Let me show you something." He walked briskly to his desk and yanked open a drawer, withdrawing two papers that he handed to me. I instantly recognized Ben's illegible chicken scratches on one and my father's Rhinehart-precise script on the other. Seeing their signatures made me gasp slightly. Both were statements of confidentiality.

"They knew about your plan?"

"Not only knew about it but helped get it off the ground by recruiting some to our party. They were loyal company men who respected the Constitution and lamented how its principles have been mangled by special interests and manipulated by partisan forces."

Although somewhat reassured by this, I thought Treadwell was crazy. My gut was churning, my brain flashed warning signs, but his vision and passion were compelling. I had to hear more. "So where do I come in?"

"Your skills are invaluable. Besides, I can keep you safe. It would be a win-win."

Treadwell might have had the resources to protect me, but I didn't know if I could trust him, not yet. As though he could read my mind, he continued, "I know you don't know me, but I know this about you. You love O'Toole, but you also love our country. You have never shirked a task, no matter how dangerous, if you thought you could right a wrong. You two are alike that way. If we do nothing, the oligarchs win, and the great democratic experiment fails. What do you say?" he asked again, even more intently.

"I'd like to think about it."

"We don't have a lot of time," he said, his voice strident, his eyes almost pleading. Somewhat unnerved, I looked away and inadvertently focused on the wall of posters, the faces of Robbie's rock icons, the voices of our idealistic, overheated generation. Treadwell followed my gaze, then looked back at me. "We have to find O'Toole, Kat. You can help us."

I didn't answer.

"Okay, time to bring out the big guns." He flashed a hopeful smile and pulled another sheet of paper from his desk. "I wasn't going to show you this because I didn't want to upset you any more than you already are." He handed me a piece of paper, a note from Robbie. I snatched it from his hand and read:

Hey Jim, long time no hear.

Making any progress? I found some stuff that may help you with your plans but can't get it while I'm here in Nevis. When things ease up a bit, I'll figure out a way to send it to you. I haven't told Kat anything—no need to put her in any more danger than I already have. I hear MacGregor's on board. He'll help a lot with recruiting. Let me know if you get wind of Beau's activities. We'd prefer not to see him again.

Thanks, and good luck, Rob

I clutched the letter and held it close to my breast. The tears finally came, and I shook with each sob. There were so many things Robbie never told me and should have.

Treadwell handed me a tissue and spoke gently. "You can trust me, Kat. Your friends are my friends. I can protect you from those who have Rob and are after you. Rob means a lot to me, and you can help me find him. In the process, you can help us build something lasting, something necessary for the country to survive. Please, Kat."

Through blurred eyes I met his gaze. His eyes were misty as well. My MO is not typically spontaneous. Normally I take facts and process them until they make sense and a pattern emerges. However, the events of the past two years had denied me that luxury, demanding instead a rapid, even instantaneous response. This was one of those times. Besides, Treadwell was growing on me. His charisma, coupled with that rare ability to make someone feel valued, was something I desperately craved in my current state.

"When do I start?" He had won this round of chess.

Chapter 7

September 10, 2001

*M*ustafa's *orders were specific. Pick up the Egyptian, take him to the car rental agency and say nothing to anyone. Adheem bristled at the instructions. He did not want to be associated in any way with this grand plan of Osama's; it could jeopardize his own. But his so-called brothers were becoming increasingly vocal in questioning his commitment to the cause. How could they, with all that he was prepared to sacrifice? He had agreed to drive this man only to placate them. That it would make it more difficult for the police to track the Egyptian's movements meant little to him.*

Adheem pulled in front of the hotel and saw an Arab checking his watch repeatedly and glancing furtively up and down the street. He appeared to be in his early thirties, a little older than Adam. When he saw Adheem, the man threw his bags into the back seat and climbed in front, wearing a self-satisfied grin.

"Take me to this address," he said as he thrust a slip of paper at Adheem.

"As you wish," Adheem replied curtly.

"Mustafa says that you're one of us, that I can trust you." Adheem nodded, and the man continued. "Tomorrow will be an historic day for Jihad. I'm told that you fought by Osama's side."

"That was many years ago, in Afghanistan, fighting the Russians. How is he?"

"He is well. Thanks to him, I will be honored as a martyr to our cause. I would follow him anywhere—even to Jannah. Perhaps if I succeed, I will be worthy of an eternal home in Firdaws."

Adheem turned to face the man. *"Firdaws is reserved for the most devout—prophets and martyrs. What will make you so worthy?"*

"Tomorrow, my friends and I will board American Airlines Flight 11." He chuckled and further mused, *"I'm glad that it's called 'American Airlines.' A nice twist, don't you think? I even have a seat in business class."*

"And where will you go on this 'American Airlines?'"

"To my place in glory. You can tell your friends that you met me."

Adheem stifled a cynical snort. *"And just how will you get there, my friend?"*

"I have been taking flying lessons here, in America. I received my commercial pilot's license last year, from the FAA. More irony, don't you think?" he laughed once more, a bit nervously. *"I will fly myself to Firdaws."*

Adheem drew a deep breath. Damn Osama. This could ruin everything he had worked for. He needed to know more. *"You think that you, alone, can make a difference?"*

"I'm not alone. There are many of us. If one of us fails, others will succeed." Pride and confidence rendered his voice firm, but buoyant.

As they pulled into the rental agency, Adheem said, *"Allah mahak (Allah be with you), Mohammed."* Atta slapped him on the back, jumped out of the car and hurried to the counter.

Adheem waited while Atta picked up his rental and drove away. Yes, this would definitely change things.

Pulling out his cellphone, he punched his son's number with rigid fingers. *"Adam, we must talk, but not on the phone."*

"What's up?"

His son's casual manner irritated him, but he let it go. The situation required calm and clear thought. "We must meet now."

"I can't. My day is booked, and I have a community meeting at seven in Dorchester." He heard Adam's muffled voice, indicating he was covering the phone, speaking to a co-worker. "How about tomorrow? My calendar is free."

Adheem clenched his jaw. "It cannot wait." He pounded the steering wheel. "Where is this meeting? I'll see you afterward."

"What's the rush? I'm prepping for my bar exam. I'm trying to establish myself as a community organizer. This is what you want, remember?"

Adheem could hear impatience pepper Adam's voice, but he knew better than to convey his displeasure over the phone. "Adam, I am your father. You must obey me."

"Okay, okay!" Adam gave his father the address of Dorchester High School and asked him to arrive no earlier than nine. "But this is all your idea."

"I understand, but if we don't meet, it will all be for nothing." After hanging up, Adheem continued to take fares around the city, contemplating the Egyptian's promise for tomorrow and what it would bring. How could he protect Adam's and his own ambitions in such an environment? He had no choice. Adam would have to distance himself from the Egyptian's actions and, in so doing, potentially incur the wrath of the brethren. He had to speak with Mustafa as soon as possible and pulled out his cell phone to call him.

Half an hour later, he drove to their usual spot. Mustafa lifted his robe and climbed in.

"So, Adheem, what is so important that we must meet now?" the old man asked.

"This Egyptian whom you asked me to take to the car rental. He told me that he has big plans for tomorrow, something to do with airplanes. Do you know what's afoot?"

"*Of course I do. Heard it from Khalid Sheikh Mohammed himself. It will be magnificent.*"

"*There will be deaths?*"

"*Many, in New York and Washington. Important buildings will fall.*"

"*The Americans will hate us even more than they already do. They will make our lives hell. It will make my plan impossible to implement unless Adam decries this action.*" Adheem checked the rearview mirror, wary of Mustafa's reaction.

"*You yourself said that attacks must occur on American soil to have any impact. Do you dare to presume that your plan is more important than Osama's? More important than carrying out the orders of Al Quran? That is blasphemy.*" Mustafa's indignation startled Adheem. "*You are already suspect within our community. We may be small in number, but we are resolute. I've warned you, people are talking. If your son speaks out against tomorrow's acts, both you and he will be dead to us.*"

"*I am no blasphemer!*" Adheem's anger would not be contained. "*You know he must appear to be one of them for the plan to work. How many times do I have to explain this?*" He turned in his seat and stared directly at Mustafa. "*You think I enjoy playing this role? You think I wouldn't rather be conspiring with all of you? No, I must sit in this forsaken cab, enduring the condescension of those whom I transport when I could be flying planes like your Egyptian or punishing the nonbelievers.*"

Mustafa shook his head. "*After tomorrow, we must stand together. If your son rebukes the actions of the Jihadists, he will be seen as an infidel by those unaware of your grandiose scheme. All infidels must die, even if they claim to be of Islam.*"

Adheem recoiled at Mustafa's words. In a more contrite voice, he asked, "*Can't you vouch for my allegiance to our cause?*"

"*I will try, but after tomorrow, our lives will be dramatically different. Our little cabal will need to know who can be trusted.*"

"*Mustafa, we have known each other for many years. We have fought, worshipped, sacrificed and suffered together. If you can't trust me, who can?"*

"A very good question. Perhaps you should ponder it carefully." Mustafa shifted in his seat and looked outside. "Let me off here. Our conversation is over but remember my words."

"You mean your threat."

"No, a promise."

Adheem stood near the rear of the high school auditorium, holding a mop so that others would assume he was the janitor waiting to clean up. Adam, dressed in a crisp white shirt and tie, stood tall at the podium, gesturing broadly. "I will work with banks to provide low-cost loans so we can establish businesses and become self-sufficient. I will see to it that business owners receive the financial counseling needed to ensure their success. We will be a community that thrives because of our own efforts, not one that is reliant on handouts from fickle politicians. We will raise ourselves from poverty and despair and become a shining example of how hard work, coupled with vision, can lead to a productive life if given a chance. We will be masters of our own fate, not slaves to an oppressive system that robs us of our own self-worth."

Adheem could not help but glow with pride as his son energized the crowd and gave them hope for a better future. He scanned the room. Adam had captivated them; they leaned forward in their seats, absorbing every word.

"Are you with me?" Cheers erupted. "Are you willing to take the next step, to attend training sessions and planning meetings, to venture forth as a united community?" More cheers, more laughter, and something else: what was it, hope? He looked into the eyes of the people and saw that they were sparkling. Previously slumped shoulders were now square. In place of skeptical silence there were now words of encouragement. Hands that had been gripping programs were now placed on neighbors' shoul-

ders. *Adam had succeeded in making the audience united in their shared sense of self-worth.*

"We can make the American dream a reality, right here in Dorchester. I'm living proof that if the son of a cab driver can make it, so can you." Adheem winced but understood. "I will do my part; will you do yours?" The audience stood and clapped. A crescendo of cheers filled the room. Adam stepped away from the podium and raised his hands in victory. He had conquered despondency by converting it to optimism. He left the stage and began shaking the hands of those in the front rows. Women hugged him. Men slapped him on the back. As the crowd dispersed, Adheem heard its members give voice to their aspirations. "I will be a dry cleaner," said one. "I will open a butcher shop," said another. "I've always wanted to teach music," said a third.

Adam was still shaking hands, thanking individuals for attending the town hall meeting. Adheem realized, possibly for the first time, that his son had a gift, a gift for rallying others to his cause by giving them what everyone wants, opportunity. Adheem was now convinced, more than ever, that his plan would succeed because Adam possessed the same charisma as a Kennedy or a Reagan.

As staff members began turning out lights, they congratulated Adam for the evening's success, adoration manifested in their beaming eyes and broad smiles. When the last stragglers had finally departed, Adheem approached his son, still high from the meeting's outcome. He hated to dampen Adam's moment, but the situation necessitated it.

"We must speak in the cab," he said tersely, then turned and walked in silence toward the exit. Adam dutifully followed.

"What's got you so rattled?" Adam asked once inside the car.

Adheem explained his conversations with the Egyptian and Mustafa and then added, "My fear is that, after tomorrow, you and I will find ourselves alone, with no one to support us."

"Holy shit. This will screw up everything. The election for

town council is just two months away. We've worked so hard. Why can't they understand?" Adam spat in disgust out the window. "I'll have to speak out against them. I have no choice."

"Yes, you must. You will have to convince the Americans that you are appalled by these acts, that you are a different kind of Muslim, in fact, that you are as American as any of them, and you must be prepared to speak out immediately. I will deal with Mustafa and his band ... somehow."

Adheem woke after a night of fitful sleep. By five a.m. he had brewed his tea and settled into the sofa, facing the television. All he could think of was that the Egyptian and his cronies would soon be boarding their flights. Maybe their plans would fall through. Maybe they'd be detained by security. Perhaps he should send a warning to the airport.

"You're up early." Baha's dreary monotone startled him. He hadn't noticed her presence. She walked to the kitchen and turned on the radio, humming along to the American music.

He didn't answer. The last thing he needed was some inane conversation with a woman he now despised. "Turn off that garbage. It's bad enough that I have to hear it in my cab," he yelled from the living room.

She turned down the volume and said, "I was thinking it might be nice to have Adam for dinner. I seldom see him anymore."

He ignored her once more, annoyed that she might complicate things further by having Adam to the house.

She re-entered the room, carrying a steaming cup of tea. "So, what do you think? Can we have Adam over? I miss him."

Still, he ignored her. In a more strident voice, she continued. "I am his mother. I would like to see him. You separate us like I'm a pariah."

His impatience peaked. *"Leave it be, woman,"* he hollered. *"You gave him birth, but he's my son."*

"How dare you deny me Adam! I will see him. You do not own him. Nor do you own me." She stomped back into the kitchen and turned the volume up once more.

He rose and followed her. *"Oh, but I do own you. You are mine and will do as I say. You're lucky that I allow you to live here. I could easily throw you out on the street with the gutter scum."*

"It would be an improvement. In fact, I would welcome it. Anything would be better than living here, with you. You are not a man, you are a pig."

He slapped her face with the back of his hand, sending her teacup flying against the wall. Her cheek bled where his ring had slashed it. *"You will do no such thing. You are nothing but a whore, but you're my whore."* He grabbed her throat with both hands and screamed, *"If you leave, I will snap your neck with my bare hands."* He pushed her away. She stumbled, then fell. *"Now, stop bothering me."*

Baha shuffled into the bedroom, stifling a whimper, not bothering to close the door behind her. He returned to the sofa. During the next two hours his anger grew as he contemplated the Egyptian's intent and its inevitable consequences.

"We interrupt our normal broadcast to bring you breaking news. A plane has crashed into the north tower of the World Trade Center in New York City." Then he saw the video. Over and over, the station replayed the tape of an a commercial plane approaching and then hitting one of the Twin Towers. Part of him enjoyed seeing the destruction repeated on an endless loop, but his satisfaction was tempered by the knowledge that this would complicate his plan. This was what the Egyptian said would happen, but was there more to come? Twenty minutes later, a second plane hit the south tower. Flames now erupted from both buildings. Smoke billowed in large, dense columns. Papers fluttered everywhere. People fled through the streets, bloodied, screaming, made ghostly by

ash. Sirens blared. Policemen waved people away while firemen rushed inside.

Then there was a loud rumble. A dark, massive, amorphous cloud enveloped one of the towers and right before his eyes, it collapsed to the ground. The Egyptian was right. It was magnificent. A half-hour later, the south tower fell, just as the first, and was equally astounding. He could not help but smile when he realized how much greater the destruction was this time than last, although seeing people jump to their death to avoid being burned alive made him shudder. This victory came at great human cost. True, they were infidels, but what if it was because they hadn't heard the truth? That would make them innocents who would find protection in the afterlife, but he couldn't ignore the screams, the blood, the agony.

"Stop it!" he commanded himself. Terrorism requires a man to focus on the prize, not the price. He continued to watch as additional reports followed. A third plane hit the Pentagon and a fourth crashed in a field in Pennsylvania. The anchorman reported that more planes were missing. Maybe there was more devastation to come. It was all so good and yet, so bad.

Although he had performed Salat at dawn, he pulled out his fraying prayer mat once more and kneeled, reciting his thanks out loud. Thousands of infidels met their death as did nineteen martyrs. The Egyptian was right; he would enjoy an eternal home in Firdaws. Adheem would join him there as would Adam. He prayed for wisdom and guidance to navigate what would now be a much more complicated path, but his supplications were interrupted when, out of the corner of his eye, he noticed that Baha had been watching him through the partially opened door.

Chapter 8

Present Day

"Are you crazy?" Jermaine bellowed, turning his eyes from the road to glare at me.

"We've been through this," I said, pounding my thighs with both fists. "I only have a week until I start working for Treadwell. I've got things to do, people to see."

"What part of 'your life's in danger' don't you understand?" He threw his hands up and let them fall back with a thud onto the steering wheel. "I've been doing my damnedest to keep you safe and this is the thanks I get?"

"Jermaine, I appreciate it, I really do, but I can't just hide out, hoping they won't find me."

"Fine, but I'm not coming with you this time. You're on your own," he barked. I had never seen him so angry. "There's a limit, and I'm not risking my neck for you anymore, not if you won't co-operate. I'll watch Scout for you. It will make your travels easier, but you'd better be back in time to start work. I put my reputation on the line to get you that job.

"I will. I promise."

"Don't make promises you may not be able to keep. If some-one tracks you down, there's no telling what will happen."

We rode home in a silence so tense that my jaw hurt. Two hours later, I was cruising on the Mass Pike in a Zipcar, heading toward the New York town of Bethel, about two hours outside

Manhattan. I'd not told anyone where I was going. Though a bit daunted about being on my own, I had to find Robbie's stash of information, even if it meant risking my increasingly fragile relationship with Jermaine, who only muttered, "Be careful," as I left.

Frankly, I was surprised that, despite his bombast, Jermaine relented so easily. It wasn't that I didn't trust him — he had saved my life — but his tight-lipped demeanor made me hesitant to share what I knew. It was clear that he didn't want me digging into the dirt of the Scions, wouldn't even discuss them, and he seemed all too eager to have me work for Treadwell without telling me why. It was almost like he wanted me to go and was only feigning disapproval.

I pulled into the snow-fringed driveway of a Best Western, in Monticello, about twenty minutes away from Bethel. In the lobby I encountered a drowsy receptionist, his head propped on one arm and his eyes glazed by *The New York Times*. I checked in and went straight to my room.

The next morning, while hotel-room coffee gurgled in the pot on the bureau, I dressed to the sound of oldies playing on the radio. Hearing Janis Joplin brought back memories of our visit to Woodstock where Robbie had proposed just before the shots rang out. I shook off the thought while pulling on my parka, gloves and boots and then gathered the invaluable gadgets that Greg had given me a couple of years before. As I bought water and granola bars in the hotel's convenience store, I reflected yet again how much I missed his quirky charm.

Snow had fallen during the night, but it was fluffy and light, and I swept it off the car with my gloved hands. Activating the GPS in Greg's headset, I drove toward Tom MacGregor's house, hoping to find a road that would take me two miles north, as Robbie had described. The day was clear and crisp and the roads, though varnished with ice, were manageable. I found Tom's house and knocked on the door, but there was no answer. Still, with a day's worth of light to guide me, I felt optimistic about finding the cabin and Robbie's secreted stash.

By noon, however, my spirits flagged. I had covered every road heading north from Tom's several times. I saw no sign that said "Bait" and no dirt roads that might lead to a cabin. The snow disguised it all. Then I began to think. If Robbie had found the cabin without a car, then maybe I had to as well. He would have had to take a relatively direct route—especially if he was in a hurry. I returned to Tom's house and prayed that this time, he might be home and could point me in the right direction.

I knocked again, but still there was no response. Pulling the car into Tom's garage to hide it from passersby, I rummaged through items scattered on a workbench. A crowbar could come in handy, and I placed it in an old burlap bag along with my computer and Greg's special gloves that left no trace. Donning the headset, I headed north on foot via the nearest road.

A few cars passed, but their drivers seemed to take no notice of me. It was cold, just below freezing, but the wind made it seem closer to zero. I kept my head down and could feel the moisture from my breath crystallize on the scarf wrapped tightly around my neck. Although I had driven down this road several times, I could only hope that the elusive "Bait" sign might be more visible at walking speed. When the headset indicated that I had covered two miles, I climbed down a short embankment and continued through the snow below the shoulder of the road, examining every tree for the sign. On what might have been the fourth or fifth pass, I happened to notice a ten-foot swath devoid of trees, next to an ancient, barren oak tree. Perhaps this was the dirt road, but where was the sign? I walked to the tree and looked up, searching for any indication that a sign may have hung there at some point.

"Menu," I said aloud into the headset. At once an array of options appeared before my eyes. "Image," I commanded. The image submenu appeared: night vision, brightness, contrast, magnification... . "Magnification," I said.

Suddenly I could see every nook and cranny of the oaken bark, and there, about twenty feet off the ground, was a rusted nail that otherwise would have been indiscernible. This might be the tree, but again—where was the sign? I made circles around its trunk, increasing the radius with each orbit. On the fifth circuit, I saw something piercing the snow. Brushing the snow away, I read the word "Bait."

I felt a surge of excitement, and my first impulse was to run as fast as possible in search of the cabin. However, I seldom acted on first impulses. I'd learned caution from my father as well as from my experience in the top-secret vault at Langley. Anyone looking for me might have found my car and could trace my steps through the snow. If I walked down the path next to the oak tree now, it would be as good as an engraved invitation to the cabin, Robbie's stash, and me.

I pitched the sign as far into the woods as my parka-constrained arms could manage. Though the snow was now obviously disturbed around the tree, I obliterated individual footsteps as best I could. I then retraced my steps, eradicating any indication of my direction, and walked at least a half mile back to the road, kicking snow upon my footprints with every step. When I reached my intended point of entry, I threw my possessions into the woods, bent my knees into a deep squat and sprang as far as I could down the embankment; it would take an expert to see my trail. Tumbling upon landing, I quickly brushed snow over my large divot, gathered my gear, and proceeded into the woods.

Slogging between trees, shrubs and rocks half-buried in snow, with the uneven footing twisting my ankles, wind chafing my face and the daylight waning, my thoughts turned to Jermaine. Perhaps I should have tried harder to convince him to accompany me. Being alone made me question the wisdom of my solitary search. But then I thought about Robbie. This was his one last request.

If I had any hope of helping him, that is, if he was still in a position to be helped, I had to find this cabin and the essential information it concealed. This thought alone suppressed any rational decision-making and pushed me onward. The moon soon began its ascent, but its meager shards of light, fragmented by the trees, provided scant guidance. Once again, I invoked the "Menu" and selected the night vision option.

At any other time, this might be a blissfully peaceful walk, especially if Robbie's hand were holding mine. But no. My feet were like bricks, my hands numb, and my thoughts fraught by an anxiety compounded by each crunch of a footfall, each creak of a tree limb and each gust of the winter wind.

Thirty minutes later, the dark forest was interrupted by an even darker void. A cabin. Instinctively, I scanned my surroundings to reassure myself that I was indeed alone. All I saw were the haunting skeletons of bare trees. I stopped to listen for any unusual sound, but all I heard was the night wind daring me onward. I approached the seemingly vacant cabin and turned the door knob. Of course, it was locked. Rummaging through the bag, I found the crowbar and wedged it between the door and its frame. After several attempts, it opened with a loud creak. I gazed behind me, half expecting that I had alerted someone, but saw nothing.

Slowly, I entered, the night vision headset revealing a room that hadn't been occupied for ages. Dust covered the decrepit furniture, which consisted of a couple of folding chairs, a couch that reeked of mold, and a teetering card table. A charred, empty fireplace was off to one side and a closet on the other. I opened the closet only to find it empty except for a couple of pages of crumpled newspaper dated from more than a year ago.

Shuffling through to the kitchen, I saw an empty sink, a stove and a small wooden table marred by gouges and stains. I turned the faucet, but there was no water. I turned the knobs on the stove, but no flame emerged. Flipping a switch on the wall yielded no light. Two doors appeared on the far wall with a window in between. The first led to a small bedroom with a bare, canvas cot next to a nightstand upon which sat an empty basin. I closed the door and opened the next, my heart pounding as it revealed a staircase leading to the basement.

Each step of my descent provoked a groan from the treads as though any one of them could give way. I heard an animal scurry across the floor below and shivered, hoping it wasn't a rat, but knowing it probably was. From my vantage point, I could see only part way into the room and resigned myself to continuing all the way down.

Upon reaching the earthen floor, I continued my search of the room, noting some saws, a hammer and nails, some dusty rifles and a few knives. I removed one of the knives, sheathed in a leather holster, and threw it into my bag. Knowing that Robbie may have once been here gave me some comfort, but it was fleeting at best. I crept along the perimeter of the room and finally reached the far corner. There, as Robbie had described, the cinderblocks were interrupted by a large piece of plywood affixed to the wall about two feet off the floor.

The nervous anticipation that I felt when I found the vault at Langley washed over me again. This had to be where Robbie had hid his stash. I dug out Greg's chemically-treated gloves and exchanged them for the ones I'd been wearing. It still amazed me that they left no trace, no disturbance of dust on any surface I touched. Greg was a genius. I pried off the plywood with the crowbar, knelt, and looked into a four-foot-square crawlspace. At first, all I saw were some rusted cans of Spam and vegetables which I pushed aside. Further behind them, out of reach, was a box, just as Robbie promised.

I reached in, pulled the carton toward the opening, lifted it out and slit the packing tape with the knife I had just swiped. I replaced the plywood and banged it so that it would stay put. Convinced that the storage site appeared undisturbed, I turned to the box and began to examine its contents, but was startled by the slow, deliberate crunch of footsteps outside.

I grabbed the box and my equipment and scurried to a small alcove under the stairs that was completely hidden by shadow. Then I waited. The steps came closer. I heard the creak of the front door and then footfalls on the floor overhead. I prayed that it was a hunter seeking shelter, but when I heard him move across the living room into the kitchen and then the bedroom, opening and shutting doors, it became obvious that the person was looking for something or someone.

I clutched the knife. My heart pounded like it would burst from my chest. I was shivering, but now less from the cold and more from the knowledge that whoever paced overhead would soon enter the basement. The footsteps stopped, and a muffled voice spoke. There was no response, and then I heard it again; this time louder.

"I found the place. Someone's been here, but it looks deserted." More silence. "No, I didn't see a car, just some footprints outside, but none on the road. Maybe a hunter." More silence.

Whoever it was must be talking on a phone. It sounded like, no, it couldn't be ... Jermaine? I almost leapt from my hiding place to run and greet him, but some latent instinct kicked in, and I listened to the rest of his conversation.

"The basement? You sure he said the basement? He's still alive? How bad is he?" Another pause. The steps were now directly overhead, and the basement door creaked open. "I'll get back to you if I find anything." There was more silence, except for the hammering of my heart that seemed loud enough to alert all of Bethel.

My arthritic joints ached as I remained hunched in the cramped space. I didn't dare move or make any sound, hardly breathing, every sense on full alert. Then the sound I dreaded began. Slow steps, down each stair, coming closer and closer, until they stopped at the bottom. The beam of a flashlight scanned the room. He walked to the far corner, where I had been just minutes before. I peeked around the frame of the staircase and stole a look. I would recognize that sturdy frame anywhere. It was Jermaine. He knew exactly where to go and pulled the plywood from the crawlspace and shined the flashlight within. A disgusted snort followed. "Damn you, Kat."

He pulled his cell phone out. "Biggs here. I found the spot, but someone beat me to it. I'm guessing it's her, but she's not here. Sometimes she's too smart for her own good. She can't be too far away." Silence. "Doubt she'd go to MacGregor's. Too obvious. Didn't see a car there when I drove by. Besides, he's out. I tried to call him." Another pause. "I'll check the woods. She must have gone that way."

My hand cramped from squeezing the knife so hard. While circling the room, he spoke again. "Of course, it's possible she went somewhere else, but I'm positive she'd want to find O'Toole's stuff first. She went through hell for him once, she'd do it again. Besides, if she doesn't have it, who does? MacGregor couldn't make it to this dump, not in a wheelchair." Another pause. "I warned her not to mess with you guys, but she never listens. I'll find her and get it but remember our deal." More silence. "Yeah, right. You'd sell your mother out if the price was right. I want proof that he's alive."

This time there was an even longer delay before I heard him again and when I did, my heart broke. "O'Toole, is that you? You okay?" Silence. "I'm trying to help you, man. Call Kat. Tell her to give me the stuff, and I'll get you out of there." Silence. "Don't be a hero. They'll kill you and her. It's not worth it." Silence. "I'm risking my fucking life for you." Silence. "I don't trust them either, but it's our only chance." Another pause. "If I get it, I'm giving it to them. It's the only way to get you out of there." The next thing I heard was Jermaine say "Shit" and put his phone away.

Knowing that Jermaine was speaking to Robbie was torture, although a different kind than Robbie's, especially if he told

Jermaine not to cooperate. I wanted to grab the phone from Jermaine's hand, if only to hear Robbie's voice. My thoughts were lacerated by my dilemma. If I gave the info to Jermaine, whom I trusted implicitly, he might be able to free Robbie, but Robbie was insistent, don't give the info to anyone, and he must have repeated that to Jermaine based on his reaction. What if I did give the box to Jermaine and they reneged on the deal? Robbie and I would die.

Robbie's captors must have forced him to reveal the information, and the methods they probably used made me shudder. Jermaine must have connected with them after I left. Otherwise, he would never have let me go alone. Now he was in danger too, putting himself at risk to secure Robbie's release. It was unbearable enough knowing Robbie was in their clutches; I couldn't lose Jermaine as well. I had to convince him to let it go. Suddenly the box took on much greater significance, and I clutched it even closer as Jermaine turned around and examined the basement once more with his flashlight. I lowered my head further into the shadow. When he started up the stairs, I finally released a deep breath and contemplated my options. Knowing Jermaine, he'd watch the cabin for a while to convince himself that I wasn't still there. I had one advantage—the night vision headset. I could watch him from the window until I was sure he was gone.

Only after I heard the front door creak shut and heard the crunch in the snow outside did I move, making every effort to keep sound to a minimum. It seemed like my footfalls on the steps could be measured in decibels. I crawled across the kitchen floor on hands and knees and only after I reached the window, did I dare raise my head. I saw his dark face in a shaft of moonlight and his flashlight aimed into the woods. He was crouched low in the shadow of a massive tree, waiting. His eyes returned to the front door, riveted. I would wait as long as he did.

Eventually, he would go to Tom's and find my car. He might even wait for Tom to return and pump him for what he knew. Thankfully, Tom could tell him nothing. Eventually, some other thoughts drifted into my psyche and no matter how I tried, I couldn't bar them from my mind's door. Robbie and I had a nice life in Nevis. If he had been more open with me about this box and its import, we could have dealt with it together. If he hadn't run off at the last minute, he'd be safe now, and I wouldn't be hiding out in a cabin, freezing my butt off, waiting for Jermaine to leave. Once again, I was in danger; once again, it was because of Robbie; and once again, I was facing it alone. Damn it, Robbie! At least Nate flew me away from danger; Robbie seemed to propel me toward it.

I shook my head, trying to scatter my feckless thoughts and focus on what mattered now. I had to alert Tom and tell him not to return home. I had to leave, but with my car at Tom's, I had no idea how to get away. I checked the GPS in my headset. Sullivan County Airport was three miles away. Could I cover that distance without detection? I had to find Tom and tell him what I knew. Robbie and Tom were tight. Maybe the two of us could devise a plan.

I ripped open a granola bar and washed it down with a gulp of water. I gazed into the woods; Jermaine was still watching. Only then did I dare open the box. If I was going to risk my life for this information, I had a right to know what it was. I peered inside and saw some files and a few flash drives; nothing else. I slumped against the wall and exhaled disappointment, having hoped for something more: pictures, a weapon, some kind of physical evidence of wrongdoing or intrigue. It would take too much time to examine the files, and time was now my adversary.

A sudden movement caught my eye. I checked my watch—two a.m. Jermaine rose and turned into the woods. He looked back at the cabin, and brusquely brushed the snow from his pants. Slowly, he slogged toward Tom's house. When I could no longer see him, I gathered my possessions. I had to act before daylight.

Not wanting to risk detection should Jermaine still be lurking about, I crawled on hands and knees to the back door, beyond his view, reached up to unlock it, and then crept outside, still on all fours. The cold slapped my face. The gusts of wind were harsh, loud and disorienting, but I remained low until I reached the far side of the cabin. Only then did I stand and run as fast as my leaden feet, gear and Robbie's box allowed; away from Jermaine, Tom's house and my car, toward the unknown.

Chapter 9

Seven a.m. found me staring at the run-down façade of a truck stop. I took a deep breath and entered, eliciting a jingle from a tiny bell attached to the door. A room previously alive with laughter was suddenly silent. I walked across the floor and could sense numerous stares following me. Perhaps it was because of my torn parka or the scratches on my face, both caused by the slashes of countless branches. Maybe it was the shell-shocked look of someone who had made a perilous choice. I took a stool on the far side of the counter.

"You look like you could use some coffee, sweetie." I looked up at the waitress, a woman whose gaunt, weathered face was softened by a pleasant smile painted with bright red lipstick. I nodded in appreciation. "Anything else?" Thin hands passed me a menu.

"A couple of eggs over easy with some toast and bacon would be great. Thanks," I mumbled.

She leaned across the counter and whispered, "You okay?"

I smiled feebly. "My car broke down. I've been trying to call a friend, but he's not answering. It was supposed to be a surprise visit."

"Someone from here?" she asked. I nodded. "What's his name? I know most of the folks in these parts, at least the year-rounders."

"Tom MacGregor. He's a friend of my husband's."

"Tommy? Lord sakes, sweetie—everyone knows him. He's a fixture around here. Let me ask the boys. They'll know where he is." She called in my order before approaching the men on the other side of the counter. A few minutes later, she returned with a loaded plate and the coffee pot. "Tommy's in Albany. Willie gave him a lift two days ago. Won't be back until tomorrow."

"This Willie, you know him?"

"I oughta, he's my cousin."

"Is there any way he could give me a ride to Albany today? It's kind of important."

The way she cocked her head conveyed deep skepticism. "Uh, sure. Let me ask him."

She was about to call to him over the counter, but my hands sprung up. "No, please. Could you ask him to come over here?"

She motioned to a lean man wearing a Buffalo Bills jacket who slowly walked our way. His bearded face was creased by a smile, and he held out his hand. "What's up, Vi?"

"This lady needs your help. What's your name, sweetie?" I told her. "Can you give Ms. Kat a ride to Albany? She came all the way to see Tommy, and he's out of town. Her car's broke down, and she's stuck."

"I'd be honored. Any friend of Tommy's ... when do you want to leave?"

"As soon as you can. I'll pay for gas."

"Don't you worry about that." His smile was kind. "Tommy's helped me out too many times to count. It's the least I can do. Finish your breakfast, and I'll be outside, warming up the truck." He started to walk away and then turned to ask, "What about your car?"

"I'll take care of that when I get back. It's at Tom's house."

"You walked all the way from there?" Suspicion flattened his smile.

"It's a long story."

"Well, we've got a two-hour trip ahead of us. You'll have plenty of time to tell it." There was a subtle change in his manner. The gregarious trucker now seemed more aloof and guarded.

I needed to win him back, telling him enough to return to his good graces, but not so much that I would put him at any more risk than I already had.

After wolfing down my meal and gulping the rest of the coffee, I left the waitress a generous tip and rushed to the truck. I found Willie leaning against it, smoking a cigarette. He tossed it on the ground and snuffed it out with a twist of his boot. He took the box and my bag and threw them in the back seat while I climbed in the front.

We rode a few minutes, his eyes darting back and forth between me and the road. "What's this all about? For real," he finally asked.

"I told you. I came here to surprise Tom. My car broke down and since he's out of town, I have no place to stay." I couldn't stop wringing my hands and, unable to make eye contact, looked down at my boots.

"Don't give me some cock and bull story. I got a sixth sense when it comes to liars. You're in some kind of trouble, aren't you?"

"It's not what you think … "

"You come into the diner, looking like hell. We got hotels, taxis, even Uber, and I'm sure you could have called any by phone. Now, you either level with me or I'm going to kick you out right here." His eyes darkened. "Tommy's my friend. The last thing I'm going to do is deliver some trouble to him, even if it is all wrapped up like a pretty lady. Should I pull over or are you going to level with me?"

We rode in silence for several minutes and when we reached a deserted section of the road, devoid of houses and any sign of business, he pulled onto the shoulder. The truck came to a stop, and he turned to face me. "What'll it be?" he asked gruffly.

"You're right. I am in trouble. If I tell you everything, you may be too. My husband is a friend of Tom's. Has been since the late sixties. They met at Woodstock. His name is Robbie O'Toole, and he's in trouble too, but he told me that he trusts Tom and that he would know what to do."

"Rob O'Toole, eh?" His face hardened. "He's been dead for over a year. Get out. Now!"

"No, he isn't! At least I don't think so." I turned to face him. "Please believe me."

"Then where is he?" he snapped back.

"I don't know. I wish I did," I answered weakly.

"Why should I believe you? How do I know that you're not going to hurt Tommy?"

"Call him. Here, use my phone."

He punched in Tom's number. At least Tom's number would be in my recent call list if Willie dumped me in the middle of no-where. "Tommy, that you?" He listened while Tom spoke on the other end. "Yeah, I know, but there's this woman here who wants to see you. Says she's O'Toole's wife." He paused again and then handed me the phone. "He wants to talk to you."

"Hi, Tom, it's Kat. Kat Hastings. Jermaine is looking for some stuff that Robbie hid in a cabin near your place. He can't have it."

"Wait a second. Slow down. I've known Jermaine since Af-ghanistan."

"I thought you met him in Iraq. You saved his life and lost both legs doing it."

"Sorry, I misspoke. Happens a lot these days." His chuckle sounded forced. "Robbie told me a lot about you and your days at William and Mary."

"Actually, we met at UVA after a keg party. He walked me back to my dorm after I had too much to drink."

"Oh, that's right. I knew it was from some place down south."

I sensed what Tom was trying to do and was growing more irritated by the minute. I didn't have time for his little test. "Look, his favorite food is a bone-in ribeye steak. Crosby, Stills and Nash and The Band are his favorite groups, and he has a tattoo of the Woodstock logo on his left shoulder. He met you at the concert where you took care of a guy who OD'd on drugs because he didn't want to die in Nam. What else do you want to know?"

"Hand the phone back to Willie."

"I will, but first, promise me you won't contact Jermaine. I'll explain everything when I see you. I know you trust him, but this is important. Robbie's life depends on it. If Jermaine calls you, don't tell him that I'm on my way." He agreed. I gave Willie the phone and listened.

"You got it, Tommy," said Willie. "We'll be there in an hour and a half." After disconnecting, he turned to me and said, "Well, it looks like you're legit. Let's go."

We rode in silence for about twenty minutes. To restore calm, I peered out at the rolling, snow-covered hills of New York, but their bleak whiteness left me uncomforted. At least I had eluded Jermaine which, for the time being, made me feel somewhat safe. Although I had never met Tom, I felt like I knew him through Robbie's anecdotes and Jermaine's devotion. Now, Jermaine was a question mark.

My thoughts were interrupted when Willie blurted out, "Trouble always seems to find Tom. Maybe because he cares too much about things and people."

"What's he doing in Albany?"

"Testifying for some damn bill. Like he needs another headache with all that's on his plate."

"What kind of bill?"

"There's a new political party that wants ballot access and the same air time as the Democrats and Republicans in the next election, you know, for the debates and all. Causin' all sorts of a stink in the state house. Guess those politicians don't want any more competition than they already got."

I instantly thought of Treadwell. Was he behind the bill that Tom was supporting? But Tom was friends with Jermaine who not only connected me with Treadwell but seemed to be working with whomever had Robbie. The hairs on my neck bristled. Something didn't compute, but I couldn't think of that now, not until I'd talked to Tom and could figure things out.

We parked in a handicap space near the state house. Willie affixed a placard to his rearview mirror, and we stepped out into the frigid air. He waved down the street to a man with longish gray hair and glasses approaching in a wheelchair. So this was the famous Tom MacGregor, the man whose identity Robbie borrowed, the man who saved our lives, and Robbie's best friend. I ran to greet him.

"I'm so glad to finally meet you. I owe you my life, Robbie's too ..." The words caught in my throat as he extended his hand. I went straight for a hug.

"Kat Hastings, I'll be damned. I finally get to meet you, but are you okay? How did you get all cut up? How's Rob doing?"

"I don't know for sure. I'll tell you everything I know when we get back," I answered.

Willie grasped the handles of the chair and wheeled Tom toward the truck. He gently lifted Tom into the passenger seat while I climbed in the back. Willie hoisted the chair into the bed of the truck and within minutes, we were off.

"Where to?" Willie asked.

"We can't go back to your place. Jermaine's watching it, I'm sure," I answered.

"Jermaine? He's fine." Tom said.

"Tom, I have so much to tell you, but ..." Instead of completing the thought, I jerked my head toward Willie.

"Don't worry about Willie. He knows my innermost secrets, don't you, bud?" Willie grunted. "Come on, Kat, the sooner you tell me everything, the sooner we can figure out what to do."

I filled Tom in on my escape from Nevis, Robbie being abducted, and his last-minute call before Nate flew Scout and me back to the States. I told him about the job with Treadwell and finding Robbie's cache of information. Then I told him about Jermaine and the conversation I overheard. "Jermaine showed up at the cabin where Robbie hid the information. He went straight to the same spot, like he knew exactly what he was looking for, and cursed me when he didn't find anything. Someone must have forced the information from Robbie and told Jermaine where to look. Robbie wouldn't have revealed it voluntarily. Whoever it was told Jermaine that Robbie is alive. I'm guessing that he's their insurance in case I found the stuff before Jermaine. They could use him to get the information from me."

"Do you have it?"

"It's in the truck. I haven't had a chance to go through it all. And there's this." I pulled out Robbie's note and handed it to Tom.

He whistled upon reading it. "Scions of Atlantis. Shit."

"You know about them?"

"Just what Rob told me, which was just enough to know this is serious business. Willie, if you want out, now's the time."

"Are you kidding? It's getting interesting," he laughed. It was good to see the smile return to his weathered face. "Tell you what. Let's go to my place. No one will look for us there. Maybe we can call the others. We can figure out our next move once we've had a chance to see what the little lady's got."

"This little lady is CIA, bro. She's tougher than she looks," Tom chuckled.

Willie whistled. "Geez, Tom, you sure know how to pick 'em."

When we reached the outskirts of Bethel, Willie turned into a drive that I would have missed otherwise. We rounded several corners as low-hanging tree limbs scraped the windshield and brushed the roof of the truck. We drove up a slight grade around a large pond and eventually came to a clearing where a small bungalow sat. Solar panels interrupted its steeply pitched roof. Willie drove to the rear of the house and parked in front of a small barn and next to a fenced-in corral. A generator abutted the house. It looked like Willie was entirely self-sufficient and off the grid.

"How far are we from Tom's?" I asked, assuming that Jermaine would be expecting me there.

"About five miles as the crow flies, more like ten by road. Let's get inside. I'll ditch the truck just to be sure." Willie lifted Tom from the seat and into the house with me following behind, box and bag in tow. It was homey inside, but definitely a man's house with little thought given to its décor or upkeep. Newspapers and books spilled onto the floor, and empty beer bottles sat on end tables with opened bags of chips. Stubs of spent joints, pinched by roach clips, rested in ashtrays.

"It's not much, especially since my wife died last year, but it's home, and my needs aren't fancy."

Willie left to move the truck while I settled into a large, over-stuffed chair with Robbie's box. The chair was perfectly suited for a reader with a good book and ample time, but given how overwhelming my current situation was, I felt like it swallowed me whole. I leaned forward to open the box and flipped through several files containing accounting forms, election results, voting records on various pieces of legislation, campaign donations larger than anything I could win in Powerball. "I'm surprised there isn't more," I said as I pulled out the flash drives.

"O'Toole had to leave his Virginia place in a hurry. I guess he just grabbed what he could. The rest was lost in the fire," Tom explained. "Can I take a look?"

I handed him the box while I opened my computer and logged on. While waiting, I asked, "Tom, I know that Willie is your friend, but do you think it's a good idea to let him in on this? What if the Scions find out he's helping you?"

"I know. I was on the receiving end of their, uh, hospitality last year when you and Rob were on the run," he said, as he leafed through the files. "Some thugs searched my place and grilled me about Rob. I told them he had been there, but split, which was true.

I honestly didn't know he was just down the road in that cabin. After roughing me up for a while, they finally believed me."

Although Tom made light of his ordeal, I knew firsthand how brutal Beau's men could be. At least I had assumed it was them. Now I was no longer sure. My apology seemed feeble; no words could convey how sorry I was for his pain. Silently, expectantly, he continued to rummage through the box, like some sort of perverted Christmas morning.

Willie walked in carrying Tom's wheelchair and returned outside to retrieve some wood. Shortly thereafter, he had a roaring fire with a meal of chicken and winter vegetables roasting over its flames.

"Kat's got some heavy shit here," Tom said. "You know I trust you and all, but you may not want to get involved with this. The last thing I'd ever want is to make trouble for you."

"Hey, gimp, if you can take it, so can I." Willie laughed heartily and punched Tom in the shoulder. "Besides, you two aren't exactly the dynamic duo. You may need my help."

He had a point. After loading our plates, we settled in, allowing the welcome heat to thaw us. I ate voraciously and then began to gather the dishes.

"Allow me," Willie said, taking the plates away. "You two get started. The room was silent except for the crackling fire, the wind outside, and the sound of Tom turning pages while I studied names on the screen of my laptop.

"Tom, look at this." I handed him my laptop where I'd been looking through the files on the thumb drives we'd found in Robbie's box and heard him whistle once more.

"Well, lookee here," he said, pointing to the screen. "That devil found the Scions of Atlantis." I watched as he reviewed the list, including members of MI6, Mossad, NSA, CIA, Joint Chiefs of Staff, some Russian oligarchs, some Arab princes, and the familiar names of industry icons, former senators and congressmen.

"That's not all, check this out." I opened another file that contained meeting minutes that read like the headlines of the day: Iranian embargo policy, decisions on the Syrian strategy, North Korean nuke testing, the Ukraine and much more. "But look at the dates. These notes preceded these events by more than a year. They were calling shots before the president or Congress authorized them." We looked at each other, stunned by the gravity of our situation.

"I think this calls for something a little stronger than tea," Tom said, breaking the tension. "Willie, we need some libations."

"Sure thing. I've got some beer, scotch and bourbon. There's a little weed if you'd prefer."

I gratefully accepted the scotch. Tom lit a joint, saying, "Hope you don't mind. Some habits die hard."

"After I found the box and hid from Jermaine, he waited a long time outside the cabin, as though he thought I was still there. I was tempted to give the stuff to him, but Robbie told me not to give the information to anyone except you. I assume he only told them after being tortured, but I must honor his request. It was his last one." I took another slug of scotch before adding, "There's something else. Jermaine arranged for me to start working for some guy named Treadwell."

Tom leaned in, surprise widening his eyes. "That's great!"

"Treadwell didn't come out and say so, but I think he wants me to dig up information on the Scions. He said I might have knowledge of 'certain things,' but I didn't let on that I knew anything about them."

"Jim's one of us." He saw my confusion and added, "He probably told you about his plans for a new party. It's exciting, just like the old days when we made a difference. But this time, we'll work through the system. It's going to be big. They won't even know what hit them until it's too late." He took another toke. "You'll see. The tribe should get here any minute now.

"The tribe?"

"We go back many years. Activists from the sixties."

"Tom, I did this for Robbie. I didn't march in the streets like all of you, and I'm not ready to share information with people I don't know."

"Rob knows 'em. He's worked with us in the past. We all saw the rough draft of his book before he sent it away to be published." Then, in a softer voice, he added, "You can trust me, trust us." I looked away, trying not to let his gray-blue eyes weaken my defenses. It went against all my training, all my instincts, to readily relinquish such potentially damning information. Sensing my reluctance, Tom broached another topic, "Does Jermaine know that Treadwell wants you to investigate the Scions?"

"No. That's another thing. I've heard of the Bilderberg group, but the Scions of Atlantis? Who are they?"

Tom chuckled. "Do you know about the legend of Atlantis?"

"I remember the Donovan song." I allowed a sip of scotch to simmer in my mouth while Donovan's voice sang in my head. "The poet, the physician, the farmer, the scientist, the magician and the other so-called gods of our legends ... ." I looked up at Tom and added, "Weren't they supposed to be an advanced civilization that escaped before the great flood? Legend has it that they established the great cultures: the Incas, Druids, Gauls, Mayans and Aztecs."

"That's one version." He took another toke. "Another is Plato's. He described them as a technologically sophisticated, but morally bereft empire seeking world domination. Only the spiritually pure, highly principled and incorruptible ancient Athenians stood in their way."

"So, which version applies to our Scions?" I asked.

Tom smiled in a vague, cannabis-altered way and replied, "Tonight, you will meet the modern-day equivalent of the ancient Athenians."

It was all Greek to me.

<<<>>>

There was a knock on the door. Willie opened it and a dozen men and women, all in their sixties to early seventies, walked into the living room. Most shook Tom's hand or patted him on the back before they settled into chairs or sat cross-legged on the floor. I shut my laptop as Tom made introductions.

"Kat, meet our fellow Athenians," he laughed before rattling off their names and occupations which included doctors, lawyers, accountants, professors—all well-educated, some retired, but all intense and curious. "I've asked you to come tonight because Kat here has hit the motherlode. Thanks to O'Toole's efforts and Kat's diligence, we now have the names and activities of the Scions."

Some applauded, others grinned broadly, and all stared at me with anticipation. I still wasn't comfortable with sharing our discovery so openly and remained quiet, studying the faces of those around me.

Tom continued, "We have records of the Scion's campaign contributions, so we know which of our esteemed elected officials are in the Scions' pockets. We have evidence of their global political manipulation and collaborations with organized crime—everything we need to out them and their control of the two parties. This is what we've been waiting for to launch our campaigns. Between Treadwell's recruitment of the last remaining honest politicians and this information, we can take back our government and restore the U.S. to a real democracy, not the oligarchy or maybe plutocracy it's become thanks to the Scions. This calls for a toast."

Willie served drinks and joints were passed. Someone asked, "So, it's a go?" Another asked, "Should we tell the others?" The room hummed with activity. I couldn't catch all the conversations, but did hear snippets about similar groups in San Francisco, Boston, New York and Chicago. I was straining to hear everything, that is, until a statuesque, earth-mother type with flowing gray-blonde hair asked, "What's happened to Rob?" It was like someone punched me in the gut. Who was she and why did she care about Robbie?

Tom frowned sympathetically and quickly changed the topic. "First things first. Kat begins working for Treadwell on Monday. He'll make sure she has all the resources she needs to expose the rest of the Scions' schemes. He will tell us what to do and when to do it."

"This is so cool—just like the old days," a balding man chimed in. "Power to the people." He raised his clenched fist.

"Yeah, and we're still fighting the same thing. I'm so damn sick of it. Thanks to Rob, Treadwell and now Kat, we have a chance to make some real change," a slender man with wire-rimmed glasses said.

"Excuse me," I interrupted, "I have no idea what you're talking about." I shot Tom a look, conveying both annoyance and dismay. My nerves were shot, and no amount of scotch would calm them. Even I was surprised when I exploded, "I haven't signed up for anything except a job to keep me alive, and I'll be damned if I'm going to join up with a bunch of geriatric hippies without knowing what's going on."

"You will, sister, you will," the balding man said.

Chapter 10

Our guests left, and I began to grill Tom. "A little more notice would have been nice."

"Sorry, Kat. I thought that it might reassure you to know there are others like us."

"Like us? You mean like you."

He met my glare with one of a weary sadness and replied, "Paul Simon once sang, 'We've lived so well so long, but when I think of the road we've travelled on, I wonder what's gone wrong.'" Then he shook his head and looked off into the distance. "What hasn't gone wrong? Each year more than twice as many people die from guns and drugs than were killed in the entire Vietnam War. A lot of them were our kids. Our schools need help. Our infrastructure is crumbling. The DOD labels climate change our biggest security risk, and yet we rolled back environmental regulations. Much of our enormous national debt is owned by many foreign powers - another huge security risk. We can't raise the minimum wage so some poor slob can afford to pay his bills yet the richest 0.5% pay almost no tax." Then he turned back to look at me, this time more intently. "All this and less than half of the country votes in a presidential election. And what is the government doing?" He grunted. "Too many people like the Scions are making too much money. We've got to fix things or we're screwed."

"Tom, I get it, I really do, but you might have explained things before ... ."

The phone rang, saving me from Tom's continued rant. I checked my watch. Midnight. Jermaine's name was on the display and I showed Tom and Willie. We exchanged startled looks.

"Hi, Jermaine," I answered, swallowing hard. "You're up late. What's going on?"

"Where the hell are you?"

"It doesn't matter. I'll make it to Boston in time. Don't worry," I replied through gritted teeth.

"What are your plans?"

"I told you, don't worry."

"I see." His voice sounded detached, like he was weighing options. "I should have never let you out of my sight. By the way, O'Toole is still alive."

I thought before reacting, not wanting to tip my hand and let him know that I was on to him. Infusing surprise, relief and any other appropriate emotion I could summon, I responded, "He's alive? Are you sure? Oh my God! How do you know?"

"Yes, but he's in serious danger. Do you know anything about some information he may have hidden somewhere?"

The time had come. I looked up at Tom and pointed to the phone. He nodded in understanding. "Robbie told me about a cabin where he hid some stuff. I found the box, but there wasn't much so I left."

He boomed, "Why didn't you tell me about this sooner?"

"Robbie told me not to say anything to anyone."

"You are impossible, you know that? How do you expect me to keep you safe?" I said nothing, so he continued, "I need to see what you have." Was I imagining it, or did Jermaine seem a little anxious? "Tell me where you are. I'll pick you up."

"Don't bother. I'll meet you in Boston," I repeated

At first, he didn't say anything. I was guessing that he didn't want to press too hard because when he next spoke, all he said was, "Okay. If that's the way you want to play it. Call me if you need me." Click.

That wasn't like Jermaine. He gave in too fast. Something was up. Maybe he was still in Bethel. Tom, Willie and I discussed the call and our options for the next day. Tom said he would call a pilot friend first thing in the morning.

"I want you to come with me, Tom. You're not safe here. Jermaine may use you to find out about me."

"I'd slow you down. I'm not exactly mobile."

"You know people. You know things. At least come with me until we have a better idea." I placed my hand on his and added, "They have Robbie. If Jermaine gets the information and gives it to Robbie's captors, they'll kill him."

Finally, I convinced Tom to join me and exhausted, we called it a day. Willie showed me a room where I could sleep while he wheeled Tom into another. Although the bed was comfy and the quilt warm, I couldn't sleep, not with various names, numbers and locations whizzing from one side of my brain to the other. Were the Scions really a sinister group seeking world domination or was that the pot talking? Wouldn't the continued prominence of the U.S. be in their best interest, at least economically? How would Treadwell use my information to bring them down? And where did Jermaine fit into all of this? How long could I maintain the ruse without further arousing his suspicions? And who was the woman who asked about Robbie? Too many questions and too few answers, but Jermaine did acknowledge that Robbie was still alive and that, alone, made me realize that whatever I did could determine his fate as well as mine, a thought that didn't make sleep any easier.

When I finally pried myself from bed the next day and stumbled to the kitchen, I found Willie flipping pancakes and frying sausage. Tom rolled in and announced that he had already called the pilot who would fly us out. I handed him a mug of steaming coffee and sat on the chair next to him.

"Have you decided where you want to go?" Tom asked.

"I need to find Greg Wheeler's son—he's a wizard on the computer, and then I want to see Martha Douglas, my former boss's wife. She's in Indiana."

"That's a lot of miles. On the other hand, I won't miss winter alone in this place, especially in this damned chair," he chuckled. "What are we talkin' about timewise?"

"A few days. Just until I start working for Treadwell. I just hope that I'm not walking into a trap."

"Jermaine is the best. If he arranged it, you'll be okay. At least, play along."

"Yeah, until I can't," I sighed, the silence that followed allowing time to muse on my prospects. Then, turning back to Tom, I asked, "So, you're still in?"

He smiled and gave me a thumbs up. I was glad, but it meant being responsible for someone else, someone who couldn't run, someone who trusted Jermaine, but also someone who also cared deeply for Robbie.

Within an hour, Willie drove us to Sullivan County Airport. We pulled into a parking space and saw a small jet idling on the tarmac, our ticket to freedom, away from the latter-day hippies, Jermaine, and anyone else who might be after the information and us. Willie pulled Tom's wheelchair out of the back seat of the car and helped him into it. After piling our bags and the box of information on his lap, we said our good-byes and watched Willie drive off. I wanted to sprint to the plane.

"I hope you know what you're doing. Jermaine will be pissed," Tom said solemnly.

I pushed the chair toward the building and responded, "I don't know much of anything anymore."

We were almost to the steps when two immediately recognizable men appeared before us: Jermaine and Nate. My heart sank. We were so close, but there was no way out, not as burdened as we were. I stopped and waited for them to reach us. It was Tom who broke the ice.

"Hey, bro, what are you doing here?"

"I might ask you the same question," Jermaine replied. His voice was brittle and his eyes smoldering. "I'll take this off your hands." He grabbed the box from Tom's lap. "I knew you were holding out on me," he added, his piercing glare now directed toward me. "Scout's on Nate's plane. If you want to see him again, you'll get on it."

I stomped toward him and when mere inches from his face shouted, "Are you threatening me?"

He leaned in even closer and replied, "If that's what it takes to get you to safety, then yes, I guess I am."

I was about to protest further when Nate said, "We don't have much time, Kat. Please."

Suddenly, a black sedan careened into the parking lot, heading straight at us. Jermaine threw the box at me and yelled, "Rob's not with them. It's a double cross. Get on the plane. I'll run interference. No arguments." He glared at me as he made his last remark.

Jermaine ran to his Hummer parked off to the side and jumped in. I hadn't even noticed it. Nate grabbed the chair and raced with Tom to the plane. I ran behind with the box tucked like a football under my arm.

Shots rang out. Jermaine was leaning out the window, returning fire. We boarded the plane; Tom was in the back seat with Scout while I rode shotgun. We sat on the tarmac, watching as Jermaine and the other car passed each other, firing shots, only to turn around and repeat the sequence like a modern-day joust until the Hummer veered and then slowed until it sat motionless in the parking lot. Four men bolted from the car and ran toward Jermaine. When they were about ten feet away, Jermaine managed to fire more shots. Two of the men dropped, but the remaining two pulled a now limp Jermaine from the car and let him fall to the ground. I wanted to go to him but could only cover my mouth to stifle a moan. I could not look away. My body shook with grief and fear.

Nate maneuvered the plane to the runway and within seconds we were airborne. All I could think of was that two men who once meant so much to me, Robbie and Jermaine, were now either dead or disabled. Despite the presence of Nate, Tom, and Scout, I felt very alone.

None of us spoke as we each processed what we had witnessed. I stroked Scout's head, now nestled in my lap, grateful that he was beside me. Jermaine had saved me once again, and yet I had doubted him. He always seemed so strong, so in control, so resilient. To see him crumple to the ground like a puppet sans strings was incongruent with everything I knew. If he was alive, they would treat him badly. If he was dead … I couldn't even think of that, not now, not with so much at stake. Finally, I asked Nate where he was taking us.

"Anywhere you want to go."

I didn't hesitate. "Washington."

We descended through heavy clouds and the runway of Potomac Airfield appeared before us. Nate landed the plane with hardly a bump and taxied to a gray hangar in front of which stood several small aircraft. A few travelers milled about, talking to pilots and maintenance men, waiting to begin their day. Nate hopped out of the plane and entered a small office while Tom, Scout and I remained in the plane.

"So, you guys know each other?" Tom asked.

"We were married once, a long time ago," I answered casually.

"Does Rob know about him?"

"Of course. I let my father bully me into marrying Nate instead of Robbie. Worst mistake of my life."

Tom whistled through his teeth. "That explains things. I was wondering why you weren't more cordial to our knight in shining armor."

"Long story," I replied, trying to cut short the topic. "Right now, all I can think about is Jermaine. Do you think he's … ?"

"Dead?" Tom sighed heavily. "Man, I hope not."

"He wasn't even trying to get away from them. Why couldn't he have run to the plane with us? At least he would have had a chance."

"Knowing him, he put our safety before his. I told you, he's one of the good guys." I sat in silence with thoughts of all the ways Jermaine had saved me flooding my brain until Nate ran toward us. "Now what's the plan?" asked Nate.

"I need to contact Cam." I withdrew my phone and punched information, hoping that Cam Wheeler had a listed number. For the first time that day, luck was traveling with us. He answered after three rings.

"Hi, Cam, it's your godmother," I said, not wanting to use my name. Though we weren't related, he called me Aunt Kat, an affectionate moniker that signified how close our bond was. "Is your phone secure?"

"It's really you? Sure is good to hear from you. I thought you were … sorry, yeah, the line's safe."

"They haven't knocked me off yet." I forced a chuckle, but knew it sounded hollow as my thoughts returned to Jermaine. We agreed to meet at BWI airport, just outside of Baltimore, thinking that we could get away in a hurry, if necessary.

When we arrived, Cam was standing at the gate, beaming. He looked more like his mom but had inherited his dad's unruly forelock which made me smile, although I winced inside. His heartfelt hug lessened my pain. "Man, it's great to see you, Aunt Kat. What's it been, three years? You made good time."

"We have a good pilot." I motioned toward Nate and introduced both him and Tom.

Cam led us to a secluded section of the concourse where we clustered around a small table. He opened his computer case and logged on. "Here's what I've found out. Jennings, the fellow you killed last year, belonged to some secret group, very powerful. Intelligence, military, government—all multinational … ."

"The Scions of Atlantis?" I asked, remembering the pictures of industry bigwigs that had adorned the walls of Jennings's office at Langley.

"You already know about them?" he asked, raising his brows.

"Not much, but Robbie, my husband, scribbled their name on a note." I noticed Nate squirm in his seat. "I did some cursory checking, and thanks to Robbie, we have some information: accounts, donations, names, meeting minutes … stuff like that. It's in a box on Nate's plane."

"Could I see it?" Cam asked. "Between what I've found and what you have, we might be able to piece things together. I think they killed my dad?"

"Why?" Tom asked.

"When Aunt Kat told Dad she needed some of his gadgets for a special project, he became concerned and began checking a few things, which led to these dudes. In my opinion, this is what got him killed, not the Kennedy thing."

"But my web searches were on his screen when they killed him. I saw them," I protested.

"What you didn't see were the sites he visited prior to that. I think they pulled your searches up to make it look like that's what he was checking into. They didn't want anyone to see what he was really working on."

"How do you know this?" Nate asked.

"My dad and I worked together quite closely. I showed him how to hack into other people's accounts. He shared his computer access with me. I was able to read everything he did." Then turning to me he added, "That was some pretty cool stuff you found about the JFK assassination, Aunt Kat. You know the Scions were involved in that, don't you?"

"So the Scions have been around for a while, eh?" Tom asked. "Are they connected to the CIA?"

"They've been in operation since World War II, maybe before. Henry Ford built Hitler's tanks. Standard Oil provided the Nazis with jet fuel and even the Zyclon-B for the gas chambers. The Harriman brothers built German train tracks—even those that led to Auschwitz. The Bushes provided munitions and taught the Germans how to manage slave labor. The Fascists stuck together; anything to thwart Communism, which might threaten their wealth. And yes, they have some connections with the Company—not the whole agency, just the few less reputable members, like Jennings," Cam answered. "Here, take a look."

Cam entered a few codes into his computer and pointed to the names on the screen. "Johnson is NSA. Powell owns the largest investment firm on Wall Street. Hughes was part of the Joint Chiefs of Staff. Katz is Mossad. Henderson publishes at least eighty U.S. newspapers. Artamenov is a Russian oligarch."

"This is incredible."

"That's nothing." He opened another file and pulled up minutes of Scions meetings that must have occurred within the past few months since I saw North Korea and China mentioned in one of them.

"I had to penetrate some elaborate firewalls to get this. It wasn't easy, but it's what I do."

"For whom?" I asked.

"Our government, of course, at least the honest part. It's my job to keep tabs on the activities of other governments, especially Russia, Iran, and some in Asia."

"I'm glad you're on our side," Nate added. "Is there anything you can't find?"

"Doubt it. If you know who to watch, you could find out anything about them. Nothing's really secure if you know what you're doing."

"We need to get going," Nate said. "It's not safe to hang around here much longer."

"Where are you headed?" Cam asked.

Nate jerked his head toward me. "This lady's calling the shots."

"Boston. I start working for Treadwell on Monday."

"Is there enough room for another passenger?" Cam asked. "I'd like to see what's in that box of yours."

"The more, the merrier," Nate answered, with a tinge of exasperation in his voice. "but you'll have to share a seat with the dog."

"We'll be quite the menagerie—a computer geek, a spy, a pilot, a dog, and Old Ironsides," said Tom, tapping his chair.

"The Scions don't have a chance." Nate smirked.

After Nate gassed up, we were airborne. By the time we reached cruising altitude I was already reading voraciously, as was Cam. Occasionally, I'd hear a gasp from him which prompted questions from Tom and Nate.

"You should see this stuff about the oil companies. Seems like they're tightening the screws on Russia and Iran," Cam said.

"This guy, Gregory, he's an oilman from Texas. That's where Beau is from. He worked for some big oil tycoon. What do you know about him?" I asked.

"Hard as nails. Been indicted for collusion, price-fixing, fraud, you name it, and got off every time. Someone's protecting him."

"Or fears him," Tom mused. "Look here, it says he was also named as an accessory to murder."

I leaned in. "Whose murder?" I asked.

"Word on the street is that he had Senator Barnes knocked

off," Cam answered. "Barnes was about to begin some sort of investigation. These guys play for keeps." He studied my face. "This guy you mentioned, what's his last name?"

"Foster. Beau Foster. Ring a bell?"

Cam whistled again. "Yep, that name sounds familiar. He's in there somewhere. Keep looking."

The cabin was quiet except for the hum of the motor and the occasional grunt or gasp as we read further. I was busy looking for information about Beau when a loud ping rang out, shattering the silence.

"Shit," Cam exclaimed.

"What is it?" I asked.

"I've been hacked. Username, TreadwellJW1."

Chapter 11

January 2008

"*A*dam, *congratulations on your election. Well earned, I might add.*"

"*Thank you, Mr. Treadwell. I couldn't have done it without your support. Well, that, and the people of the 7th district.*" *The young man fought the urge to gape at the opulent office and the sophisticated electronics contrasting with vintage rock concert posters that adorned the walls. He read the names: Jimi Hendrix, Janis Joplin, The Beatles. He had heard of them, of course, and knew the signed posters must be worth hundreds of dollars but could not figure out why a man of Treadwell's stature would choose these for his professional space.*

Treadwell seemed amused by Adam's interest in his posters. "Before your time, but they're an important part of my life. I saw Janis pass out right on stage. Our music united us against a senseless war. That same feeling drives me today."

Adam studied the man. Mid-sixties, he guessed from the hair, the creases surrounding the eyes, and prominent jowls, but also fit and tan; with an energy and enthusiasm that rivaled those many years younger. Adam guessed that, once, Treadwell was probably like his fellow students at Andover, the ones from affluent families who vacationed in Hobe Sound during school breaks, flew abroad during the summer and would return to beach houses on the Vine-

yard, the same ones who mocked him, calling him towel head or Ali Baba, that is, until he excelled in soccer, bringing honor to Andover. The memory made him wary and, suddenly, a little resentful.

"When I see someone who is willing to work for his beliefs and remains uncorrupted by the political machine, I take notice. I especially like your 'Make Experience Matter' program, getting retirees to tutor and train inner city youth. Fiscally responsible, yet socially progressive; a man after my own heart." Treadwell sat back in his chair and clasped his hands atop his desk. "You know, this could be just the beginning."

"Sir?" Adam leaned forward, eager to hear more.

"I represent many people who are dissatisfied with the way things are going. We need honest men and women who are more interested in the country's best interests, not their own. You were born in Pakistan, right? Are you a Muslim?"

Adam tensed, stunned by Treadwell's frankness. "Yes, sir, I am. Is that a problem?"

"No, it may be a plus. I heard your comments after 9/11, how you decried the actions of Al Qaeda. You are a voice of reason in an unreasonable world and bring a perspective that most Westerners lack. If we are to govern effectively at the national level, we need insights like yours: a moderate American Muslim who loves his country, wants to give back, and isn't afraid to speak out against the radical fundamentalists. You may be that person."

"What are you saying?" Adam didn't dare overstep his position, not if he thought Treadwell was dangling an even greater prize. Nor did he want to seem too eager to please.

"The state senate is just a stepping stone. Keep doing what you're doing at the state level and when the time is right, maybe we start thinking about the U.S. Congress—a representative or even a senator. It will depend on what's winnable. What committees will you try to join?"

"*I was thinking of the Ways and Means Committee,*" *Adam replied, assuming that Treadwell would approve.*

Treadwell shook his head. "*Too much corruption. How about Ethics? It would be better for your image.*"

"*I'm less concerned with my image and more interested in how I can get things done. Just because others have been bought, doesn't mean I will be.*"

Treadwell's smile seemed condescending, as though Adam was naïve. Adam clenched his jaw but remained calm.

Treadwell held up his palms as if to stifle further argument. "*If you say so. Just join as many committees as you can while remaining effective. Make a name for yourself. Raise your visibility beyond Route 495. Get people to see you as a competent leader, not just a Muslim who helps the down-trodden. I'll get you invited to fundraisers, parties, openings.*"

"*Mr. Treadwell, I appreciate your confidence in me, but my work is my top priority. This position will give me the platform to finish what I've begun.*" *Sparring with a man like Treadwell was risky, but Adam knew that this was exactly what the situation called for. If Andover and Harvard taught him anything, it was how to read people—who was real and who wasn't.*

"*Spoken like a man with integrity. I like that. In fact, it's the main reason I endorsed you and the others we've selected.*" *Treadwell sat up in his chair and leaned across his desk.* "*We have a plan, Adam, and you can be a part of it. We will return our country to the democracy that our forefathers intended, not the oligarchy we've become.*"

"*Plan? What kind of plan?*" *Adam said, but inwardly was thinking, great, I'm part of my father's plan and now, Treadwell's. When do I run my own life? Still, Treadwell piqued his interest.*

Treadwell began, enthusiasm raising his voice and animating his actions, gesturing with his hands and occasionally pointing his finger to emphasize a given point. "*It's a couple years away from full implementation so it would be premature to discuss it now, but if you stay with us and don't compromise yourself in any way or for anyone, I can promise that you will be an integral part of it."*

It was time to seal the deal. Adam stood abruptly, straightened his suitcoat, and grabbed his briefcase. "With all due respect, Mr. Treadwell, my only interests are those of my constituents. I appreciate your support, but will not deviate from that, not even for you and your plan."

Treadwell jumped up and stood immediately by Adam's side. "Bravo." He slapped Adam on the back. "I would think less of you if you did. Have I ever asked for anything in return?" Adam shook his head. "Nor will I. Now have a seat. There's more to discuss."

Adam returned to his seat but kept his eyes on Treadwell.

"You're a Harvard man, aren't you?" Treadwell asked. Adam nodded. "BC Law as well. Andover. Quite a pedigree. Your father drives a cab, and your mother works in a laundromat. Self-made. Perfect. You personify the American dream. No one could write a better script. I only ask that you stay above the fray. No special interests, no kick-backs, no trading favors for votes, got it?"

"I would never ... that's not why I entered politics." Adam's indignation seemed genuine.

"That's what I want to hear. I'll be in touch." Treadwell returned to his desk and picked up the phone, signaling that the meeting was over. Adam took a couple of steps toward the door but paused and turned to face Treadwell. "Just to be clear, you'll support me no matter how I vote or what projects I endorse?"

"That's it. Now, if you'll excuse me."

Adam shook his head in disbelief and only after he exited the office did he allow himself a smile. He had completely fooled one of America's wealthiest moguls. His father would be pleased.

Once the door was shut, Treadwell spoke into the phone. "Josh, keep an eye on him."

"That's what he said, no strings attached," Adam repeated into his car's speaker phone, waiting for his father's response, expecting him to be elated by this latest news.

"We need to get you a wife. No American politician is a bachelor for long."

"What? That's all you can say?" Adam's impatience flowed through to his fingers, now drumming repeatedly on the steering wheel. *"Besides, I haven't had time to meet someone. I've been too busy."*

"I will find you one. I'll talk to Mustafa, if he'll still speak to me. Maybe this will help win him back."

Adam bellowed into the phone, *"I will not have an arranged marriage. If I marry, it will be to someone I love. Besides, an American wife will make me more acceptable in the eyes of voters."*

"Our ways aren't good enough for you?" Adheem's voice was steely. Adam braced himself against the lecture he was sure would follow. *"Our people have had arranged marriages for hundreds of years. My marriage was arranged ... ."*

"And that's been so successful," Adam replied with uncharacteristic sarcasm.

"Who do you think you're speaking to? Do I need to remind you ... ?"

"You remind me every day, father, but our ways are not the American way. If you want this to happen, I must appear like one of them."

"Remember who you are, the lessons you've been taught, Al Quran. *You must not compromise yourself. I fear that your success is going to your head. You are becoming too much like them."*

"If I don't, your plan will fail, won't it?" Adam could not believe he was being so blunt with his father. It felt good. He had worked so hard, yet it was never enough. At that moment, he realized that it was he who now held the power in their relationship. Without him, his father's plan was nothing. He was the one who would die, not his father. Seconds passed as Adam sensed that his

father was choosing his words. When he spoke at last, Adam was staggered.

"I've been expelled from Mustafa's group. They will have nothing to do with me. I've been labelled a Khie'yen. I have received death threats. I've been betrayed by those I thought were friends and banished by the cause I swore to defend. You are my last hope."

"I didn't know, father. I'm sorry," Adam replied softly. "Don't they know what you're ... we're trying to do?" Adam's compassion was tempered by anger; anger toward the shortsighted Mullah, his father's and Treadwell's attempts to coerce him. It boiled over. "It's just that you can't have it both ways. I can't be trusted as a public servant if people suspect that I am anything but a moderate, law-abiding, America-loving Muslim."

Adam sensed his father seething and was glad they weren't speaking in person. "I'm sorry, father. I just want something more, something that at least approaches love and companionship in the time I have left."

"I warn you, Adam. You may be a politician whose star is on the rise, but you're still my son. You will obey. Do you hear me?" His father was yelling now and would no doubt strike him if they were speaking face to face. Adam could hear him thrashing about and fervently hoped that his mother would not bear the brunt of his anger.

"Father, you always tell me to think of the big picture, the great prize, the grand plan. Have I not done everything you've asked? This is a minor request and still, you would deny it to me after all that I've done and all I must do." Adam gripped the wheel, bleaching his fingers, and swore under his breath.

"If you marry for love, how do I know that you will not place your relationship above my wishes? How do I know that you won't betray me as the others have? Women are not worth it."

"Because I am your son and you have taught me well." Adam had used that line in the past, and it always seemed to placate Ad-

heem, but now he wasn't as certain, so he added, "I am willing to die to make your plan successful."

"Al Quran promises a martyr an eternity of pleasures that are far more meaningful than the transient dalliances of this world."

Adam raked his hair in frustration and said, "Father, I must go, but I will not change my mind. I will marry a woman I love, not a stranger."

For the first time ever, he hung up on his father. He stared at the speaker, realizing that on one level, his father was right. Adam couldn't name a single politician who wasn't married. He took a deep breath and punched a number in his contact list.

"Meghan? It's Adam. I was wondering, do you have plans for tomorrow evening? I would like to discuss the Dorchester project over dinner."

Chapter 12

Present Day

We returned to the Beacon Hill apartment in Boston with no further incidents. Tom somehow maneuvered his way across the icy cobblestone sidewalks, into the phonebooth-sized elevator and through the narrow hallways of the building. Once inside, he immersed himself in more reading. Nate left to forage for groceries. Cam immediately established a command center and began the task of making both of our computers impenetrable. That Treadwell discovered Cam's hacking was unsettling on several fronts. How did Treadwell have the capability to detect Cam's computer? Would his efforts extend to me? Was my computer still as safe as Cam's father, Greg, had once assured me?

Despite my best efforts to concentrate, my thoughts drifted to Robbie and Jermaine. Both might be dead by now, which left me feeling like a stark white canvas with splatters of guilt, anger, and fear splashed upon it. Tom interpreted the angst of my brain art and took my hand. "We have no control over what might have happened to them, Kat. Jermaine acted on his own. You did as Robbie asked and now the best way to honor him is to finish what he started."

"I'm afraid for him, but I'm also angry with him. He knew that finding the information would put me in danger; you too. He never said what he wanted me to do with the information. He never mentioned Treadwell, or your band of friends, or Treadwell's plan for a third political party. No, he ran off, leaving me on my own. What kind of person would do that?"

Tom's smile warmed like comfort food. "Rob loves you, Kat. He also respects you and trusts that you would know what to do. You were right to come to me. With the information that Robbie discovered and you retrieved, we can expose the Scions for who they are—powerful, wealthy, ruthless people who put their own interests above the law and the well-being of our country."

"I thought I was done with all of this intrigue. I want to be back on Nevis with the Robbie I thought I knew, running in the sand, soaking up the sun and free of care." I petted Scout who had curled up on the sofa next to me. My soul felt as cheerless as the stolid brick buildings along Pinckney Street and the gray sky above it.

"Is that what you really want? You don't strike me as someone who would knowingly let a wrong persist. It's part of the reason Robbie loves you. He said so many times." Tom sat back and released my hand. "These are trying times, Kat. The world is blowing up because of flawed policies, partisan politics and internal strife. There are many honest, hard-working people who want to unite behind something and someone they can believe in. We can give that to them."

"You don't need me. Treadwell doesn't need me. You have your information. I want what's left of my life back."

"On the contrary, Kat. We do need you. You're not only an analyst, you know the workings of the CIA, and the rest of the secret government that really runs the show. You have an intimate knowledge of that arcane world and the people in it. You know who we can trust."

"You mean like my dad?" Cam asked, joining the conversation. I tried to smile and wanted to remember the Greg I knew—brilliant, funny, a friend—but the only image I could muster was that of him slumped over his desk. "Aunt Kat, what my father knew about the Scions got him killed. Please, for him and all the others who are trying to set things right, you've got to stick with this."

I felt outnumbered by this tiny, diverse group of rebels. I thought back to those I knew at the Company. Cam's father Greg was gone; so was Ben.

"I'm not sure who I can trust."

Cam showed me a list he had just printed. "Do you know these people?" he asked.

I recognized some of the names but didn't really know them; Ben would have.

"I want to give you a little tutorial. I've found a way to hack into the databases of the CIA, DOD, FBI and NSA. I've written down the steps. You should probably memorize them; it would help," he smiled sheepishly as though giving me orders seemed inappropriate to him.

I read though his notes. It would take me forever to grasp this, but he was probably right. If this was found in my possession, I'd go straight to jail, or Russia like Snowden.

"How did you do this so fast?" I asked, waving the paper at him.

He chuckled. "This took the better part of this past year. I just retraced my steps, so I could give it to you."

I breathed a sigh of relief which Cam must have construed as concern, for he added, "You're not alone in this."

"There are more of us than you know," Tom added in agreement. "The stakes are too high. We need you, but if you really want out, that's fine. I don't want to pressure you. If you decide to help, don't do it for us, or even Robbie. Do it because it's right and necessary."

My shoulders seemed to bow under an intangible weight. Hadn't I already gone through enough trying to do what was right? And look where it got me; almost killed, possibly losing my husband, perpetually on the run, not knowing who I could trust. But then I looked from Cam to Tom, their expectant, hopeful eyes tugging at my will, waiting patiently for my response. At this point in time, they were the only people I could trust; everyone else was dead or captured. If I turned from them, I'd have no one. An imperiled life on my own was far more frightening than doing analysis for Treadwell but putting myself through this again was almost too daunting to imagine.

Nate returned, and over dinner we discussed what the next two days might hold. Nate and Cam would fly out to Indiana to see Martha Douglas, while Tom and I would stay in Beacon Hill until Monday when I would begin working for Treadwell. By the time we finished our meal and washed the dishes, it was late. Cam and Tom said their good-nights. I remained in the living room unable to think of sleep, my mind churning.

"You're not going to bed?" asked Nate. "You must be exhausted."

"I'm not even halfway through Cam's stuff. I want to be prepared for Monday."

"You know, you don't have to do this."

"So I've heard, but they're right. If we don't do it, who will?"

"Kat, I'm worried about you. I don't want to see you get hurt. I'll take you somewhere safe. I have some contacts ... ."

I gazed into his eyes, eyes that once offered security and strength—until those same eyes lied like the rest of him. "You really think that I would go anywhere with you, by myself?"

"You don't think that I regret what happened between us every single day?" He leaned toward me and placed his hand on my thigh. For some reason, I didn't pull back. "Kat, I never stopped loving you. I was a fool, but O'Toole ... he's a dreamer, always tilting at windmills. I may have had affairs with women, but he left you for his cause. At the end of the day, we both left you alone.

Well, I'm back and once I return from Indiana, I'm not going to leave you."

His voice was as soft as his touch. I was weakening, wanting more, but then Robbie's face appeared in my mind. "Nate, I ... I can't. If Robbie really is still alive, I'd never forgive myself."

"Just tell me one thing. If O'Toole isn't alive, would you take me back?" His face was mere inches from mine. A kiss would be so nice; his arms so comforting.

"I can't think about that, not now." I stood and walked toward my room. Before I entered it, he grasped my shoulder.

"Let me know when you can."

Nate and Cam left early the next morning, leaving a void that was quickly filled with work and a sense of relief. It was too dangerous to be alone with Nate.

Tom and I pored through various documents until we decided some fresh air was in order. While I pushed his wheelchair along Charles Street, he broke the silence of our thoughts. "Are you sorry Nate's gone?"

"What makes you say that?"

"Gut feeling. He makes me nervous—for a few reasons."

I stopped pushing and stared at the back of his head. He knew.

"Once he gets back," I said, "I'll ask him to leave."

"Glad to hear it. I know he's a friend of Jermaine's and your former boss, but what we're doing needs to be kept secret or the whole thing will fall apart."

Tom was too much of a gentleman to acknowledge what he must have overheard. I followed suit. "I don't think he'd sell us out."

We spent the remainder of the weekend alternating between reading files and Tom regaling me with stories of his hippie past— the concerts, the protests, the commune in which he lived, his road trips and his drug experiences, a world I never knew. He told me of the woman he loved but never married. She left him when his legs were blown off, and he despaired about meeting anyone who'd accept him in his current state. "I guess it makes it easier to get involved with this stuff. Makes me feel useful without getting anyone else in trouble, at least not with their consent," he chuckled.

"Like me?" I asked.

"You, Willie, the others. Once upon a time, we stopped a flawed war. We got unethical presidents out of the White House. But until Treadwell gave us one last chance to have an impact, I'd come to feel marginalized. Let's face it, our culture idolizes youth and not only aren't we young, we're dinosaurs."

"Have you ever met him? Treadwell, I mean?"

"I knew him back in the day. He was into the SDS and Weathermen, a little too radical for me. He wanted to blow it all up, total anarchy. He was at the Democratic convention in Chicago too, the so-called battle of Michigan Avenue, whipping the crowd into a frenzy, throwing rocks and glass, screaming into a bullhorn—like nothing I ever saw before. That's when I first met him, right before they hauled him away in the police van. The next time I met him was twenty years later at a rally in Albany. By then, he had already made a fortune and was heavily courted by various candidates from both parties but didn't really like either. It was always a case of the lesser of two evils in his mind. When he first conceived his plan for a new party, he called me up to discuss it. Now, I'm in control of his media campaign and help organize his efforts in New York State."

"Each state has an organizer?"

"Many more."

"You're kidding! How is it possible to keep a secret between that many people?"

"We do our homework and allow only the most trustworthy folks to join. They all know the importance of keeping this under wraps. Frankly, I'm not surprised that Treadwell was able to detect Cam's computer activities. His system is far more secure than the U.S. government's and most companies. It has to be, given the level of corporate espionage in his industry. If anyone of us is not completely loyal to the cause, it will destroy everything we've worked for since 9/11 when this all began."

"Why 9/11?"

"It showed how little we understood the Mideast and how fragmented our intelligence systems were. The two-party system polarized us so much that we couldn't respond effectively. We now knew that we were no longer truly safe on our own soil. Vietnam should have taught us that we can't fight a traditional war against a nontraditional enemy. Now here we are, watching the atrocities of Syria and seeing no end in sight to the war in Afghanistan."

"I still don't understand how you're going to keep this secret and then suddenly reveal these new candidates and expect them to get elected."

"When the time is right, about a third of the existing Congress and state governors will suddenly announce they are leaving their parties for ours. We will expose the illegal relationships between the Scions and the remaining Republican and Democratic candidates and will have a quality candidate to run against each, using a social media blitz that makes Obama's look archaic. We will expose the complicity of mainstream media so people will not trust the rhetoric of standard news stations or newspapers and will seek out our vehicles. Thanks to Treadwell and other businessmen of integrity, we have the money it will take. They won't know what's hitting them."

He sounded so much like Robbie—his enthusiasm, his idealism, and his belief that we could actually change things for the better. Sure, I was skeptical as I often was with Robbie. I didn't see how it could possibly work, not after a decades-old status quo, but that was not a legitimate reason for not trying. "Silence is compliance," as Robbie would often say. But how could I best help them? They didn't need me to expose the Scions; they now had enough for that. Treadwell must have something else in mind, but what was it? Monday could not come soon enough.

Nate and Cam returned late Sunday afternoon. I wasn't sure what I had expected, but it was more than the single piece of paper Cam waved in front of me. The uncertainty in his voice belied his satisfied grin.

"I'm not sure this will help or confuse you even more," he began. "We looked through everything—books, papers, keepsakes. This was the only thing that seemed relevant."

I took the paper from him. The logo at the top center jumped out at me as I read:

11/18

Dear Ben,

We are grateful for your service on our behalf. In return, we will maintain our end of the agreement as stipulated. As previously requested, please destroy this document and any other materials related to this matter.

With appreciation,

Wentworth Hughes

"Ben was working with them? It can't be!"

"Let me see that." Tom rolled his chair closer and I handed him the note.

"Wentworth Hughes. He was head of the NSA," Cam said. "He asked Ben to destroy the note, but obviously he didn't. Why?"

"Maybe he wanted us to find it," I mused. "This was written a month before Ben was killed. Look at the symbol. That was on some of the stuff Robbie had. It must be the Scions' logo."

"An adaptation of the original symbol of Atlantis," Tom explained. "Plato's version of the story is that the gods divided the earth amongst themselves; Poseidon got Atlantis. He mated a mortal woman and had a daughter named Cleito. Poseidon built a shrine to their love which was enclosed within a golden wall surrounded by concentric rings of sea and land, like the rings of this symbol, basically a 'Keep Out' sign to humans."

"It seems that the Scions have adopted this symbol to claim that they are powerful like the gods, and they don't want anyone interfering with the way they rule the world," Cam added.

"In a nutshell, yes," Tom answered.

"But we still don't know why Ben had this. What did he do to earn their appreciation? Was he part of their group? Maybe he was investigating them. Did Martha say anything when you showed this to her?" I asked.

Cam sighed. "I never showed it to her. Just stuck it in my pocket. The less she knows the better."

"Smart move," I said.

Cam snorted, "Maybe it was Ben's insurance policy. Guess he wasn't in good hands."

"Cam, really? This is serious," I said.

"Speaking of serious," Nate interjected, "I'm not sure, but we may have been watched. I circled the block a few times while Cam was inside and saw a drone overhead. Maybe I'm paranoid, but unless one of Martha's neighbors was playing around, her house may be under observation. If so, they'll question her. We may have been tracked. I took a few detours to get here to throw anyone off, but we need to be careful. Maybe we should split up." He let his words sink in before adding, "Kat, let me take you somewhere else."

"No!" Cam and Tom cried in unison. Then Tom continued, "She's not leaving my sight. Maybe you should go. We'll be fine."

Nate studied Tom; his eyes were slits; his fists tight. "Not to be disrespectful, but there's not much you can do to defend her."

"I can defend her from you." Tom shot back, with an equally intense glare.

I stepped between them. "Stop it, now, both of you. I can take care of myself." I paused to contemplate our options. "I'll call Martha and ask if anyone has contacted her. If they didn't see you leave with anything, they may not know about the paper. Nate, check with your contacts to see if anyone has been dispatched to find us. Cam, you check for any messages that may have been sent—email, Twitter, etc., and who may have sent them. I'll talk to Treadwell tomorrow and see if there's another place we can hide out. The last thing we need is dissension among us." I reached for the phone, but before I could punch in Martha's number, it rang.

"Kat, it's Martha. Some men just left. I thought you should know. "

"I'm so sorry, Martha. I didn't mean to get you involved with this. They didn't hurt you, did they? What did they want?"

"I'm all right. I just told them that two men showed me badges and wanted to look at Ben's things. They asked if I knew them, and I said no. They also wanted to see Ben's things, so I showed them. I hope that's okay."

Thinking her line might be tapped, I didn't want to say too much. "It's fine. Thanks for letting me know." I hung up and looked at Nate, Tom and Cam who were hanging on every word. "They're onto us. Since they saw Cam and Nate it might be best if you guys both leave. Cam, you should go back to DC. Nate, I don't even know where you should go, but you can't stay here."

"I told you, I'm not leaving." Nate folded his arms and tightened his mouth into a thin seam that stitched his face.

"I'm not asking you; I'm telling you. Four of us in one apartment is too much." I touched his arm, partly with affection, but more as a command. "Nate, I appreciate your help, but Treadwell knows Tom. He can help two of us easier than four."

Nate didn't budge, so Tom, in a stern voice that seemed incongruent to everything I knew about him, said sharply, "You heard her, Nate. Leave."

"Like you're going to make me?" Nate snickered at Tom.

"That's it," I yelled. "Nate, leave. Now. If you really want to help, find out what happened to Jermaine. Find out what's happened to Robbie. Take Cam to DC. Just go."

He stared at me before saying in a barely audible voice, "You'll be sorry, Kat," and then stormed toward the door. Gripping the knob, he said, "If you change your mind, call me. Come on, Cam. It seems we're not wanted here."

I closed the door behind him, leaned against it, and closed my eyes. He was wanted. That was the problem.

Chapter 13

At seven-thirty a.m., the expected knock on the door sounded. "Who's there?" I asked. It was Josh. I followed him to his car and sat pensively in the passenger's seat as he navigated Boston's former cow paths that now passed for roads. I warmed to the idea of being under Treadwell's care. I wasn't safe anywhere. At least someone was trying to help me, and if what Tom said was true, he was trying to save the country as well. I just wished I knew more about him. My thoughts came to an abrupt halt when the massive façade of Quantum Bioinformatics appeared before us. We rode in a private elevator to the top floor where Treadwell was waiting.

"You've been busy," he said. Noting my dropped jaw, he added, "I've been keeping an eye on you. I hear you met my friend, Tom. Good man. We go back a ways."

"Mr. Treadwell … ." He told me to call him Jim. I nodded. "Tom and a few of his friends elaborated about your plans. I must admit, I'm skeptical. I don't know how you're going to keep this under wraps until the time is right. How will you even know when the time is right?" He gazed at me but said nothing. He obviously had no intention of revealing anything, so I tried another tack. "You probably also know about Jermaine and Robbie." He nodded. "Are they … ?"

"Alive? I think so, but since neither has the information that you do, they're merely bargaining chips until the Scions get you.

We won't let that happen." Then more quietly, he mused, "Don't know how long they'll last." That thought hung like smoky air until he asked, "Can I get you anything, coffee?" He poured himself a cup, as though he needed any more caffeine.

I shook my head. "How do you know?" I was hoping he'd say something to indicate that he was connected to Robbie's captors or had heard from Jermaine.

"I don't think it's wise for me to tell you. You were in the CIA; you know all about compartmentalization. If you don't know something, you can't slip up, and no one can glean information from you. All I can say is that they are as well as can be expected given the interrogations I'm sure they've had to endure, but time is not on our side. We have to find them, so what do you say? Ready to start?" I nodded, impressed by his energy and proactivity. "You'll have an office, two doors down. No one is allowed on this floor without special clearance. You'll have direct access to me at all times, either by phone, computer, or in person. I expect the same from you. You'll be picked up every day at a different time. Josh or one of the others will tell you where and when." He took a sip of coffee and gauged my reaction.

"Uh, sure, no problem," I muttered, although there was a problem. Treadwell had hacked Cam's computer. But Tom trusted Treadwell, and Robbie trusted Tom. Did three degrees of separation count for anything? It had to. Wanting to honor Robbie's admonition, I couldn't share all I knew, but I had to test Treadwell's sincerity. "I want to show you something." I handed him a list of names. "Do these mean anything to you?"

"Where did you get this?" he asked, obviously stunned. "These people belong to the Scions." He passed the first round.

"I've done some cross-checking, and I think there may be an upcoming meeting. At least twenty of them will be in Munich next week at the Hotel Torbraeu."

"This is fantastic," he said as he scanned the paper. "Maybe we can beat them at their own game." Then, looking up, he added, "We're going to be a great team."

If we were going to be a great team, we had to be straight with each other. A second test was in order. "I can continue digging for more information about them, but there's someone else already doing that—Cam Wheeler. I used to work with his father."

He smiled sheepishly. "Yeah, I know. We caught him snooping around." Treadwell passed again.

"He's a good person," I responded. "His father was my friend. In fact, Cam encouraged me to work for you. He could be a big help."

He carried his coffee cup to his desk and sat down, motioning me to take the chair across from him. "I've got many computer whizzes around here. One more could be a complication. We can't take any chances."

If I were to make a case for Cam, I needed to cement Treadwell's trust in me. "I think I can best help you by monitoring the actions of people out to compromise your candidates—you know, smear campaigns, entrapments schemes, that kind of thing. People in the Company are experts at that."

"Ah, the Company. That's where you can really help. We need to enlist the help of anyone who you think can be trusted. People like you who haven't sold out to the Scions. Have you maintained contact with anyone there?"

"I've been busy trying to stay alive." My tone teetered toward sarcastic, but I kept it in check. "Especially since the people I knew best are dead. I'd probably be dead too, if I'd kept in touch with anyone, inside the Company or out." Suppressing my remorse over the intensity of my isolation, I saw an opening and took it. "Cam showed me how to access the CIA database on my computer without being traced. I'm not sure I'll be able to tell who's trustworthy, but I should be able to determine who's questionable, based on what they've been up to."

"I'm listening."

"Cam gave me this list." I pulled out another sheet of paper and handed it to him. "I've already checked half the names. Most of them are clean, but these two—" I pointed at two names—"I wouldn't trust. They staged some false flags in the Mideast that resulted in escalation of our military presence. Someone had to benefit from that."

He scanned the list and said, "Way to go, Kat. This is good stuff. There's someone else I want you to check into. His name is Adam, Adam Zuabi. We're thinking of supporting him for Congress. I want to be sure he's legit. Here's his resume." He handed me a sheet of paper. "Good schools, impeccable voting record, innovative thinker, good organizer ... almost too good."

"I'm on it. Anything else?"

"I've got another place for you to stay. It's in Beantown, but it's nicer and safer. Your, uh, friends won't know where to find you."

My eyes widened. "I see you know about Nate and Cam." Feeling suddenly exposed, I replayed our conversations in the apartment, hoping we hadn't said anything too revealing.

"My top priority is your safety. I didn't have a chance to warn you before Biggs brought you there. He should have told you the place is bugged. I'm sorry. By the way, the new place is bugged too. We can't be too careful." He sounded sincere, but it was still unsettling to know he could spy on me. "If it's any consolation, I have a target on my back too." Then, in a lighter voice, he added, "Bring Tom sometime if you'd like. It would be good to see the old son of a gun control advocate." He pressed a button and then stood, which was my cue that our meeting was over. Within seconds, Josh appeared at the door, the creases in his khakis looked like they could slice paper.

"Show Kat to her office." And then, turning back toward me, he said, "If you need anything, call Josh. Let me know what your investigations turn up, okay?" He paused and chuckled. "Now that you're here, maybe we can get in a few games of chess."

I followed Josh out of the room and a few steps down the hall, thinking that I would get slaughtered playing chess with Treadwell but was pleased by his willingness to take me on.

"Here, place your index finger on this pad," Josh said proudly, as though it was all still very cool to him. He programmed the entry system, then told me to press the button once more. When I did, the door disappeared into the wall, revealing a beautiful office with plants, artwork and leather-bound furniture, including a large reclining chair behind a mahogany desk on which sat three computer screens and a box covered with buttons.

He pressed one of them and a large panel slid into a recess, revealing a large screen. "This is for when Jim's out of town. You'll be able to telecom with him at any time." He pressed another. An array of images appeared on the screen before me. "This accesses our various security cameras. You'll be able to see anyone anywhere on site at any time." He pressed another button. "This one turns on the TV. You can watch congressional hearings in real time—even those not publicly available. In fact, you can watch every TV station in the world. This blue one," he pointed to another button, "will connect you to me. Call if you need something."

"What's this red button do?" I asked, trying to keep them all straight.

"Jim. Don't hit it unless it's an emergency, I mean, a real emergency." Moving away from the desk, he pointed to various areas of the office. "You have a stocked fridge over there by the window, and your private bathroom is in the corner. You can log into our entire library online as well as the Library of Congress and the National Archives."

I scanned the room with its opulence, efficiency and solitude; prison never looked so good. "Looks like I'll be busy."

"We're counting on it. There's one cardinal rule. No paper.

Everything you do must be digital. We can keep things secure that way."

I was thinking that, by banning paper, they could monitor all my activity and would know if I passed information to someone else. But I kept that to myself. "When do you leave for the day?" I asked.

"When you do," he grinned, probably realizing how overwhelmed I was. "Just press that blue button." I remembered Jermaine had said the same thing when I worked in the vault at Langley and flinched. "Oh, there's one more thing." He pulled a debit card from his pocket. "You'll need money. This should cover anything you need. Jim says you're to be paid five-hundred thousand a year but he doesn't want a paper trail. It's for your own safety. We don't want to tip anyone off that you're here, working with us. If you need more for any reason—trips, rentals, etc., just let us know." He scanned the room and added, "This must seem daunting. Don't worry. Jim takes good care of his friends."

I stared at the desk before me, trying to digest my situation, wanting desperately to believe Josh's words. Not sure where to begin, I decided to start with what was troubling me the most— the note Cam found in Ben's possessions. Removing Cam's cheat sheet from my case, I hacked into the CIA database and performed a search using "Ben Douglas and Wentworth Hughes." Enough links flashed onto my screen to occupy the remainder of my day. By the time six o'clock rolled around I had delved through just half of them but learned that Hughes was on the payroll of at least three foreign governments, personally netting almost twenty million dollars in kickbacks over the past five years. I couldn't help but wonder why Ben had assisted him, and how.

I lurched back in my chair, staggered, and hoped that Treadwell's computers were as safe as claimed since I was certain that someone, somewhere had been alerted to my electronic trespassing. A chill sped down my spine but stopped short when I realized that Ben must have lured Hughes in, possibly by providing him with valuable information, hence the note with the Scions logo. Hughes must have used the intel for personal gain, providing Ben with enough evidence to indict him. Perhaps Hughes realized what Ben was up to and had him killed. It was the only conclusion that made sense.

I hit "escape" and abruptly changed course, hacking into the DOD database and conducting a search for Hughes's travel plans. He was a busy man, flying to places like Russia, Saudi Arabia, China and Iraq. Eventually Munich appeared, as did the complete itinerary for an upcoming trip, including times and rooms for various meetings at the Hotel Torbraeu. At the top, it read "Emergency Meeting." I wondered if Robbie's information had prompted it.

I quickly fired off an email to Treadwell, describing what I had found and concluded with a mention of the warning I received by phone. I pressed the blue button to signal Josh that I was ready to leave for the day. He knocked on my door within a couple of minutes and pressed the button for the security cameras, checking the various parking lots and exits.

"Looks like we're good to go. Hope you don't mind, but your stuff has been moved to the new place. MacGregor's there too." Josh shut everything down and then asked, "So how was your first day?" Before I could answer, he opened the fridge. "Food okay? Would you rather have something else? I'll make sure it gets stocked."

I realized that I hadn't eaten anything all day and admitted as much to him. He grimaced, but cheerfully added, "I know, it's easy to get caught up in this stuff, but you have to eat."

I liked him. I really did. I was old enough to be his mother, but if I had a son, I would want him to be like Josh—bright, enthusiastic, friendly. I asked him, "So what do you do the rest of the day when you're not taking care of me?"

"I'm at Jim's beck and call. 'Aye, aye,' and all that. I don't think he sleeps ... ever. But he treats me well and more importantly, I believe in him and what he's trying to do. It makes it all worthwhile." He said it with pride. I liked that too. "I wish he would run for some office. He'd make a damned fine president."

If Treadwell's plan to create a viable third party was successful, and he became president, he would be the most powerful person in the world. That kind of drug would be stronger than anything he took in the sixties. I shoved the thought aside. There were more pressing matters at hand. Besides, he was a prosperous businessman. Why would he want to be president?

"Are the computers here really secure?" I picked up my case and began walking toward the door, not wanting to make his day any longer than it already was. "I mean, could anyone trace my investigations?"

"We knew the Russians were hacking into the government's computers before the government did. We're the ones who told the feds, although very discreetly. Our entire line of work necessitates total security or else we'd be open to all sorts of corporate espionage. Once Treadwell developed his plan for a third party, we ramped it up even more." Then he paused and must have realized that I was asking more out of out of fear than interest. "Kat, you're safe with us. We'll take good care of you"—chuckling lightly—"whether you like it or not."

As we descended in the private elevator, my curiosity got the better of me. "Josh, I hate making such a long day for you. What about your family? I can drive myself to and from work."

"Don't worry. I won't be your chauffeur every day. We'll mix it up a bit. I'll ride with you tonight just to make sure things are okay at the new place. By the way, I hear you're a runner. Treadwell would prefer that you use the gym downstairs as a precaution."

He deftly avoided my question, revealing nothing about his personal life. Interesting. They knew everything about my life but would not share aspects of theirs. I hoped the plastic smile on my face hid my growing discomfort about the gilded cage being constructed around me.

We arrived at the new apartment on Marlborough Street in the Back Bay. It was another brownstone, but fully furnished in an Art Deco style—multiple geometric shapes, bright colors, ornate designs and a jukebox sitting in one corner. I half expected Noel Coward to walk in and select some Cole Porter. Instead, Tom rolled in wearing a grin that split his face in two. Scout rushed past him and began his dance of combined jumps and circles.

"Pretty fancy digs, eh?" Tom exclaimed. "Check this out." He wheeled himself to the wall and pressed a button. A door slid open and revealed a fully stocked bar—lots of chrome, crystal glasses hanging from a rack, and bottles of top-flight liquors inverted into dispensers for an easy pour. "Can I get you two something?"

Josh declined, but I asked if there was any wine. Tom found a wine cooler and pulled out a bottle of Opus One ... of course. While Tom uncorked, Josh led me on a brief tour, pointing out various amenities. He also showed me a control panel, similar to the one in my office, that would provide instant access to him, Treadwell, the police and security cameras. It should have been reassuring, but it only heightened my paranoia.

"I've got to go," he finally said, "but tomorrow I'll pick you up at seven forty-five." He was all business now. "I'll be in the alley behind the building. Check the cameras first and then exit through the back. If you do go out, you may see a guard watching the place. Tomorrow, it will be a white guy, about six feet tall, brown hair, wearing a Red Sox jacket and carrying an umbrella. Any problems, yell, "My dog!""

More scrutiny, more limitations, and more anxiety in return for security. I nodded and walked with Josh to the door. After closing it behind him, I closed my eyes and lowered my head. Josh seemed trustworthy, maybe a potential ally. I needed an ally now. Between him and Treadwell, I was beginning to believe I was safe, but still, it baffled me that someone who once wanted to blow up the system was now willing to spend billions of his own money to fix it. With his wealth and influence, he seemed better suited for the Scions and make the system work for him.

Scout must have sensed my disquiet because he walked over and rubbed his head on my leg. Reflexively petting his head, I looked over at Tom. "I guess it's just the three of us now— you, me and Scout. No Robbie, no Jermaine, no Cam ... ." I stopped short of saying Nate's name and instead walked over to my wine glass and took a healthy gulp.

"Yeah, well, uh, there's something I need to tell you," Tom said. "I'm going with you to see Treadwell tomorrow, but after we meet, I'm flying back." Seeing my disappointment, he added, "I'm needed in Albany. Plus, to be quite honest, Jim thinks I'll be too obvious on the streets here, you know, with the chair and all." He grabbed the wheels and moved closer, taking my hand. "He's right, Kat. You know it too. You'll be fine."

His eyes glistened. I knew he was worried. Now, it would be just Scout and me.

Chapter 14

"Good work on the Munich meeting," said Treadwell when I saw him the next morning. "We've got some guys over there to repair their wiring, if you catch my drift." Seeing my raised eyebrows, he explained, "We installed a sophisticated electronic surveillance system. They won't be able to detect it if they do a sweep, and it will let us know what they're up to."

"How did you pull that off?" I asked, thinking that no matter how wealthy Treadwell was, even he couldn't accomplish this without some help, not when he was up against governments and an elitist cadre of people as wealthy as him.

"Called in a few chits," he answered casually. "Now I need you to start working on Adam Zuabi. Find out everything you can about him. I have a gut feeling. I can't put my finger on it, but doesn't it strike you as odd that a devout Muslim is pro-choice and advocates for gay rights? Yet he's remained unscathed. I can't let my concurrence with his views blind me to what else might be going on."

Thus began my investigation into Adam Zuabi. For the next few days, I dutifully checked all the databases, but found nothing incriminating. His background, which I already knew, was pristine, as were his voting records and even his health records. But his father, Adheem Zuabi, was a different story. He fought alongside Osama bin Laden in Afghanistan. He'd been cited several times for domestic violence, called in by neighbors, all dismissed because his wife wouldn't press charges. The mosque he attended included a few individuals who were listed in the Terrorist Identities DataMart Environment database, better known as TIDE, compiled with the collaboration of more than sixteen intelligence organizations within the U.S. I was all too familiar with its use from my days chained to a desk in Langley.

Pushing one of the buttons on my desk, I flipped through channels until I found the one that aired hearings of the Massachusetts legislature. Members of the Senate Ways and Means Committee sat at a table in front of a hearing room. I examined them carefully. One man differed from the Irish, Italians, African Americans and WASPS. He had olive skin, dark hair and chocolate-brown eyes, and was neatly groomed and impeccably dressed. It had to be Adam.

The committee was discussing Boston's mass transit system, the MBTA. In response to a question, Adam leaned into the microphone. "People can't afford the T as it is. Fare hikes are not the answer; volume is. To handle the volume, we need to stagger use. I've already spoken with some of the large employers in the area who seem willing to adjust their work shifts so that fewer people are riding during peak times, and more are riding during off-peak times. Greater volume means greater revenue. We get people out of their cars and onto the T by increasing tolls into the city. Not only will this reduce congestion on the major arteries, it will reduce highway maintenance and pollution. Costs saved there can support the T." He said it all without a trace of an accent and answered questions with a mixture of humor and confidence. I could see why Treadwell thought highly of him.

That day's debrief was a command performance issued by Treadwell. After filling him in on what I discovered, I told him that I wanted to meet Adam Zuabi in person to learn more about his family. I could tell he wasn't thrilled with the idea because he pointed out the risks and tricky logistics. After my persistent protestations, however, he relented, recommending that I visit Zuabi at the State House, a public place with minimal danger. I would use a different name, wear a wig and claim that I was from *The Alternative*, a new media outlet owned by Treadwell and, I presumed, one of the vehicles he would use to communicate to the masses as Tom had described. Treadwell would arrange everything, including an unseen escort who would shadow me. Such was my new life. I nodded my head in resignation. Nothing was simple anymore, but he was concerned about my safety. At least, that's how I reassured myself. It was the next order of business that proved to be more alarming.

In a voice laden with concern, he continued, "There's something else you need to hear." He lowered a screen and pressed a button to initiate a videotaped recording. There were the normal murmurs and scrapings of chair legs that preceded any meeting, and then a man at a podium began to speak. Treadwell told me that his name was Stuart Johnson, a former high-ranking member of the NSA.

"Thank you all for coming on such short notice." The room went silent save for his voice. "We've had a major security breach. As you know, we trusted Ben Douglas from the CIA to provide us with pertinent information upon which we have acted and, I may add, benefitted from, both professionally and financially. Douglas leaked our names, our activities, and our contacts to a reporter, Robert O'Toole, who is now in our custody."

I gasped at hearing Robbie's name and listened even more intently. "We believe that O'Toole hid the information, and it might be in the hands of a woman named Katherine Hastings, who has also used the name Carla Banks. She used to be with the CIA and has significant analytical capabilities, but her location is unknown. I don't need to tell you that if this information gets into the wrong hands, we could be exposed. Despite significant, uh, pressure,

O'Toole will not reveal any information about her or what Douglas gave him. We will all need to take extreme caution until this issue is resolved. I'm sure you all have questions and concerns, so I will now open the floor."

"Why would O'Toole give the information to a CIA agent?" a man asked.

"She and O'Toole are married. She used to work for Ben Douglas and gave O'Toole the hidden evidence from the Kennedy assassination. We've suppressed that, but he wrote a book about it and other events. Fortunately, our influence with the publishing industry has enabled us to prevent its distribution and enabled us to track him down. Unfortunately, Hastings and O'Toole split up before we could get them both. Next question."

"There's self-publishing and the internet. She could use either or both to get the information out," a woman stated. I looked questioningly at Treadwell; he said the speaker was Bette Collins, a successful lobbyist for the Scions' interests.

"True, but Hastings is smart," Johnson replied. "She knows that if she leaks anything, we'll find her and kill O'Toole." Then he snorted. "Of course, we can use the normal channels to discredit her and paint her to be a lunatic or a pervert."

Collins persisted. "Do we have any proof that she actually has anything?" I scanned the room. She appeared to be the only female member of the group, suggesting that she must be important to them, but her stooped frame and constant adjustment of her glasses betrayed her discomfort. She might be a weak link in their chain of control.

"A man named Jermaine Biggs was to have intercepted her at an airport in New York state. We convinced him that if he got the information and gave it to us, we would release O'Toole. Of course, that wouldn't have happened, but he didn't know it. We sent people to the airport to take it from him, but he gave it back to Hastings, and she disappeared. We've got him locked up as well."

Not only had Jermaine tried to save Robbie; he was alive. I

was relieved on both counts, but my consolation vanished when I realized that he was probably being tortured as well. I checked Treadwell. His face was like stone.

"Where are they?" someone asked.

"O'Toole was in Saudi Arabia. They have unique ways of obtaining information, but when we took Biggs, we brought O'Toole back to the States. People are more likely to talk if they have to watch someone else being, uh, interrogated. We'll use them as bait to get to her. She's soft on both of them and if squeezed enough, she'll cave."

His allusions to what Robbie and Jermaine were enduring was devastating, and although Robbie's stash was not my doing, it still grieved me that he and Jermaine were suffering. Even if I had been honest with Jermaine, it would not have made a difference. They double-crossed him. Still, I was guilt-ridden; Jermaine was their captive because of Robbie and me.

I bristled at Johnson's description of me as soft. Women could be every bit as tough as men under pressure, and I'd proved myself more than once. On the other hand, being "strong" in this case could mean abandoning two people I loved for a cause I wasn't even sure I believed in. I snuck a look at Treadwell, searching his eyes for any reaction to Johnson's words. His attention was riveted to the screen like he was watching it for the first time. Though not calm, he seemed more detached than I, like a chess savant thinking several moves ahead.

"You said we don't know where she is, but do you have any guesses?" a lanky man near the back asked.

"She was in New York when we took Biggs. She escaped on a plane flown by a CIA contact who worked for her father, H2. They flew to BWI, but then returned to Boston. We think she may still be there," Johnson answered. My spine went taut.

"Then why don't we just take her out? Boston's not that big," someone with a thick Slavic accent asked.

"We haven't been able to find her, which makes me think

that someone's protecting her. We'll get her. You can count on it."
Murmurs of disgust filtered throughout the room.

A stern-looking man in the front broke in. "And then what?"

"I'm surprised at you, Hughes. You know better than anyone.
We'd have to eliminate her," Johnson answered in a voice so cold,
so devoid of emotion that my chest tightened, and my breathing
stopped. "We can't afford another debacle like your Ben Douglas."

Now I had a face to go with the name, Wentworth Hughes, the
man who had written the note to Ben. I detested him on sight.

Johnson's pronouncement silenced the room; no more questions were raised as the audience absorbed his words. He surveyed
the room and the facial expressions of the fifty or so people gathered, trying to discern any dissent. Collins' shaking hands held a
shredded tissue; others looked at the floor. To reinforce the need
for solidarity, he added, "I don't need to remind you that we're
all in this together." He glared at Collins. "United, we are more
powerful than any government in the world. We have all reaped
the benefits of this union, from money laundering to lucrative contracts, and will do so as long as we act as one." He took a sip of
water to allow his words to sink in. Satisfied that his message was
received, he moved on. "While you're all here, I want to make
sure that we're on the same page regarding the stock sell-off next
Wednesday at three p.m. We need to force the EU's hand once
again … ."

Treadwell pressed the button, and the screen went dark. He
stared at me for a few seconds before saying, "Now you know
what we're up against. I can keep you safe, but only if you let
me." His voice was gentler than I'd yet heard it. Still, it provided little comfort. I was on the hit list of one of the world's most
powerful organizations. The same organization held my husband
and my guardian. Terror consumed me. I sat, stunned, unable to
speak. Instead, I stared beyond Treadwell to a photo of Crosby,
Stills and Nash, the original one taken on their porch in Laurel
Canyon and signed by all three. I looked at their faces, young, un-

kempt and relaxed. The world was different then … or was it? JFK had been killed by a collusion of the powerful. They perpetuated the Vietnam War while making billions of dollars, and who knows what role they played in Iran-Contra, Afghanistan, Iraq, and Syria? Thoughts collided in my brain like cars in a demolition derby, until only one remained; I was in serious trouble.

Treadwell took my hand. "We can beat them, Kat. We have the resources. We have a plan, and we'll have the people, but more importantly, we're guided by something more powerful than wealth and power. It sounds corny, but we have what's right on our side, and that's more important than you, me, O'Toole, or Jermaine."

I gazed into his eyes, soft and brown like Scout's, brimming with compassion. He draped his arm over my shoulder and then pulled me close. I thought of the iconic picture from Woodstock, a man and woman wrapped in an old, mud-splattered blanket, sharing a moment of peace in the midst of bedlam. I could feel his heart beating slow and strong. I could smell his full-bodied aftershave. I could have disappeared into his arms forever, but he pulled away, took hold of my shoulders, and looked into my eyes.

"Your father once told me something that I will always remember. 'Never underestimate the power of a people united by an ideal or threatened by the loss of that same ideal.' Kat, we can restore that ideal and expose those who would destroy it."

The mention of my father's name yielded the desired effect. I wanted to throw myself back into his arms. I would follow this man anywhere.

Over the next few days, I became resigned to the security measures taken on my behalf. I dutifully met my driver each day, limited my workouts to the gym at Quantum Bioinformatics, walked Scout only on well-travelled streets, stayed inside at night, and confined my research to assignments given me by Treadwell. But despite my best efforts, the solitude of each evening made it impossible to avoid thoughts of Robbie and Jermaine, and how they were suffering so that the Scions could learn of my whereabouts and activities. That's why, when I finally got the green light to go to the Massachusetts State House, I welcomed the brief respite and my meeting with Adam Zuabi.

When the designated day arrived, I donned glasses and a brunette wig, dressing down to look the part of Emily Ferguson, an unremarkable reporter for an edgy news publication, and my third identity. Exiting the T at Park Street station, I crossed Beacon Street to the gold-domed State House overlooking Beacon Hill. The statue of John F. Kennedy reminded me that my investigation into his death had led to my being here. Another statue, of Daniel Webster, reminded me of the need for truth. The statue of General Joseph Hooker made me smirk. Despite his heroics during the Civil War, his name would forever be associated with ladies of pleasure.

At the visitors' entrance, a security officer barely glanced at the fake ID furnished by Treadwell and gave me directions to Zuabi's office. Passing through an imposing rotunda with Siena marble columns and a stained-glass skylight, I climbed a flight of stairs, wandered down a corridor of offices and conference rooms, and at length found Zuabi's suite. The door was hospitably open, and to my surprise, the congressman himself was standing just inside, talking to an assistant seated at a desk.

"Ah, Ms. Ferguson, welcome." A broad smile brightened his face, and he waved his hand to usher me into his private office.

"Thank you for meeting with me," I said, perching on the edge of an office chair and handing him my business card, also courtesy of Treadwell.

"My pleasure. Always available to the press." Walking behind a handsome antique desk, he looked at my card for a moment before placing it atop a day planner and sitting down. "How long have you been with *The Alternative*?"

Remembering the profile that had been established for me, I

answered, "I've free-lanced until recently, but you know how it is, a friend of a friend of a friend got me hired fulltime. It pays the bills mostly." I had to go on the offensive and make sure that I was asking the questions. "How are you finding the Ways and Means Committee? There's been a lot of turnover since the indictments."

"I like it. I feel like it's the best place for me to get things done," he replied casually. "I'm sure that I've ruffled a few feathers during my short tenure. Some of the people with whom we do business are, shall we say, unaccustomed to our exacting methods," he said with a wink. "So what kind of story do you want to write? Perhaps you want to know how an American Muslim can succeed in the current political environment. That's the question I usually get."

"That's as good a place to start as any, but I'm not looking for the usual story," I answered. His eyebrows arched slightly, and he seemed to assess me more closely. I took out my cellphone and hit the record button. "You don't mind?" He shook his head, and I began. "I've done some research and know your background, so let's cut to the real story. Your father fought beside Bin Laden in Afghanistan and now drives a cab here in the city. He attends the same mosque as some radical Islamists. Yet you now hold a political office of significant stature here in Massachusetts. Our readers might find that disturbing. What can you say to assure them that you are not a radical as well?"

His eyes grew wide and dark. Reflexively, he crossed his arms, shifted in his seat, and paused to gather himself. Trying to keep things light, he chuckled. "You do not mince words, Ms. Ferguson. Let's set the record straight. My father is well-educated but could not get a job in the states commensurate with his skills. That's why he drives a cab, a cab which he owns, by the way. He worked long hours yet home-schooled me until ninth grade to ensure that my future would be better than the life he's led. Importantly, he instilled strong values and has set an example that I can only hope to match." He stood and began to circle the room, as if to reassert control over the interview. "It is true that he fought with Bin Laden against the Russians, but he did not share Bin Laden's hatred of the West, just the Russians. As for the mosque, there may be a few extremists, but the rest of us love our country as much as you."

I studied him. His eyes were no longer looking directly at me. I needed to get him back on the defensive. "You were vehement in your condemnation of the 9/11 attacks. You've supported ideas that are counter to your faith." I pointed to a picture of a sandy-haired woman on his desk. "Is this your girlfriend? If so, are you dating a non-Muslim? I guess what I'm getting at is, why isn't the Islamic community more critical of you?"

He held up his hands as if to stop any further barrage. "Ms. Ferguson, please. Not all Muslims are extremists. Mostly, we are a peaceful people who do not hold the same violent, archaic notions as those you have read about in the news. Yes, I have experienced some backlash, but my constituents support me because of the progress I've made. Do not stereotype me because of Al Qaida or ISIS. I am as American as you." He returned to his chair, but stood behind it, grasping its frame with clenched knuckles that belied the calm in his voice. "Now, if you want to discuss some of the initiatives I've been working on … ."

"Certainly, but first, you claim to be independent of any influence, yet James Treadwell was a major donor to your campaign. Why would someone like him be so supportive of you and your work?"

His smile disappeared, and the relaxed tone vacated his voice. He sat in his chair and leaned across his desk, his hands balled into fists. When he finally spoke, it was as though another person sat before me. "I assure you that no one, including Mr. Treadwell, has any influence over me. He supports me because he feels the same way as I about the problems confronting our state. He has not asked me to vote a certain way on any issue. I have not sold out to anyone, nor will I. Frankly, I resent the question," he paused, realizing that he had reacted too strongly, and then added more quietly, "But you're a reporter so I know you must ask it. I, too, have wondered why he has been so supportive, but he strikes me as an honest man who cares about current events. I welcome his endorsement. Now, I hope you'll ask me about what we've accomplished."

"Sure, but first, you mentioned a backlash earlier. What, exactly, have you endured? I only ask because I want to describe the personal sacrifices you've made."

He sighed heavily, obviously wanting the interview to end, but not wanting to antagonize me and perhaps create bad press. "Nothing worth printing. I've had a good life with many opportunities. It's time to give back to the country that has given me so much." He clearly was pleased with his answer. The smile was back. His voice had a lilt to it.

"Do you know a man named Mustafa, Mr. Zuabi? He attends the mosque of your father. Some have said that he had dealings with the 9/11 terrorists."

Zuabi slammed the desk with his fist and, in a voice consumed with malice, answered, "I don't know what your agenda is, Ms. Ferguson, but you clearly care more about speculation than fact. My record is impeccable, and I am working hard to improve our state. I resent your innuendo. I hope you write your damned story with more integrity than you've demonstrated in this interview which, by the way, is over. I have more important things to do than answer your inane questions."

I had struck a nerve.

When I returned home later that evening, I poured a glass of wine and listened to a recording of our conversation. While I had learned essentially nothing from his words, I gleaned a great deal from his body language, tone of voice and the topics that elicited the most disingenuous responses: his father, the mosque, Treadwell's support. He never answered the question about Mustafa, which was most interesting and suggested that he did, in fact, know of him, a thread I must unravel.

I was logging off my computer when my phone rang, causing me to jump. I pressed the green button and heard, "O'Toole's cracked. We know what you have and where to find you."

My breathing quickened and my heart pounded as I screamed into the phone, "Who is this? What have you done with Robbie? How do I know he's still alive?"

I heard an evil cackle until the phone was handed over and another voice, one I knew so well, came on the line.

"Kat, it's me. I'm, uh, okay." His voice was feeble, broken, like someone talking under hypnosis—no affect, no emotion, only a quiet monotone devoid of any personality. "I'm sorry ... for everything."

"What have they done to you? Where are you? Who's holding you?" spraying questions like bullets from a bump-stocked semi-automatic gun. I wanted to keep him on the line, just to hear his voice, fragile though it was.

"Don't worry about me ... ." He paused for several excruciatingly long seconds, as though he were summoning strength to speak again. "Don't give them anything. They'll kill us no matter what you do. Save yourself ... ."

I heard a loud crack and then his moan. I bent over and began to rock back and forth, overwhelmed by feelings of helplessness and horror. I buried my face in my hands and tried to staunch tears. Then the raspy voice came back. "We know you have O'Toole's information. Destroy it. If you leak it to anyone, you've talked to your husband for the last time. Got it?" The line went dead.

I stared at the phone, wanting to hurl it into the octagonal mirror and shatter the image of the once happy, self-assured person who now was beyond recognition. It was too late to consider compliance. Once they found out what I had already done, Robbie would die. Robbie didn't know where I was, or who I'd shared his information with, so the people who had him couldn't know either. Hopefully, that would keep him alive a while longer.

Chapter 15

A different driver met me the next morning and, because he didn't know me, was probably less startled than Josh would have been by my tear-stained eyes embedded in dark circles over ashen cheeks. This driver was a large man with hands that seemed more accustomed to working fields and a face that saw too much sun. He lacked the lean efficiency and polish of a typical Treadwell minion, but could probably break a man's neck with a single flick of his wrist. Once in the car, he handed me a cup of coffee accompanied by a ragged smile, both of which I needed, and won me over.

He left me alone with my thoughts, most of which concerned Robbie, some of which centered on what I needed to tell Treadwell, and a few wondering what I would investigate first at work. I was intrigued by the woman at the Scions' meeting in Munich. Like the child's game, "which of these do not belong?" she looked out of place in the room of ruthless powerful men and seemed to show a smidgeon of distaste when it came to the fates of Robbie and me. I wanted to learn more about her. I also wanted to see what I could find out about Zuabi's father, Adheem.

At Quantum Bioinformatics, my chauffeur flashed another smile as he helped me from the car. "Sorry you had such a tough night. No one will hurt you while I'm on your watch." I stared in surprise as he drove around the back of the building and out of sight, but then I remembered; my place was bugged. Someone in

Treadwell's organization had probably heard my side of the conversation. Though maddening, it did mean that I wouldn't have to recount the entire scenario at work.

Once logged in at my desk, I sent an email to Treadwell asking if he had time to meet with me. I had hardly typed the last word when he was at my door.

"Here's what we know," he began. "O'Toole's alive. They can't know where you are for sure. At least they couldn't have gotten it from O'Toole because he doesn't know where you are. Apparently, you have some additional information that you haven't shared with me —" he shot me a mildly indignant look—"but they don't really know that you've done anything with it." He paused. "They may figure out that you are working for me because, if I do say so myself, there aren't many people who have the resources to help you that I have. We think last night's call came from in state. They can't be far away."

I stood abruptly and walked toward him, hoping to see a glimmer of compassion underneath this all-business recital. "I looked at the display. The call was blocked. How do you know?"

"As soon as you received the call, we put a trace on."

"You've compromised my phone too?" My phone was the one device I thought was still private, and despite his wanting to keep me safe, I resented it.

"Guilty as charged, but that call gives us access to their network and maybe will lead us to Rob. If they don't toss that phone, we'll be able to tap into it. We might learn who's calling the shots, what their next step is. I don't mean to sound insensitive, but your privacy is a small price to pay for that kind of intelligence." He turned toward the door and pulled it open, but before leaving he added, "There's one other thing that we know. O'Toole is in a bad way. We need to find him soon."

Everything he said was right, but for some reason, it didn't console me. As though he could sense my inner turmoil, he added, "Kat, I think we have them on the ropes. Please don't hold out on me. If you have something else … ." When he saw that I wouldn't budge, he said, "'There is nothing more difficult to carry out, nor more doubtful of success, nor more dangerous to handle, than to initiate a new order of things.'" He looked for my recognition of the quote and added, "They are scared that a new world order will destroy everything they have."

Damn, more Machiavelli. Why was Treadwell so enamored of him? This time, I didn't acknowledge the source and merely said, "I know that your new party is important to you, but Robbie is important to me."

"He's important to me too. Let's hope they use that phone again before too long." He silently left the room, his head down.

I stared at the closed door for several minutes as I contemplated what had just transpired. My life was no longer my own, my privacy extinct. My husband could die, painfully. The Scions wanted me dead. And this man, whom I simultaneously admired and doubted, held our fate in his hands and somehow believed that his phantom power base could change a political system as old as the country itself. And this same man was betting on the likes of Adam Zuabi, whose father fought beside Bin Laden, to pull it off. I was screwed.

What would my father have done? He certainly would not be sitting idly by and letting things happen to him. No, he would act; cautiously, invisibly and intelligently. He would lurk in the shadows, glean as much information as he could, and never tip his hand. When the time was right, he would pounce. So must I.

I scoured the CIA database and found Adheem Zuabi's unlisted address as well as video surveillance tapes of the mosque. On at least twenty of them, I saw a man who resembled Mustafa's mugshot get into a cab, the same cab on all twenty tapes. I stopped the video and enlarged the picture, so I could jot down the number on the license plate. If I was lucky, it might match Zuabi's.

The question now was, should I tell Treadwell about my plans? If I went to Adheem's home on my own, whoever was watching me that day would tell him. But if I told Treadwell of my intentions, he might prevent me from tracking Zuabi down. In this instance, I thought it was better to ask forgiveness than permission.

I logged off, called Josh to let him know I was leaving, and met my escort in the parking lot. I was glad that it was the same ruddy-faced man who had brought me to work in the morning. Our conversation was a pleasant change from the day's events. Though originally from out west, my driver stayed on the east coast after his return from Iraq. He'd been working for Treadwell for the last five years, mostly to counter corporate espionage, but he alluded to other "special tasks." I assumed they included protecting assets like me and possibly others as well.

After he dropped me off, I entered my apartment, dumped my computer case on a chair, and changed into jeans, a sweater, and some running shoes. I pulled on a parka, leashed Scout, and began a brisk walk, scanning the sidewalks for tonight's guardian. I saw a thirtyish man in a leather jacket sitting on a stoop, reading *Sports Illustrated*, who wouldn't meet my eyes. Half a block away, there was another man, slightly older, speaking into a cell phone while his eyes darted back and forth, watching every movement around him. Across the street was a third man sitting in a car. It could have been any of them.

I proceeded down the block and took a quick look over my shoulder to see if any of them followed. None did. I turned left on Dartmouth and then right on Commonwealth, choosing the center path where others were also walking their dogs past the various statues or memorials. At Gloucester, I took another left, crossing Newbury Street to Boylston. That's when I saw the guy who had been reading *Sports Illustrated*, the magazine now jammed in his pocket. He was about six feet tall, clean-shaven and wearing a black wool hat with the gold B of the Boston Bruins emblazoned on front. He walked past me with no look or comment. He was tonight's shadow.

I quickly returned to my apartment, fed Scout, and then donned my brunette wig before picking up a pocketbook and stuffing a notebook inside. The game was on.

I peeked out the window. It was dark now, making it difficult to see if the Bruins fan was nearby, although I was sure he was. I exited through the rear of the building into the alley and ran to the Dartmouth Street garage to pick up a Zipcar, a gray Honda Civic, paid for with Treadwell's debit card. I hopped in and drove across the Harvard Bridge to Cambridge, feeling freer than I had in weeks.

My phone's GPS led me beyond Harvard Square to Norfolk Street in East Cambridge. I parked across from the sad-looking house I thought might be Adheem Zuabi's, turned off the engine and waited, hoping I'd see someone enter or exit. It was cold, but I didn't dare turn on the engine for heat. Instead, I slid down in my seat and thought about what I might do should anyone appear.

A sharp rap against the passenger side window caused me to jerk upright. It was the Bruins fan. Busted.

"Nice try," he said. "I work for Treadwell."

I lowered the window. "How did you find me?" I asked with frustration.

"Your phone. I hopped in a cab. Can I come in?" Not waiting for an answer, he opened the door and climbed inside. "What are you doing here?" He removed his hat and rubbed his hands over his buzz-cut auburn hair. He looked so young.

Incensed that my phone betrayed me again, I answered, "This politician that Treadwell is supporting, Adam Zuabi, has a father who lives here. I want to check him out."

"Why didn't you ask us? It'd be safer than you sneaking out on your own," he said, attempting to smile.

I was about to make a flippant remark when a black cab pulled in front of the house and parked. A man approaching sixty got out. His shoulders were hunched as he flipped a wad of bills, evidently counting the day's earnings. I thought I saw him glance at us in the car, but he turned toward the house, climbed the steps and entered. A light went on in the first floor, and I could see him walk to the window and move the curtain aside. He was checking us out.

I could do several things: drive off, which would suggest we'd been watching for him; or continue to wait, which, if he had seen us, would also seem odd. I had to think of something quick because I could feel his eyes on us.

"Kiss me. Pretend we're making out." I embraced the Bruins fan and pulled him close.

"What the hell?"

"He's looking at us. We need him to think we're here for some other reason."

We remained entwined until we heard footsteps on the pavement. Looking up, we saw a small woman who, though walking quickly, seemed to have a hitch in her step, like she was dreading something or someone. Seeing a light on in the house hastened her pace. Adheem, if it was him, let the curtain fall and moved away from the window. He must have been looking for her, not at us. Phew.

His rant began immediately upon opening the door. The woman drew back and flinched as though bracing herself for an expected attack. He grabbed her arm and yanked her inside. She must be Adheem's wife, Adam's mother.

"Can we go now?" the Bruins fan asked.

"Not yet." Removing my notebook from my purse, I opened the car door, dashed to the back of the cab and jotted down the license plate number. Without checking, I knew it matched the number in the surveillance video. I climbed the steps and was about to knock on the door when I heard slaps and screams.

"I expect my dinner to be ready when I get home," a deep male voice bellowed.

"One of the ladies did not come to work. I had to stay late," a timid voice responded. "If I didn't stay, I'd lose my job."

"Am I not more important than some silly job? You get too many ideas from those bitches you work with. Quit. Find something else. Scrub floors if you must. I don't care. You are here to serve me."

Another slap, more screams.

"Please stop," the woman begged.

What to do? Even though intervening would blow my cover, I couldn't let this continue. I had to help this poor woman. Ignoring thoughts of what my father would do, I banged on the door.

"Mind your own business. Leave us alone," the man yelled within.

"I'm a reporter from *The Alternative*. I'd like to interview you for a story I'm doing on your son. It will just take a few minutes."

The door opened, and the thin man glared at me with deep-set eyes, glowing with hot coals of malevolence. I was sure that he'd be just as happy to hit me as his wife. I peeked inside to see a dreary apartment with a threadbare rug on the floor and dingy gray walls. The woman was nowhere in sight. "Who is that man in the car?"

"He's my photographer. Please, just a few questions. It won't take long."

He looked back and forth between the two of us as though he was trying to decide whether to agree to the interview or not. "Okay, but five minutes, that's all. I haven't had my supper."

I motioned for Treadwell's man to join me when Zuabi blurted out, "No pictures."

I hollered, "Leave your camera in the car. No pictures," relieved because my escort had no camera. Still, I wanted him nearby.

We stepped inside, and I casually looked around. The harsh glare of a computer screen illuminated the living room where a prayer mat lay on the floor. A picture of an old man with coal-black eyes, wearing a turban and a dark, flowing robe stood watch over the room. Newspapers were strewn everywhere. Numerous books and papers were jammed onto shelves. What I wouldn't give to see what was written on them.

"Thanks for speaking with us. I was wondering if you could comment on your son's success and your hopes for him."

"I am very proud of my son. He has accomplished much and has proven to be an excellent advocate for the people. The state is fortunate to have him. I wouldn't be surprised, in fact, I hope he serves at the national level one day."

I was stunned by the ease with which he transitioned from the ranting, violent husband to the proud, articulate father. His resonant voice and thick accent made him seem like a sage scholar instructing a philosophy class, not a lowly cabdriver who beat his wife.

I could hear pots clanging in the kitchen behind the foyer and asked, "Is that Adam's mother in the kitchen? Could I speak to her?"

He shook his head. "She is busy preparing our dinner. We are late for prayers. I'm afraid I must say no."

"Please, just a few words."

"I … said … no." Gone was the rich base voice, now replaced with clipped words, cold and mean. "You must leave … now."

He slammed the door behind me. But at least I had met Adheem Zuabi. I detested him. I didn't trust him, and he made me very nervous, all good reasons to investigate him further as well as his son.

When I saw the text from Treadwell the next morning, I knew there'd be hell to pay when I got to work. I was right.

"What were you thinking?" he boomed as I entered his office. "You could have been hurt." His face was red and taut. "I've gone to great lengths to ensure your safety, and I'll be damned if I let you destroy everything I've worked for. Not now. We're too close. Don't do this ever again. Promise?" He paced the room attempting to calm himself as much as chastise me. I had to restore myself to his good graces.

"I'm sorry. I'm just used to a little more autonomy, but I did learn a few things. Adam's father meets with a guy named Mustafa, who is in the TIDE database and had ties to the 9/11 pilots, among others. I checked the intel photos, and Zuabi has picked up Mustafa dozens of times. As Adam's career progressed, the meetings have become less frequent. Adheem no longer attends the mosque."

He stopped pacing. "Go on."

"Maybe Zuabi did something to tick them off. Or maybe he was concerned that any association with the mosque would hurt Adam's ambitions; I don't know. I told Zuabi that I was doing a story on his son, and he barely spoke to me. As soon as I asked to talk to his wife, he kicked me out. Why wouldn't a father want to speak about his successful son? Why doesn't he want me to talk to the mother? He's hiding something, something beyond beating his wife. I can feel it."

"I'll take it from here. Please be careful and let me know next time." he said in a softer tone. "Maybe you should focus on the Scions and what they're up to."

I was surprised he seemed so dismissive of Zuabi, especially since he could sabotage Treadwell's plans for Adam and the role he might play in the new party. But Treadwell had given me sanctuary, and I owed him. Still, I countered, "Okay, but I'm telling you, Adheem is more dangerous than either you or I know."

He thought for several agonizing ticks of the clock. He was onto something but wouldn't share what it was and only replied, "And that's exactly why you shouldn't be the one to investigate him."

"I'm not so sure about that. Zuabi won't be threatened by me.

Women mean nothing to him. He thinks of me as a woman reporter, a nuisance. If he suspects he's under surveillance by your
men, we'll never discover what he's up to." Then I began to think
out loud. "Maybe I can get to his wife or maybe I can talk to his
neighbors. He's away most of the day."

"What about the Scions?" Once again, he dismissed Zuabi. I
told him I could do both, but then he said, "There's been a devel-
opment." He paused as though he was contemplating whether to
share his news. "Governor Ryan called me last night. It looks like
Representative Samson will be found guilty of income tax evasion
which means a vacant U.S. House seat. He's been impressed with
Adam's performance and is considering him as Samson's replacement. He asked me what I thought, and I requested some time."
Treadwell must have sensed my shock because he continued, "I'm
willing to try it your way, but only if you keep me informed. I want
to know everything you're doing and when you're doing it. Deal?"

My jaw went slack. He had relented and importantly, he trusted me with this new information. "How long do we have? If Adam
goes to Washington, we won't have the same access. I need to get
on this now."

A rueful smile crept onto his face. "Your father told me you
could be a bit feisty." He rubbed the stubble on his chin and waited for me to speak. When I didn't, he reminded me that I hadn't
consented to his terms.

"Alright, fine. I'll let you know everything I'm doing, I
agree ... ," shaking my head and waving my arms before focusing
directly on him. "but no limits. If I need to travel or move closer
to Zuabi, I'm going to."

"You're taking a big risk. Do you know what you're getting
into?"

I smiled coyly and answered, "Not a clue."

Chapter 16

Present Day

"*I* *tell you, Mustafa, the plan is taking shape. Adam has been selected to fill the vacant representative seat. He's going to Washington. He will be a heartbeat away from the president.*" *Holding the steering wheel with one hand and gesturing wildly with the other, he continued,* "*Everything we've dreamed of, it's coming to pass. I told you it would work. You must tell the others. Make them understand. I've never betrayed them. I am a loyal soldier in Jihad.*"

"*This is your dream, Adheem, not mine, and in truth, that's all it is, a dream. Your plan is too complicated. It relies too much on people and events beyond your control, not to mention fortune. Your son is now a big celebrity. What if it has gone to his head? How do you know he will obey you?*"

Adheem looked at him in the rearview mirror, failing to disguise his disappointment and anger. His jaw was clenched, and his hands were wrapped as tightly as a leather cover on the steering wheel. In a low, vicious voice he growled, "*My son will obey, I can assure you.*" *Hearing no response from Mustafa, he continued, but in a more plaintive tone.* "*Will you at least tell the doctor who attends the mosque? We need him to give Adam a physical and create a medical record that states he has high blood sugar. We need the insulin vials. It's vital to the plan.*"

"You need the diagnosis, and you need the vials, not me. You are mad. Why not just kill the president with a gunshot if Adam's to be so close?"

He pounded the wheel with his fist. "Was hijacking four planes madness?" he snapped. "I've explained this a million times. We will kill them all, the entire government. A president can be replaced, but if the whole government is destroyed, the country will be in ruins. The market will collapse. Panic will ensue. It will be total pandemonium and ripe for the taking."

"Do you realize how long it will take him to smuggle in the materials for such a bomb using tiny insulin vials?"

"I did the calculation. Two years, maybe less." Adheem reassured himself that, since he asked questions, Mustafa was still interested. That was good. "All he needs is enough to destroy the U.S. House of Representatives chamber, a place where he will be well known. Two years will provide ample time for him to earn the trust of his colleagues. No one will suspect him of anything." Then, more reflectively, he added, "They will all be there—the President and Vice President, the Congress, the Supreme Court, the Joint Chiefs of Staff. No one of any import will be left."

"And you don't think they will check every person who enters the room? You are a fool, Adheem. Drop me off at the next block. I can listen to this nonsense no longer."

"Mustafa, please," he forced himself to be calm. "Once Adam has the fake medical record, no one will care if he carries the insulin vials with him to work every day, but instead of insulin, they will be filled with PLX or ANNM. I'm still sorting that out. PLX blew up that building in Oklahoma in 1995. ANNM took down the Korean airplane in 1987. I need to determine which requires less liquid and which resembles insulin, but those details can be easily resolved. Adam will have the detonator in his office near the Chamber. The night of the speech, when the time is right, Adam will detonate the bomb. It will work, I am sure of it."

"You can be sure of nothing, Adheem. I've seen many men fal-

ter when faced with the reality of their own demise, men with much less to lose than the celebrity your son now enjoys."

"Just promise me you will speak to the doctor. I'll take care of the rest."

The old man closed his eyes and sighed. "As you wish, but you must tell me everything. If you fail, you will ruin us. If you succeed, I will deny knowing you."

"When I succeed, you won't have to deny anything. We will win the Jihad."

The cab pulled to the curb and the old man exited, so deep in thought that he didn't even notice a woman with auburn hair standing across the street, partially hidden by shadow, who seemed to be speaking into a cell phone, but was really snapping pictures.

Adheem returned home and called Adam. "Mustafa is with us. He will arrange for you to have a physical, and the doctor will diagnose you with high blood sugar as we discussed. It will be glorious, and you, my son, will be an honored martyr. Our name will go down in history."

"Geez, you need to chill." He was glad that his father could not see him roll his eyes. "By the way, it's called diabetes." He tapped his desk with his pen, its rhythm directly proportional to his impatience. "You realize, that if I do go to Washington, there will be greater scrutiny. I already have reporters wanting to interview the American Muslim politician. You should have seen the one who spoke to me last time. She was determined to dig up some dirt— even asked about Mustafa. You need to be careful."

"A reporter stopped by my house last week. She had brown hair, said she worked for The Alternative. *I've never heard of it."*

Adam sat up in his chair. "That's her. What did you tell her?"

"I told her I was proud of you and hoped that you would serve at the national level. Then I sent her away."

Adam thought for a bit and then responded, "If she comes back, be polite, but say as little as possible. She could be a problem."

"If she persists, I will take care of her."

"Father, relax. We might be able to use her to our advantage," Adam countered. "I have found that the press can be an ally if properly stroked. How would Mustafa react if I publicly decried the mosque and him?"

"No, you mustn't. Not now. He's finally back on board," his father replied, anguish raising his voice. "We need his help."

"Even if it helps me execute your plan? It's not enough that I'm willing to die for you, I have to play by your rules? Do you realize what you're asking of me?" Now Adam's voice matched that of his father's in both volume and anger.

"Such insolence. Your death will give you honor throughout our world. You know what will happen if you fail me."

"You've reminded me more times than I can count. I'm so lucky to have such a loving father. Is that all I mean to you? A pawn in your plan? Maybe it is you who should bomb the State of the Union address. Maybe you should go to Firdaws. I'd hate to deprive you of your glory."

"Adam, I'll not have you speak to me like that. You have an opportunity to achieve greatness. We have worked so hard for this. It's within our grasp."

"No, I'm the one who has worked hard. I'm the one who is making a difference. Without me, your plan is worthless."

"I'm beginning to think that you will betray me. If you do, your mother will die. Do you hear me?"

"I've heard you a hundred times. I will do it, but if you do anything to mother … ."

"Then you must obey me." He slammed the phone down, totally dissatisfied with his son and their conversation. He swiped at the table top, sending the cup crashing to the floor where it

shattered it into pieces. That's when he heard her gasp. "How long have been listening?" he yelled. "Come here, now."

Baha slowly entered the room, her head bowed. "I heard nothing. I just got home."

"You lie!" He stood abruptly and struck her face with the back of his hand. "What did you hear?"

"I only heard you tell Adam that he must obey you and then you hung up," she replied meekly.

"Do not take me for a fool. You sneak around here like a common rodent." He yanked his belt from his waist and lashed her with the buckle. She tried to shield herself from his blows, but many found their mark, and blood flowed from her face and hands.

"Please stop. I heard nothing," she screamed.

He grabbed her shoulders and threw her against the wall, causing pictures to fall and cracking the plaster. She crumpled to the floor and curled into a fetal ball. He yanked off her hijab and pulled her hair until her face pressed at his knees. He kicked her repeatedly until the screams stopped and then stormed out of the house.

When she came to, her head was throbbing. The house was dark and silent. She crawled from room to room to reassure herself that he was indeed gone. Using the dresser for support, she pulled herself up and gathered some clothes. Then she took the little money she had set aside as well as a phone number that one of the women at work had given her. With unsteady fingers, she punched the number into the phone.

After what seemed like an eternity, a white van pulled in front of the house. She hobbled from the house, and a woman helped her inside. She took one last look at the place she never called home, knowing that if she stayed, she would die. She never saw the curtain move in a window two houses away.

<<◇>>

"Please help me," she said in voice barely louder than a whisper.

The woman at the desk looked up. Her face blanched and her hand rose to her mouth. It was then that Baha realized how bad she must look. The woman rushed to Baha's side and helped her into a chair.

"Who did this to you? Have you called the police?"

"It was my husband. He's done this before, but not quite so bad. I haven't told anyone. I've been too afraid."

"Does he know you've gone? Will he be looking for you?"

"I don't know."

"How did you hear about us?" the woman asked gently.

"Some of the women at work told me to call you after the last time, but I resisted. I didn't know if you would help someone like me. But after tonight, I have no choice. Will you help me? Please?"

"Of course. Let's get you cleaned up. You'll need to see a doctor."

"No, please. I'll be okay. I just need to hide out for a while."

"It's policy. And we'll need to take some pictures in case the police get involved. Unfortunately, we deal with this type of thing many times. Our staff is totally discreet. You can trust us. We'll take good care of you."

"I don't want the police involved. I can't. My son .... "

"I'm afraid I have to insist. It's really for your own good."
The woman grabbed a camera from the shelf and grimaced as she snapped shots of bruised eyes, swollen cheeks, bloodied skin, sights that she had seen all too often. She heard Baha whimper each time she raised an arm or moved a leg, and it made the woman ache as well. She took Baha into her arms and held her gently.
"We're all done with the pictures. Do you want to shower? Would you like anything to eat? Some tea? Is there anyone you'd like to call?"

Baha shook her head. "Just a shower if that's all right, and then I'd like to go to bed."

"It will be okay. I know it seems awful now, but you've done the right thing by coming here. You'll be safe."

Baha didn't think that she would ever be safe. Her son had abandoned her, and she was convinced that Adheem would find her and kill her.

After two weeks, the wounds were healing, and Baha began to feel human again. She helped with the cleaning and the dishes and often prepared some of the traditional meals from her home-land for the other women. Her version of Aloo Matar Gosht was a particular favorite with its curried flavored beef, vegetables and desi spices. Occasionally, she would babysit when one of the other residents had to go out. It reminded her of Adam's youth, before he was under his father's control. For the first time, she was making friends who shared the same challenges and shame. The counselor told them that they had nothing to be ashamed of, but Baha couldn't hear it. No matter how often she attended the sessions, she left feeling inadequate, a failure.

The woman in charge of the staff trained her to do some work on the computer. Baha could earn money and pass her days. Importantly, she didn't have to leave the center. She was forbidden to tell anyone her location, but that was not a problem. She never wanted to see Adheem again, and her son had no desire to see her; Adheem told her as much. "Your son is a success," he'd say. "You're an embarrassment to him and his career. Don't ruin it for him. Think of someone besides yourself for a change."

The other women at the mosque became strangers once Adheem had been expelled for his western ways, and Adam spoke out against them. There really was no one to whom she could turn except the other women here. But eventually, they, too, would leave, *moving on to new lives. Would she ever have the courage to do the same? Where would she go? She knew no one.*

That's why, one day, when a new volunteer arrived, she felt a shred of excitement. She was the same age, kind and friendly. She, too, had suffered many years as Baha had, and now, wanted to help others. At least that's what the woman in charge told her. The volunteer's name was Carla. No one here used last names. She was pretty in an athletic sort of way. She seemed very smart, too smart to have allowed herself to be abused, but as Baha knew, abuse did not discriminate. Women from all social strata walked through these doors.

Carla worked during the day, but when she visited, they ate dinner, shared many hours of pleasant conversation, watched TV, and she helped Baha with her chores. Baha knew that one day, Carla would leave as the others had, but maybe by then she would find a way to do the same. For now, it was good to have some company. But it was more than that; she now knew someone who genuinely seemed to care, someone she could trust. She hadn't felt that since she left Pakistan years ago.

Spring seemed to arrive all at once on a bright Saturday morning near the end of March. The winter had been so cold, and snow seemed to fall every other day. How she wanted to walk out-side and see the buds on the trees, hear the birds sing, and smell the fresh air, but she didn't dare. Adheem drove a cab. He could be anywhere, and with her luck, he'd find her.

Kat bounded into the room wearing a broad smile and jewels in her eyes. "Baha, I have a car. Let's go to the beach. I've made a picnic lunch. We can watch the waves and walk the sand. What do you say?"

She jumped up with excitement, ready to blurt out, "Yes!" but just as quickly sat back down. "I don't think I should. It may be too dangerous." She lowered her head, disconsolate in her cowardice. She wrung her hands repeatedly as though trying to cleanse the sadness away.

"We'll go up to Crane's Beach. It's an hour from Boston. No one will look for us there. You can't stay inside on a day like today." Kat came to her and knelt beside her. "Please, come with me. I could use a friend now." Her eyes were warm, pleading. Baha could not refuse her.

The ride along the coast mesmerized Baha. She could not keep her eyes from the small towns with their shingled houses and seafood restaurants. There'd be an occasional glimpse of waves pounding the shore. It was so beautiful, but still, she also could not refrain from checking the other cars for the menacing black cab that might be lurking in their midst.

Kat described the fishing industry in Gloucester, the witch trials in Salem—ever chatty and knowledgeable. Baha wished she was more like her, confident, poised and beautiful. "I've made us a nice lunch. I hope you'll like it. Are you hungry?" she asked.

"That's so kind of you. This whole adventure is so kind. We have no waves in my country. We are landlocked. This is beautiful, so liberating. So .... " She turned to face Kat. "Why are you doing this for me?"

Kat laughed, not in a mean way, but lightly. "This is not an adventure, just two girls doing something fun for a change. I needed to get out and thought you might too. You've been cloistered in that house for weeks."

"You said you needed a friend, why? A person like you must have many friends."

"None that I can talk to, not about my problem. I trust you, Baha, and I know that you will keep my confidence. I'll explain when we get to the beach."

They pulled into the long driveway, passing Crane Castle and the beach grass and beautiful grounds, still brown and dreary from the winter's cold. Kat took the picnic basket and led the way to the broad beach, sheltered by dunes, and totally empty.

"Let's go over here, out of the wind."

They found a small alcove and Kat spread a blanket on the

sand. *"I've got chicken salad, chips, some vegetables and dip. There are also some nuts and cheese, if you'd like." Kat pulled the items from the basket, placed them on the blanket between them, and handed Baha a plate. "Please, help yourself."*

Baha smiled at her and hesitantly took a sandwich and some vegetables. The two women ate in silence, scanning the waves and the gulls overhead. After several minutes, Baha asked, "So what is it you are troubled by?"

Kat placed her sandwich on the plate and looked off in the distance as though searching for words. Then she sighed deeply. Turning to Baha, she said, "It's very difficult to talk about. You promise you won't say anything to anyone?"

"I know very few people, and those I know I would say nothing to. You have my word."

"Baha, there are many things about me that you don't know. My husband, well, uh, he was abducted by some very powerful people. He wrote something that could expose them. I'm afraid that they will kill him." She buried her face in her hands and tears that were meant to be feigned were all too real. "I'm scared for his safety, and I don't know what to do."

"Have you told the authorities? They might be able to help," Baha answered.

"That's just it. This group of people controls the authorities," Kat answered, wiping her eyes. "My husband was trying to let the people know that their government is not as legitimate as they want to believe. I don't know who to go to."

"There are some battles that cannot be fought. I, too, feel helpless sometimes. It's a horrible feeling, I know."

"But you're safe now. Your husband won't find you. You can begin a new life. I'm afraid that mine is ruined."

"I am not free. I, too, have a burden that haunts me at night and lurks during the day." Baha's voice grew meek and low. "Can I share something with you in confidence, Carla?"

"Of course," Kat gently touched her arm. "You listened to my tale of woe; it's the least I can do."

"Have you heard of Adam Zuabi?"

"Who hasn't? He's the hottest politician in the state and soon could be in the national government. Talk about a success story."

Baha paused in thought yet could not suppress a smile of pride. "He's my son."

Kat's hand shot to her mouth to indicate her sham surprise. "Your son? I don't understand. Why … ?"

"I overheard a conversation between him and his father. It's what led to our last fight. I told Adheem that I heard nothing, but he didn't believe me. That's when he started to beat me. But he was right, I did hear more, and I don't know what to do."

"What did he say that could be so bad? I mean, only if you can tell me." Kat leaned forward. This was the opportunity she'd been hoping for but didn't want to blow it by pressing too hard.

"You see, when Adam was a small child, his father taught him at home, not just science and math and literature, but Al Quran. But his version is not what I was taught. My religion is one of peace and goodness. When I first met Adheem, he was different, kind and gentle. After Afghanistan, he changed, but I was his wife. I made a promise, and I was to be his for life. That's what Al Quran teaches us. How I prayed that he would return to his old ways, but things only got worse. He kept me from my only child. Adam would sometimes see me in secret, but eventually, the visits stopped. His father told me that I was an embarrassment and could hurt his career." Baha stopped as though the thought was too painful to continue.

Kat couldn't let her stop, not when she was so close to finding out what she needed to know. "Do you think Adam really feels that way?"

Baha waited before answering, afraid that she had said too much. Just when Kat thought she had lost her, Baha answered, "I cannot believe Adam would forsake me. His father is keeping him from me and … ," she paused once again, biting her lip, "I think I know why."

Kat said nothing, hoping the awkwardness of silence would be enough to prompt Baha to continue. Seconds passed. Once again, Kat thought she had lost her and was ready to let it go for another day. "If this is too difficult, you don't need to tell me. I'll understand." She didn't move, praying that Baha would be comforted by the absence of pressure. Kat began to gather the food and return it to the basket.

"No, I need to tell someone. I just didn't want it to be you. I don't want you to hate me or my people. We are not all like my husband. This country, it can be so wonderful, but it can also be mean. After 9/11, we were all outcasts, thrown into the same basket as those terrorists. I despised what those men did, but I did not deserve to be spat upon and scorned. You should have seen the horrid things that were painted on my home."

"I can't imagine how hard it must have been for you, but Adam's success shows that people can change. He's accomplished so much. Perhaps that's some solace."

Baha looked directly at her for the first time that day. Her eyes were searching, pleading, but mostly darkened by a fear that made Kat grow cold. "Carla, you don't understand, you can't understand. Adheem has a plan. I don't know what it is, but it involves Adam. If Adam does not obey, his father told him that he will kill me. I didn't hear the whole conversation, but when Adam goes to Washington, he will become a martyr. I'm afraid he's going to do something very bad."

For the first time in her life, Kat was sorry that she was right. She leaned over and held Baha close, but her thoughts were elsewhere—not with this poor woman who bore such a heavy burden. Kat would not tell Treadwell until she knew more lest he denied her further inquiry.

Chapter 17

"Cam, it's Kat. Treadwell has compromised my phone, so I'm calling on a burner cellphone. I'll explain everything when I see you, but can you get your hands on an electronic surveillance device that I could place in someone's car?" Cam didn't speak right away, and I ducked a little further into a doorway hidden by stairs that led to the brownstone above.

"Are you safe? Where are you?"

"I'm on the street," I answered, watching several people pass by. "I moved to another apartment, but I can't risk talking there. Treadwell may have bugged it like the other places I've lived. His people are watching me night and day. Can you help me?" I tried not to sound too desperate.

"Uh, sure, but I don't understand. Can't Treadwell get one of his guys to do this? You don't need any more trouble."

I paused, wondering how much I could tell Cam without jeopardizing him or Baha. "You have to trust me on this, Cam. Please. Will you help me?"

"Of course. Always. If I assemble it tonight, I could be there tomorrow afternoon." Cam paused again before adding, "I'm worried about you, Aunt Kat."

"I'm fine, really," I lied. "There's one more thing. Treadwell may have also hacked my computer. Would you be able to look at it?"

"I'll bring another one with a new account, but I don't get it. I thought you were working with him."

"I am, but I need some leverage. If he knows what I'm up to, I'll lose it,"

I was glued to the window and was thankful when a yellow cab pulled in front of my apartment. I ran outside and hugged Cam so tightly that I'm sure he sensed the urgency that now consumed me. The look of concern on his face confirmed it.

He took one look at the shabby exterior of my building. "You live here?"

"A man named Adheem Zuabi lives over there," I responded, pointing across the street two houses down. "I've been keeping an eye on him. I'll tell you all about it." Looking back at my own apartment, I added, "I admit, it's not the Ritz, but it will do for now."

We climbed the stairs, but before entering, Cam held a finger to his lips and pulled out some sort of wand from a large suitcase. He waved the wand in broad strokes as we walked inside. Once in the tiny living room, a light on the wand flashed as he neared an end table. He looked inside the lamp shade and pointed. We crept in silence to the kitchenette and the light flashed again; he aimed the wand at the ceiling light and winked. Proceeding to the bedroom, Cam found another bug; this one was behind the alarm clock. Lastly, we entered the bathroom, and I was relieved that he didn't find a bug there. Still, Treadwell's men had been thorough.

I motioned to the door and led Cam outside. Once on the sidewalk, I said, "If we remove the bugs, Treadwell will find out. He'll be suspicious and start asking too many questions."

His brow creased, and he was working his jaw. "I can temporarily deactivate the ones in the living room and kitchen but will leave the one in the bedroom on so if someone's listening, they can still hear ambient sounds."

"Good idea," I replied. "I'll turn on the TV to cover our conversation."

We returned to the apartment, and I grabbed some soft drinks from the refrigerator as noisily as possible. Cam promptly shut down the two bugs while I turned on the TV. Once he was convinced that we could not be heard, we set to work. He removed the surveillance device from his suitcase, programmed it into the new computer, and showed me how to listen in. Then he downloaded the files from my old computer onto the new one, so I would have access to everything I'd discovered. He also showed me how to check security on the new computer, so I would know if someone were to hack it as well. Lastly, he gave me a new phone for me to use going forward. Cam had thought of everything, just like his dad.

Now we had to wait until Zuabi came home so we could plant the bug in his cab after dark. With time to kill, we went to a nearby Thai restaurant that was small enough to notice anyone who seemed out of place, but large enough to find a secluded table where we could discuss the recent events that had led to my current situation. The smell of curry was comforting and woke my taste buds. Some foreign music played in the background, which would help camouflage our conversation. Still, we spoke in hushed tones.

After I finished filling Cam in, he whispered, "I don't get it. Adam Zuabi seems to have it all. Why would he risk it to appease his father? Do you think he'll really go through with it? Any clue what he plans to do?"

"I have the same questions. Unfortunately, I have no idea what their plan is. That's why we need the bug. His father occasionally picks up this guy, Mustafa. He's bad news. I'm sure that Zuabi discusses his plan with him. I need to hear what it is."

"Have you told anyone?"

"No, just you. I've told Treadwell about my suspicions regarding Adam and his father, but he seems unfazed by it." I took a sip of That sweet tea and sighed. "I feel like Treadwell's stringing me along, knowing that I'll stick with him as long as there's a chance that he'll find Robbie and Jermaine. But there's something else that I can't put my finger on. As you saw earlier today, he's keeping me under tight wraps. Someone might be watching us now, I don't know. I'm just not sure what Treadwell's real intentions are. The problem is, I feel trapped. I can't tell anyone in Intel because I'm on someone's list somewhere after the Kennedy stuff. The Scions want me dead. I don't dare go to the local police." I took another sip of tea and stared off into space, musing, "I'm afraid I'm on my own."

He leaned across the table flashing a smile that made his eyes sparkle. "No. You've got me."

I returned his smile with one veiled in sadness. "Do you know how much you remind me of your father?" I said as I brushed the unruly wisps of hair from his eyes. "I miss him so much. I can't let anything happen to you too."

When my watch read nine p.m., we left the warmth of the restaurant for the cool spring evening. We slowed our pace as we approached my street. I tensed slightly when I saw Zuabi's cab parked in its normal spot. The lights were still on inside his house, so we entered the apartment, leashed Scout and returned outside, covering many blocks to reassure ourselves that no one was watching us. The only people we saw were walking home; heads down, moving quickly, paying us no attention. Any one of them might work for Treadwell. By ten p.m., Zuabi's lights were out. We returned to the apartment, packed the device to plant in the cab, changed into dark clothes, turned off the lights, and watched the street.

At midnight, I gave Cam a look. It was time. We crept down the back stairs, through the postage-stamp-sized yard still fringed with the last vestiges of winter's snow piles. Before crossing the street, we hid behind an evergreen bush and scanned our surroundings one more time. The moon was the size of a nail clipping and gave scant light. The street was empty, and long shadows cast by an occasional streetlight provided some cover. Only a siren wailing in the distance and the whistling of the wind pierced the stillness of the night.

Using a Slim Jim that I picked up at Wal-Mart the day before, I unlocked Zuabi's cab and watched the street from behind the rear bumper while Cam activated the device and placed it under the dash, out of sight. He locked the door and shut it as quietly as possible. We sprinted back across the street and hid behind the same bush, straining our eyes for any sign of movement. It had taken less than five minutes.

Once back inside my apartment, Cam dashed to the new computer, punched some keys, and confirmed the bug was working. Mission accomplished.

Cam settled onto the sofa for the night. I silently entered my room and lay in bed, cuddling Scout, alert to every sound inside and outside my apartment.

It was six a.m. when I heard a car door shut. I raced to the window in time to see Zuabi drive off. I pulled on a robe and ran to the living room where Cam was already on the computer, listening to the sound of the news station on Zuabi's radio.

"You're up early," I said, as I leaned over to see what he was doing.

"Once we re-activate the bugs in your apartment, you'll need to use these earphones so if anyone's listening, they won't hear Zuabi's conversations." He plugged the headset in and let me listen. "I've typed in some keys words. Maybe you can help me think of more. I've programmed it so you can skip right to those. Otherwise, you will get your fill of NPR."

"Hmm," I muttered. "How about Mustafa, Adam, president, Washington, Jihad, bomb, gun ... Baha ... ."

"Who is Baha?" Cam cut in.

"Zuabi's wife," I answered quickly, and he asked why I wanted to add her. "Just a hunch," I responded and left the room, ostensibly to make some coffee, but also to avoid further questions.

When I returned, Cam said, "I think it's all set. If you think of any more words, this is how you can program them in." He showed me the steps and then took out the new phone. "This one has a few more bells and whistles than the one my dad gave you. For one thing, if you press here, you'll be able to receive any calls made to you on your old phone without worrying about being tapped. Treadwell won't have a clue that you're using a new phone, and you'll have some privacy. I put a camera outside your house, so while you're away, you can use your phone to watch your place. I've copied all your contacts too. Let me show you a few other things."

My tutorial took until eleven a.m. when Cam called a cab for the airport. I didn't want to see him go.

"I hate leaving you here alone, Aunt Kat, but I have to get back. Be careful, and please, call me if you need anything. By the way, which of the calls was from the guy who has O'Toole?" he asked, pointing to my contacts.

I showed him the number. He wrote it down and then re-activated the bugs. Within minutes, the cab arrived. I watched as he strode down the walk. Before climbing in, he gave me one last wave. With one hand on my chest, I waved with the other, praying that no harm would come to one of the finest young men I knew.

"It's definite. Adam is going to Washington," Treadwell announced with pride. I looked down. "You don't seem very excited."

"I've told you, I don't trust him," I said.

"With all due respect, I need more to go on than your gut instinct."

"What about these?" I handed him the pictures of Adheem meeting with Mustafa. "Zuabi meets with this guy. His name is Mustafa. He's known to associate with radicals, some of whom attend his mosque. Why would Zuabi consort with him—especially if he wants his son to succeed?"

"Adam told me that he and his father are estranged. You can't blame him for his father's acts." I seldom saw Treadwell so defensive.

Making every effort not to raise my voice to match his, I said, "And I think you're being naïve. Just because he fits perfectly into your grand plan, you can't ignore the obvious. His father could be a terrorist."

He stood and walked to my chair, leaned over and asked testily, "Where's your proof?"

"I'm following a lead, and when I have something concrete, you will be the first to know, but for now, here's this." I tossed a folder onto his desk. "It's a communication between Hughes and Johnson. I think you'll find it interesting. It appears that Senator Mendez has joined their ranks. I think they were involved with the H-bomb North Korea just tested."

Treadwell flipped through the pages. While he was doing so, I went on the offensive. "Speaking of progress, have you made any on Robbie and Jermaine? We had a deal."

"We're getting closer," he said offhandedly as he continued reading the file.

"That's not good enough," I snapped. "When you find something and tell me, I'll give you more, but until you do, I'm giving you nothing."

His laughter was laced with condescension, and it drove me nuts. "Are you trying to manipulate me?" he asked. "You promised to tell me everything you've been up to, but you haven't, have you?"

He was watching for my reaction; I gave him none. "I know some guy came to see you yesterday. Who was it?"

"My godson. He came to visit."

He asked several questions about Cam which I answered without divulging anything of import, but then he asked, "So why have you been going to the women's shelter?"

"I told you, I'm following a lead."

"Uh-huh, and what kind of lead is this? Does this have something to do with Zuabi?" A tiny vein in his neck now looked like a thick cable.

I would not raise my voice, despite an intense desire to do so. "I will tell you everything when you can tell me Robbie's location and your plans to get him back. You've had three months and nothing to show for it. I've given you a ton of intel; you've given me nothing."

"Nothing? I've given you nothing?" Another derisive laugh. "How about safety? How about money?"

"That means nothing without Robbie." I stood to leave, unwilling to endure any further interrogation. Perhaps he decided that his previous tack was not working because when he spoke next, his voice was softer, kinder, and he wrapped his arm around my shoulder.

"I'm sorry. I'm under considerable pressure right now and I'm not reacting well to more. We're on the same side, remember? We're going after the bad guys. We're trying to make things right. If I'm short, it's because the national election is less than a year away. We don't have much time. Please, work with me. I am not your enemy, they are."

"Find Robbie and Jermaine. Then we'll talk." I could feel his eyes on me and heard a pencil snap as I left the room.

At my desk, I logged onto the computer Cam gave me and plugged in the headphones. While listening, I also logged onto my work computer and began cross-checking the movements of various members of the Scions. Multi-tasking was now second nature. From inside Zuabi's cab came the familiar voices of Steve Inskeep and Rene Montagne, and I switched to the tape, punching in the key words. When I typed "Baha," the tape jumped to a conversation between Adheem and an unknown contact.

"Baha's been gone for over a month. I haven't been able to find her. She may know too much, but I don't think she would go to the authorities. She'd be too scared." It was Zuabi.

"Have you told Adam or Mustafa?" the unknown voice answered.

"I can't. If Adam knows she's safe, then he may not follow through. Mustafa would use this to condemn me and my plan. I need you to find her. She used to work at a laundromat, but no one there will speak with me. You may have better luck. Also, there was this reporter who came to the house while Baha was there. Baha may try to contact her."

The man responded, "Adheem, you became my father when the Americans killed mine. You have shown me the true way. I will do whatever you wish, no matter what."

As Zuabi gave the man additional information about the laundromat and me, I sat back in my chair and buried my face in my hands. This changed everything.

Chapter 18

After contemplating options, I called Tom and explained Baha's predicament. "I have a huge favor to ask, Tom. If it's a problem, I'll understand. Could I bring her to your place for a week or so until I can find something more permanent? I've got to get her out of Boston. Her husband is looking for her and if he finds her, he will kill her. By the way, she's Adam Zuabi's mother."

There was a long pause on the other end of the line. I knew I was asking a lot and prepared myself for a barrage of questions. I was surprised he didn't say more than, "Shit, Kat, I'm not much protection. Treadwell could help her better than me. He can't afford a scandal with a member of his party, not now."

"No one will look for her in Bethel; certainly not her husband. I don't think you'll be at risk. Besides, I need to see you. There are a few other things that we need to discuss, including Treadwell. A lot has happened."

"Maybe Willie can help. Between the two of us, we'll figure something out. I'll get back to you."

He called back within an hour and said it was a go. I thanked him profusely and appreciated, yet again, his generosity of spirit. Now I had to figure out how to convince Baha to go and, if she agreed, how to get her away before Adheem found her, and without alerting Treadwell's men, who watched me twenty-four/seven.

I quickly threw some clothes and toiletries into a suitcase and called a cab. Once it arrived, I turned my old phone off, all too aware that Treadwell's men could use it to track me once more. They would know that I was up to something, but it was a risk I was willing to take. I had to.

We pulled in front of the shelter. I asked the cabbie to wait and ran inside with an empty duffel bag. Baha was in the kitchen, chatting with another woman. She seemed so serene, so comfortable. How I hated to tear her away from this newfound oasis. Upon seeing me, she smiled brightly and invited me to join them.

"Thanks, but I need to talk to you … in private." I kept my voice steady, not wanting to alarm her any more than necessary.

She excused herself and led me to her bedroom. "We can talk here." She offered a chair, but I remained standing. "You look upset."

"I need to get you away from here. You're in danger. Adheem's been looking for you and has enlisted the assistance of another man. It won't be long before they figure out where you are. I can't let them hurt you again. Please, Baha, you have to trust me."

"But Carla, I'm finally free. I've made friends. I feel useful. How can they find me?"

"Adheem told this man to go to the laundromat. There's no telling what lies he may use to find out that your co-workers recommended you come here. I'm begging you. It's for your own good. I have a friend who will let you stay at his place until it's safe. He's a good man."

"I cannot stay under the same roof as a man unless I am his. It is against our teachings." Her former tranquility disappeared. She shrunk before my eyes, her arms wrapped tightly around her chest as if shielding herself from my request.

"It's only temporary. I'll help you pack. There's not much time." I opened her closet and grabbed some dresses and coats. She was too stunned to speak. "Please Baha, there's not much time. I'll explain everything, I promise."

She didn't move as I opened bureau drawers and removed scarves and underwear. That's when a loud pounding sounded at the front door. We froze a second before instinct took over. I jammed her belongings into the bag, yanked her arm and pulled her out the back door, scurrying to the side of the house. Crouched behind some shrubbery, with Baha behind me, I craned to see who was at the door. It was a slender, olive-skinned man, trying to explain that Baha was his sister, and he had come to take her away. I looked at Baha. She shook her head. When the woman from the shelter denied him entry, he shoved her aside and ran into the house, screaming Baha's name. We sprinted to the cab.

The cabbie took us to a rental agency where I used Treadwell's debit card to secure a car. He would soon realize that I had left, but with my phone de-activated, he had no way of knowing our destination. He'd be pissed off, but so was I. It was only when we were on the Mass Pike that we could breathe easily.

It pained me to see the horror in Baha's eyes. She hadn't spoken a word since we left, but only stared out the window, occasionally dabbing her face with a tissue.

"I owe you an explanation," I began. She said nothing. "What I told you at the beach is true. I can't tell you everything; it would only place you at more risk, but I've been investigating your husband. I'll admit, I wanted to meet you to learn more about him, and what you told me confirmed my fears. I'm so sorry if I misled you, but right now, you are my only concern. I am your friend, Baha. I will do whatever it takes to keep you safe."

She remained silent and would not meet my eyes. She must have felt betrayal at some level, but I had rescued her from the man who stormed into the shelter. That had to count for something. Maybe it was dread that her old life might return. Maybe it was a sense of loss for the fleeting new life that she found. I could empathize with both, having been on the run or hiding for the past two years myself. I ached for her. No one deserved this less than she. I let her be alone with her thoughts, whatever they were.

When we reached the rest area in Ludlow, I told Baha that I

needed to stop. She accompanied me inside. I bought us some tea and sandwiches, and we found an empty table near the window.

"Why were you investigating my husband?" she asked meekly.

"Actually, I was investigating your son." Her eyes flared with both pain and anger, so I quickly added, "It was only then that I found out about your husband."

"Why were you interested in my son? He's done you no harm. He's helped many people in his district. He's accomplished so much."

I reached across the table and took her hand. "Baha, you yourself said that Adheem has some sort of scheme that involves your son. If I get you to safety and can let Adam know that your husband can't hurt you, maybe he won't execute Adheem's plot. If Adam's as good a man as you claim, he won't."

She closed her eyes, rested her chin upon her knotted hands, and sighed. "It's been so long since I've seen him. I don't know what he'll do. Adheem has been filling his head with wild ideas since he was a child."

"He must love you very much to risk all he's achieved to ensure that Adheem doesn't hurt you."

"There was one time, when he was no more than twelve. Adheem struck me, and Adam ran to him, pounding him with his fists, screaming for him to stop." Her voice began to quiver. "Yes, he does love me. I'm sure of it." She lowered her head as though embarrassed by her emotion.

I stood and walked to her side, gently saying, "Let's go. We can talk more in the car, if you'd like."

I did most of the talking during the remainder of the trip, describing Tom and his colorful past. Baha asked few questions, clearly apprehensive of this next venture in her traumatic life. I asked her about Pakistan and her life before coming to the States. Though she had never been formally educated, due to the strictures of her culture, Adheem had once cared enough to teach her to read. Like many soldiers who survived a war, he battled with depression, random anger, and little opportunity to deal with it. When he uprooted his family and replanted them in the states, he was driven by something Baha could not identify, scouring the papers, listening to the news on TV and discussing politics with the men of the mosque. She said it was like he had a new purpose in life, and though only a cab driver, he held his head high among his peers. I soaked it all in, my brain processing the most minute details and filing them for future reference.

Tom was at the door when we arrived, his hand beckoning us in and his eyes flashing welcome. I think that seeing him in a wheelchair helped quell some of Baha's misgivings, made him seem less threatening to her. I smelled the rich scent of Mideastern food, a testament to Tom's efforts to make Baha feel at home. Baha excused herself for evening prayer while I played sous chef in the kitchen, stirring sauces, washing pots, slicing vegetables. By seven, the table was set, and the food served.

Baha, though quiet, listened intently to Tom's stories of the past and present. She smiled frequently and asked about his accident, which he described without a drop of self-pity, in fact, made light of it. The two of them seemed to hit it off—especially since his time in Iraq familiarized him with some customs shared by Baha. This might just work, I thought inwardly.

By ten, Baha was ready for bed, so I led her upstairs to a room of her own.

"Carla, I can't thank you enough. You saved my life. How can I repay you?"

"Don't worry about that. Seeing you laugh again is all the payment I need." I meant it. "There's one more thing." I hesitated, reluctant to reveal one more layer of duplicity. "My real name is Kat, short for Kathryn. Carla is a cover. If we're to be friends, the least I can do is tell you my real name."

"Good night, my friend. Sleep well."

I descended the stairs and Tom led me to the back room, out of earshot lest Baha was still awake. He poured some scotch for the two of us and said, "Sounds like we have some catching up to do."

I described the events that led Baha and me to his doorstep. He listened quietly, periodically asking a few questions, nodding in understanding. When he asked me about my work with Treadwell, this time I couldn't hold back; not after all he had done for Baha and me.

"I don't know what to think, Tom. I like him one minute and suspect him the next. He's an enigma." I paused over my scotch, more to decide how to frame my words than savor its flavor. "He's had ample time to find Robbie and tells me nothing. I gave Cam some information about a call I received; the time, my location and my cellphone number, and he located them in three days. They're keeping Robbie and Jermaine in a high security base about six miles from Camp David called Raven Rock. Surely, Treadwell has many more resources than Cam. Either it's not a priority, or he's using it to keep me under his control."

"He's really busy, Kat. His party is about to be announced, any day now, and he wants an all-out media blitz. He knows Robbie and wants him back as much as … ."

"What? He didn't say anything about that to me." I placed my tumbler on the table with a loud thunk. "Dammit, we had a deal. He was supposed to tell me everything."

"Well, he's going to use the governor's press conference to announce it."

"What press conference?" I asked. A curious tingling made me wriggle my shoulders, sending a chill down my back. I could guess the answer before he gave it.

"The one where Adam Zuabi is officially named to replace Samson. It's all set, day after tomorrow."

"I've got to get back," I said, thinking out loud. "This is very bad."

"What is it, Kat?"

I swore him to secrecy before saying, "Zuabi has concocted some sort of plot that involves Adam once he goes to Washington. Whatever it is, Adam will be a martyr, and if he backs out, Adheem will kill Baha."

Tom sat up in his chair and wheeled himself to a canister on a table across the room. He pulled out a joint, lit it, and took two deep puffs. "Does Treadwell know?" I shook my head. "You've got to tell him."

"I conveyed my suspicions about Adam to Treadwell, but he doesn't seem to take them seriously. When I know more, and Robbie is safe, I'll tell him everything. Cam put a bug in Zuabi's cab, that's how I found out Baha was in danger. I'm hoping to learn more about this plot, but until Treadwell levels with me, he's getting nothing."

Tom rubbed his jaw and inhaled another toke. The room was silent except for some song by The Byrds playing in the background. It should have been "Eight Miles High," given Tom's proclivities. I was beginning to think he had zoned out altogether when he asked, "Wouldn't there be background checks on Adam? Governor Ryan wouldn't appoint someone unless he was squeaky clean—especially since Samson screwed up."

"Adam's clean as a whistle. As for his father, other than fighting the Russians in Afghanistan and some domestic violence incidents that aren't even on his record because Baha wouldn't press charges, there's nothing. Believe me, I've checked. Adam claims Adheem came to the States because he didn't approve of bin Laden's violent ways. No one knows about his activities except possibly this guy at the mosque, Mustafa. To the rest of the world, Zuabi is an immigrant cab driver whose son exemplifies the American dream. Treadwell said so himself."

I sat back in my chair and, while waiting for Tom to respond, had a thought. It was more like a hunch, but worth checking out tonight after we turned in, and before I listened to more NPR and Adheem Zuabi's conversations. Tom told me that I had given him a lot to digest, and he needed to sleep on it. Sleep, now that was a novel concept.

The sun rose way too early, barging through my window like an unwelcome guest. I rubbed my eyes, willing them to stay open, and checked my watch—seven a.m. Although the night had yielded little rest, it did impart some interesting findings. Adheem was livid that Baha was not at the shelter. The women there said they didn't know of her, despite the threats issued by the strange man. Their courage was nothing short of amazing. Baha really was safe, at least for now. I hated the thought of telling her I had to leave.

The other item I discovered was the record of Adam's physical which, except for newly diagnosed diabetes, was perfect, above reproach, just like everything else appeared to be in his life. The rest of his background check indicated nothing, but set me thinking. If Adam were to back out, could his father implement his plan? Evidently not, since he applied tremendous pressure on Adam. It must have something to do with Adam's going to Washington. As a U.S. House member, he would have access to other men and women in Congress, the capital building, maybe even the president at some point. Was that it? But if Zuabi wanted to kill the president, he could try it himself with a long-range rifle and telescope. Plenty of snipers did so in Iraq and Afghanistan. What could Adam do that Adheem could not? It had to be more than sponsor a friendly bill or help implement policy; that would not make him a martyr.

With questions swirling in my head, I stumbled down the stairs where Baha and Tom were sipping tea. She wore a beautiful magenta robe with a matching hijab on her head. I almost envied that she didn't have to style her hair daily. More noticeable was her demeanor. She seemed far more animated than the night before, laughing, telling stories of her own, helping Tom by refilling his cup and clearing his dishes. I almost felt like an intruder when I entered. Tom had a way of disarming people and putting them at ease. I was relieved to see him work his magic once more.

"It's about time you got up," Tom greeted me. "We were about to send out a search party. Late night, huh?"

I headed straight for the coffee pot.

"Allow me," Baha said, and jumped up to beat me to it. "Have a seat. I'll get it for you."

I didn't argue and plopped down into a chair across from Tom, who asked quietly, "Find anything?"

I nodded and whispered that I was certain Baha was safe. She brought the steaming cup of coffee and an almond croissant and set them before me. I thanked her and savored the strong, hot liquid, hoping for a rapid effect. We chatted lightly for a while, and Tom mentioned that he wanted to show Baha the sights in his backyard, meaning Bethel. I chimed in that it would be a good idea.

"You'll join us, of course," Baha said, making it sound more like a question than a statement.

"Normally, I would. Bethel is very special to me. In fact, it's where my husband proposed, but I'm afraid I can't. I learned last night that I'm needed at work." The look on her face could break a heart of granite; it shattered mine. "I'm so sorry, Baha. I'll be back in a few days, I promise. Tom will take good care of you."

"Is this because of the man you told me about, the one who has you investigating my son?" she asked, her voice brittle.

"I'm afraid so. He's a taskmaster," I answered trying to keep it light, not even thinking of telling her that I was going to hear her son be officially named to his new office and detesting the fact that she couldn't see it as well. It made me wonder, would Zuabi, the elder, be there?

Tom came to my rescue. "Baha, I have a friend, Willie. He can chauffeur us anywhere we want to go. It will be a blast, you'll see. They don't come any better than him."

170

"I cannot stay alone with a man. It is forbidden. I'm sorry, but I must find a hotel. If you'll let me borrow some money, I will pay you back."

"I understand, Baha, but your husband wants to kill you. Even the *Koran* says, 'The Holy Prophet has instructed that she would not be beaten on the face, or cruelly, or with anything which might leave a mark on the body.' Your husband has exceeded that which is allowed by the *Koran*. He's the one who broke Islamic law; not you. You owe him nothing." Baha and I stared at Tom, astonished that he could quote the *Koran*. "As for staying in the house of another man," he continued, "welcome to the MacGregor Hotel. I'm merely the proprietor." He chuckled lightly, but then leaned toward her and said, "You are safe here, Baha, and I will do nothing but take care of you. Kat will be back before you know it."

Realizing that she had no choice, she bowed her head and left the room. I felt like I betrayed her yet again, but knew that Tom would do nothing to make her uncomfortable. Now that she was safe, I had more pressing matters to address. Someday, she would understand.

Chapter 19

By the time I arrived at the press conference wearing my reporter's disguise, the room was bulging with people and alive with animated conversations. I squeezed in between two reporters who were griping about being stuck in the back of the room. It was the perfect spot to observe others without being noticed myself. Cameras clicked like cicadas when the governor approached the dais, followed by Adam Zuabi, the lieutenant governor, and senior members of the state legislature. The air was warm and charged like a summer's night awaiting lightning.

"Ladies and gentlemen, it gives me great pleasure to announce that I have selected Adam Zuabi to fill Massachusetts' vacant Second District seat in the U.S. House of Representatives. Adam has been a champion of the people, and through his efforts we have reduced our welfare rolls, improved our transit system, cut health-care expenses, and restored the integrity of our Ways and Means Committee, all while reducing the state's operating costs. Importantly, he has given the citizens of our state hope: hope for a better job, hope for crime-free neighborhoods in which they can raise their children, and hope for a better life than their parents had. Although we will miss him here in the State House, I am confident that there is no one who can better represent our interests at the federal level. And now, I'd like to present Adam Zuabi."

The room erupted in applause and it was then that I realized why the room was so packed. More than half of the people gathered were his constituents. Across the room, one of those cheering was more animated than the rest—Adheem Zuabi, dressed in a loose-fitting suit and clapping vigorously as he scanned the room to gauge the reactions of others. His smile was like that of a poker player who just bluffed his way to the pot he was raking in.

The governor stepped away from the dais and waved his arm, motioning Adam to speak. Adam was beaming as he strode to the dais with an air of confidence and perhaps, triumph. He pulled a piece of paper from his pocket and placed it on the podium but never looked at it. He had been groomed for this very moment.

"Governor Ryan, distinguished members of the legislature, my fellow citizens, I am deeply honored by the governor's kind words and appreciate his confidence in me."

His father hung on every word, nodding and smiling; his chest puffed out, making his suit seem less baggy than before.

"You have my solemn vow that I will not disappoint him; nor will I disappoint you, the people whom I am privileged to serve. I am living proof that anyone can succeed in this great country if given the tools and the opportunity. I am fortunate to have had both and that is due, in large part, to my parents who sacrificed much so that I can stand here today before you."

Adheem's smile was now mixed with discomfort. He drew back against the wall. His dark glare at Adam suggested that he wanted no notoriety.

"I will work just as hard, dream just as much, and fight, if necessary, to ensure that the best interests of our state and, indeed, our country, are served with integrity, diligence and compassion. I will not be bound by party lines, only by what is right and good for the people of this great land."

Adheem, the poker player, was back, practically licking his chops.

"I thank the governor for this profound opportunity. I thank the good people of this state for their belief in me, and on a more personal note, I'd like to thank Meghan Callahan for her unwavering support."

Adam's smile seemed genuine as he extended his arm toward a smartly dressed, diminutive woman with sandy, neatly coiffed hair who approached the podium with small steps. She embraced Adam and waved to the crowd, now euphoric, except for one person whose eyes narrowed, jaw dropped. and fists clenched. Adheem hadn't known, and he did not approve.

Adam and his girlfriend stepped back, allowing the governor to approach the podium once more. This was it.

"And now, I'd like to make another statement." He paused, ever so slightly, as though fully aware that he was about to drop a bombshell and desired maximum impact. "Massachusetts has always been at the forefront of political and social change, whether it was the Revolutionary War, abolition, marriage equality or education, all of which ensure the preservation of human rights and the provision of opportunity for everyone. Thus, it is fitting that it is here, in this great state, we make history once again. Today's political climate makes bipartisan cooperation a thing of the past. Party interests have taken priority over what was once the *United* States. The majority of our country is no longer represented by the radical right of the Republican party, nor the extremist left of the Democratic party." He paused to look around the room and ensure that he had everyone's attention. "Today, I proudly announce the launch of a new political party, the Constitution Party, a party that is fiscally conservative, but socially inclusive, a party that will not pander to the powerful but rather, will represent the people ethically and with the best interests of the country as our core mandate."

A tide of murmurs swept through the room, now a lightshow of flashing cameras. Reporters poked tweets into their cell phones. Adheem looked confused and troubled, but when he looked up, our eyes locked. His expression morphed to a sneer. I did not look away, nor did he, as the governor continued.

"At least a third of the U.S. Congress and twenty-one governors have pledged their commitment to the Constitution Party. I am proud to say that I am one of them, as are both senators and three representatives from our state, including Adam. They have been selected on the basis of their records, their integrity, and independence from any special interest. We did not take all comers, only the best and most trustworthy."

Adheem turned at the mention of his son's name. Once again, he seemed stunned and angry. Adam must have kept this from him as well.

The governor continued, "Unlike the campaigns of John Anderson, Ralph Nader, or H. Ross Perot, we have vast resources, a critical mass of politicians in our fold, and a network in place to position us as a viable option for voters who are frustrated by the choices they've been given previously. We also have a newspaper, TV station and a website to counter the rhetoric of extremist talking heads; all are called *The Alternative* because that's what we're about, an alternative to biased reporting and special interests. Unlike existing news outlets, our outlets are not influenced by the intelligence community, the power brokers, or either the Democratic or Republican party. They will provide pure information, which will allow people to make their own intelligent, informed decisions. Together, we will return our government to us, the people, as the Constitution intended. You will be hearing much more about us in the coming days, and I think you will be as excited as we are. Thank you."

A forest of hands sprouted. Voices barked out questions. A riot of lights and sounds destroyed any semblance of decorum. History was being made, and everyone realized it. That was when I saw Treadwell, wearing a thin, nervous smile. He stood on the side of the room, surrounded by several men and women, some of whom I recognized from Quantum. There was no way that I could navigate the sea of people between us, so I decided to go to the office and confront him there, in private. It would give me a chance to prepare both my plan of attack … and my defense. We both had plenty to answer for.

Back at my desk, I booted up my computer and while waiting, hit the buttons that lowered the screen and allowed access to various news outlets. News of Treadwell's party was everywhere. Pundits both praised and ridiculed the new party. Politicians both scoffed and admired the "new experiment." Several confirmed their allegiance to the new party. It was really happening. Treadwell had pulled it off, and ironically, so had Adheem.

I logged onto my personal computer, followed the steps outlined by Cam to enter the once-secure DOD network, and searched Raven Rock, where Robbie and Jermaine were being held. Floorplans, staff names, and a litany of security measures and procedures appeared before me. I was studying access routes when my door flew open and Treadwell stormed in.

"Have a nice trip?" he asked sarcastically. "Washington is nice this time of year; don't you think?" His smug expression was maddening and indicated that he expected me to be shocked and defensive. I opted for the opposite. A rant would accomplish nothing. At least he didn't know my real destination or my reasons for going.

I minimized my screen so he wouldn't see what I had been searching and hoped that he didn't notice that I was using my personal computer. Looking up at him calmly, I answered, "Yes, as a matter of fact, I did. By the way, congratulations on today. You must be pleased."

"You were watching it on TV, I see," he replied, gazing at the banks of screens before me.

"Actually, I was there. So was Adam's father." His eyebrows arched, almost imperceptibly. "It looks like you're off to a good start," I added. "I've been trying to monitor the response of the

Scions but have found nothing yet. In fact, I think they've blocked me. I've seen no communication from them."

My nonconfrontational approach seemed to throw him off balance as he did not acknowledge my comment and flubbed a few words before responding, "We had a deal and you broke it."

"As did you. It was supposed to go both ways. You didn't tell me about the announcement, and I didn't tell you about my trip. I say we're even." My voice was still steady, and I was determined to keep it that way. "What about the Scions? Aren't you concerned about that?"

"I told you about the third party and Adam's potential appointment. I just didn't say when both would be announced. Perhaps if you'd been around more, I would have."

"How about a text or a phone call? And what about the Scions?"

"Why did you go to Washington? If I'm paying for your boondoggles, I have a right to know." I could tell he was trying to match my even tone but was having difficulty because that same bulging vein betrayed him once more. His refusal to answer my questions about the Scions awoke my gut with an uneasy feeling.

"Yes, you do. And I have a right to know what you're doing about Robbie. That was also part of our deal. When you level with me about that, I'll tell you everything." He played with a pen on my desk, a delaying tactic, so I pressed further. "Well? It's been months."

He hesitated. I couldn't tell if he was thinking of an answer that would placate me or was reluctant to share what he knew. "He and Biggs are someplace in western Mass, either Westover or Barnes."

"That's a lie," I snapped. "You said that Robbie is your friend. We both know that you're stalling his rescue, and I want to know why. You have pull. You know people. Hell, we both know you have the resources. What kind of person would let a friend be tortured? What did he do to deserve that? Maybe you're glad he's locked away, so he can't investigate you. Or maybe, you're not his friend at all." So much for the calm approach.

His face turned ashen, and his eyes winced as though I had struck him. For the first time, there was no pretense, only remorse. He began to pace the room in slow plodding steps, his shoulders drooped, his hand rubbed the back of his neck. He turned away and gazed out the window, far into the distance. It was several minutes before he spoke and when he did, his voice seemed nostalgic and sad.

"We were young and like most young people, we felt invincible and that our cause was right and good. We were taking on 'the man' and were part of something bigger than ourselves. The fire inside was stoked by every demonstration, every time we felt the butt of a night stick, and every joint we shared. When RFK got killed, and Humphrey won the nomination, we were crushed. Then Nixon got elected, and I lost it. Maybe it was an excuse, but I started getting into some heavy shit. It wasn't long before I was on the street, begging for money until I had enough for the next hit." He pulled up his shirt sleeve, revealing an arm puncuated by the scars of ancient needle marks. My jaw dropped.

"Rob heard I was in bad shape and came looking for me. When he found me, he took me home and didn't leave my side until all the night sweats, seizures and sickness were gone. He was strict and told me I was wasting my potential. He would bust my butt until I got a job, went back to school, ate right, and exercised, you know, tough love. We lived together for a couple of months until he was certain I was clean. It's because of Rob that I'm here today and not dead. I owe that man my life."

"He never told me," I said solemnly.

"Doesn't surprise me. The man you married is the best."

"That must have been hard."

"You know what makes it hard? That he doesn't know I'm still trying to change a corrupt system. What's hard is hearing you question how devoted I am to him. Nothing could be further from the truth. I admit, I lied about his being in western Mass. I didn't want you getting hurt trying to find him. If I could spring him tomorrow, I would, but Raven Rock is impenetrable. It's tearing me apart that I can't help him the way he helped me. Since I can't free him, I'm doing the next best thing. He loves you, Kat, very much. If you mean that much to him then I must keep you safe … for him."

I didn't speak. Even if I could, I wouldn't know what to say. My mind was a morass of gnarled thoughts and feelings, sucking me down into a void which suffocated reason. He rose and moved toward the door. When he pressed the button to open it, I blurted out, "What if I could figure out a way to get into Raven Rock? Would you help me?"

He shook his head sadly. "It's impossible. The only way is to broker a deal, so they'll release him. Anything we came up with could endanger you, me, and everything we've worked for." Even though he pounded a fist into the palm of his other hand, he seemed small and limp. Without looking my way, he added, "Please keep what I told you to between us. Do I have your word?" I nodded. "I will be away for a week to attend announcements in other states. Try to stay out of trouble."

Saying something was impossible was like waving a red flag at someone as bull-headed as me. He should have known better. As soon as he left, I returned to the DOD website and spent several hours scouring the information on Raven Rock, including watch schedules, delivery times and days, the duties and clearance of onsite personnel, electronic surveillance, defense mechanisms, various cells where prisoners might be held, the underground tram from Camp David to whisk the Commander in Chief to safety in an emergency, everything I could find. There was so much, and yet no chinks in the armor jumped out. I had only the week Treadwell was gone to figure something out.

I called for my escort, later than usual, and spent the ride home contemplating all that was on my mind. Baha was safe—check.

Adam was going to Washington. How could I keep an eye on him and his father? The Scions were silent—why? And why didn't Treadwell express more concern when I told him? Maybe he had already known. Treadwell. The mere thought of the man spawned another slew of questions—was his admission one more attempt to elicit my cooperation, my sympathy? It seemed like too much to confide in a peon like me, but it would explain a lot. Eventually, as always, my thoughts turned to Robbie. I was desperate to get him out, no matter what.

After dinner, I took Scout for a walk and saw a strange car outside Zuabi's. Silently, I pulled Scout to a side window where there was a gap in the curtain. Even though the window was shut, I could hear Zuabi bellowing at his son. He was angry about Adam's girlfriend and the new party, thinking that both put his plan at risk. Adam assured him that nothing had changed, and he was still on board. But then he asked about Baha.

"She left me, but I will find her."

"You beat her again, didn't you?"

"I told you, I wouldn't hurt her. She left while I was out. She'll come back. She always does."

Adam stood abruptly and grabbed his coat. He picked up a small vial, like some kind of medicine, and jammed it into his pocket. It looked like an insulin vial, but why would it be sitting on a table? There was no sign that they had dined, nor were there any syringes. If he was taking insulin, why wasn't he using the newer pens that were much less painful? He headed toward the door, but before leaving, yelled, "I want to see her when she does. If anything has happened to her ... "

"She's fine. Now go to Washington and do your job. The real one." Adheem slammed the door behind him.

I heard the front door open and ducked down, stroking Scout to keep him silent. Adam did care about his mother, and Adheem could ill afford to alienate Adam further. I wondered, if he didn't find her, would Adam go through with the plot?

After Adam's car roared down the street, I returned home and checked Zuabi's conversations for the day. Nothing there. I went back on the DOD website and read until two a.m., when a crazy idea took root. I jotted down a quick note and turned in. It was incredibly risky, and I'd have to wait awhile before I could even think of pulling it off, but with Cam's help, it just might work.

Chapter 20

A proficient hunter must have a dependable weapon loaded with lethal, but precise ammunition. He must be nimble enough to pursue his quarry, through hill and dale, heat and cold, wind and rain, and once he has it in his sights, his shot must be true. Sightings are infrequent, and the opportunity to land his prey is often lost if he fails at any step.

I began my search for the right ammunition; only when I found it could I begin to think of how to pursue my target and when to deliver the devastating blow. Few people in positions of grandeur achieve their status without compromising themselves along the way—a kickback here or there, deceit in their professional dealings, using their influence for illicit personal gain. I hoped that Bette Collins, the only woman member of the Scions, was one of them.

Bette Collins' ascent to leadership of Innovative Policy and Implementation, or IPI for short, had been nothing short of meteoric. Born in California, she attended Stanford as an undergrad where she majored in political science, graduating summa cum laude, before attending Harvard's John F. Kennedy School of Government, studying national policy. It was there that she met her mentor, Proctor Banks, and hitched her wagon to his rising star. Actively recruited by the Manhattan Institute in 1979, Collins spent four years immersed in urban issues before deciding, according to her cover letter to the newly formed National Center for Policy Analysis, that her interests leaned more toward global affairs. She and Banks left together after ten years and formed IPI with Banks as its head and Collins his second in command.

It was when I read a tabloid headline from 2005, "Think Tank Head Dies in Fire," that things got interesting. As is often the case with tabloids, the story lacked substance; however, it provided enough substrate to dig deeper. By the end of two days' ferreting, I deduced that Collins had not only benefitted from Banks' death; she, and not Banks' wife of twenty-four years, had been with him in bed just prior to it. Police logs, newspaper clippings and insurance reports provided nothing damning when considered individually, but together they painted an impressionistic picture of a woman who, deliberately or not, hastened Banks' death and got away with it. When Banks' wife realized that she would not receive one cent of insurance money should her husband's death be deemed anything but an accident, she refused to authorize an autopsy, let alone a criminal investigation. Her husband drank a lot, and when he did, there was no rousing him from sleep, she told the cops. Her pride would not allow her to acknowledge the presence of another woman. He was alone, she said. Bingo.

Collins was named president of IPI within days of the fire and gained the ear of every right-wing politician and a firm hold on other body parts of several key political influencers as well. Collins' influence, whether intellectually or carnally acquired, grew such that with each election cycle, she raked in millions. Never married, but never lacking for male companionship, she was now a multi-billionaire with ample dirt on enough people that no one dared expose her for what she was.

She lived in Georgetown, ground zero of the country's power base, but also owned homes in Grand Cayman and Switzerland, where she enjoyed the benefits of offshore banking. Hers was a life of private jets, personal trainers, beauticians and nutritionists, plus a yacht that sat in the canals of Fort Lauderdale, its full-time crew ready to spring into action at her command. But Collins also had enemies who would salivate upon hearing the salacious details of her rise to power.

What I wanted to know was how much of this did the Scions know? Was she a member under duress or had I read her incorrectly? There was only one way to find out, but it meant matching wits with a brilliant, ambitious and potentially ruthless adversary. Great. It was time to pull another iron from the fire. I picked up the phone and called Tom. "Hey, stranger, how's it going with Baha?" I asked.

"Hey, Kat. Good to hear from you. Things here couldn't be better. Baha and I are hitting it off, I mean, really hitting it off." It was good to hear him so upbeat on several fronts. Not only was his personal happiness gratifying; maybe it would allow me to focus on Robbie and Adam.

"Would you mind if she stayed a while longer?" I hated to impose on Tom but couldn't guarantee my own safety, let alone Baha's.

"Mind? I would love it. We've already discussed it. She doesn't want to go back. She said that she feels free for the first time in her life."

"And you're okay with that?" His response was a resounding yes. Relieved, I asked, "Could I speak with her?"

"Sure, but I have to get her back to my friend's place soon. She's fine staying at the Hotel MacGregor during the day but is still very concerned about propriety. Let me go get her." After a few minutes, Baha's lyrical voice was speaking in my ear.

"Hi, Kat. How are you?" I told her I was fine, and she continued, "It's so nice to hear from you. Thank you for bringing me here. Tom is wonderful. He's taken me places and has cooked for me. We …"

"I'm glad. Don't mean to interrupt, but I need to ask you a couple of questions. Did you know that Adam has diabetes? Also, do you know a Dr. Khatib?"

"Khatib?" Her voice became strained with concern. "He attends the mosque where we used to go. He's one of Mustafa's friends. He's dangerous. Please stay away from him."

"He's the one who diagnosed Adam's diabetes."

"I don't trust him, Kat, nor should you. Adam did not mention diabetes to me the last time we spoke, about a few months ago."

"If I gave you Adam's number, would you call him and ask him about it? But if you do, please don't say where you are. Just that you are safe. Please don't mention Tom or me."

There was a long pause on the other end. Finally, she answered, but all emotion vacated her voice, leaving it hesitant and muted. "I, I guess I could. Do you think he would speak to me?"

Hearing her question was painful. How hard it must be for her to think her son didn't care about her. I replied, "I'm sure of it. He's very concerned about you. Please don't ask me how I know." I immediately added, "Whatever you do, don't stay on the phone longer than thirty seconds. We can't chance someone tracing the call."

"Is he in danger?" she asked, as any mother would.

"Remember what you overheard? I'm not sure how, but I have a vague suspicion that Adheem's plot may have something to do with Adam's diabetes diagnosis. If he knows that you've found out, maybe we can derail things and save Adam in the process. He may ask how you know, but please don't tell him. In fact, don't tell him anything. Please call me right after you've talked to him. Tom has my number."

She agreed and promised to call as soon as she could. Another item checked off my list.

The next day I was on a plane headed for D.C. to see Cam. I'd planted several red herrings throughout my apartment, as before, to throw Treadwell's moles off, but took some solace that he was out of town, the expectant father awaiting the complete delivery of his new party. Reluctantly, I put Scout in a kennel. It was just one of numerous concerns that clogged my head during the hour-long flight. Even seeing Cam in the pick-up area, his face beaming with conspiratorial enthusiasm, did little to console me. On the ride to his apartment, I filled him in on everything, but mentioned the two items that required his help, the Scions' silence and my scheme to confront Collins.

"Your confidence in me is flattering," he laughed, but the set of his jaw suggested that he thought I was nuts. Maybe I was.

As soon as we reached his apartment in Arlington, I pulled out my computer and pointed out the various ways I had tried to search the Scions. He asked me when I first noticed that I couldn't hack in, and I thought for a bit. "It was when I returned from Bethel, right before the governor's announcement. Interesting timing, now that I think about it."

"Hard to believe they wouldn't be commenting on that. You might be on to something."

"The way I see it, there's really two things we need to find out. First, we need to find where in cyberspace they're communicating. The second is potentially more concerning. Someone had to know that I was hacking in. Otherwise, why would they block me? The question is, who knew?"

"I know where you're going. You think it's Treadwell."

"No one else knew but you and him," I said.

He pressed his fingers together and raised them to his lips as he mulled over various possibilities. "Maybe there's a snitch in Treadwell's organization. You said they can track what you're doing, right" I nodded. "Either way, I think I can figure it out. I'll hack into the computers of the members we know and find out what websites they've been using. Maybe that will tell us something. What else have you got?"

I logged onto the DOD website and showed him the information about Raven Rock, pointing out various procedures, places and people within the facility. I pulled away from the screen and said, "Treadwell's right. It's impossible to penetrate. Even if I got in, I'm not sure I could get out—not with Robbie and Jermaine. That's why I'm contemplating another approach."

After further explanation of my straw man plan, he exclaimed, "You could get yourself killed!" His gaze returned to the screen, and he punched a few keys to home in on some of the details I had mentioned. "And you really think you can get Collins to cooperate?"

"I won't give her a choice." Seeing his face darken, I added, "Cam, if I don't try, I doubt that I'll ever see Robbie again." The sobriety of that single notion instilled a clarity that sliced through the tangle of thoughts short-circuiting my brain. "Let me show you something." I pulled up the recording of the Scions meeting that Treadwell had shared with me and showed it to him.

"Geez, Aunt Kat, you're in deep shit. If your plan doesn't work … ."

"But look at Collins. Her questions, her body language … I don't think she has the stomach for their methods. Either they have something on her, or she didn't know what she was getting into. We've got to find out what it is. If you can access their communications, we might just find out what it is and can use it to get to her."

I knew it was a long shot, and there was no way I would involve Cam beyond his computer work, but I had to do something. Treadwell wasn't helping other than unknowingly giving me the idea. At least I thought it might have been unintentional; with him, I was never sure. He said the only way to get someone out of Raven Rock was to broker a deal. He could be manipulating me the same way he moved his chess pieces around a board. But who better to target than someone like Collins who might not be fully committed to the Scions?

Cam said nothing as he punched the keys of his computer, so quickly, so adroitly, that I couldn't follow all he was doing. One page would appear only to be replaced by another, then another.

He'd type in some code and pull up an entirely new set of websites. He asked me for some of the Scions by name, and I rattled off the ones I knew. While he was occupied with that, I reviewed the search I had done on Collins—where she lived, the location of IPI, what kind of car picked her up—anything to help establish her routine.

A couple of hours later, I was in the kitchen, trying to find something edible when I heard Cam shout, "Sonofabitch." I raced to his office and looked at the screen. It was black. "Oh, sorry, Aunt Kat," he said, seemingly embarrassed by his outburst. "They crashed my computer. They've got this thing buried behind more firewalls than I've ever seen." Seeing my dismay, he added, "That doesn't mean I can't break in. It just means it's going to take some time."

A sense of dread consumed me as my renewed fear for Cam's safety emerged. "They can't tell you're trying to hack, can they?"

"If they're monitoring things, they might be able to figure out someone's trying to hack in, but they won't know who," he answered, while typing some more.

I placed my hand on his and said, "Please stop. Treadwell thinks that I went to D.C. last week when I really went to Bethel. If he is connected to the Scions in some way, he may be able to figure out I came to see you. I can't allow you to keep doing this. If anything were to happen … "

"I'm not using my account. I'm using one that belongs to Russian intelligence, FIS." His smile seemed simultaneously innocent and mischievous, like a little boy who stole the last cookie and blamed it on his big brother.

"That's supposed to make me feel better?" I checked my watch and said, "I've got to get to Collins' townhouse in a few hours if I'm going to get that surveillance camera. It's the only way to monitor her schedule and see who visits her. Let's get something to eat besides the biology experiments in your refrigerator. Maybe you can tell me why my plan won't work." He laughed lightly, but

I could see the strain in his face. There was something he wasn't telling me. We both logged off, and Cam locked his laptop in a safe. While he was busy, I removed my home surveillance camera from my suitcase and threw it in my purse. Cam slung my computer case over his shoulder, knowing I'd never leave it behind.

We decided to walk to a restaurant half a mile away. It was a pleasantly warm spring day, though the sun had begun its retreat in the west. We could have left our coats at home. Commuters were making their way home in cars and on foot. I watched each one pass by, looking for any sign of familiarity or danger. It was second nature now.

We walked in silence for a couple of blocks until I asked, "So what is it that you're not telling me, Cam? I've known you too long,"

"Geez, you sound like my mother." He walked a bit more before saying, "It's just that something's weird about that website. Whoever put it in place really knows what they're doing. None of our government agencies has encryption like that, and I don't know any businesses that do either."

"Except maybe one."

"Treadwell? But why?"

"Think about it. I suggested that you should work for him, and he dismissed the idea. Maybe he didn't want you to find something in his files that I couldn't. I was blocked from the Scions' websites right before the announcement of his new party. If I was able to access their new communication channels, I might be able to confirm it."

"But why would he show you that tape from their meeting?"

"I know; it doesn't make sense. Maybe he was setting me up, but his assistant said something that haunts me. He said that Treadwell would make a great president. This may be a stretch, but what if Treadwell is still a member of the Scions, and his ultimate goal is to be president? He would have many legislators in his camp which would give him an enormous amount of power and, by extension, the Scions as well."

We kept walking while Cam pondered my speculation until we reached a small Thai restaurant squeezed between a couple of shops and offices. He asked if I would mind Thai again. Never. It was my favorite, and time was tight. Lights were low in the room, but still, gold statues of Buddha could be seen against bright splashes of red and gold on the walls. Luk Thung music, with its distinctive vibrato and use of western instruments, played in the background. We took a table in the back, under an arch adorned with electric lanterns, which partially hid us from the other customers. The waiter handed us some menus and filled our glasses with water.

After perusing the menu, I said, "I think I hear red curry shrimp calling my name. You?"

"I'm feeling a bit more adventurous. You must be rubbing off on me," Cam replied, trying to keep things light. "Pad Kee Mao with a bottle of Singha. That should do it." He closed the menu and continued our previous conversation. "It doesn't compute, Aunt Kat. The Scions already have a lot of power. Shoot, they practically run the country as it is. Why would Treadwell go to this much trouble if he wasn't legit?"

"Haven't figured that part out yet, but when I told him I was blocked, he didn't seem surprised at all. You would think he'd be concerned that they were onto me. There's another thing. When Tom spoke of Treadwell in the old days, he said that Treadwell was too radical, that he wanted to blow everything up, total anarchy. Treadwell supports Adam and didn't want me checking into his father. What if Treadwell knows about Adheem's plot, and will be waiting in the wings when it happens?"

"Then why would he give you access to all that he has? He knows how good a data miner you are." Seeing me shake my head, unable to answer him, he continued, "Have you even considered the possibility that he's on the level?"

"A little, maybe not enough," I responded. Inwardly, I was thinking that there were too many instances where I couldn't understand his actions or, in the case of freeing Robbie, inaction.

"Have you been up front with him?" he asked, before scooping up the last bit of his meal and washing it down with a slug of beer.

"I'm afraid to. I feel like I have no privacy as it is."

Cam nodded in acknowledgement, but asked, "Isn't he trying to keep you safe? Hasn't he paid for all your needs? He explained why he couldn't rescue Robbie. It's not like he's superhuman. Your father, Ben, Tom—they all believed in him. Why don't you?"

"It's a gut thing, I guess. I can't explain it." Wanting to change the topic, I continued, "Time is getting short. Can I go over that plan with you?"

Despite Cam's desperate objections, we finished the meal outlining the steps I would take and what I needed from him. I wiped my mouth and placed my hands on the table. "It's dark out. I've got to go. Let's get the check."

"You sure you want to do this?" he asked. "If so, I'm going with you."

"No, Cam. I'm not going to put you in any more danger. I'll text when I'm done and on my way back to your place."

He protested once more, but I was resolute. We agreed to leave the restaurant separately. I grabbed my computer case and, once outside the restaurant, hailed a cab. As we drove away, I saw Cam exit the restaurant and head toward his apartment, shoulders stooped and head down, apparently deep in thought. Then I saw something else. Across the street, illuminated by a streetlamp, a man was speaking with three others. I'd recognize that face anywhere. Beau Foster. He didn't seem to notice Cam, but his presence could not be an accident—not in a large city with 1600 restaurants and not when it came to me.

Had Beau seen us enter the restaurant together? I quickly texted a warning to Cam and prayed that Beau and his buddies would not follow him home. Should I go back? If I did, what could I do? How did he find me? A hundred more questions popped up like whack-a-moles, and I couldn't beat them down with answers. Finally, a text reply flashed on my phone. Cam was home and saw no one lurking outside. I slumped back in the seat, relieved. We were okay for now, but how long would that last? Did I dare return to Cam's and place him in further jeopardy?

The cabbie pulled to the curb two blocks away from Collins' townhouse. It was time to complete the task at hand. I would deal with Cam's predicament later. I paid the cabbie, scanned right, then left, and walked briskly to the spot I had identified through Google Earth. It was a cluster of shrubs across the street from where she lived. The night cloaked the area in darkness, and few people passed by on the street.

I ducked behind the shrubs and pulled the camera from my purse. I crouched for several minutes to ensure that my presence was not noticed by anyone. Confident that I was undetected, I positioned the camera to allow a clear view of the front door. I checked the view on my cellphone. Perfect. If my computer search was correct, Collins should be arriving shortly. I decided to wait a few more minutes on the chance that I might spot her and also to get a feel for the rhythm of the street. Maybe I was just stalling until I figured out what to do about Beau, a new variable in my personal multifactorial equation.

It was just before nine when the svelte, stylishly-clad think tank member walked arm-in-arm with a dark-haired man who held her close. They seemed to be without a care in the world, laughing, smiling, as if their only concern was how quickly they could reach Collins' apartment and let nature takes its course. I quickly snapped a close-up of him on my cellphone and sent it to Cam who could use facial recognition software to determine his identity.

Within minutes, a light appeared on the ground floor. A window framed a silhouette of the two of them, locked in a long embrace, which eventually disappeared, only to be repeated in a second-floor bedroom, and then the entire apartment went black.

After a brief check of the area near me, I emerged from the bushes and brushed my pants to free them of pine needles and dirt. I walked a couple of blocks and called Cam. He picked up on the first ring.

"I've been worried sick, Aunt Kat," he said.

"I'm fine. What about you?"

"Things here are fine. I did a check on that photo you sent me. Your pal rubs elbows with some high flyers. It's Washburn, the head of the SEC. By the way, he's married. Looks like Collins is an extracurricular activity."

"Good. Another piece of ammunition. I'm going to stay in town tonight as a precaution. If Beau is watching your place, I don't want him to link you with me, and I certainly don't want to waltz in if he's waiting there. Could you send my suitcase here? I don't know how long I'll be staying."

"Uh, sure, if that's what you want, but there's something you should know ... ."

The ominous sound of his voice made me impatient. "What is it, Cam?"

At first, he was silent. I prodded some more. "I'm really worried about you, Aunt Kat. I broke through the Scions' firewall. They're meeting again in two weeks, this time in London. Collins is going too." He paused once more before adding reluctantly, "You and Treadwell are on their agenda."

Chapter 21

Beau's menacing face invaded my dreams and loomed above my hotel bed like a taunting specter who remained all night and robbed me of much-needed sleep. How had he found me and why didn't he pursue me? Was he intentionally letting me know he had tracked me down or could it have been coincidence?

Room service could not deliver my coffee fast enough and when it arrived, I savored it like it was the first I'd had in months. I checked Collins' house. Washburn had left around eleven p.m., and the livery service picked her up at eight this morning. Then I checked Zuabi's cab conversations. The one with Adam jumped out.

"Father, I've heard from mother. You're lucky." He sounded angry.

"Where is she?" Adheem snapped back.

"I asked, but she would only say that she was safe. Why would she say that? What did you do to her?" Hearing no response, he continued, "She told me that she heard I had diabetes, I asked her how she knew, but she only said that she was worried about me. Did you tell her?" Now his anger was laced with an accusatory tone.

"Of course not. The fewer people who know, the better. What was your reply?"

"I told her not to worry, that it was recently diagnosed, but under control."

"Don't they trace calls to Congressmen? You could find out where she is."

"And deliver her back to you? No way. You will not hurt her again. Besides, she hung up before the trace would kick in. She's being coached by someone, I'm sure of it."

"But who? Who knows where she is? No one knows about your blood sugar but you, me, Mustafa, and Khatib." The strain in Adheem's voice indicated that he was clearly agitated but seemed less concerned about Adam than his plan. "Maybe your benefactor. Maybe he's the one who has her and mentioned it to her. I knew that this new party was a mistake. I warned you of such things."

"Treadwell? He's the one who made my appointment possible. It would have taken me years to get elected to Congress. His ambition makes him blind to minor details like diabetes. Besides, my health record is public. Anyone could look it up," Adam explained impatiently.

"But your mother wouldn't know that." Adheem thought a bit before adding, "If anyone mentions it to you, be wary of them. I mean it, Adam. This could ruin everything we've worked for. We're so close. If she calls again, do whatever you can to keep her on the line. You must find her. I'm, uh, worried about her."

The line went dead. Relieved that I heard the conversation before my interview with Adam, I continued to listen. Within seconds, Adheem placed another call on speaker phone and told an unknown person about this new wrinkle. The detached voice said that they would have to speed up the plan somehow, before someone figured it out.

My enhanced paranoia made me jump at the sound of a knock on the door. It was the bellhop delivering my suitcase that Cam sent over. He placed it on the bed and received a nice tip. Before getting dressed for the day, I did one last search. Although I had seen the summary of Adam's physical, I had not checked actual laboratory values. These were a bit more difficult to find, but persistence and Cam's tutelage paid off. Both Adam's HbA1c, at

5.5%, and a blood glucose of 87 mg/dL were well within normal range. He was no more diabetic than I.

I called Adam's assistant, provided my fake name and told her I was a reporter with *The Alternative*, Treadwell's media outlet. The mere mention of Treadwell's name did the trick. I scored an eight a.m. interview for tomorrow. He had to be in chambers for a vote at nine, so it would be short, but maybe long enough. I asked when he arrived in the morning and she proudly announced, "He's in by eight every day, rain or shine."

With a day to prepare and my mind a kaleidoscope that seemed to change design with every random thought, I pulled on my running clothes, laced my Asics, and set out for the Washington Mall. Nothing would restore reason and provide a fresh perspective more than a run around the monuments to honorable men and fallen heroes. I punched Pandora on my cellphone, plugged in my ear buds and selected the Classic Rock station, which somehow made Robbie feel closer than the seventy miles that separated us. It might as well have been a million.

Passing the various museums of the Smithsonian, I jogged toward the east end of the Mall and headed toward the Capitol. The two sets of steps led up to the main entrance, but only tourists seemed to be entering there. To my left was the Rayburn Building, where Adam's office was located. A couple of guards stood outside. I jogged over to them, identified myself as a reporter who was to meet with Zuabi the next day and asked about the procedure for entry. One of the Capitol policemen described the security measures in place and told me what kinds of things were not allowed.

There are very few advantages to being a woman in her sixties, but one is that no one expects any nefarious intent. Once the guard checked the list and saw my name, he became chatty, asking me if I had met Adam and saying what a nice man he was. I told him that I had interviewed him in Boston and was doing a story on his transition to the national stage. I learned that Adam arrived on the underground train that links the various buildings in the

Capitol complex, not the main entrance, and that the train was for the exclusive use of Congressional members, their staffs, and invited visitors. I encouraged him further with my own trumped up accolades of Adam—man of the people, dedicated public servant, yada, yada, yada, and finished by saying, "Massachusetts' loss, the country's gain. I hope he's feeling better. He was having a rocky time with his diabetes."

"Yeah, he never goes anywhere without his insulin, hard candy, and a bottle of water. Good thing he's a Congressman. He'd never get through regular security with that," he said. "We're used to it now." I thanked him and moved on, having learned more in a five-minute chat than I could have in five days on the computer.

I allowed thoughts of Adam to simmer on my brain's back burner while I mentally transitioned to Bette Collins. I had committed illegal acts before, either because of my job or to ensure my survival, but nothing like I was contemplating now as a private citizen. I needed to be alone with her, in a place where she could not sound an alarm or call in the police, where I would have the upper hand. I had to arrange things so that she would follow through. If she did, and Robbie was released, I had to ensure that he would not be followed and that we could safely connect somehow. I had an idea but wasn't sure I had the guts to carry it out.

I had reached the Washington Monument on the far end of the Mall. Now I took a left toward the Jefferson Memorial, thinking of the many quotes ascribed to him. "A little rebellion now and then is a good thing," or "When the government fears the people, there is liberty; when people fear the government, there is tyranny." What would our country's architect of both buildings and the U.S. government have thought about the Scions or, for that matter, Treadwell's Constitution Party?

I turned right and ran by the Tidal Basin and the Lincoln Memorial and headed back, passing the Ellipse behind the White House. Was that really Treadwell's goal—to be his party's nominee one day and ultimately the most powerful man in the world?

197

There was so much to learn. It was time to take a new tack with him. If we kept butting heads, I'd learn nothing. I needed to regain his trust, even if I couldn't reciprocate.

I had almost reached my starting point when my phone rang. It was Baha.

"I spoke to Adam," she said. "He told me that his diabetes was recently diagnosed and that's why I didn't know about it. He was very curious as to who told me and where I was. He asked several times. He said that he wanted to move me to a safe place, away from Adheem."

"What did you tell him?"

"Nothing, but then he said something odd. Something like, 'I now can do what I must.'" Her voice was contorted with pain. "Kat, I'm worried. Now that he knows I'm safe, I think he means to obey his father's will."

I could only imagine how terrified she was, knowing that Adheem intended to make a martyr of his son. "Did you ask him what he meant?"

"No, my time was up. I didn't even have a chance to say good-bye."

I could tell that she was in a fragile state and didn't want to distress her further. "Perhaps you can call him again and tell him what you know and how you feel. Maybe you can change his mind. Let me see what I can find out."

"Yes, yes, I will do that, but you must be safe as well. Please call soon."

I promised that I would, but inwardly wondered how a person could compartmentalize his thoughts the way Adam was. He seemed to be enjoying his new-found stature yet was prepared to sacrifice it all for Adheem's plan. I had to find out how.

I finished my route and returned to the hotel where I logged on to find the location of Collins' livery service. I was jotting down the address when Cam called on my secure phone. I told him about my morning's conversations with Baha and the Capitol policeman. Then I told him about my plan for confronting Collins.

"I don't need to tell you how risky that is, Aunt Kat. What if the other driver shows up? What if Collins calls the livery service? What if she agrees to help you and then reneges? You will have exposed yourself for nothing. How will she get Robbie and Jermaine out? Even if she does, how do you know that someone won't be waiting to knock them off?" By this point, his voice had risen several octaves.

"I know, I know. It's a huge risk. I have to work on some of the details. When I have it set, I'll run it by you. Did you find anything out?"

"You bet." He cleared his throat and began, "Collins is the newest member of the Scions. It's almost like she's their Mata Hari, entertaining U.S. government officials and communicating what she's discovered to the Scions, so they can benefit. What's interesting is that she told Hughes she no longer wanted to play their game. Hughes told her that she didn't have a choice, that they would leak information that could ruin her."

"What kind of information?" I asked, although I was thinking about Banks' death.

"Don't know yet, but it must be pretty bad if she's willing to continue."

I took a moment to contemplate what Cam had told me. Was Banks's death, Collins' dalliance with the head of the SEC, and this latest news enough to blackmail her into helping me? "Can you give me printouts of what you found?"

"Sure, I'll bring them by tonight, say seven?"

"That would be great. Use evasive measures in case someone's watching you. With Beau on the loose ... ."

"Funny you should mention him. I found out who he works for—George Bradley, the oil magnate, a member of the Scions, who has holdings in the Mideast, Russia and the U.S. Bradley brought Beau on board after he got out of jail, and it seems like his duties keep expanding. Online, he's known as 'the facilitator,' a euphemism for hitman as far as I can tell."

Given my own experience with Beau, I wasn't surprised by Cam's findings but pushed for something more concrete. "Was Beau connected with the death of Senator Barnes?"

"All indications suggest that he was, but nothing came of it. There are other mysterious deaths, but I can go over those with you later." He said this dismissively, but then his voice became sharp and ominous. "There is one other thing you should know. The Scions like the current world order. They are making lots of money and have a hand in every power base on the globe. They are not happy with Treadwell's new party or Treadwell himself. If they lose influence in the U.S. because of it, all hell will break lose. You know that meeting I told you about? There's an email from Johnson to Hughes that was sent within hours of the Boston announcement and in it, he wrote, 'We'll have to discuss the Treadwell situation.'"

I didn't speak right away. I was too busy thinking about the implications of Cam's words. Maybe Treadwell wasn't one of them after all. "That explains why Treadwell is on the agenda, but why me?"

"I was afraid you'd ask that." I could hear him take a deep breath and could almost see him blowing it out through puffed cheeks. "They think that Rob still has some information that he's not telling them. Nothing they've tried has worked. They think they can get him to talk if they find you and use you to get to him. The fact that Beau is nearby can only mean one thing. He's after you, Aunt Kat."

I had known that Beau's presence outside the restaurant may not have been a coincidence, but this news struck me like lightening. "Cam, don't come over. They may be watching you, which may be why they didn't pursue you before. Email me what you have. It will be safer for both of us. I don't know how he found me. I used the ID Treadwell gave me. Damn. Leave town, Cam. Go somewhere safe. I'll be in touch."

At seven-thirty a.m. I entered the Rayburn Office Building, a modified H shape with a marble façade that sat upon a pink granite base. I walked to the security station and placed my bag on the conveyer belt, put my cellphone and watch in a dish, and handed an all-business, fortyish guard my ID. After glancing at it, he looked me up on the list of visitors and provided directions to Zuabi's office.

While I was retrieving my things from the scanner belt, another guard approached the security checkpoint from the direction of the underground train. The name on his badge was Ghauth Malak. I asked if he knew whether Zuabi had arrived. This guard was younger, thinner, with dark eyes and an olive complexion who spoke in clipped sentences like many from other countries. He told me that he had just seen Zuabi coming in from the parking garage and checked him through. I could feel his gaze upon me as I walked past the statue of Sam Rayburn, a former Speaker of the House and the building's namesake. As I entered the elevator, I wondered why the guard's voice seemed familiar.

I left the elevator on the third floor and found Zuabi's office. A young black-haired woman greeted me and introduced herself as Su Ye Chen, Zuabi's intern, and explained that she was filling in for his assistant who was out that day. Seeing an opportunity to capitalize on her inexperience, I chatted her up a bit: where was she was from? what were her career ambitions? how did she like D.C.? When I thought I might have gained her trust, I told her I was having some issues and asked there was a nearby restroom, one that was private, that I might use. She led me to Zuabi's restroom, which was adjacent to his private kitchen, and left to get me some coffee. No assistant would ever leave a visitor alone in a congressman's office. I was in luck.

I took the opportunity to ensure that my wig was perfectly placed and did a little snooping. Six insulin vials sat on the shelf of the medicine cabinet but otherwise, nothing was out of the ordinary. I met Zuabi's assistant in the kitchen and asked if there was any milk. She opened the refrigerator, and I peeked over her back and saw several more insulin vials, a six-pack of water bottles, and some soda bottles. They were not sugar-free.

We walked toward Zuabi's desk, and she offered me a chair. After she left, I scanned the room and saw some built-in file cabinets, a picture of John F. Kennedy on the wall, a bowl of candy on a table, a picture of his girlfriend on his desk, and many books. I pulled one from the shelf and opened it. It was hollow and empty, as was the next one. I was about to pull out another when I heard Zuabi's voice in the next room. I quickly returned to my chair and dug through my purse for my cellphone when Zuabi walked in.

"Good morning, Ms. Ferguson. I hope you haven't been waiting too long." His manner was professional, but his eyes were like ebony, and his voice measured. He was carrying a Styrofoam box and a cup of coffee which he placed on his desk.

I made every effort to be friendly and nonconfrontational, which was difficult knowing what I did. "No, not at all. I'm early. Ms. Chen was kind enough to let me in. If you would like to eat your breakfast, I can wait outside."

"If you don't mind watching me eat, that won't be necessary. I don't have much time. I'd like to review a couple of items before our session at nine." He opened a desk drawer and pulled a couple of sugar packets out and emptied them into his coffee.

I pointed to my cellphone and asked if he minded me taping our conversation. He waved his hand, indicating he was fine with it. "I feel like you and I got off to a bad start. Clean slate, okay?" He nodded while he opened the box and cut the syrup-drenched pancakes and sausage into bite-sized chunks and shoveled one into his mouth. "I'm doing a story on the members of the new Constitutional Party—how it's impacted their ability to collaborate with and influence Democrats and Republicans and, in your case, how the transition from the state level to the national level has been."

He swallowed and took a sip of coffee before answering. "It's going well. I have a lot to learn to be sure, but my colleagues have been helpful."

"Even the members of the traditional parties?" I asked.

"I think we're all still figuring out what it means. My priorities haven't changed. I'm still fiscally conservative and want to maintain a strong defense, but I'm also trying to create opportunities so the average person isn't mired in debt, can find a job, go to college, learn a trade, and can live their life as they choose. The point is to find common ground and eliminate the gridlock that has strangled progress."

I asked him for some details, which he freely provided, and we moved onto several other topics. He seemed happy to have a forum to communicate his message, and I was a willing conduit. With each question, he became warmer, friendlier, and seemed less defensive than when I first arrived. Our time was growing short, so I finished with one last question, "You've lived in New England all of your life. Your family is there and, I presume, your girlfriend," pointing to the picture. "How has the transition been on a personal level?"

He smiled, as though he appreciated the question, and looked at the photo on his desk. In an almost dreamy voice, he said, "Meghan is moving to D.C. in two weeks." Then his tone changed. "Her parents and mine are not thrilled, you know, the religion thing, but maybe by then we can convince them that our happiness is more important." He took another bite and thought for a bit while chewing. "Could we keep that last part off the record?" I nodded, and he added, "Thanks. Don't want to make matters worse. Let me just say that the transition has been generally good."

"Believe me, I understand. I once married someone to please

my father, and I regretted it the rest of my life. I'll email you a draft of the article, if you'd like. Change anything you want. This series is meant to help people get to know you; it's not an exposé." I pretended to turn off the cell phone and commented, "Other than your personal life, your parents must be proud."

He handed me his business card with the gold seal of the United States at the top. Underneath, his name appeared in bright blue letters: Adam B. Zuabi, Member of Congress, Second District, Massachusetts. Contact information for his Boston and Washington offices was to either side, and his email address was at the bottom center. As I looked it over, he said, "My father always pushed me. Nothing is ever enough for him. His goals for me are different from mine. In some ways, I'm glad to be away from him, but unfortunately, that also means that I don't get to see my mother. Can you understand?"

"Completely. It sounds like your father and mine were cut from the same cloth," I answered as I began to pack my things together, trying not to be overtly intrigued by his remarks.

"In some ways, yes. In others, definitely not." He shut the breakfast box, threw it into the trash, and rose to shake my hand. "It's been a pleasure, Ms. Ferguson. Please stop by anytime."

I thanked him, rose, and shook his hand. He told me to call him Adam. I smiled warmly and asked, "One last thing, Adam, could you please tell me where I might get a bottle of water? My morning run has made me really thirsty and it's a long trip back."

He held both palms out and shrugged his shoulders. "I wish I had some to give you. There's a vending machine down the hall or you might try the cafeteria."

I thanked him once more and left, thinking he was either stingy or hiding something in those bottles I saw in the fridge. As I walked down the hall to the elevator, I processed what I had learned during the last twenty-four hours. If my suspicions were correct, nothing was imminent. Adam was still on board with his father's scheme, but I had an inkling that he was faltering. The question was, could his commitment be eliminated in time?

Chapter 22

The cab dropped me off at Lincoln Livery near DuPont Circle, and I walked to a corrugated-roofed building where a balding, corpulent man sat at a desk, watching ESPN on a wall-mounted TV. He was dressed in black Dockers and a white shirt, both craving an iron. His loosened tie freed his neck to spill over his chest. A limp black jacket was thrown over a hook on the wall. A buzzer sounded as I entered the door, and he quickly donned the jacket, tightened his tie, and hiked up his sagging pants.

"Sorry, Miss. I'm just a dispatcher. We don't usually get foot traffic here. I wasn't expecting … ."

I held up my hands to reassure him. "Please, no worries. I'm hoping to arrange transportation for my boss. He's very particular—that's why I came in person. He needs to be picked up at his home at nine a.m. sharp Monday through Friday, unless he's out of town, and would have to be driven home at seven p.m. Would you be able to do that?"

He replied, "Sure thing," and proceeded to explain that all their cars were Lincolns, hence the name Lincoln Livery. He paused and smiled as though waiting for me to appreciate the play on words. I pleasantly complied, which provided enough encouragement for him to continue, stating that the standard model was the MKZ, but they had larger models available, if necessary. I asked to see the sedans, repeating that my boss was very picky, and he led me through the spotless garage, proudly explaining that they performed their own maintenance to ensure dependable service. We exited through the door to a lot in which a dozen black cars were parked; each had a Lincoln Livery sign with a decal of the Lincoln Memorial attached to the rear right window.

We circled the cars, and he proudly described the various amenities Lincoln Livery offered as part of its service. I feigned interest, adding that my boss was a businessman who worked with many high-ranking government officials, so it had to be perfect. Then I asked if he had a brochure that I could show my boss. While on the far side of a car, I pressed the "send" button on my phone so that it would dial the phone at the desk. We both heard the ring, and he excused himself to answer the call, saying that he would bring a brochure back with him. While he was gone, I opened one of the car doors, grabbed the Lincoln Livery sign, and stuffed it in my bag.

By the time he returned, mumbling something about a wrong number, I was standing near the garage and told him that I thought these cars would work just fine. He handed me the brochure which I thumbed through and asked about the drivers, explaining that, because of my boss's position, the driver had to be above reproach and, in fact, would have to clear a background check.

He nodded his head in understanding and acknowledged that many of his drivers had gone through this. "We transport lobbyists, politicians, CEOs ... you know, the movers and shakers. What does your boss do?"

"I'm not at liberty to give you his name just yet, only after the deal is signed, but I can tell you he's head of a very influential think tank here in D.C." I spoke in hushed tones, as though I was sharing a deep, dark secret, in hopes of gaining his confidence.

"No problem," he repeated, in an equally discrete manner. "We have another client who is a member of one of those think tanks. Maybe you've heard of her. Bette Collins. Our driver, Steve, takes her to and from work every day, well, except Fridays. She doesn't go in on Fridays."

"Bette Collins?" I responded, trying to sound impressed. "Well, if you're good enough for her, you're good enough for us." I paused before asking, "What happens if your driver can't make it, you know, because of illness or something?"

"I, or one of the other dispatchers, call to explain the situation and tell our client who will be driving instead. We don't want our clients to be surprised or concerned. You know, some of them are quite powerful, and their security is important."

"Excellent. I will share that with my boss. He'll be pleased to know about your high standards. Do you have a business card?"

He checked his pockets. "Sorry, it's inside. Come with me."

We walked back to the desk where the business card for each driver sat in a box on a shelf to the right of the desk. He handed me his with a picture of his much younger self. I asked him if he could draw up an agreement for my boss to sign, and while he went into a small office behind the desk, I searched the boxes for a business card with the name Steve on it. There was only one, and I slipped it into my pocket. I checked the other cards and saw the names of three dispatchers, one of whom was a woman named Mary Sanchez. A stroke of luck. I took that one too.

"Here ya go," he announced as he ambled back to the desk. "Have your boss look this over. If he's okay with it, just send it back, and we'll be happy to assist you." He handed me the form, and I pretended to read it.

"I most certainly will. You've been very helpful, uh ... ." I looked at his card.

"My name is Charles, Charles Finch, you know, like the bird, but I go by Slim." He chuckled with mild chagrin.

"Thank you, Slim. I'll be in touch." I began to walk out the door, then turned. "I'm curious," I said. "I don't want to seem like I'm prying, and if you can't answer, I'll understand, but does Ms. Collins ride in an MKZ? My boss is very competitive and would want to ride in a limo of equal prestige. You know how these power types are." I rolled my eyes, trying to elicit his empathy.

He smirked and replied, "Do I ever. The stories I could tell you." He laughed and shook his head. "Come over here, and I can show you." We went to the window, and he pointed. "She rides in that car, right there. Just like the one I put in your contract. You can assure your boss that he'll be riding in style." Another chuckle.

Once again, being a middle-aged woman was an advantage. He didn't suspect a thing and told me way too much. I thanked him again and left, silently reciting the car's license plate number in my head. When I was out of sight, I entered the number into my phone. Being in my sixties had disadvantages as well, one of them being that I no longer trusted my short-term memory.

At the hotel, I withdrew $400 from the ATM in the lobby, as I had every day for the last two months, trying to amass as much cash as possible. I rode the elevator to my floor and, once inside my room, looked up various rental agencies to find a black Lincoln MKZ that I could use the next day. Eventually, I found a place in Alexandria that rented a Lincoln that was identical to what Steve drove. I told the agent that I would be by later in the day to pick it up.

Then I called Cam. "Where are you? Did you leave as I asked?" I tried, unsuccessfully, to keep from sounding distraught.

He replied that he hadn't yet but would soon. I reiterated my plea and reminded him of the potential danger he was in. He assured me that he was fine. I made him promise to be gone by the end of the week, if not before. "Is that why you called?" he asked, trying to move on from the subject.

"That, and I want to tell you about my visit with Adam Zuabi. I think I've figured it out, Cam, at least part of it. Adam's diabetes is a smokescreen which enables him to bring insulin vials and water bottles to his office. I think there's a guard who lets him pass through with both. I couldn't place his voice right away, but I'm sure he's the one that Adheem speaks to over the phone, and the one who went to the women's shelter to find Baha."

Cam grunted. "That's not much to go on. Besides, Zuabi's in Massachusetts. The guard works in D.C. Why would he ask him to find his wife?"

"Still working that out, but regarding Adam, no diabetic would eat what he eats, and when I asked for some water, he told me to use the vending machine or go to the cafeteria when he had six bottles in his refrigerator. Besides, some of the insulin was on a shelf in his bathroom when it should be kept cool. Also, a couple of the books on his shelf were fakes with compartments inside. I only had time to look at a couple, but I'm sure there's more. If he's stockpiling whatever is in the vials and water bottles, he could hide them there."

I heard Cam whistle on the other end. "What do you think it is? A liquid explosive of some sort?"

"That's my guess," I answered, all the while browsing online for stores that sold men's suits. "Adheem's plan will make Adam a martyr, which means Adam will die when the bomb goes off, suggesting that he plans to detonate while in the chamber. The question is when and where. Blowing up the Rayburn Building would only kill a third of the representatives. That's not enough of a prize, to hear Adheem talk. I think Adam means to blow up something bigger. Maybe the Capitol. Depending on when he does it, he could take down the government."

The line was silent for a while, long enough that I asked Cam if he was still there. When I heard him reply, I added, "Think, Cam. When is the entire government assembled? I mean every-one—the Congress, the President, the Vice President, the Supreme Court justices, the Joint Chiefs of Staff, the Cabinet."

"The inauguration, but that isn't for a couple of years." He thought deeply and then uttered, "Shit. The State of the Union address. Do you think that's it?"

"I'm positive. Adam's girlfriend is moving to D.C. in October. I think he wants to enjoy life for a bit before martyrdom. He rides the underground train to the Capitol every day. That would give him the opportunity to stash the liquid explosive somewhere inside. Once he's in the Rayburn Building, no one would bother him for a bottle of what they assume is water. He could make some excuse about his diabetes if they did. The fact that he wouldn't offer me any of his water is suspicious to say the least."

"Why don't you bust him now? Wouldn't that be safer than waiting?" Cam asked.

"We have until January. If Adam thinks we're onto him, he may go for a smaller prize, like his own office building. I can't risk outing myself just yet. If I report this, I'm dead. If I'm out of the picture, Robbie and Jermaine will die too."

"Couldn't you report this anonymously?" Cam asked, almost pleadingly.

"Nothing is anonymous anymore. You know that better than I. We need more proof, and I need to be able to prove Adheem is behind it. The evidence you and I have collected has been obtained illegally."

"But it's still evidence." Neither of us spoke for several seconds, long enough that I could hear Cam sigh in exasperation. Then he asked, "Will you tell Treadwell?"

"Probably, but I need to get my hands on one of those vials and find out what's inside. I didn't want to risk taking one. He probably knows the exact number he has. We can't screw this up, Cam. It's going to take Adam a while to accumulate enough of the liquid to blow up the Capitol. We need to find out who's supplying him with the explosive. We need evidence against his father and that guard, if he is indeed involved. If we don't pull this out by the roots, it will grow back, but in a different form, in a different place."

We continued to argue until Cam reluctantly relented. Pressing my luck a bit further, I asked, "One last thing. Can you find Collins' cell phone number? I need you to call her Wednesday morning at seven a.m. Say that you're "Slim" from Lincoln Livery and that Steve will not be able to pick her up, but that another, equally qualified and trustworthy driver will meet her at eight a.m. sharp."

Once again, he grudgingly agreed. I told him I had to go but reminded him to be careful. The last thing I wanted was for Cam to experience Beau's hospitality as I had. Cam said something about the pot calling the kettle black. After we hung up, I checked the video of Collins' house on my phone. Steve had picked her up promptly at eight that morning. His limo had the same plate number as I had noted, and he wore a black suit. I left the hotel on a quest to find the same.

The suit was a little large in the shoulders and waist but would do. A sardonic grin creased my face when I realized that it hung on me like Adheem's had when the governor announced Treadwell's new party. The next item on the agenda was to buy a car. I needed a more anonymous means of transit than a commercial jet to escape Washington and Beau, but that would have to wait until the next day. Night had descended, and streetlights dotted the road below my window. Horns still sounded, and an occasional voice could be heard above the din. Despite being surrounded by hundreds of thousands of people, I felt very alone and, if I was honest with myself, very scared.

I thought back to that day in Nevis. It seemed like eons ago when Robbie left to divert Beau, and Nate flew me to safety. Nate said I could call him if I needed him. Josh had said the same thing. It would be nice to have someone around. I missed Scout more than ever, but someday, he would leave me too. Baha accepted what the world had thrown at her, and now she was happy. I envied her. What I wouldn't give to be somewhere with my special someone, away from the mess I was in.

The anxiety I felt knowing I had put Cam at risk gnawed at me too, like I was doubling down on the guilt I felt about his father's death. I couldn't let anything happen to Cam. Sure, he was bright enough, but he was alone as well, and I wasn't sure how savvy he was when it came to the world of the street where evil did not discriminate—especially as the stakes grew. Maybe I could convince him to leave Washington with me.

Still, I had to take the risk. I had to confront Collins and convince her to help me. Otherwise, I had no hope of ever seeing Robbie again. When Treadwell mentioned brokering a deal with the Scions, had he done so hoping I'd take the bait? If he was sincere in his aspirations for a new party to right the ship of state, his loss might be even greater than mine. Was it a coincidence that the Scions had us both in their sights? Had they figured out that I was working for him? Josh or any one of the men who escorted me to and from work could have told them.

I wanted to be back in Nevis with Robbie, not in this damned hotel room where the walls crept closer together while the bed grew far too large.

The rental Lincoln was immaculate, looked every bit like the limos I had seen at the livery service, and had that unmistakable new car smell. Importantly, it had door locks that could be operated by the driver. With its plush seats, high-end sound system and a small bar in the back seat, I felt like I was driving a living room more than a car. Once back at the hotel, I parked it in the garage. Check.

Then I took a cab to a nearby Audi dealership that had advertised certified pre-owned A4's for sale. Through one of the websites, I had obtained a price to avoid any haggles and minimize my time with the salesman. After a brief test drive to assure the acceleration was as advertised, I presented a bank check for the agreed-upon amount and drove off; no questions asked. Check.

On my way back to the hotel, I took a short detour through Shirlington, the neighborhood where I once lived. I could not ignore the feelings of nostalgia for the life I once led and the friends with whom I shared it. So much had happened in the last year and so much unraveled, miring me in profound loss and swirling in a downward spiral. Like Janis once said, "Freedom's just another word for nothing left to lose." She could have been singing about me.

No sooner had these thoughts emerged when the storefront of Pam's antique shop appeared before me. Pam had been a close friend. Her husband, Trevor, a history professor at Georgetown and a CIA contact, served as my father's eyes and ears and apprised him of all my activities while I delved into the Kennedy assassination a couple of years ago. I missed Pam so much. She had provided a measure of normalcy to my increasingly abnormal life. She and Trevor were responsible for reuniting Robbie and me.

After circling the block a couple of times to ensure that Beau was not lurking about, I parked my new car and walked to the store window, pausing briefly to look inside. Pam sat at a desk in the rear of a showroom of vintage antiques—chairs, armoires, lamps, end tables, all of which looked like they once furnished fine homes of the rich and famous. She seemed to be absorbed in some reading that made her oblivious to my presence and, if it weren't for some intangible strain that furrowed her brow and paled her skin, I would have said that she hadn't changed a bit. It may have been my imagination, but her characteristic aura of joy was gone, making her seem small and frail.

Perhaps my loneliness made me too needy. Or maybe I craved the sanity check only she could provide. Perhaps I just wanted to know if she was okay. Whatever the case, no amount of reason or fear could keep my feet from walking inside, while contemplating how much I could share without harming us both.

Upon hearing the door open, she looked up and her face brightened, illuminating an array of emotions too varied to describe: surprise and curiosity, joy and concern, shame and angst. She jumped from her chair and ran to me, hugging me tightly, and then she pulled away to look me over.

"Kat, it's so good to see you. I never thought I would see you again. How are you? How is Rob?" Tears appeared in the corners of her eyes, and she quickly brushed them away. "Let's go in back where we can talk." She turned the "open" sign to "closed," and I followed her into a musty stockroom bulging with boxes and file cabinets.

"I'm sorry to barge in without warning, but I was in the neighborhood, and I needed to see you. I've thought of you so often. I never got to say good-bye." Seeing Pam was like a key that unlocked many months of emotions from the psychic cages in which I'd incarcerated them. Words tumbled freely, but nonsensically. She held me again; this time until I stopped trembling. I looked up at her and shook my head, unable to form a cogent thought.

She made some tea and handed me a cup steaming with the soothing aroma of chamomile, its warmth welcome and steadying. With little prompting, Pam told me that Trevor and she had separated because the trust between them had been shattered by the life he had kept secret from her. She found it difficult to forgive him, even though his actions probably saved my life. After some time to compose herself, she sighed and said, "I want my old life back. I signed on for a weekly soiree with good friends and fine food, for theater, and music." Then, turning to me, her eyes darkened, and she added, "Even you, someone I thought was my friend, turned out to have a secret life that forced you to leave. Now, I am alone, not knowing who to trust, who to believe."

I lowered my head, knowing that her feelings were justified and ashamed that she felt I had betrayed her. "I am your friend,

Pam. That's why I'm here. I've been running since the day I left. Things are crazy, more than you could know, and I'm in the thick of it. Beau is still after me, and he's working for some powerful people. They have Robbie. I haven't seen him for months."

I began to say more, but she interrupted, "Why, Kat? Why do you do it? People get hurt. You can't save them all. You're one person, one person who has everything to lose. What did your father do to you that makes you so, so robotic, so damned responsible? Leave it to the authorities."

"That's just it. I don't know who in authority is legit and who isn't. Maybe it doesn't affect the average person now, but one day, it will." I brushed my hair back and stared beyond her, talking almost to myself. "Besides, I'm in too deep. It's too late for me to get out. I doubt I'll ever live a normal life again."

She was silent for what seemed an eternity, but when she spoke it was in a low voice, ragged with sadness and resignation. "Then I need you to stay away. I can't handle any more drama in my life. I need friends that I can depend on and have fun with, friends who aren't going to get themselves killed. I'm sorry, Kat, but it's too hard to be your friend. I will miss you." She laughed bitterly. "What am I saying? I've missed you for over a year. Now please leave. Don't come back, okay?"

I began to protest, but she raised her hands and turned away, adding, "Please turn the sign around before you close the door."

I left the building feeling even lower than I thought was possible. My desolation was complete. But what did I expect? Another life of someone I cared for was turned upside down. Could Nate whisk me away to some unknown Eden, free of intrigue and danger? Even if he could, how would I convince those that would kill me that I was out of the game? Knowing what I did, could I live with myself if I left it to others?

Once back in my shiny new car, I slumped over the steering wheel. The truth was, I had very little choice. I could act, or die … or both. It was a simple as that. Tomorrow would change everything, and I needed to dig down deep and find some resolve buried somewhere. I would not forsake the country that I had dedicated my life to. My father's words echoed in my ear. "Some things are worth dying for." Was Robbie one of them? I was no longer sure.

Chapter 23

I was almost grateful when the alarm buzzed at 5 a.m. I had spent most of the night rehearsing the words I would say to Collins. Still, I edited, rephrased, and stumbled as I practiced in the shower, as I dressed, and as I downed both cups of coffee. Everything hinged on today. The choreography, the words, my bearing, my timing all had to be perfect. Anything less promised disaster. It was now or never.

I took a deep breath and punched the number of Collins' driver into my phone. "Hi, Steve, it's Mary from Lincoln Livery. Slim's out sick today. We have a special request from the Saudis. You need to be at their embassy at eight-thirty sharp. We've already told Collins that someone else will pick her up." Steve seemed a little surprised but said okay.

I was at Collins' Georgetown home at a quarter to eight, repeatedly wiping my sweat-drenched hands on my pants and pushing my sunglasses up the slick skin of my nose, scanning the roads for anything unusual. It was eight, and no Collins. Damn. My eyes were riveted on the door of her building. Come on! I was fervently hoping that she hadn't changed her mind about going to work today. It would ruin everything. Steve would arrive at the Saudi embassy and realize something was wrong, and I'd be screwed. She had to show up.

She did, but not alone. My throat tightened as though squeezed by two strong hands. Beau Foster. He swaggered alongside Collins, wearing a self-satisfied smirk. They must have spent the night together, but I wondered who was the conqueror and who was the conquered as she wore an equally arrogant grin. He may have been there to keep her in line, ensuring her allegiance to the Scions. Alternatively, she may have seduced him into forming an alliance with her. It was difficult imagining that their ilk did anything out of pure emotion, only for gain.

"Come on. Come on, leave!" I thought to myself. Each minute that passed ushered in a wave of dread that peaked when Collins entered the back seat, and he climbed in next to her. My throat went dry. Thank God for the sunglasses, but would he recognize my red hair? If so, I was in trouble. I should have worn the wig.

"Driver, drop my friend off at the Rayburn Building. Do you know the shortcut?"

Damn. I had memorized the route to IPI but not anywhere else. Every livery driver in Washington would know the way. They would realize that I was a fraud.

"Shortcut?" was all I asked, in an intentionally altered voice.

Collins sighed in exasperation, irritated by my ignorance. As she rattled off a list of streets, I tried to lock them in, but knew I'd screw up. A different tack was necessary. I punched the address into my Waze app and said, "M Street is a mess—construction. It will take forever. I know another way."

"Whatever," she replied, obviously annoyed.

I pulled away from the curb and into D.C.'s rush hour traffic. Collins shut the sliding door between us, not knowing that I could hear everything they said once I activated a mike in the back seat. Perfect. Let them focus on each other, not me. While they talked, I contemplated contingencies should something go wrong, which now seemed all too likely; at least my gun was under the seat. Still, I managed to catch part of their conversation.

"She's here in D.C. We're watching the apartment of this guy named Cam Wheeler. She worked with his father at the Company. Wheeler's been helping her with IT stuff, keeping her off the grid.

We'll find her and when we do, I'll finish what I should have done last time," Beau said.

I clenched the steering wheel hard. The hairs on the back of my neck prickled. It was all I could do to focus on the traffic. They knew about Cam.

"Why bother? She means nothing to us," Collins replied.

"It's personal. Hastings has fucked me over too many times. Besides, she has ways of getting what could be very dangerous information, and I have a hunch that she's working for Treadwell."

Damn. It was getting worse. Sweat seemed to ooze from every pore in my body. I failed at any attempt to keep calm.

"Why doesn't he turn her over to us?"

"That's the part I can't figure out. Maybe he's trying to keep an eye on her. He's watching her every move. Or maybe he's playing both sides. Johnson and Hughes are losing patience with him. I say we bring him down, but the others aren't there yet."

"You're too damned impulsive. Use your head for once. Has it ever occurred to you that it might be more expedient to use him to our advantage?"

"I'll take her down and anyone who's helping her, including Treadwell. I don't care how big he is. He wants it all, and it's pissing people off. Speaking of which, they know you're making a play for Washburn. Be careful."

"I'm always careful. Tell Hughes to back off. I'm a big girl."

"The bigger they are, the harder they fall."

"And if they asked, would you take me out too?"

"You know who pays my bills."

"You're such a fucking mercenary. You'd kill your own mother."

"If the price was right ... "

"Nice, really nice. What about O'Toole? Can you use him to get to her?"

It was like someone stuck a knife in my spine, causing my

back to visibly arch. I could feel my hands tremble on the wheel, hoping that I wasn't causing the car to shake in response.

"He's one big blob of mush, blathering like a little baby, ready to do whatever we ask, but Hastings won't know that. As long as he's alive, she'll keep trying to find him. Stupid bitch. Once we get her, our problems are over."

Despite my frantic state, I remembered to turn off the mike as we pulled up to the Rayburn Building so they wouldn't know I had heard their conversation. Treadwell was one of them. He knew my movements, what I was doing, and could have me killed in an instant, but hadn't. Why? Who was Beau going to see in the Rayburn Building? What if it was Zuabi? Robbie was in a bad way and even if I could get him out, I'd be signing my own death warrant if I met up with him. It was over.

Beau opened the door and in my rearview mirror, I saw him smile lustily at Collins and say, "Last night was fun. Let's do it again ... soon."

"Yeah, right, but make sure you tell Hughes to lighten up. I'm not screwing anyone over except Washburn, and the Scions will thank me for it."

A flood of relief washed over me as Beau left the car. It was only then that I felt the ache in the muscles of my neck and shoulders. I loosened my grip on the steering wheel and could feel tingling in my hands. But what I felt most acutely was the soul-shattering emptiness of realizing that Robbie and I would probably never be together again.

I pulled away from the curb toward IPI while Collins pulled out some papers and read, allowing me some time to mentally prepare for the task at hand, more determined than ever to bring the Scions down, and angrier than I had ever been in my life. Few things were as dangerous as the actions of someone with nothing left to lose just like Janis said.

Ten minutes later, I turned into a vacant lot, one I knew to be devoid of surveillance cameras. Then I locked the doors and aimed my gun directly at Collins' face.

"Hand over your phones, both of them. Now."

She looked up, more outraged than startled. "Who the hell are you? What do you think you're doing? Do you know who I am?" All asked in rapid succession. No stammering. No fear. No concession. Not the response I'd been hoping for.

"Shut up," I snapped. "I said now." I held out my free hand, waiting for her to comply.

"How dare you? I'll have you ... "

I fired the gun into the seat, just inches from her face. She jumped at the bang of the report and gasped loudly. Her previously defiant façade cracked slightly, further emboldening me. "The next one won't miss, I promise." Glaring at me, she practically threw her phone in my direction. "I've been watching you for days. Give me the other one. Now," I ordered. Slowly, she pulled a phone that was strapped to her leg. "Give me your purse and that valise as well."

She hesitated, and I aimed the gun directly at her face. Reluctantly, she handed them both over, I briefly looked through each one, my gun still levelled at her head. When I saw the small handgun in her purse, I gulped silently. The valise held many papers and another phone. Who carries three phones? Was one a special link to the Scions? As I continued rifling through her belongings, she rallied. "You realize that I can have you killed. You also realize that when I'm not at the office, people will look for me, people that you don't want to antagonize, believe me."

"Like Beau?" I asked, spitting out the words.

That caught her off guard, prompting her to ask once more, "Who are you?"

I had to admire her poise. She didn't seem fazed at all, just very, very pissed. I silently pulled back on the road and continued to drive, ignoring her questions and protests. Once the city was well behind us, I turned onto a deserted dirt road and jumped out. "Get out of the car."

"Why should I? You're not going to kill me. You need me or you wouldn't be going to such lengths."

Damn, she was tough. I had to be tougher. "Killing you would give me great pleasure, I assure you. If you want to live, you'll do as you're told. Now get out of the car."

She slowly climbed from the car, smiling condescendingly, as though humoring me, but it only strengthened my resolve.

"Put your hands behind your back," I snapped.

She didn't move so I grabbed one, then the other. She resisted, trying to pull them from my grasp, but my training, though many years past, kicked in. Within seconds, she was cuffed. I pulled a blindfold from my pocket and covered her eyes. She spat at me but missed. It made me angry enough that I pushed her hard, causing her to land on the back seat with her legs waving in the air like an overturned turtle. The image made me feel stronger, and I enjoyed seeing her helpless and pathetic. In that instant, I hated her.

She righted herself as I climbed behind the wheel, grateful that she couldn't see the tremors in my hands as I maneuvered the car back onto the highway. The car was silent as we passed the hills and forests of Howard County and remained so as we entered Ellicott City, the site of Jermaine's safe house where he had helped me recover from the wounds inflicted by Beau and his henchmen and had finally earned my trust. I felt secure here, like I had the upper hand, at least temporarily. I knew the house well—how to enter it, how to secure it, and some of the tricks the house had up its sleeve.

As we turned into the driveway, I lowered the window, lifted a flap, and pressed my index finger on a square black screen posted discretely on one of the trees that lined the driveway. The garage door opened, and we disappeared inside. Motion detectors triggered lights and lowered the door behind us. I walked slowly to Collins' door, hoping to heighten her angst and concern. I wanted her to know that I would stop at nothing, maybe even let her think I was unhinged; maybe I was. Ripping the blindfold from her eyes gave me some perverse pleasure as did waving the gun in the direction of the door inside. I was unaccustomed to being in control, even if it was transient, but I would savor and use it while suppressing my conscience's comparison of my actions to those of Beau. "You first."

She flashed a look of utter disdain, but acquiesced. The house was as I'd remembered it: spartan, with minimal décor, immaculate, but boasting a mountain of electronics that far surpassed any satellite intelligence branch I'd ever seen. I told her to sit in one of the ladder-back chairs in the kitchen and yanked her hands back and cuffed them to its posts. Then I covered her mouth with a piece of duct tape. Once convinced she was secure, I returned to the car and collected her things.

Upon returning to the kitchen, I found the phone number of her office and called to say that she had a family emergency and wouldn't be coming in for the next few days, making sure that she heard the conversation and realize that she might be here for a while. The duct tape had prevented her from yelling something while I was on the phone, but now that it was no longer needed, I ripped it off, eliciting a small yelp and an irate glare. I didn't mind either. Next, I pulled the results from my investigation of her and threw them on the table in front of her.

"Start reading." She gazed at the thick stack of papers and released a sigh of disgust. She didn't seem alarmed, not yet. After she had read about thirty pages, she looked up, although there were many more to go. Distress had replaced her fury. Finally.

"What do you want? Money? How much?"

I laughed derisively. "You should wish it were that easy. You have someone that I want—you and your Scions friends."

Her jaw dropped, and her eyes bulged. "How do you know…?"

"I know many things, far more than what's in those papers in front of you. The Scions are holding Rob O'Toole and Jermaine

Biggs. I want you to get them released. Free and clear. Without surveillance. Without consequence. If anything happens to them, you'll regret it."

She snickered bitterly, not the response I had hoped for. "You've picked the wrong person. I can't get them released. It's beyond my control. I'm just their pawn." Then her eyes grew clear as a realization dawned. "You're Kat Hastings. They've spoken about you. You're as good as dead."

"And so are you if I leak these," I shot back. "In exactly one week, an email is scheduled for transmission. It will go to the President, the entire Congress, the Supreme Court, the DOJ, and the media. It will expose you and every member of the Scions. The only way to prevent it is if I delete it. If I'm dead or detained, it will go out anyway. There's enough in these papers to put you and the Scions away for life. You will all be charged with treason."

In a voice devoid of emotion, she responded, "The government could do no worse than what the Scions would do to me. I told you, you've got the wrong person for this job."

"The way I see it, you are the perfect person to do this. You are far too smart a woman to not cover your ass. You have too much on too many people. The Scions fear what you know." I paused to assess her reaction. She wasn't wavering, not one bit. It was time to play poker. "I know that the Scions are watching you, demanding that you serve them, making you do things you don't want to do, threatening you if you betray them. I also know that you regret joining them and want a way out. I can give you that."

"You?" she scoffed. "I don't have time for this."

"I have all the time in the world. You, on the other hand, do not. Like I said, nothing would give me greater pleasure than killing you right here, right now." I tried to sound like I meant it. I pressed the gun against her head for good measure.

She didn't flinch. I pressed harder. "I know that the Scions are meeting in London next week. Now that I have your phones, I will tell them that you ratted out Hughes, Wentworth and the others. If you're not there, they will conclude that you've defected. I don't need to tell you what they will do."

She smirked again. "You're out of your league. They will hunt you down and if they can't find you, they will find your friends. They already know about that young computer whiz you've been seen with." A sinister smile crossed her face. I couldn't react and let her see my fear.

"This is how it will go," I said. "You'll contact Hughes. You will tell him what I have on him and the others and state my demand. He gets Robbie and Jermaine released."

"The hell I will," she snapped.

I ignored her once again and continued. "Once I'm convinced that Robbie and Jermaine are safe and not being followed, I will send the email anyway, but will remove anything about you, although you deserve the same fate. The Scions will be exposed, and you will be free to leave."

"You're an even bigger fool than I thought," she laughed mockingly. "No one can bring them down, especially you."

Her condescension unnerved me and without thinking, I smashed her face with the butt of my gun, slashing her skin, sending rivulets of blood trickling down her chin. Hatred oozed from us both, but I had to rein in my emotion. She was my only hope.

"I've given you a way out. You can take your chances with me or hope they're in a forgiving mood when they find out what I know and blame you it" She didn't respond, but only stared down at the floor. After a prolonged silence, I rose and said, "I can wait as long as you. The difference is that I have food and access to the bathroom. Think hard. This is your last best chance. When I return, I want your answer. Otherwise, the email goes out. It's as simple as that." I left the room. It was time to let her stew a bit, and I needed to regroup. If she didn't agree, my options were limited.

During the thirty plus minutes I spent away from her, I obsessed over her conversation with Beau about Treadwell. I had planned to use his media outlets to spread the word on the Scions.

Beau and Collins made it sound like Treadwell was one of their cronies, although currently not in high standing. If he was, why were his and my name listed on their next agenda? Perhaps Treadwell was sincere and just pandering to them until he could break away, but I could not ignore the possibility that his new party was just as sinister as everything else the Scions were into. It would explain why he didn't take my investigations of Zuabi seriously. I had to confront him, but at a time and place where he could not hurt me, not knowing if that was even possible.

The house was quiet except for the hum of the computers, radios and fax machines. I had expected a test of wills, and Collins did not disappoint, but time was growing short. I had to get out of D.C. and convince Cam to come with me, but not until Collins complied. It could be a long day.

The silence was shattered by her voice calling out. I took my time walking back to the kitchen. I couldn't appear too anxious, too desperate.

"I need to use the restroom."

"Too bad." I turned to walk away.

"Let me see what you have on Hughes and Johnson."

I pulled another stack of papers from my bag and placed them in front of her. Her eyes widened as she read, either in disbelief regarding the extent of their actions or that I had so much on them; maybe both. Several minutes later, she looked up at me and asked, "And I have your word that you will release nothing about me?" Her face had grown purple and swollen from the wound I inflicted. In another time, I might have tended to it, but not now.

"The only way I will release anything about you is if I discover that Robbie and Jermaine are being followed or are in any danger." In my mind, I'd accepted that they would no longer be part of my life, and this realization brought a deep sadness to my soul. Saying the words made it real.

After what seemed like eons she said, "They're too powerful. They control the media. Hell, they control the government. Do you realize that every presidential candidate is vetted by them? I don't think it will work."

"I have nothing to lose. The Scions have cost me my husband, my friends, and my life as I knew it. The target on my back gets bigger every day. If I go down, I will take every Scion I can down with me, including you. You can be a hero, or you can die."

"I guess I could call Hughes when I return to my office."

"I may be crazy, but I'm not an idiot. You'll call from here. I want to hear both sides of the conversation. If I'm satisfied, I'll release you. If not, you can rot here for all I care. Your fate is now in your hands. You're a smart woman. Make it happen."

"The bathroom?"

"Like I said, I'm not an idiot." I walked away once more. Maybe nature had more sway than me. During the next few hours, I looked through the contacts on her phone and was stunned by the names listed, all the way up to the president. Maybe I really was crazy to play their game. It felt like one of those movie scenes in which the desperate poker player shoves all his chips into the center of the table for one last-ditch chance to win the pot.

When the clock read ten p.m., I strolled into the kitchen and flicked on the light. She squinted and squirmed, her skirt soiled by nature's call. "I'm going to bed. I'll be leaving in the morning with or without you. And by the way, no one ever comes to this place. You'll be dead in a couple of weeks."

She spat at me as I taped her mouth shut again. I had placed her in a horrible position, but one of her own making. I did not feel the least bit of guilt.

I woke at six after spending much of the night writing a script that I needed her to read. After showering, I dressed and headed toward the kitchen. Collins was slumped in her chair, her head hanging down, veiled by her dull, listless hair. The stench of urine was strong. I started the coffee maker and began cooking some eggs and toast, not even acknowledging her presence until she grunted. I ripped the tape off and saw that her wound had grown, leaving her face dark and misshapen. "You have something to say?"

"Okay, you win. I'll do it." Her voice was weak and resigned.

I shoved a piece of paper in her face. "Read this. I want you to say this to Hughes, word for word." I finished making breakfast and devoured it in front of her. She eyed the food with envy. After the last bite, I released her from the chair, jammed my gun into her back and pushed her into the living room. I re-cuffed her to another chair and sat beside her in front of a microphone, reminding her that if she deviated at all, she was dead. Then I punched in Hughes' number and held my breath.

"It's Bette. I need to read you something so please let me finish before you say anything." She dutifully read the document which took about ten minutes but contained enough information to grab Hughes' attention. At the end, she read the terms of the deal.

"Are you alone?" he asked at the end.

She took a quick look at me and I nodded. "Yes," she lied.

"Then I assume we can speak freely," Hughes said. "Who has put you up to this?"

I shook my head.

"I don't know where this is from," Collins answered. "It came to me in the mail. There's much, much more than what I've read to you."

"It must be Hastings. We'll take care of her. Don't worry."

"I'm not sure about that. Besides, the email will go out no matter what unless O'Toole and Biggs are released. Beau told me that they're useless now anyway." Collins was agitated now as though she, too, knew this had to work.

"Maybe not." Hughes paused as though he was thinking. "Maybe if our techniques have been successful, we can manipulate them to do our will once they're out. We've embedded chips under their skin so we can find them at any time. Their release could prove useful. Maybe they can lead us to Hastings. It's be a small price to pay to keep this under wraps and get Hastings."

"I'm not sure it's her. Maybe Treadwell. He's the only one who could find all this out." That wasn't in the script, and her ad lib was perfect.

"Let me get this straight. All we have to do is release them and none of this gets out?" Collins grunted agreement and Hughes continued, "How do you let this mystery person know?"

"I have a number to call."

"Come to my office. We'll need to run this by Johnson."

"I can't. Not for a few days at least. Talk to Johnson, but you need to do this quickly or the email will go out to everyone in the government. I'll call back in an hour."

I disconnected the line. She had done well. Now all we had to do was wait an hour. While she was still cuffed to the chair, I took my phone and went to the bedroom, shut the door and called Cam.

"It's Aunt Kat. Listen carefully. They know all about you. You need to leave the city right away. Go to the first place Jermaine took us. The code for the door is 0-2-6-1. Wait there, and I will meet you within the next day or two. If I'm going to be late, I'll let you know. If you don't hear from me, well … I'm so sorry I got you into all of this, Cam. Please be careful. They're watching you and may use you to get to me. Go now."

I didn't give him a chance to respond. I hung up and returned to retrieve Collins. We had an hour to kill. The least I could do was make her breakfast. She had done her job.

"They're out," Hughes stated flatly. "They're en route to the train station in D.C. We gave them some money for a ticket. Johnson is bullshit about it, but I finally convinced him we could use them as bait. They don't know anything about the chips so hopefully, they'll go someplace that will lead us to Hastings. Call your blackmailer and let him ... or her know. We want to see everything you have so we can start damage control just in case. Don't say a word of this to anyone, got it? And get your ass here ASAP."

That was my cue. I disconnected the line and pulled Collins to the bathroom to clean her up and gave her some of my old sweats to replace the formerly smart, but now pungent outfit she'd been wearing. Within minutes we were on the road. The beauty of the day belied the deed at hand; blue cloudless sky, fresh air, and with light so bright, I donned sunglasses to tame its glare. Just before we reached Columbia, I pulled onto a deserted road, hidden by trees and shrubs, that split wide farm fields tinted green by early crop growth.

"There's a gas station about a mile that way," I said, pointing. "You can call someone from there." I uncuffed Collins and handed her her purse, now devoid of phones, gun and a few other items. "One false move and the email goes out with your info in it. Play by my rules and you're safe. I keep my deals."

"You're leaving me here? I did everything you asked."

I almost felt sorry for her, but not enough to change my mind. I needed a head start desperately. "You'll figure it out."

In the rearview mirror, I saw her staring at me. She somehow looked smaller than when I first picked her up. I didn't know who was in worse trouble, her or me, but I couldn't dwell on that now, not with all that I had to do. It took every ounce of self-control to remain within the speed limit. The last thing I needed was to be stopped by an unsuspecting cop. After what seemed like eons, I pulled over and replaced the original license plates on the limo before returning the car. Thankfully, the agent only looked the outside over and didn't notice the bullet hole in the back seat. I walked the block to my waiting car, grateful that it was still there. Trembling, I climbed in and headed to the beltway and, I hoped, freedom ... at least for now. It was only when I was on Route 95 North that I could begin to think how or if I would confront Treadwell.

Chapter 24

*A*dam saw the red awning of the Ezme restaurant and felt *his nerves kick into high gear. Everything had to be just right, so he arrived well before the time he had asked Meghan to meet him. He had selected this restaurant near Dupont Circle for several reasons: It was easy to get to, it was quiet and unpretentious, and the food was good; but most important, its Mideastern cuisine was symbolic of the life he would ask Meghan to lead—that as his wife.*

The receptionist led him to a small table in the corner next to a large wine rack and under a Turkish tapestry. Although she left him a couple of menus, he couldn't even think of food just yet. Instead he rehearsed—again—the words he would say.

"Hey, there. Have you been waiting long?"

She looked stunning and wore her hair long, the way he liked it. She was wearing a flowered print dress which, though demure, revealed her petite, fit figure.

"No, not at all. I'm glad you could make it. Can I order you a drink?" Adam responded, trying his best to remain calm. She asked for a Chardonnay and he continued, "Did you have any trouble finding the place?" She laughed in that light-hearted way that sent him over the edge and said it had been no problem. "I hope you like Mideastern food. It can be a little spicy."

"I'm Irish. After a life of boiled potatoes and corned beef, I crave spicy." Her lips curved into a simultaneously innocent and

beguiling smile. Adam was so mesmerized that words wouldn't come. "Is there something wrong?" Meghan asked.

"No, no! I just, well, I want you to enjoy the evening." Pull yourself together, he admonished himself. "I want tonight to be special, like you are to me."

"Oh, Adam, don't be silly. I always have fun with you. Have you been here before?" He told her it was one of his favorite restaurants, prompting her to ask, "What do you recommend? Better yet, why don't you order for both of us? I don't have a clue what to get."

He loved her carefree way, her reliance on him. He asked the waiter for her wine, adding an order of Karides Guvec, a seafood stew, and Durum Adana, a spicy ground lamb and beef wrap.

"So how was your day?" he asked. Meghan described the various triumphs and pitfalls familiar to a legislative staff member. He listened patiently until she finished but felt ready to burst by the time she was done. Still, the words he had practiced so diligently would not come.

"You're quiet tonight. Are you sure there isn't something bothering you?" She gazed into his eyes, and he thought he would melt into his chair.

It was now or never. "Meghan, I am so glad you were willing to move to D.C. It's been wonderful having you here. It's a new place for both of us, and I'm hoping you have no regrets. You and I have been dating for a while now, and I'd like to, I mean, I'm wondering ... well, is the religion thing a problem?" Damn, that's not how it was supposed to come out.

She took his hand, and he could feel warmth in places he didn't want to acknowledge. "If it were, do you think I would have made the move?" Her smile was even more captivating, paralyzing him into silence. "Wait, you're being serious, I'm sorry." She took a breath as though wanting to be careful of her words. He leaned in, anxious, alert as she continued "We may call God by different names, but He's still God. By the time Jesus came around,

He must have realized that we needed the Ten Commandments for dummies, because he gave us just two; love God and love each other. That's what I strive for, although I don't always succeed." She winked and added, "All that matters to me is that the people I care about feel the same way, regardless of their religion."

Hearing her words stripped away any pretense, any decorum. The words he'd been waiting to say since he met her tumbled out, and he was unable to control them. "I do. I mean, I ... Meghan, I care for you very much. I've never met anyone like you. I want to be with you for the rest of my life. I know we haven't been dating very long, but is there any way, I mean, could you, dammit, Meghan, would you marry me?"

Her eyes widened. She shifted in her seat. Her hands repeatedly folded over themselves. Just when he thought he'd blown it, she answered, "Wow, I wasn't expecting this. It's so soon." She took a sip of water and tried to collect herself. He waited and waited. Finally, she said, "Adam, I'm not saying no, just not yet. I care for you too, very much. I know you've gone way out on a limb, and I appreciate your feelings, which I think I share. Let's give it a little more time so we can be sure, okay? When I say yes, I want it to be for keeps."

Though not the answer he had hoped for, it was encouraging. Thankfully, the tension was eased by the arrival of their dinners. She took a spoonful of the stew and sighed with delight. "This is delicious." She scooped some more into her mouth. "You understand, don't you?"

"Yes, of course," he responded quickly, too quickly. "I shouldn't have ... ."

"No, don't apologize. I appreciate knowing how you feel. In fact, I admire your honesty. You're different from other men I've dated. Most bury their feelings, and it's hard to know where they stand."

"Thank you for saying that. I just wanted you to know that I'm in this for the long haul, not just a whim." He looked at the food

before him, unable to take a bite. "Speaking of honesty, there's something else. I have this, uh, friend. He's been involved in something very bad and doesn't know how to get out of it. What do you think I should tell him?"

"How bad is it? Murder? Drugs?" She laughed nervously.

"It's bad. He's a wreck. I don't know what to ... , I mean, what he should do."

Her gaze pierced his soul, leaving him feeling defenseless. Her light, airy demeanor disappeared, and her smile flattened. "I would tell your, uh, friend to do whatever it takes to make things right. Nothing is worth compromising one's values, and it's never too late to make a change."

It was what he'd expected her to say. In fact, her morality was part of her appeal. She had no hidden agenda and seemed incapable of deceit. With Meghan what one saw is what one got, and he loved her for it. He nodded, and quietly said, "You're right, as always. I'll tell him."

Meghan could tell Adam was still preoccupied. To lighten the mood, she joked, "You don't expect me to wear a burka, or anything, do you?"

"Never. The last thing I'd want is to hide your beautiful face."

They finished the dinner, exchanging small talk, and left the restaurant. He told her he had a lot of work and needed to get back. He opened the door of the cab for her, and before she climbed in, she turned to him and stroked his cheek. "I know you'll do the right thing, Adam."

Chapter 25

As soon as I got back from D.C., I drove straight to the kennel. Between Scout's wagging tail and devoted brown eyes, the anxiety of my drive from Washington to Boston melted away. I knelt, hugged him and rested my head on his broad, strong shoulder. We drove back to my tiny apartment which now seemed like an oasis. I thought about sending Treadwell a quick email indicating I was home, but with Collins' words replaying in my mind, I decided to wait. One more day would not make a difference, and the last thing I needed was another confrontation.

I dropped my bags, donned my running attire and led Scout back out the door for a much-needed jog around the neighborhood. The sun was bright, though low in the sky. The air was fresh and inviting. Despite logging far fewer miles recently, I fell into an easy rhythm, nothing ached, my breathing was smooth, and before long, I entered the zone where random thoughts come and go. I must have been crazy to attempt such a plan. What if Collins didn't comply? Or worse, what if she and the Scions figured out a way to extract their revenge? I thought about Cam and worried about his safety. Would I ever see Robbie again? What condition would he be in if I did? I had no idea what I would say to Treadwell, if anything. I did not want to tip my hand, especially now that my trust in him had vanished.

After several miles, I rounded the corner and turned back onto my street and saw a small girl in torn jeans and uncombed hair, playing with her doll on the steps of a house close to mine. How I envied her innocence. I couldn't even remember the last time I enjoyed such bliss, and I craved it now more than ever. I gave her a quick wave, and she jumped up and ran toward me.

"Can I pet your dog?" she yelled.

"Uh, sure," I responded, regretting instantly that I had made contact.

"He sure is big. What's his name?"

I told her, and she volunteered that she was Ashley and her doll was Anna, named after the heroine of her favorite movie, "Frozen." Scout wagged his tail vigorously as she petted him.

"What's your name?" she asked.

"It's um, Mary."

She mentioned that she knew where I lived because she had seen Scout and me before. I learned that she liked school, except when the boys teased her about her clothes, and that she lived with her mom, but only saw her dad on weekends when he took her to movies or the park, or made dinner for her. Our pleasant chat came to an abrupt halt when an all-too-familiar black cab slowly pulled up beside us. Adheem. Damn. I wasn't wearing my reporter's disguise and prayed that he didn't recognize me.

"Hello, Ashley. How is Miss Anna today?" he asked as he opened the car door. The little girl smiled. She seemed comfortable around him. "I brought you some candy," he added, handing her several pieces of what looked like taffy wrapped in paper. "Looks like you've made a new friend."

"Her name is Mary."

He studied my face. "Mary, eh?" His gaze intensified, as though he was trying to place where he had seen me before. Maybe I could confuse him further.

"Hello, uh … ."

"Adheem. Adheem Zuabi." He shook my hand. "I believe we've met."

"Hmm, I don't think so," I responded lamely. "I just moved here." Scout's hackles stood at attention, and his eyes were riveted on Zuabi. Scout could always sense my mood and now was not the time for him to react. "Well, I need to get home and feed my dog. Nice to meet you."

Before he could answer, I was gone, passing my house and jogging until darkness veiled the sky. Only then did I dare return home.

Cam called before I could make it into the shower. He was safe and had booked a room at the Lenox Hotel in Boston. Hearing his voice brought instant relief. He said that he had scanned his car for surveillance devices and was sure that he wasn't followed. I was grateful that he was such an obsessive electronics geek. We would meet the next morning to discuss everything and chart a course of action.

Collins called as I was undressing. She confirmed that Robbie and Jermaine were indeed free as Hughes had claimed and asked me to remove the incriminating information about her from the email.

"Hughes said they had chips embedded. Until they are removed, no way," I replied flatly.

"You bitch!" she erupted. "We had a deal. I can only do so much."

"Well, you'll have to do more. Contact Jermaine and tell him to get them removed and then call me so I know for sure."

She complained bitterly, explaining that if she did that, Hughes would know and suspect her of selling him and the Scions out.

"How stupid do you think I am? You heard him say that they would use Robbie to get to me. Until those chips are gone, so is any hope of you being deleted from that email." I hung up, relieved that I could finally shower.

I let the water pour over me for several minutes. It was delightfully hot and soothing and though I knew its comfort would be transient, I savored every second. I grabbed the loofah sponge and lathered up, letting my mind wander and indulge in thoughts of happier times in Nevis with Robbie, our runs on the beach, our quiet dinners, and the love we once shared—all gone, never to be shared again.

But something wasn't right. It might have been a change in the lighting, a subtle sound, or some sixth sense. I abruptly turned off the water just as Zuabi ripped open the curtain and stood before me, his eyes ablaze and waving a knife. I shivered, not from the cold, but from feeling totally exposed and vulnerable.

"It's amazing how a little girl can be so helpful," Zuabi sneered. "She was more than happy to tell me where you live. I didn't recognize you right away, but then it came to me. You're that reporter who asked so many questions. My son said you came to see him as well. You have some answering to do."

"How dare you come into my house. If you don't leave, I'm calling the police." Where was Scout, I wondered. Had Zuabi hurt him? "Your son is our representative. Why wouldn't I want to interview him?" I asked, forcing calm into my voice.

"If you were a real reporter, I'd agree, but why the disguise, eh? And why would my wife leave shortly after you came to my home? And isn't it a coincidence that you live here, so close to my house?" He paused and twisted the knife in his hand. Its tip glowed with reflected light. It looked very sharp and very deadly.

Though probably close to my age, Zuabi was lean and strong. I wasn't sure I could take him, even with my training. Besides, he was armed, and I was cornered in the shower.

He laughed scornfully. "I have learned how to, shall we say, encourage people to talk, Miss Banks, Miss Ferguson, Mary, or whatever your real name is. It isn't pleasant and from the looks of that scar on your breast, you already know what real pain is."

"Get out," I screamed. Where was Scout?

He seized my arm and threw me against the shower wall. My head hit the tile with a loud crack. "Do not take me for a fool! You will not leave this room alive, you know that, right? You will not destroy all I have worked for. However, you can make your death far less painful and much faster. Tell me, where is my wife? Tell me what you know, or you will soon wish you had."

I heard muffled barking from my bedroom. Scout was alive. I had a chance.

"Okay, have it your way. Besides, things are in motion. You can't stop it now. This time next week, I will have my prize. Too bad you won't be around to see it." Zuabi laughed, his evil eyes gleaming. "I will enjoy this."

He raised his knife, but before he could strike, I quickly grabbed the shower brush and smacked his head. Then I pushed him hard against the sink and raced from the room with him inches behind me. Scout was barking from behind the closet door. I flung it open and lunged for my purse, hoping the gun inside was still loaded. Zuabi tackled me, and we fell onto my bed, his weight pressing upon my naked body. I could feel his sharp breath against my face and smelled its stench. Scout jumped onto the bed and sank his teeth into Zuabi's neck, eliciting a piercing scream. Zuabi rolled over, writhing in pain. I jumped up, found my gun, and aimed it at Zuabi's head.

"Drop your knife, Zuabi."

He smiled smugly and stepped toward me. He didn't think I would shoot him. It only made me angrier, more desperate, and ready to kill. But then Scout barked, shattering my hate. What was I doing? Taking a deep breath, I shifted my aim from his head and shot him in the thigh. He dropped the knife and doubled over in pain, I struck him as hard as I could with the butt of my gun, and he fell to the ground with a deep groan. Slowly, I bent down and checked his eyelids. He was out cold. I dug out the handcuffs that I had used on Collins and clamped one ring to his leg, the other to the bed frame.

I couldn't go to the police. They would ask questions and might expose my identity and location to the wrong people. I couldn't tell Treadwell, either. Only one option seemed viable, and I pushed it from my mind. I wasn't desperate enough to call Nate, not yet.

I dressed and packed my things, all the while thinking that, once again, Scout had saved me as he had over a year ago. As I scratched his head, I thought about that little girl, Ashley. Once I had been an Ashley, sweet, gentle, trusting. Now, I hardly knew the person I'd become. I had killed a man in New Orleans on my last case, kidnapped an influential member of the Washington establishment, and had just deliberately maimed Zuabi. Now, I trusted no one except my dog. I had become my father, a man I simultaneously revered and detested. I had once wanted his life. Now, I had it. I stole a look in the mirror and was horrified by the dead eyes that stared back at me. There was no hope of experiencing the tranquility and grace of a Baha or the friendship of a Pam. The Kat Hastings I once knew was dead.

I called a hotel in the Seaport area of Boston that allowed pets and booked a room for two nights, plenty of time to meet with Cam and figure out next steps. After gathering as many of my belongings as could be crammed into my car, I left the house, door unlocked, and called 911. Scout and I would be long gone by the time an ambulance arrived for Zuabi. Probably foolish, but Zuabi would bleed out without care, and I didn't want another murder staining my hands.

Thankfully, it was an easy drive with little traffic. The city was alive with the lights from tall buildings and the sounds of horns from Boston drivers, not known for their patience behind the wheel. I parked in a nearby garage, foregoing the valet service. We walked briskly to the hotel, passing many people, mostly young, mostly on their way to or from the many new bars and eateries that had sprung up along the once run-down waterfront of Boston Harbor. Now, the Seaport was a prestigious address, affordable by few except those who worked in the financial district or the nearby biotech firms.

I checked in with just my computer, a few clothes, and Scout. Once in the room, I leaned against the double-locked door and sighed deeply. So much had happened so quickly, it made my head spin. I needed to catch up with myself if only to prepare for the next challenge.

Famished, I called room service and treated myself by ordering wine with dinner. Tonight, no one knew where I was or what I was doing, and I was glad. There would be no logging onto the computer. No phone calls. Just Scout, me, a nice cabernet, and the TV. For the first time in what seemed like forever, I could relax. Or so I thought. The news anchor announced that the president had called a special session to present his sweeping plan to deal with North Korea, Russia, Syria, China, and Iran to the entire Congress … next week.

So that was it.

Cam's knock upon my door the next morning was insistent and rapid. He burst into the room and promptly announced, "There's something you need to know." His eyes were large, and fear carved deep furrows in his brow.

"Before we get to that, I … ."

"Aunt Kat, this is important. The Scions … ."

"Cam, please. I need to tell you … ."

"Dammit, Aunt Kat, the Scions have an all-out hit out on you, not just a few of Beau's guys—they're pulling out all the stops."

I recoiled. My hand jumped to my mouth and my body seemed paralyzed. In faltering steps, I moved to the nearest chair and sat, like a rock, immobile and cold, while his words sunk in.

"It's all hands on deck, Aunt Kat. They know you're in Boston. They know what kind of car you're driving. Several men are on their way here right now, if they're not already here. Beau is in charge. Collins told them everything, and she wants you bad. They know you're working for Treadwell, and they think he's keeping you under wraps, so he can use you as a trump card when the time is right. You need to get out of here, and you can't go to Bethel. They know about Tom. You can't go back to D.C. either. And wherever you go, you can't use your car."

He finally took a breath which allowed me to say, "It's not just me I'm worried about. They know about you. Collins told me." I stroked Scout's head mindlessly while adding, "We both have to run. I'm so sorry. I should have never dragged you into this."

"I was a willing accomplice," he said, attempting a smile. "Anyway, it doesn't matter now. We're both in too deep. The question is, how do we dig our way out? We can't drive, and they'll be watching the airport and train stations."

I stood, walked over to the window, and gazed out at Boston Harbor below. Boats were docked on the pier next to the World Trade Center where flags of the world's countries rippled in the wind. Planes soared overhead on their way to Logan Airport. Tourists crowded the sidewalks. I was resistant to the one idea I had, but it could work. It had to.

I opened my laptop and did a search for Bay State Cruise Lines, whose sign I saw across the street from the hotel. A ferry was leaving in thirty minutes, and there were spaces available. I asked Cam, "Could you work your magic and get us two tickets under another name and credit card?"

"No problem. Where are we going?"

I pointed to the dock. "Provincetown. There's an airport there where Nate could meet us and fly us out."

"Nate?" Cam's eyes narrowed. He was not pleased.

"Do you have a better idea?" He shook his head in resignation, and while he began typing, I gathered my things, thinking we had one more week until Zuabi's plan was realized, and the email went out. I could only hope to see both through.

Cam logged off the laptop and shoved it in the case. I leashed Scout, grabbed my bag, and we left for the ferry. There was no time to retrieve anything from the car. We dodged the traffic on

Seaport Boulevard and ducked into a 7-11 until the line of passengers began to move. Only then did we dare join the queue. That's when we heard the explosion and saw smoke billowing from the parking garage where my poor little Audi was parked. I looked at Cam and, without speaking, our eyes acknowledged the obvious.

We scrambled onto the ferry, possibly the only two people who weren't craning their necks to see what was happening on the street. It was sheer bedlam with people shouting, running and gesturing wildly. Only when we reached our seats inside the cabin did we see smoke billowing from the hotel. Guests and employees ran from the building, screaming, tripping, pushing.

I looked at the sidewalk and saw a group of men clustered near the hotel, the only unruffled people in a swirling mass of humanity. Beau's cruel, handsome face stood out like a flashing warning sign. They were watching everyone as they fled the hotel, waiting, waiting. They spoke amongst themselves, and Beau pointed a finger to the four exits. They split up and ran to cover each. We sunk down in ours seats lest one of Beau's henchmen happened to scan the boat. I prayed that Scout wouldn't begin to bark and tried to relax him while my heart felt like it would burst through my chest.

Fire engines and police cars converged on the area. The Seaport was now a riot of people, smoke and sirens. Flames now consumed the hotel and garage. Screams competed with sirens for decibels. The ferry left the dock, but it seemed so slow and plodding. Hurry, hurry, I thought to myself. Only when we passed the harbor islands did I begin to de-tense. We had cut things too close. We had been too lucky. The fates always had a way of evening things out.

Chapter 26

The ferry buzzed with passengers speculating who was behind the events we had left behind, and why, and how, allowing us to speak quietly at a small table in the midsection of the boat. Cam tried to convince me not to call Nate, but I was already onto other pressing concerns. I told him about my close call with Zuabi and how his plan had been moved up to next week. "He's incapacitated, but Adam isn't. I hate to involve her, but Baha may be our only hope. Maybe she could convince Adam to change his mind."

"You have to think of yourself, Aunt Kat. It's time to tell the authorities. Let them deal with it." He stared out the window as the shores of Nantasket beach came into view. "Besides, how are you going to reach her? Tom's lines are probably tapped. You can't go there yourself."

"I don't know which of the authorities to trust. Some of them are in the pockets of the Scions."

"How about Treadwell? Maybe there's something he can do."

I filled him in on Collins' comments and how I no longer could trust him either, before adding, "If Adam succeeds and the government is in shambles, the Scions will take over, maybe with Treadwell leading the way. Perhaps that's been his scheme all along."

We were passing the distant shores of Plymouth when a new thought occurred. "Maybe we could get the special session of Congress cancelled. If I send the email now and include information about Zuabi, the president or maybe the Congress would have all the proof needed to indict the Scions and pick up Zuabi."

"But what about Robbie? If you send the email before he's safe, the Scions will kill him and Jermaine."

"You're right. Collins is supposed to have them call me once they're safe. Then I'll send the email out. I don't give a damn about any of them or the deal I made."

The Race Point lighthouse appeared as a small speck on the horizon. We were getting closer to our destination even if we were no closer to coming up with a plan. I couldn't be sure that Nate would come to our aid after I'd kicked him out. I didn't know if Robbie or Jermaine would call in time. There were too many moving parts.

Once we arrived at MacMillan Wharf in Provincetown, I called Tom and told him that we had to meet as soon as possible. "It's important. Don't say where; your line is not secure. Just give me a hint that I can figure out."

There were a few moments of silence before he said, "Do you remember the name of Robbie's second favorite band?" I told him I did. "Okay, meet me at the place where they recorded their first album." I knew exactly where he meant: 56 Parnassus Lane, West Saugerties, N.Y., the location where The Band recorded "Music from The Big Pink" after backing Bob Dylan for several years.

As soon as we hung up, I called Nate, who, thankfully, answered immediately.

"I knew you'd call. In fact, I was hoping you would," he began.

"Nate, nothing has changed between us, but if you're still willing to help … ."

"What is it, Kat? You sound horrible."

"I've been better. Could you pick Cam, me, and Scout up at the Provincetown Airport and fly us to Woodstock? I need to see Tom right away."

"I'll be there in five hours. Just be safe."

We walked to Commercial Street, festooned with rainbow flags, Portuguese banners and Old Glory, its many shops and eateries bustling with tourists from a recently docked cruise ship. We grabbed a slice of pizza at Twisted Sister and found a vacant spot on the park benches outside Town Hall where we discussed our limited options. Neither of us mentioned the Scions, their threat all too real, too immediate, too deadly. The phone vibrated in my pocket.

"Kat, it's Jermaine." I closed my eyes as relief flooded every artery, every vein. He asked if my line was still secure. I answered that it was, courtesy of Cam, and he continued. "We're safe. The chips have been removed. They hurt O'Toole pretty bad, but he's alive."

Upon hearing that Robbie was safe, I exhaled as though I'd been holding my breath for a lifetime. "I won't ask where you are, but can you tell me, exactly how bad he is? And how are you?"

"Been better, but I'll be okay. O'Toole's not the same, if that's what you mean. It's going to take some time. I'll watch him." He was obviously shaken. His voice was detached, distant. I could only imagine what he'd been through, but before we disconnected, he said, "Thanks, Kat. We wouldn't be here without you. Take care of yourself."

I sank back into the bench and threw away what was left of my pizza, thinking that Jermaine wouldn't have been captured in the first place if not for me. I gazed up at the Pilgrim Monument, towering behind us, and thought about what it represented, a new nation, one that would grow to be the most powerful on earth, established by the simple yet profoundly revolutionary Mayflower Compact that would serve as the foundation for the U.S. Constitution.

So many had fought, suffered and died to protect this new experiment, but many others took it for granted, or worse, manipulated it to achieve their own ends. It was because of this vicious minority that I ran, hid, broke the law and—if they caught me— would almost certainly be killed.

I told Cam what Jermaine said, and this time I couldn't staunch my tears. He wrapped his arm around my shoulder. "It will be okay. We'll get through this."

I wanted to believe him, but we were up against overwhelming odds. Even if I did get to see Robbie again, it wouldn't be the same; neither of us were the same. Too much had happened ... to both of us. "Let's get out of here," I said.

We walked west, passing by more shops, more restaurants, beyond the Coast Guard station toward the jetty. The massive granite rocks interrupted the black and blue water, leading to the Woods End Lighthouse. Seagulls squawked overhead. Neither of us spoke, so absorbed were we with our own thoughts. In another time, this town, with its magnificent beauty, hectic summers and acceptance of diversity, could be the type of place I'd want to land. But now it provided only fleeting sanctuary while we waited for Nate. If only Robbie were here. We could get jobs, lie low in a small beach house like we'd done on Nevis, join those hearty souls who called it their year-round home, and maybe have normal lives again. Like Thoreau said, "Here a man may stand and put all America behind him."

Cam pointed to his watch. It was time. We hailed a cab to the airport, saw Nate deftly land the plane and, after boarding, watched Long Point Light fade from view. Nate was all business; I wasn't sure whether it was because of our last encounter or because of the gravity of the situation. In either case, I was glad. The less drama, the better.

Within three hours, the runway of Stewart International Airport appeared, and I had recouped some composure. A few cabs were waiting outside, and I gave one of the drivers the address. Once at The Big Pink, we saw Willie pushing Tom toward us. Their expressions were unusual; no smiles, no waves, just a somber demeanor that didn't bode well. Robbie must have been worse than I thought.

I gasped when Treadwell appeared from behind the raised ranch. "You're not the only one who knows Rob's favorite bands." He gazed up at the modest old house and added, "The place hasn't been the same since Levon died. He was the heart and soul of The Band. I used to love jamming with him." His smile was rueful. Josh emerged behind him, along with some of the drivers who had escorted me to work during the past few months. "Tom, let's go back to your place. We're too obvious here," Treadwell said. "By the way, how do you like the new digs?"

"Hated to leave Bethel, but the new place is fine, thanks. Appreciate your help. Too many people knew about it, and I could use a little less notoriety," Tom replied.

Treadwell said, "Kat, you ride with me. Josh, take the dog." I protested, but he took my arm, saying, "You and I have much to discuss ... in private. We'll meet the others after we've had a chance to catch up."

Outnumbered, I gave Cam a look of resignation and prayed that Treadwell wouldn't try anything malicious. On the way to the car, Treadwell was humming "Cripple Creek," attempting nonchalance, but the vein in his neck betrayed him. My body tightened as I climbed inside.

"Anything you'd like to tell me?" His voice was steady, but his fingers were white as his grip tightened around the wheel.

"I told you I'd try to get Robbie released," I said, squirming in the deep leather seat of the McClaren 650. "You weren't doing anything."

"It's time you leveled with me. There's something else, isn't there?"

His voice remained calm, like he knew he was in control. He was. I guessed he was referring to the Scions. If I told him what I had learned, he might press his advantage. Who knew what he might do?

"I don't know what you're talking about," I muttered.

He veered to the shoulder of the road and turned to me. "Collins told you I'm involved with the Scions, didn't she? After all I've done for you, for Tom and Rob. I'm sick of your bullshit, your mistrust."

"What are you going to do? Kill me?" I forced a brittle laugh. "You'd be doing your buddies in the Scions a favor."

"What are you talking about?" He pounded the steering wheel. "Dammit, I've been trying to help you, but no, you've questioned me at every turn. Yes, I was involved with the Scions, but that was until I learned what their true motivations are. They're like a cult; once you're in, you can't leave. I had to string them along, make them think I was still one of them."

"It would have been better to hear it from you. What do you expect? You'll benefit greatly from party leadership. You'd have ultimate power and make even more money. Is that why you ignored what I told you about Zuabi? You want to blow up the government like you did in the sixties? You've hacked my phone and my computer. You've bugged my apartment. The mistrust has gone both ways."

He sighed deeply as he rubbed his forehead in exasperation. "I was trying to keep you safe, and you haven't made it easy. The way I see it, we have two choices. You can either work with me and avoid prosecution for all you've done, or you can continue to distrust me, in which case, I will ask your friend Nate to fly you somewhere safe where you can't ruin what we're trying to do. Your choice. Now, our friends are waiting. Which is it?"

"I want to talk to the others."

He swore in disgust and roared back onto the road. We drove two miles in silence until we reached Tom's new place. Treadwell's anger was palpable, but at least I was alive, and I might see Robbie again.

Tom's living room was packed with the assembled group, their faces questioning as we walked in the door. Baha came to me and asked if I was all right. I discreetly nodded, then ran past her to Robbie. His head was lowered; he didn't even acknowledge my entrance, let alone my light touch on his shoulder. When I leaned over to kiss him, he turned away. Tom and Jermaine, who sat on either side of him, gave me sympathetic looks as, despondently, I found an empty seat across from them.

"It seems as though we have a breach of trust," Treadwell began. "Kat is questioning my intent, and we have reached an impasse. Can anyone here persuade her? She won't believe me."

A murmur of protest grew throughout the room. Even Jermaine questioned me. Tom pleaded Treadwell's case. Treadwell's men told me I was just plain wrong. Except for Robbie, who remained stone-faced, it was unanimous. They were all totally devoted to Treadwell. Despite his manipulation, he was the Messiah who would lead them to the promised land where he would restore a sense of wholeness. But it didn't work on me. Perhaps it was the cumulative dose effect of all I had experienced, but I remained unconvinced. Treadwell was right; we had reached an impasse.

The only sound in the room was Jackson Browne singing about dashed hopes and dreams in "The Pretender." Treadwell slowly walked toward Robbie and knelt, placing his hand on the bruised and knotted hand resting on the chair. "Rob, if you can understand me, nod your head." Robbie looked up at Treadwell and slowly nodded. It pained me that he reacted to Treadwell and not me. "That's great, bro. Now, this is important. If you trust me, I mean really trust me with all your heart, nod your head again." Robbie paused, as though he somehow understood the gravity of the situation. After glancing at me, he looked back toward Treadwell and nodded once more.

Tom and Jermaine both grabbed Robbie's shoulder, and then they looked at me as well, waiting for my response. Treadwell rose and stood aside while I returned to Robbie's side and said, "It's me, Kat." He looked up. His bruised, vacant eyes sucked the life from me. I took his trembling gnarled hand and held it tightly; the others seemed to hold their breath in anticipation. "I need to hear it from you, Robbie. I need to know if I can trust Jim. Everything depends on it. Please, tell me if you can."

The room was quiet. Robbie said nothing. I leaned in closer, my ear to his mouth. Once again, I urged him to say something, anything, but he was silent. I pulled away and looked at him. Seeing his battered face, his frail, starved frame and his skeletal limbs was devastating. Soon my entire body shook with heaving sobs as though the weight of the events during the past six months descended all at once, causing me to collapse on the floor at Robbie's feet, my head on his leg, my tears forming a growing dark circle on his pants.

After a few moments I felt Robbie's hand gently stroke my hair. My head snapped up, and I saw his eyes moisten as well. I reached up and wiped his face with my fingertips. I had breached the wall of trauma that enveloped him. He motioned me closer, and in a foreign, strained whisper, he rasped, "Jim's okay." I asked him if he was sure and he slowly nodded his head. I gently placed my hands on his face and lightly kissed him. It was more than I could have hoped for.

I dragged my arm across my face, wiping my wet eyes, and stood next to Jermaine who whispered, "The doctor said that with therapy, it might take six months or longer until he's back to himself. He's on some serious medication. It's amazing that you got any response."

It took a moment to let that sink in. Once I had collected myself, I looked at Treadwell and said, "It seems I've misjudged you. What's next?"

"We have a government to save." Treadwell forced a chuckle, then more somberly added, "If you're up to it, Kat, I'd like you to come with us to Washington. I need you to confront Adam with all you know and prevent him from executing his father's plan. My guys will come as back-up."

"You have all the information you need. You can handle Adam on your own. My place is here with Robbie."

Treadwell pressed, but I continued to protest until Baha stepped forward. "I'd like to go. I can talk to Adam. He'll listen to me, I'm sure of it." Then, glancing at me, she added, "Besides, Kat could use a friend."

"Baha, please. You don't need any more trouble. Neither of us do," I replied.

"You don't understand," Baha said. "Adam might do something drastic if he feels cornered. I couldn't live with that. You must let me come with you."

"We can't guarantee your safety, you know that," Treadwell said though gritted teeth. He didn't want her to come.

Baha lowered her head in acknowledgment. Tom embraced her. "Baha, please reconsider. Think about what we have together. I want you to be safe."

"Tom, you have been wonderful, and I appreciate all you have done for me. I will return, I promise, but Adam is my son. I can't let him do anything evil, and I will do whatever it takes to prevent him from killing himself and hurting others. I must go. Please try to understand."

I couldn't let Baha go by herself and reluctantly agreed to accompany them.

Now that he knew his mother was safe, Adam had to act quickly to prepare for his onerous task at the Capitol. He needed to concentrate, but numerous thoughts of his father's actions flashed into his mind: the constant repetition of Jihadist propaganda, the isolation from the outside world, the heartless mocking of his mother if she dared speak against his father's perversion of Islam. But these were nowhere near as bad as being locked in a closet for days, beaten severely, or deprived of food for saying anything even slightly contrary to his father's dogma—all designed to brainwash

him into submission. For a while, it had worked. Adam had hated the infidels, was intent on their destruction, and had been willing to die to achieve it.

But that was before he became a public servant and earned the respect and gratitude of his constituents, many of whom hadn't experienced the opportunities he had, and virtually all of whom appreciated his efforts on their behalf. One wrote, "You saved me." Another said, "Thank God for you." He had worked diligently to help them find a better life and, in the process, had given them hope and a slice of the American pie, even if it was a smaller portion than that enjoyed by more privileged citizens. All they needed was a chance, and once they were given that chance, they felt like they belonged. It was impossible to hate them.

Instead, his loathing now was transferred to his father, though he acknowledged that Adheem had been right about one thing. Adam's love for Meghan had overcome his father's attempts to twist his mind. He had been transformed by her lilting voice, her sense of humor, the way she listened and above all by the fact that she somehow seemed to understand the challenges he faced. She didn't care that he was a Muslim. In fact, she said it made him more interesting than other men. "Being with you is like going on a trip to a foreign land." The prospect of a life with her had annulled the years of coercion and turned him from his father's hate. He felt good about that, grateful. But still, he needed to act. He must remove the bomb before he could be held accountable for planting it.

His father's friend, Ghauth, was on duty. That was both good and bad. Ghauth would not be suspicious about seeing him at this late hour, but he was also his father's eyes, watching Adam and ensuring his allegiance to the cause. Ghauth greeted him when he entered the Capitol, remarking only that he worked too hard. Adam told him he had to make another delivery. Ghauth flashed a complicit smile and walked away.

After checking the hallway in both directions, Adam opened the door to a small room lined by shelves that held cleaning supplies, boxes of toilet paper, paper towels, and hooks on which mops and brooms hung. Against one wall was a deep sink. Across from that, Adam opened a door to a stairwell that led to the maze of tunnels below the Capitol.

Except for the occasional whoosh of steam and clanking of pipes, it was silent, eerily so. Dim lights illumined his way, although by now he could make the passage blindfolded. The musty odor assaulted his nostrils. It had to be ninety degrees inside the tunnels. He removed his jacket and left it on a railing. Though alone, he tiptoed, trying to be as silent as possible. Turning this way and that, he reached the spot directly beneath the podium where the president would speak. Three water-cooler jugs with wires attached sat on the floor, taunting him, impossible to remove in one trip. He had to take them, one by one, and dump their contents in the sink at the top of the stairwell. If he could do so, no one would be the wiser.

Removing a pair of wire cutters, he realized that his hands were trembling. One wrong move and the whole thing would blow. He took a deep breath and vigorously shook the nerves from his hands. Satisfied that he was steady enough, he snipped the wire that led to the primer. So far, so good. Then he took another deep breath before cutting the reactor wire. Still okay. Lastly, he clipped the ignition wire that would disable the remote detonator. He had done it.

He hoisted the first jug onto his shoulder, straining under its weight and dreading how long it would take to complete the task. He'd have to move slowly to avoid shaking the liquid and having it explode on its own. He grunted with every step until he reached the staircase. He groaned as he gazed up the stairs before him. They seemed endless, but with no other option he took the first step, then the next, and the next. Sweat poured off his brow. His muscles ached. He drew on every ounce of strength he had left, and then he did something he hadn't for a long time. He prayed, *not to the vindictive and blood-thirsty Allah imagined by his father but rather to the compassionate and loving God invoked by his mother.*

Once on the landing, he gingerly lowered the jug off his shoulder. Two more, he thought, wondering if he could make it. This would take far too long, but what else could he do? He couldn't ask for help. What would he say? "Oh, hey, I was gonna blow up the Capitol and bring down the government, but I've changed my mind. Can you give me a hand?"

By the time he was lifting the third jug up the stairs, he was panting heavily, his shirt soaked. He remembered his father's admonition. "Women are worthless except for bearing sons. They should never interfere with one's destiny. You've been placed on this earth for one thing, to bring glory to Allah." Adam thought of Meghan. He was going through this ordeal for her and for his mother. Surely, they were worth it, weren't they? His father was wrong, wasn't he?

Distracted by his thoughts, he missed the step and rammed his knee against the edge of the next stair. The jug wobbled, and the sweat on his hands made it slip from his grasp. If he dropped it, he was dead. He fell over onto his back, cradling the jug onto his stomach, and felt the sharp edge of the tread cut into his spine; a yelp of pain escaped. His knee throbbed, his back ached, and his vision blurred. He shook his head to chase the dizziness away and slowly lifted the jug onto the stair and rose. With tremendous effort, he hoisted the jug once more and made it into the room. He placed the first jug in the sink, pulled out a knife and punctured the plastic to allow the slow escape of liquid into the drain. When that was emptied, he returned for the remaining two jugs and as precious minutes lapsed, he thought of Ghauth. If he was suspicious, he might check the bomb site in the tunnel. If he saw nothing there, he would tell his father, or worse, kill Adam.

Half an hour later, when the task was finally completed, he limped to the loading dock as quickly as his quivering legs would allow. Allah was with him. Many empty water jugs waited to be picked up. He grabbed three and, scanning the hallways once more, returned to the cleaning closet and filled them with water. He lugged each one to the bomb site, grimacing from the effort. He positioned the jugs, meticulously attached the wires and then hobbled back toward the stairs. He had done it, but no sooner did the thought form when he heard footsteps approaching from the far end of the tunnel. Adam froze.

"You're still here? I thought you'd be done by now," Ghauth asked, his eyes narrowed by suspicion. He held Adam's jacket in his hand.

"Uh, well, now that the date has been moved up it took a while to load enough explosive into the jugs. This stuff's unstable, as you know. Didn't want to risk a premature detonation. Man, is it hot down here. Need to get out and cool off." Adam realized he was blathering. He had to stop before the guard grew more apprehensive.

Ghauth eyed him carefully. Adam realized that he needed to placate him somehow and added, "I'm a little nervous, but I think this will work. There's enough stuff down there to blow the dome off. When it does, I will find my place in Firdaws. Father will be proud."

"I'd like to see them one last time," said the guard, his voice steely. They walked together to the bomb site where the guard inspected the jugs carefully while Adam held his breath. He threw Adam's jacket at him and grabbed Adam by the throat. "What are you up to?"

"Get your fucking hands off me. I don't know what you're talking about. I have done everything that my father has asked."

The guard pulled out his service revolver and pointed it at Adam. "What has you down here so long that you had to remove your jacket and are sweating like a common pig?"

Adam braced himself. "You're going to kill me? Who will be my replacement, you?" He laughed derisively. "Be my guest."

Adam donned his jacket and said, "I told you, it's hot down here. Didn't want to ruin my coat."

"You worry about a coat when you're going to die tomorrow? That makes no sense. You're up to something. What is it?"

"I'm spending my last night with my girlfriend. Surely, you don't begrudge me that. Now lay off."

"Show me where the detonator is," the guard commanded, waving his gun.

Adam sighed and turned back, walking through the tunnel in silence, up the stairs, to his office. "Why are you limping?" the guard asked. Adam opened the drawer to show him the detonator and explained that he had a tough workout at the gym. "You're going to die and yet you worked out? Why?"

"Just because I am willing to die for our cause it doesn't mean that I'm looking forward to it. A few miles on the treadmill took my mind off tomorrow. Now, if you'll excuse me, I plan to enjoy my last night on earth."

Adam closed the drawer, shut off the light and left his office. The guard accompanied him down the hallway toward the exit. Adam limped off into the night, relieved to be away from Ghauth. He stole one last glance behind him. The guard was still watching.

Chapter 27

I followed Treadwell, his men and Baha onto the plane for D.C. with debilitating trepidation. Seeing Robbie so incapacitated had been beyond soul-shattering, and I'd wanted nothing more than to stay behind and care for him, but Treadwell was right. I needed to support Baha in convincing Adam to abandon the plot. I needed to support Baha, period. Though she barely said a word, she was clearly terrified, and I felt deeply responsible for her. Willie and Tom could take care of Robbie.

During the flight Treadwell tried to lighten the mood by regaling us with stories of his time in Woodstock. He spoke of jam sessions with Bob Dylan, Van Morrison, Todd Rundgren and Janis. He lamented the toll that drugs and alcohol took on Rick Danko and Richard Manuel of The Band. He looked at me. "That could have been me if it weren't for Rob," he said.

His affection for Robbie comforted me, and I admired his ability to stay calm despite the situation. He sounded so at ease, so natural. The more he spoke, the more my frostiness thawed. I wanted to hear more, if only to take my mind off the matter at hand.

Baha was not as easily calmed. She knew nothing of the icons of the sixties and had to be thinking of Adam. According to Adheem, the bomb would go off tomorrow when much of the government would be gathered like sitting ducks, about to be blown to shreds. Her son would die in disgrace. If we had any chance of thwarting the plot, we had to get to Adam immediately.

My thoughts were interrupted when Treadwell asked, "So this email you've generated about the Scions, where is it and when does it go out?"

"How do you know about that?" As soon as I asked, I remembered that Treadwell knew everything I'd done and must have gained access to the laptop that Cam had given me; his asking was a mere formality. I tapped my case and answered, "Unless I delete it, it goes out tomorrow." He stared at the case too long, his interest disconcerting.

It was late afternoon when we landed. As we climbed into the waiting limo, Treadwell called Adam and said they needed to meet, that something urgent had arisen. Adam agreed to come to Treadwell's D.C. office within the hour. Baha's lip quivered slightly, and I placed my hand on hers, trying to calm her, but Treadwell's mention of the email had rekindled my own apprehension.

We parked near a towering office building and rode an elevator to Treadwell's office, less technically appointed than his Boston digs but opulent nonetheless. A massive desk sat to the right; across the room stood a credenza topped with highball glasses, champagne flutes and decanters of clear and golden liquors. In between was a large table surrounded by leather-bound chairs. Large floor-to-ceiling windows filled two walls, but the light they provided could not defuse the percolating tension as we waited for notification of Adam's arrival. I jumped when the phone rang. Treadwell walked to his desk calmly and answered it. "Zuabi's here."

I silently practiced my spiel. I was as ready as I'd ever be. All of our efforts depended on it.

A minute later, the door flew open and banged into the wall, but it was not Adam who entered. Bette Collins, Wentworth Hughes and Stuart Johnson strutted in, followed by Beau and three of Beau's henchmen. They all wore smug smiles of triumph. Collins marched over to me and slapped my face, hard. "That's for all you put me through, bitch," she snapped.

Treadwell smiled at the group. "The email hasn't been sent yet," he said. Josh snatched my laptop and moved away. My faith in him was now shattered as well. They were all complicit.

I swung on Treadwell, pounding my fists into his chest. "You lied to us! What about Robbie? What about Tom? They trusted you, you bastard!" The ruddy-faced man who had seemed so nice when driving me to work pulled me away, pinning my arms behind me as I called him every name I could think of.

Beau strode over and punched me in the face. "Shut up, you fucking bitch." Then he laughed scornfully. "I've been wanting to do that for a long time. This one is mine."

Though my arms were immobilized, my legs weren't, and I kneed him viciously in the groin. He doubled over in pain, but his eyes blazed with malevolence. He'd be even more brutal next time.

"Take it easy, Beau. We have some things to discuss first." Treadwell sat and propped his feet on top of his desk, giving me a smirk before asking, "What is the arrangement with Zuabi?"

Baha cringed. As horrible as this turn of events was, it must have been worse for her. She whispered, "What about my son? Where is he?" I didn't look at her, and Baha shrunk suddenly as the reality of our situation dawned on her. She knew I was helpless.

Hughes answered, "As soon as he gets our okay, the plan is a go. You give us the laptop and Hastings, and we'll let you blow it all up and have your elections. Of course, we expect your continued cooperation once you're the president. We have as much on you as you have on us. Insurance sounds so much better than blackmail." The other Scions snickered.

The double cross was complete. I should have trusted my gut. The Scions had known about Zuabi all along. How had I missed that? Treadwell must have shared my findings with them. His disinterest had been an act.

Treadwell would take over the country, and I had given him everything he needed to make it happen. People would die, and

I'd be first. I would never see Robbie or Scout again; I hoped that they could take care of each other. Baha would be crushed, and I prayed that they would not kill her, or worse, return her to her husband. Everyone I cared about, even the country I loved, would all be destroyed.

"That's the deal," Treadwell said. "I think this calls for a celebration. Josh, would you mind getting the champagne?" He looked at the Scions with great self-satisfaction. "I got Dom Perignon just for the occasion."

Though nearly blind with fury, I was still an intelligence operative. Scanning the room, I made an inventory. Treadwell was seated at his desk. The ruddy-faced man still held me from behind. Collins, Johnson and Hughes stood around the center table. Beau, not yet fully upright, was recovering near the credenza. His henchmen were near the windows. Baha stood trembling near the door, a few feet from Josh, who now placed my laptop on a small stand and walked toward the mini-fridge. The Bruins fan walked over to the credenza to get cocktail napkins and champagne flutes, which he placed on the center table. A fourth man I didn't recognize popped the cork and began to pour.

Treadwell swung his legs off the desk and invited everyone to take a glass. If I hadn't been restrained, I would have scratched his eyes out.

"The Scions will let me rule without interference?" Treadwell asked. The group nodded. "Then I give you a toast: To the new world order." This time they flashed smiles that would have shamed the Cheshire cat.

As they raised their glasses, Treadwell reached back to his desk and subtly pressed a button before adding, "Our work here is done. She's yours."

With everyone's hands holding a flute, I saw my chance. It was now or never. I stomped down hard on the instep of the ruddy-faced man and rammed my elbow into his solar plexus, hard enough that he lost his grip on my arms. I bolted toward the door, yanking Baha's arm with one hand and grabbing my computer case with the other.

Not fast enough. Baha and I reached the hallway only to encounter a dozen CIA agents, some of whom I recognized, rushing toward us. My immediate reaction was a sense of spectacular betrayal, but when one of them grabbed us and told us to take cover, I realized that the opposite was true: we'd just been saved. As the agents stormed Treadwell's office I told Baha to run, but she followed me back to the entrance and stood behind me.

We watched as Collins shrieked, fists were thrown and bodies collapsed against walls, toppling furniture and smashing glasses, showering everyone with premium champagne. Guns were drawn. Josh and the others in Treadwell's group subdued the Scions, wrestling their arms behind them and tying them with restraints. Beau and his men put up more of a fight but were overpowered by my former associates, one of whom winked and said, "Great to see you, Kat." Within seconds, all were bound.

It had all happened so quickly. The immaculate office was now in shambles, but we were safe, and the core of the Scions had been taken down. I gazed at Treadwell in disbelief. Almost sheepishly, he said, "Remember those agents you told me you trusted? I knew we'd need reinforcements, so I took the liberty of contacting them. I'm sorry I put you through this, but the ruse would not have worked otherwise. It was the only way we could get them here all at once and not risk them getting to you first. I was still in shock as he continued, "Think of chess. You can't let your opponent know what you're planning, and you have to stay several steps ahead."

It was a depraved chess match, but my relief far outweighed any resentment I felt for being Treadwell's pawn. Baha and I hugged, sharing a moment of joy, but then I realized that we weren't completely safe. "What about the other Scions? You've only captured three of them."

"You probably already know I hacked your new laptop. I shared your email with the CIA, at least those you told me we could trust. They're in the process of rounding them up. It may take a few days, but they can't hide forever." He gently placed his hand on my shoulder. "We couldn't have done this without you, Kat. You are a bona fide hero."

"What about my son?" Baha asked, the pain in her voice palpable.

"Ah, another loose end." I had barely reacted to Treadwell's nonchalance when he pressed another button on his console and asked, "Has Congressman Zuabi arrived?"

The agents and Treadwell's men were still picking up glass and broken furniture when Adam entered, about ten minutes later, his eyes widening at the disarray. Baha gasped and ran to him. He folded his arms around her.

"Adam, I've missed you so much. What are these things they're saying about you? I can't believe it. Please tell me it isn't true." She stroked his face with a gentle hand and gazed into his eyes, searching for the truth.

"I'm so sorry, mother," Adam answered, his voice cracking, his eyes moist. "Father said that if I didn't obey him, he would hurt you. I couldn't let that happen, but it's okay now. I've taken care of everything." He told them about the plan and where he'd initially planted the bomb, but now it was dismantled.

The group was stunned by his words. It was Baha who finally spoke. "Where is your father?"

"I don't know. I haven't heard from him in over a week."

I filled them in on what I had done to Adheem and added, "He may still be in the hospital. Jim, could you find out?"

"That's the first time you've called me Jim," said Treadwell. "Finally. Thank you." His smile was electric. Turning to his men, he said, "Check it out." To Baha he said, "Why don't you go back to Tom's? I'll let you know when your husband is in custody."

"I'll go with her," I said. "It looks like things here are under control. I'm sorry I doubted you, Jim." Using his name seemed easier this time, more natural. Adam said he would come along to spend some time with his mother as long as he didn't have to do another interview with me. I promised.

Treadwell hugged me in a friendly way and agreed that I should accompany Baha, assuring me that he would keep me apprised of Zuabi's status and that of the Scions still on the loose. "You need to be with Rob, help him get back to his old self. And Kat, thanks for all your help. If you need anything, anything at all, just call. Okay?"

Chapter 28

Once we were airborne in Treadwell's plane, I could relax somewhat, but it was impossible to fully shake the anxiety that had gripped me for so many months. My fears about Robbie remained, as did the nagging resentment of Jim's manipulation, however necessary it may have been.

My reflections were interrupted when Baha made a quiet declaration. "I will divorce my husband," she said, "though it is contrary to everything I've been taught."

"He's put you through so much, mother, more than anyone should endure," Adam said, placing his hand gently on her arm. "Maybe in some Arab countries, a man can beat his wife, but not here. *Al Quran* says that marriage is supposed to provide tranquility, love and compassion. Father did not give you that, far from it. You may divorce a spouse who does not meet this contract and may marry another as long as he—or, in my case, she—believes in the one true God, regardless of religion."

"You learned your lessons well, Adam," Baha said with a smile, "but what is this about your case?"

"I've met someone, mother. She's means a lot to me. She makes me a better person. In fact, it was she who convinced me to abandon father's scheme, once I knew you were safe. I want to marry her, if she'll have me. After what I have done, I wouldn't blame her if she didn't."

"She sounds like a special person. Is she a believer? If so, I'm happy for you. What is her name?"

"Meghan. I want you to meet her and hope you'll give me your blessing."

I sensed that Baha was skeptical, and reluctant to have this discussion in my presence. "I'm sorry, Kat. We should not be discussing such things when you must be distraught about Rob."

"I don't know if things will ever be the same between us. He seems so broken."

"Trust time and friendship," she replied gently. "Tom is a warm and patient man. He will help pull Rob through. We all will."

I had my doubts. I had seen what PTSD could do, and Robbie had certainly experienced enough for more than a lifetime. All I could manage was, "I hope you are right."

Tom met us at the airport with Willie pushing his chair. His eyes were glowing, and Baha returned his smile with one equally warm and tender. "It's so good to have you back. I've missed you," Tom said.

"Tom, this is my son, Adam. With the guidance of a woman he loves, he's been able to undo years of his father's coercion. Adheem treated us both very badly, but I think Adam endured worse. I am proud of him for overcoming years of mistreatment."

Tom shook his hand firmly. "Welcome. I've been wanting to meet you. You did the right thing, and we're grateful. That took guts."

Adam thanked Tom but was ashamed that he'd considered the plot in the first place. As they returned to Willie's truck, Tom turned to me and more somberly added, "Jim called and filled me in. You must be a wreck. Are you okay?"

"I guess so. At least it worked," I replied dully.

"With the Scions decimated, Beau back in jail, and Zuabi's plot foiled, we can all focus on getting the new party underway. I'm psyched."

I could tell he was trying to lift my spirits, but all I could say was, "Right now, Robbie is my only concern. I want to see him and Jermaine as well."

"Jermaine left. Once he knew Rob was safe, he said there some things he had to catch up on."

I was disappointed but understood. He'd been in custody almost as long as Robbie and risked his life for us. As we approached town, Tom played tour guide, pointing out various landmarks. "Over there is Zeno Road where Rick and Grace Danko lived. Seems like the guy was itching for an accident every time he drove." A little further on, he added, "Levon Helm lived in that house in the late sixties and once he got clean, held concerts for local bands up there in The Barn." As we turned onto Camelot Road, Tom pointed and said, "That's where Bob and Sarah Dylan lived when they first moved here. I can't believe I live on the same street as Dylan. Rob will love it here. He'll be among the ghosts of days past."

His travelogue did little to ease my anxiety, and I still feared for our future. If our first encounter was any indication, it would be challenging at best. But Baha was right that at least we'd be among friends, and safe in this rustic community. With its resident memories, it might just be the balm that Robbie needed to make his journey back to me.

When we arrived, Scout came bounding out the door and ran to my side. I hugged his thick, furry neck gratefully, letting him slobber my face with licks. Tom's cozy house was a welcome sight. Like the communes of the sixties, we could work together and rebuild our lives with friends who would become family. This would be my new life, and hopefully Robbie would rediscover himself, find a way to contribute, and dream his dreams instead of the nightmares he'd experienced.

Ghauth arranged for Adheem to enter the Capitol and could

avoid the scanner well before anyone else arrived. By the time the video from the security cameras was reviewed, the damage would be done. He hobbled in on his wounded leg and with each painful step, cursed the vile woman who shot him. The guard told him to remain in a small AV room to the side of the chamber, twenty feet from the podium, and locked the door so no one would walk in unexpectedly. Then he left to attend to his responsibilities, promising to return once he found Adam.

Adheem pulled out his cellphone and called Mustafa, whose initial cynicism about the plan's feasibility justified a moment to gloat. His excitement made his chest tight, his heart race. Adheem prayed that the bomb would kill them all. His only regret was that Adam had not served in the House longer; he could have accumulated much more explosive.

It was close to nine when he heard the politicians filter in. The room hummed with conversations, questions and—oddly, Adheem thought—mild laughter. Soon they would laugh no more. Adheem was startled when the guard unlocked the door, his face grim. "Adam is not here. They said he had a family emergency."

"We have no family emergency! Perhaps that man, Treadwell, found out about the plot and did something to Adam. All of my plans, my dreams ... !" Adheem's eyes widened in horror as he considered this possibility.

"He was here last night, acting strange. Said he was making a last deposit, but I sensed something was up. He was sweating profusely and limping. He also said he was spending his last night with his girlfriend. I should have killed him on the spot. At least I have the detonator." Ghauth waved the device in front of Adheem. "The coward lost his nerve."

"Let me see that." Adheem seized the device from the guard and stared at it. "He must have betrayed me for the girl. I am ashamed that a son of mine is so weak, so worthless. After all I did for him." Adheem spat out his words like they were laced with arsenic. After a moment's pause, he said more somberly, "Perhaps *this is how it was meant to be. The plan was mine and so shall be the glory." The guard nodded. "Promise me one thing, that you will kill my son and wife. They are worse than these infidels."*

"You have my word." The guard checked his watch. "It is almost time. I must go to my post. Allah mahak, Adheem."

After his many years of planning, his patience and the trials he had overcome, Adheem's goal was finally within reach. He could taste it. He took a deep breath, preparing himself for the promise of Firdaws where he would join Osama, Mohammed Atta and the many others who died for Jihad. His thoughts were jarred by the bang of the gavel. A deep voice announced that the president was entering the room. He heard those assembled rise.

Mustering as much discipline as possible, Adheem waited a few minutes to allow those assembled to believe that all was well and would let down their guard. The room was quiet except for the president's speech and the persistent clicks of cameras from the balcony. Normally, these might have annoyed Adheem, but now there would be a historical account for this monumental event.

The time had come. He made a quick supplication to Allah and pressed the remote. Nothing. He pressed it again and again; still, no explosion. He cursed Adam and his deceit. This was his doing. In a blind rage, he bolted from the room into the chamber and ran toward the podium, ignoring the pain in his leg. He was within a few feet of the podium when guards caught up to him. Just as one grabbed his arm, he screamed, "Allahu Akbar!" and pressed the button on his bomb-laden vest.

A loud roar followed by screams and the thunder of feet stampeding from the room were the last sounds he heard.

Chapter 29

When we entered Tom's house, Robbie was sitting in a corner chair staring at the TV with glazed eyes. In my most cheery voice, I greeted him with a light peck on the cheek. He continued to stare at the screen. I wanted to weep, but instead I just sighed and smiled at the others. Penetrating the emotional walls Robbie had constructed would be a challenge, but it was one I had to overcome, for both our sakes.

I had turned to find a chair that I could pull beside Robbie when the news anchor announced, "This just in. A suicide bomber has breached the Capitol chambers ... " —our heads whipped around as one— " ... where the president was addressing a joint congressional session to outline his national security strategy. The perpetrator activated a powerful explosive that killed the president, vice president, and Speaker of the House. The Senate majority and minority leaders, who were sitting nearby, have been critically wounded and were airlifted to Bethesda for treatment. This is a national emergency. I repeat, the president and vice president are dead. The president pro tempore, Senator Joe Bernadi from Ohio, has been sworn in as president. Stay tuned for further updates."

I collapsed in a chair as the anchorman repeated the news and correspondents interviewed survivors, still in various states of shock. I looked at my friends, searching for answers they didn't have, straining to understand how this could have happened. Adam had promised that everything would be okay. Adheem couldn't have done this on his own, not with the bullet hole I planted in his thigh. All I could think of was Treadwell and the Scions. I had heard them speak of Zuabi while in Treadwell's office, but I had assumed they'd been referring to Adam.

A boiling rage raced up my spine, careening toward my brain. I had been played by Treadwell. I gauged the expression of the others, but saw only vacant, dumbfounded masks. We were all as immobilized as Robbie who, oddly enough, seemed riveted to the news, more alert than I had seen him since his return.

I followed his gaze to the screen, where the news anchor continued. "A Capitol guard, named Ghauth Malak, is unaccounted for. Anyone with information regarding his whereabouts should call the police immediately. He may be armed and dangerous."

My cellphone rang, and I quickly pulled it from my bag. "Kat, it's Jim. Have you heard the news? This is horrible. I don't know what to … ."

Something inside me snapped. Reason fled, replaced by panic, helplessness, despair and fury. "You planned this all along, didn't you?" I screamed. "Checkmate. You won. Machiavelli would be proud."

His voice rose an octave. "What do you mean? Kat, I didn't do this."

"You're a businessman. What do you know about governing?" Now I was shrieking.

"You don't know what you're talking about. I'm as stunned as you."

"Just tell me one thing. What kind of leader will you be? Plato's philosopher-king?"

"Kat, calm down. You're not yourself. You're not making sense. I had no part in this. You have to believe … ."

I threw the phone across the room and raced outside with Scout at my heels. I ran and ran, livid, trying to exorcise the demons who had invaded my soul, feeling responsible for Robbie's decision to sacrifice himself and suffer for me. Now, he was a ghost, a shadow.

I didn't kill Zuabi when I had the opportunity. My father would have. Now the president was dead, and the country was in chaos. And then there was Treadwell, one huge question mark for which I had no answer, only a gnawing fear that I screwed up something there as well. It was too much to bear.

My anger and guilt transformed me into a running machine, unaware of fatigue or pain. Even Scout, who normally would have asked for a break or two, seemed to sense my turmoil and matched me stride for stride. Eventually, we found ourselves on the Glasco Turnpike, with Overlook Mountain looming ahead. I was drawn to its stature, its strength, and the way it seemed to shelter the town below. We slowed to a trot and continued for another hour until we reached the trailhead on Meads Mountain Road, where red blazes led to an uneven gravel path. Slowing to a walk, we trekked its length until we reached the abandoned Overlook Mountain House, now in disrepair. Desperate for a distraction, I paused to take it in.

After years of wind, rain and snow as well as the contributions of countless graffiti artists, the house was in shambles. I tried to imagine it during its heyday when it was solid and grand. Now it was merely an oddity weathering the assaults of nature. Nonetheless, it stood its ground, defying the insult of birches growing up through its floors, the absurdity of staircases leading nowhere, the futility of windows wide open to the elements.

We slogged on for another half-mile until we reached the fire tower. Despite my growing fatigue, I climbed the eighty-plus steps, with Scout faithfully trailing behind. We were rewarded with a magnificent panorama of the Hudson River, the Ashokan Reservoir and the undulating landscape of the Catskill Mountains blanketed in a lush green quilt that stole any remaining breath I had.

I felt small as I stared out at the great expanse, but, elevated by the tower, I did not feel insignificant. Although I couldn't see them, I knew there were millions of people below, wondering how the country would survive its loss. Some of them would use the president's death as an excuse to hate. Fear does that. But the large majority were good and hard-working people who help their neighbors, join the military to defend us or donate money to the less fortunate. Despite the divisions and mind-numbing rhetoric of late, we couldn't allow our differences to diminish us. Like the Overlook Mountain House, our democracy had weathered much over the years and, though abused and battered, it still stood. This was not the time to give up; not on Robbie, not on the country, and not on myself.

What had happened to me? My father had been able to handle the danger, the intrigue, the moral confusion, but it occurred to me that he had grown darker over the years: more guarded, distant and unapproachable. I doubt that he trusted anyone, and my own ability to trust was in short supply. Perhaps he and I had more in common than I'd been willing to admit, and it frightened me, but he'd tried to make things right in the end. I had to do the same, even if it meant becoming like him to survive.

Adam was dreading the call he had to make, knowing it would prompt a raft of questions which he didn't want to answer. "Hi, Meghan, I'm okay. I wasn't there."

"Oh, my God. This is awful. They killed the president, and so many died. I was afraid you were ... I've been a nervous wreck. The police and FBI have been hounding me like crazy. What's going on? Where are you?"

Hearing the anxiety in her voice, he hated adding to it, but he had no choice. Hesitantly, he said, "You're going to hear about this sooner or later, and it's only right that you should hear it from me. The bomber was my father."

It was several moments before she spoke, in a much more subdued voice. "I don't know what to say. I'm glad that you weren't there, but why? Wasn't it a special session? Is this what was both-

ering you that night at dinner?" There was another pause. "Adam, my god. Did you know?"

Adam gulped reflexively. "We need to talk."

"Talk to me now," she demanded. Adam replied that it was too complicated, especially over the phone, which heightened her concern. "I want to see you, and you'd better tell me everything. Where are you? I'll get there as soon as I can."

"That might not be a great idea. We should wait until things cool down, maybe in a couple of weeks. It's not safe, and I don't want you to take the risk."

"I can't wait that long. Where are you?"

The more he tried to evade her questions, the more irritated and adamant she became. Finally, he answered, "I'm in Wood-stock, New York, staying with some friends."

"Woodstock? Why there?"

"My mother's been staying here to hide from my father. It's a long story."

"I'm flying up there. Don't try to stop me. Hold on." She did some clicking on her computer, and after several minutes she said, "There's a Jet Blue flight tomorrow afternoon. Pick me up at Sullivan County Airport at one p.m."

Tracking the woman had paid off. Ghauth now had all the information he needed. Adheem would get his revenge.

The sinking sun tie-dyed the sky with bright reds, oranges, yellows and purples. I checked my watch and realized I'd been gone for five hours. Faced with a long hike back, Scout and I descended the stairs of the fire tower and retraced our route. By the time we could see Tom's house, the sky was black and the air cool. As we approached the house, I heard the voices of my friends and listened undetected.

"Man, I hope nothing's happened to her," Tom said. "Now, we have Rob to worry about as well. He's been looking for hours."

Hearing that Robbie cared enough to search for me was an unexpected consolation, but I felt badly for causing the others concern. I was about to go inside and apologize when I heard a voice I hadn't expected. Treadwell.

"It's my fault," he said. "I put her through too much. I should have been more open with her, earned her trust. I should have listened to her warnings about Adam's father. I was too preoccupied getting the party off the ground and neutralizing the Scions. I should never have mentioned brokering a deal. I knew she would do whatever it took to get Rob back." He paused a moment while the others tried to calm him, but he continued. "She had too much to deal with. I was wrong to lay more on her. She was talking crazy, like I had something to do with the assassination. Do any of you feel the same way?" Maybe it was my exhaustion, but the tone of his voice didn't match his words. It was like he was rattling off a list, not remorseful. And why would he need their reassurance?

"That's crazy, Jim. You gave Kat a job that you knew she could do. It was her decision to pursue Zuabi. She confronted Collins on her own. You gave her a place to land, kept her safe. Whatever risks she incurred, she did so voluntarily." Tom said.

"Yeah, I know, but I still feel like I'm to blame. I'd like to hang out until I know she's all right. Do you mind?" Treadwell asked.

He might have been sincere, but he might also be making sure I hadn't run to the authorities instead of the mountain. He would wait until he knew where I stood. I would give him the confirmation he sought but would remain watchful.

"What about the convention next week?" Tom asked. "You've got to get the party organized, especially with all that's happened today. We'll let you know about Kat."

"I'm not needed. Governor Ryan has agreed to chair the party. He can run things. Because we're new, there's just a few candidates running so it's basically a rubber stamp and a means to raise our visibility. It's time to turn over the reins and watch from the sidelines."

He wasn't planning to take control; he had no hidden agenda. But why was I still so suspicious? I had to face him. I took a deep breath and opened the door.

Baha sat on a chair next to Tom. Treadwell and Adam were on the sofa. They jumped when I entered. "Sorry to make you all worry. I needed to clear my head."

"Thank God you're safe, Kat," Tom said. "Rob is out looking for you. I'll call and let him know you're back."

Baha left to retrieve some water, a glass for me and a bowl for Scout; her gentle smile conveyed support.

"I left as soon as I got off the phone," Treadwell said. "You sounded horrible, like you thought I was behind the assassination. You don't, do you?" Interesting that he began with that, but I didn't let on.

"I wondered for a while, I'll admit, but while I was running, I did a lot of thinking. You couldn't have anticipated what Adheem would do. I certainly didn't, not after I shot him." I noticed Baha gasp. "We both thought Adam was totally responsible for executing the plot and that it was foiled after he had a change of heart. It was the guard. We must find him. I'm afraid he will come after Baha and Adam."

"Ghauth threatened to kill me the night I disassembled the bomb," Adam chimed in. "I think you could be right." His manner was unusually guarded, like something else was bothering him. "Ghauth wouldn't think of coming here." It was like Adam was simultaneously relieved and nervous.

When Baha returned with the water, Tom said, "You and Adam should stay here. He won't find you in the wilds of New York state."

"We can't put you in danger. You've already done so much. Adam and I will find another place to hide."

Tom began to protest, but Treadwell jumped in. "Tom's right,"

Treadwell said. "You're safe here, and he has many friends who can help." Then, turning to me, he added, "I assume you'll stay with Rob?" I nodded. "I'll have some of my guys come up and watch the place." And watch me, I thought, unable to dispel my doubts. "But now that I know you're okay, I'd better go back," he continued. "We need to pull the country together. Tom, I'll leave it to you to decide whether you can make it, but I'd like your help at the convention."

Tom turned to Baha and asked, "What do you think? If Jim's guys come up, they can protect you, but if you want me to stay, I will."

"You should go. You've worked so hard for this. We'll be fine," Baha answered, her voice thin.

Over the next half hour, we discussed Treadwell's party, the state of the country, and what precautionary steps we would take while Tom and Treadwell were at the convention. Adam was very quiet and did not participate in the conversation. I assumed he was still feeling remorse for all that had happened. Then the door opened, and Robbie appeared, worn, but disturbed. I ran to him and wrapped him in my arms.

"I'm so sorry, Robbie. I didn't mean to make you worry. I appreciate that you went looking for me."

"Damn it! You put everyone through hell. You had no right." His eyes were like hot coals.

Taken aback by his outburst, I quietly responded, "I went to the mountain, like we did so many years ago. Remember how you said it gave you perspective? You were right." I touched his arm.

He abruptly pulled away and trudged up the stairs. My eyes followed him longingly, desperate to somehow bridge the distance between us.

Chapter 30

I rose early the next morning to see the others off. The aroma of bacon and eggs made me realize how ravenous I was after yesterday's quasi-marathon. Baha poured me some coffee, which I immediately gulped down, and dove into the plate she had prepared for me.

"How are you feeling?" Treadwell asked. "I was hoping I'd get to see you before we left."

"Much better. I'm sorry for putting everyone on edge."

"Forget it. You're okay, and that's all that matters. By the way, Josh called. They've found the remaining Scions. They won't be bothering anyone for a long time, at least not the ones we can extradite. The Russians and Saudis won't cooperate, I'm sure."

Adam solemnly announced that Meghan would be arriving later that day, which explained his preoccupation. He must have been thinking about what he would say to her. If Baha was excited, she didn't show it. She simply told Adam he needed to be truthful … about everything. Adam nodded his head, and then walked distractedly toward the window and gazed outside.

The bustle of comings and goings was interrupted as Robbie entered the room. He walked directly to the counter where he poured himself a cup of coffee and took two strips of bacon. I went to him, but he walked past me out to the porch. I followed as he silently took a chair and sipped his coffee.

"Will you ever be able to talk to me?" I asked. I couldn't determine if he held me responsible for all he endured or if his PTSD was at work. Whatever it was, I couldn't break through.

Just when I was about to give up and go back to the kitchen, he said, "It's hard, Kat. The nightmares won't quit. No matter how hard I try, I can't stop thinking about what they did. It's … ." His voice trailed off, and his eyes fell to the ground. I wondered if he blamed me.

"I love you, Robbie O'Toole. I can't imagine what you've been through, but I won't press. If and when you want to talk, I'll be here. I'm not going anywhere." He pursed his lips. His eyes were glistened. I had made a dent, not much of one, but it was something.

The house seemed deserted once Treadwell and Tom departed. Robbie left with Scout for a walk, declining my offer to join him. Baha did her best to remain upbeat; Adam was still preoccupied. We watched the news for updates on the nation's status, Adam robotically filling in details about various individuals involved. When Baha excused herself to shower, Adam and I were alone, and he tentatively asked, "Are we okay, you and me?"

"Your mother is my friend, Adam. I don't want to see her hurt by anyone, especially you. You're all she has. Well, you and Tom. She's told me what your father put you through. It must have been horrible, but still, you planted the bomb." I pointed my finger at his face. "Think of this as a second chance. Don't screw it up."

"It was crazy. For a while, I didn't feel like I had a choice, like I was hard-wired to do such a thing, but you're right. I must take responsibility." He held up his hand and said, "You have my word. I will do everything I can to set things right with my mother, Meghan, and you. I know what it's like to be on your bad side." He smiled weakly, but then checked his watch and gasped. "Shit, I've got to get to the airport. Please tell my mother I'll be back as soon as I can. I have no idea how I will explain things to Meghan."

Once he was gone, Baha cleaned, and I peeled some vegetables. "She must be very special to convince Adam to change his mind. His father had such control over him. I pray we get along. I hope she can understand what he's been through. It would mean so much to Adam ... and to me as well. What do you think will happen to him?"

I felt sorry for her, but I understood. Adam's fate was unknown. His role in planning the explosion was known to very few people, but one of them was the guard. Would he risk his own fate to expose Adam? Despite the fact that Adam foiled the original plot, there would be investigations. We might even be deposed. I knew what his father was planning and hadn't reported it. The ripples of this plot had grown to a tsunami that could overwhelm us all.

He boarded the plane the same time as the sandy-haired, freckled woman and fought the urge to watch her during the flight. Instead, he occupied himself with a newspaper. He enjoyed reading about the attack and regretted Adheem would never know how successful he had been. The woman paid him no attention. She would before too long.

When the plane touched down, he raced to pick up his rental, threw his gear into the trunk and drove into the arrivals area. To his relief, Adam had been late; the woman was just coming out of the terminal to meet him. He leered when he saw them embrace. He would follow at a distance until he knew where they were staying, then he would watch the house for a couple of days, perhaps listen to their conversations. This would allow him time to obtain the materials for a suicide bomb. He would pick the perfect time. It had all been so easy.

When we heard a car pull into the driveway, Baha hopped up and tucked errant strands of hair into her hijab, straightened her dress, and took a deep breath. I joined her at the door and supportively placed my hand on her back.

"Mother, this is Meghan," Adam announced tentatively.

Meghan's eyes were red, her skin blotchy. Adam must have told her. In a quivering voice, she said, "Hello Mrs. Zuabi. Adam speaks so highly of you."

Baha's smile was strained, but surprisingly, she hugged Meghan tightly. "This must be so difficult for you. I'm sorry. Please, come inside. We have much to learn about each other." Adam looked disconsolate.

At that moment, Robbie and Scout returned, for which I was grateful. He had been gone most of the day. I took a chance and asked, "Why don't you and I get dinner ready and let them have some time to themselves?"

Amazingly, Robbie followed me to the kitchen. He seemed calmed by his walk, and as we worked side-by-side, I was reminded of our days in Nevis, where we cooked together every evening. Tonight, however, the only sounds were of pots clanking or plates being removed from cabinets. My periodic attempts to draw him into conversation were futile. On the other hand, the silence in the kitchen allowed us to overhear the conversation in the living room between Baha, Adam and Meghan.

As we set the table, Adam came in and offered to help. "I told her about my father and how he treated me. But when I told her what I did and undid, she freaked out. There's still so much to explain, and she said she'd be willing to hear the rest, but then she needs to leave to think about what it means to us. It doesn't look good." I felt badly for him but was not surprised.

Early the next morning, we took Meghan on a tour of the town, including Bethel and the site of the famous concert. I was hoping that it would jar memories for Robbie, but if so, he didn't let on. At least he'd joined us, which was encouraging. That evening, while Adam and Meghan were presumably continuing their talk, Robbie, Baha and I watched the news, still loaded with announcements concerning the interim government and coverage of the funerals of those who died.

We also saw news about the Constitution Party's convention and heard about it during Tom's call, set on speaker phone. His enthusiasm was contagious as he described how energized the delegates were, especially now that there would be no incumbent. The field was wide open. Treadwell's party had nominated two politically moderate candidates, a man from California for president, and a woman from New York as vice-president; both had been senators known for their integrity and bipartisanship, both had years of experience in government, and their states were loaded with electoral votes. Tom said he was coming home tomorrow evening. Now that the nominees were selected, he wanted to be with Baha to ensure she was okay.

Jim also called me to provide his take on their progress. "I think we can really make this work, Kat. The energy here is amazing. People are ready for a real change, and they believe in what we're doing. Have you seen the press coverage?" I told him I was impressed. "Coming from you, that means a lot, really. By the way, now that the Scions are under wraps, my guys will return to the States. They'll be there in two days to keep an eye on things. Is everything okay up there?"

I told him it was and asked about Jermaine. He responded that Jermaine was working with Cam to track down the guard, but nothing had turned up. He would let us know as soon as they learned anything, leaving me to wonder how long we'd have to wait for resolution.

The next day, Willie dropped Tom off late in the afternoon. When Baha ran to greet him, he pulled her close and kissed her lovingly. She seemed mildly embarrassed that their emotion was public, eliciting a light chuckle from Tom.

Over a meal of corn on the cob, steaks, snap peas and salad,

Tom regaled us with stories from the convention, mentioning that Jim was as excited as a father of a newborn, though he let others take the lead. The two candidates had a clear vision for the country and were eager to share it with voters. Their platform was a mix of socially progressive, financially accountable and strong national security proposals, as Jim had envisaged. "You would have loved it, Rob. Maybe next time." Robbie nodded, his smile crooked.

Tom's enthusiasm thankfully eased the collective tension created by Meghan and Adam's relationship, Baha's concern for them both, and Robbie's return to silence. Seeing my friends in various emotional states intensified my own despair. I wanted to be alone and turned in. As I lay in bed, half-listening to their conversation from the room below, I wondered for the millionth time if Robbie and I would ever experience a normal life again.

Sleep eluded me. All I could think of was the Robbie I used to know: kind, gentle, caring and with an internal moral compass that guided him to do good and right wrongs. Yes, some of his dreams led to my nightmares, but he had returned to my life at a time when I needed to look outside myself and think of others. He put his life on the line to save mine. I remembered his words when he proposed to me a couple of years ago, although it seemed much longer. He said he couldn't imagine life without me, that I was the missing piece that solved his life's puzzle. I wanted to believe that was still true, but with all that had passed, was that still realistic?

My memories were interrupted by the sound of leaves crunching outside. I bolted upright. The hairs on my neck stiffened. The steps were slow and deliberate, like those of a wolf stalking its prey. Nearing the house, they slowed and became undiscernible. Scout was already at the window. Quietly, I joined him, straining to see in the dark while stroking his neck to calm him. Other than trees and bushes under the moonlit sky, I saw nothing. Except for the conversation downstairs, I heard nothing. Whoever or whatever it was must be on the porch, possibly peering inside. I waited, hardly breathing, straining to see in the dark. Fear took hold, and I felt cold, enveloped by an eerie sense that something was very wrong. There was only one person who would be hunting for someone here, seeking revenge—the guard. Somehow, he had found us.

I gave Scout the silent sign. He wouldn't give us away.

Regretting that my gun was locked away in Tom's safe, I scoured the room for a weapon, something large and heavy, but light enough to wield. Seconds were ticking away and with them, the fate of my precious friends dimmed. In the corner by the dresser, Tom's old crutches were propped against the wall. They'd have to do.

Scout and I got to the bottom of the stairs without making a sound—when suddenly, from the living room, came a horrific crash of glass. Peering around the corner of the staircase, my heart sank. The living room was in complete disarray, with overturned chairs, lamps and tables. Tom's wheelchair was on its side, and he lay unmoving on the floor, his glasses bent and broken. Baha knelt next to him, her face already growing purple. Adam was bent over in pain. Meghan clutched him closely, shrieking epithets. In the corner was Robbie, the one strong, brave man I loved, curled up with his head buried in his hands; the attack had sent his fragile psyche into overload. The intruder, wearing a suicide vest, was wildly waving a detonator in one hand and a gun in the other.

"Tie them all up," he ordered Adam as he threw a coil of rope at his face. "I only want you and your mother. Obey me, and the others will live. If not, we will all die together."

Adam broke away from Meghan. Her eyes, wide with fear, followed him as he dutifully affixed the rope to the hands of my friends. The guard checked the ropes to confirm they were secure. Adam apologized repeatedly for placing his friends and mother in such a predicament. His face contorted with terror as he anticipated the guard's intent. "Please, Ghauth, don't hurt the others. They've done nothing wrong."

"You coward," he sneered at Adam. "You built the bomb and

didn't have the guts to detonate it. You betrayed your father." Then to Baha the guard yelled, "And you betrayed your husband and disobeyed the teachings of *Al Quran*. You are a common whore. You both deserve to die. A gun is too easy. Your suffering will be far greater than what you caused Adheem."

He raised the gun and shot Adam in the thigh. Adam howled and collapsed, thrashing in agony. The guard dropped the gun and pulled out a knife with a gleaming six-inch blade. "I lied. You will all die, but not until you witness these two being sliced, over and over, until their last drop of blood is spilled. You first," he said to Adam. "I want your mother to see you suffer." He straddled Adam and taunted him, his eyes ablaze as he yelled something in Arabic. Then he placed the detonator on the ground beside him, freeing one hand to clutch Adam's throat. Adam desperately tried to avoid the vicious slashes and swipes; each time he tried to fend off the knife, the blade lacerated his arm. This was my chance.

"Attack!" I hollered. Scout lunged at the guard who looked up just in time to see the large black dog sink his fangs into his neck, eliciting an ungodly screech. I leapt to kick the detonator out of his reach. With every milligram of strength, with all the rage, fear, frustration and guilt that had festered in me for months, I swung the crutch at his head. He fell atop Adam in a limp, motionless heap.

I pulled the guard off Adam, who lay motionless on the floor. Blood was everywhere—the guard's, Adam's, and with horror I realized, Scout's too. I ran to Scout and tried to staunch the flow of blood from his chest with my hands, screaming that I had to get him to a vet. I couldn't get both Adam and Scout medical help and expect either to live.

I grabbed the guard's knife and used it to cut the ropes binding the others. Ripping the belt from my robe, I used it as a tourniquet around Adam's leg. Meghan called 911. "Please send someone to the gray bungalow on Camelot Road. We've been attacked.

There's someone here who is bleeding badly. Come quickly," she cried.

Scout was too heavy for me to lift. I looked at Tom beseechingly, but he could only stare at me helplessly. Our savior was panting rapidly, his breaths increasingly shallow, his fur matted with blood. My grief was unbearable as I watched my companion, my protector, and yes, the most important being in my life, dying before my eyes.

Then two large arms swooped down and gently lifted Scout. A firm, urgent voice I hadn't heard in months said, "Let's go, Kat." It was Robbie.

Epilogue

In the six months that had passed since that horrific night, many things transpired, almost too many to relate. Adam survived, but spent a long time in the ICU. He had explained everything to Meghan, but their relationship had taken a hit, one from which they probably would never recover. He received a reduced sentence due to his father's abuse and his cooperation, including the identification of those in Mustafa's cell.

Jermaine took a job in Treadwell's organization where he applied his unique skills to track down any threats to the new party and address them. Cam returned to DC to continue in his work in identifying foreign meddling in the US election process, the power grid, and financial institutions. Unfortunately, he would never lack for gainful employment.

Tom and Baha were married and remained in Woodstock. While we still lived there, Robbie and I took long runs with Scout, who fully recovered, and hiked the mountain, holding hands and reminiscing about days past. There was still enough of a spark to rekindle our love.

Eventually, we moved to Boston where Robbie could pursue his passion for investigative journalism as a reporter for Jim's media outlets. Jim demanded that he not pull any punches. The new party had to be beyond reproach – no lies, no corruption, and no hidden agendas, just the truth, which Robbie pursued as zealously as he always had. When Robbie unearthed damaging information about a Constitutional Party's member, Jim made sure the entire story was reported, and forced the congressman's resignation. This bolstered my growing trust in Jim, but when he offered me a job, I turned it down. I wasn't ready to jump into anything just yet. I still had some nagging guilt about how I could have prevented the assassinations, and there was something else gnawing at me, but I couldn't identify what it was.

I frequently stopped by to visit Ashley, the little girl I met near Zuabi's house, who was my yardstick for all that is good and innocent. She gave me hope and as my father once said, "If a person loses hope, then he's lost everything. As long as good people do the right thing, there's hope," something that he and I both clung to. In fact, I had come to embrace our many shared qualities and finally admitted to myself that I missed him very much.

Jim stopped by periodically for dinner, and each time I warmed to him a bit more until I finally admitted to myself that I liked him. We played a few games of chess, which he always won. However, during the last game, Jim's first move was the knight, not a pawn, which was unusual for him. I looked up, questioning, and saw him wink. "Thought I'd try a new strategy."

After several moves I asked, "Do you think I should have killed Zuabi?"

His eyes left the board and focused on me. "Is that what's been bothering you? You haven't been yourself since the assassinations."

"Yeah, I guess so. It's just that I can't believe the EMTs didn't tell the police they found Zuabi handcuffed to the bed."

"Let it go, Kat. It's over." He moved his bishop putting his king in jeopardy.

He would never make a move like that. My words must have distracted him. It was time to go fishing. I nonchalantly asked, "Doesn't it strike you as odd that the queen is a more powerful piece than the king? She can move diagonally, vertically, and horizontally in any direction and any number of spaces. A king can only move one space in any direction yet, he's the one that must be toppled. He's just a little more versatile than a pawn."

"The Scions were evidence that power is not always where it appears to be." He smiled as though relieved I had changed the subject. "A king is just a symbol. A pawn does his dirty work."

That was it. "You mean like Adam versus Adheem." He said nothing, so I continued. "You made out pretty well from the situation. Your party stepped right onto a more level playing field." I moved my rook one row up from his king and waited for his next move.

He stared at the board, his face scrunched. He was rattled, but I couldn't tell whether it was because of my move or my observation. I was hoping he would shift his king up one space, so I could use a move my father had taught me more than forty years ago.

"I guess we did now that you mention it, but like I said, it's over. Time to move on."

"You had my apartment bugged. You must have heard my altercation with Zuabi and the gunshot."

His eyes met mine. They were dark and hard. "Don't go there, Kat."

"It's the democracy thing, isn't it? You don't trust that it can right itself when things go wrong."

He released a deep sigh and paused a moment before speaking. "Churchill said, 'Democracy is the worst form of government, except for all the others.' There must be a better way to govern."

"So you got Zuabi out before the EMTs arrived."

He exposed his king and then replied, "For your sake and mine, I will neither confirm or deny that."

My queen went in for the kill. "Check mate."

The End

Acknowledgements

I have been blessed with many wonderful family members, friends, and unknown readers who purchased, read, and provided a review of my first book, *Scars and Stripes Forever*. Many of these same people helped me spread the word by recommending my book to others and hosting book presentations. Venturing into creative writing after more than thirty-five years in science has been a daunting experience, and your kindness and support means more than you'll ever know.

For this, my second book, I would like to acknowledge in order of the creative process, the following people for their help. I am grateful to Mary Wasmuth, Alyssa Haywoode, and Elizabeth Bernhardt of my writing group for their thoughtful, but gentle critique of very rough drafts and for providing valuable insights and ideas.

In addition, I immensely appreciated the review and edits of my sister, Priscilla Daniels, who asked cogent questions, changed the odd word, fixed punctuation and, along with my other sisters, Cyndy Pollard, Beth Rousselle, and Judith Rust, consistently encouraged me throughout the process.

I would especially like to mention Marge Davis, my friend and former college classmate, who is a copy editor extraordinaire. Her generous contribution of significant time and expertise improved the manuscript considerably. I am in her debt.

Robin Nelson of the Leaning Rock Press has my deep appreciation for agreeing to make *The Scions of Atlantis* into an actual book. Her patience, professionalism, and commentary were indispensable.

Lastly, Luanne, how can I ever thank you for reading multiple iterations of the manuscript? At various times you were a treasured sounding board, cheerleader, counselor, and reality check—all necessary, all welcomed, and all a testament to your belief in, and love for me.

About the Author

Claudia Turner was born in Baltimore, Maryland. She earned a B.S. from Bates College, an M.S. from Pennsylvania State University and a PhD from Johns Hopkins. At various times, she has been an athlete, teacher, scientist and finally, a writer. Claudia lives in Massachusetts where she enjoys spending time with family, friends, and her dog, Rosie.

This is her second novel, a sequel to *Scars and Stripes Forever*.

Previous book by Claudia Turner

Scars and Stripes Forever

Ben Douglas. of the CIA. comes across a memo that mentions a secret room in Langley, established by the men of Op-40. He orders his subordinate, Kat Hastings, to find the room and tell him what's inside. Kat unearths missing evidence from the Kennedy assassination that will expose the government's duplicity regarding the official version of events. She must decide whether to honor her CIA oath, her conscience, or her heart. Her survival depends on it as those who hid the information, including her father, will stop at nothing to keep it secret.